Death
in a
Bush Camp

by

Hugh Chare

Publication data

Death in a Bush Camp © Hugh B. Chare, 2023

Book and cover design by Hugh B. Chare
ISBN: 978-1-940012-24-7
www.kilihune-books.com

 Kilihune Books

Marieke Englebrecht mysteries
Death in the Mopane
Revenge after twenty years
Death in a Bush Camp

The James Martin series
African Encounter
Across the Zambezi
Just off the Great North Road
Well, there you go!
Back to Africa
We don't make glass
The Sagitta Mishap
Carbon Copy
Flight 5 to Johannesburg

Other books
The journal of Jan Englebrecht
British Spy in the Bushveld
Federica
First to the Cape

Preface

Bush camps are part of the fabric of the African tourist industry. They typically accommodate eight to ten guests, in relative luxury, and usually do not have all the trappings of safari lodges, so no pools, no spas, no masseurs, just a closeness with the bush and all that is wild.

Animals in the wild tend to avoid humans, which is why walking safaris are a completely different experience from vehicle safaris. Animals may avoid humans, but that is not to say that animals do not sometimes come really close; they do, and the camps typically have protocols to manage those situations. However, there are often no particular protocols to deal with deadly human-to-human interactions.

The Lufupa River Camp is a real camp situated at the confluence of the Lufupa and Kafue rivers, and the Radisson Blu and Latitude 15 hotels are real, as is Sky Trails, a local air charter company. Otherwise, Air Safari, all camps, people, events, etc., are fictional, and any resemblance in the featured characters to actual persons, living or dead, is purely coincidental.

My thanks go to Namukolo Ngenda for her thoughts when this novel was first conceived, and to James Duncan-Anderson of Wild N'Beyond Safaris for his help and guidance on arachnids, and to Phil Jeffery and Tyrone McKeith, and Classic Zambia Safaris for hosting us year after year at one of their bush camps, and to Diane Bédat for looking after us so well.

Contents

La vacance

"It's been almost a year now since we retired," Marieke said in French to her partner, Melisende.

"Already?" Melisende said. "I think we should treat ourselves to a holiday. Didn't you get something from Bridget that they had opened a new camp?"

"She did say that," Marieke confirmed. "I should call her and see if we could go and spend a couple of weeks there."

"Let's do that," Melisende said. So, Marieke called Bridget and was told that they would be delighted to have them as visitors, if they did not mind staying in a staff tent and helping out occasionally. That suited Marieke, so arrangements were made. Marieke, Marieke Englebrecht, and Melisende, Melisende Garnier, had both retired in 2013 from the *police nationale* of France, which used to be called the Sûreté. They had met at university in Lyon and had formed a strong bond that had grown over the years, even when Marieke had returned to Africa and had been working in the Botswana Police. She had decided that separation was not desirable and had moved to Paris to be with Melisende and had joined the police there, and had worked alongside Melisende for years.

The Bridget Marieke had referred to was Bridget Martin, related by marriage in a very roundabout way to Marieke. Marieke's cousin, Katrina Englebrecht, was married to James Martin, Bridget's brother-in-law. Bridget and William ran safari camps in Zambia in the Kafue National Park. They had previously run one in northern Botswana, which is where Marieke had first met them. She had been called in to investigate a potential crime and had discovered the family relationship. She had been aware of her cousin Katrina, but they had never actually met. Under the old South African apartheid rules, the marriage between her parents was illegal, because although her father was a white South African, her mother was a black Botswanan, something not permitted under the arcane laws of the time. They lived in the wilds of Namibia, far away from officious

1

government bureaucrats, so Marieke grew up on a farm in remote Namibia and spent time in the bush and with the San who were on the farm. Growing up, Katrina had lived in Zambia where her parents ran a heavy haulage business, moving mining equipment and other large pieces of machinery around the country. She had met James when he had gone to Zambia to work on one of the large copper mines in the famed Copperbelt. Partly because they lived in different countries and partly because of the supposed family disgrace brought on them by Marieke's parents, the two sets of parents did not socialise and rarely, if ever, talked to each other, so Marieke and Katrina did not meet until they were in their forties and by then a reconciliation between the parents was not possible as Marieke's parents had both been killed when their car had hit a landmine laid during the war of independence of Namibia.

In the latter days of her career, Marieke had worked mainly on security issues in old French territories in Africa, but also on other issues where there was needed cooperation between the French and other African countries. She had been assigned to many of those and had visited Zambia a few times and had established a good working relationship with Commissioner Joseph Bwalya of the Zambia Police. It had also given her the opportunity to take trips into the bush and to renew her acquaintance with Bridget and William. The new camp that they were going to was a bush camp also in the Kafue National Park, and it was run by Alessandra Martin, one of the two daughters of Bridget and William.

"How do we get there?" Melisende asked Marieke.

"Air France to Johannesburg and then South African to Lusaka or Emirates to Dubai and then direct to Lusaka," Marieke replied. "Once in Lusaka, Bridget and Will run that small airline that serves the parks, so we'll get tickets out to where we need to go, I'll get details from Bridget."

"When shall we go?" Melisende asked.

"They open usually in June, I'll get dates from Bridget," Marieke replied. "We'll need to take some warm clothes, at least hats and gloves, because the mornings will be cold."

"This will be fun," Melisende said. "Get us dates and I'll make the bookings with Emirates. I like the idea of skipping Jo'burg, and I'd like to see what Emirates is like."

"What do you know about them?" Marieke asked.

"From what I've been briefed on, they started up in 1985 and have grown substantially since. They operate the largest fleet of Boeing 777 aircraft and also have quite a few of the Airbus A380 super jumbos," Melisende said. "From what I've heard, they look after their customers well, so it should be an interesting experience."

Bridget sent them dates, so Melisende made travel arrangements that would put them into the camp on the twenty-fifth of May, a few days before the camp actually opened to paying guests. They would not be flying out to the camp, but would take one of the camp vehicles that had been in for a complete overhaul and was due to be taken back out to the camp. That promised to be an adventure in itself as it was over three hours' drive on the Great West Road to the turn off into the park, then another two hours on a dirt road before they parked the vehicle and went by boat the last leg of the journey. Marieke also let Commissioner Bwalya know that she was going, but that it was not business but a holiday trip. Although it was a holiday trip, both were taking along their MacBook laptop computers, Marieke because she was working on her autobiography and Melisende because she was working on a cookbook that she was creating. Marieke was also taking along her iPad Mini, packed with apps for animals, birds and trees.

"What do we wear to travel?" Melisende asked on the day of their departure.

"I think just khaki trousers and shirts, light boots and the green jackets we have," Marieke suggested. "We might be driving out, but we could be flying back, and there's probably a weight limit on luggage of 15 kilos."

"I'm really looking forward to this," Melisende said. "We haven't taken vacation in a while."

"Well, I'm packed and ready to go," Marieke said. "All I need to do is change clothes."

"As do I," Melisende echoed.

"Are we ready?" Marieke asked Melisende after they had both changed.

"Ready," was the reply. They took a taxi to Charles de Gaulle and found the Emirates desk and checked in for both their flights, to Dubai, then onward to Lusaka. It was their first experience with Emirates, as most of their travel before had been with Air France, mainly because when travelling on official business, they were required to use the national carrier whenever possible. Their Emirates aircraft to Dubai was one of the new Airbus A380 planes.

"This thing is gigantic," Marieke said as they boarded.

"Does it actually fly?" Melisende asked.

"Must do," Marieke laughed. "Or it will be a long taxi to Dubai. Let's see, where are we seated, there, 9E and 9F, those seats in the middle, this is the only way we could sit together, the window seats are just single seats, but we do get to sit upstairs on the upper deck."

"A bit like the old Brit show, Upstairs Downstairs, at least looking around, there's plenty of room," Melisende said.

"What's the flying time to Dubai?" Marieke asked.

"Just under seven hours," Melisende replied. "We'll get there tomorrow morning, then get the Lusaka flight a short while later."

"I'm glad we spent the money to fly Business Class," Marieke said. "God knows how many people are down there in Coach, all jammed in together."

"I found some recent travel reports, and all that I've read are positive," Melisende said. "Nice seats, nice menu and nice crew."

"These seats go flat, so we'll be able to try and get some sleep," Marieke commented as they took their seats, stowed their bags and got comfortable.

"Good afternoon," a flight attendant said. "My name is Marie. You are Melisende Garnier and Marieke Englebrecht?"

"That is correct," Melisende replied.

"May I get you something after takeoff?" Marie asked.

"Some white wine, please," Marieke said.

"Moi aussi," Melisende echoed.

"We have a nice Latour Meursault," Marie suggested.

"That sounds wonderful," Marieke said.

"Are you visiting Dubai?" Marie asked.

"No, we connect there for Lusaka," Melisende replied.

"Are you going on a safari? It looks as if you're dressed for it." Marie asked.

"We are," Marieke confirmed.

"Well, I hope you enjoy your flight with us," Marie said. "I will be back with the wine as soon as we have taken off and reached a safe altitude. These are the wine and food menus. I'll be back later for your orders."

They took off, with the plane rumbling down the runway until it eventually lifted off and climbed out of Paris and then turned east for Dubai.

"Look at this entertainment system," Marieke said to Melisende as she experimented with the remote control she had found. "It must have thousands of movies."

"That sometimes seems to me a double-edged sword, Melisende said. "There's so much choice, what do you pick?"

"I suppose if there's something you really want to see, pick that; otherwise, just pick something and see if you like it," Marieke said.

"I'm not sure I'll be doing much movie-watching," Melisende said. "I'll think I'll eat, then try and sleep."

"Good idea," Marieke agreed. "Tomorrow might be a long day."

"I wonder what this new camp is like," Melisende said. "It sounds fairly isolated, hours of driving from Lusaka and then a boat ride."

"The camp we went to before on the Busanga plain was quite a drive too, but from what Bridget said, they now fly into the Ntemwa strip and it's not too far a drive from there," Marieke added.

"Excuse me, ladies," Marie said. "Your Meursault."

"Thank you, Marie," Marieke said.

"Do you ladies live in Paris?" Marie asked.

"We do," Melisende confirmed. "And you?"

"I live in Dubai now. I used to work for Air Inter, but I prefer Emirates, it gives me more scope for international travel," Marie replied. "We are a very international crew, I think there are twelve countries represented and at last count, fifteen languages spoken.

Here are your amenity kits. I think you'll find everything you need in them. Have you had an opportunity to review the menu?"

"Thank you, we have," Melisende replied. "We were thinking of the mezze to start, then the grilled beef steak, and to finish, the cheese board."

"For both of you?" Marie asked.

"Yes, please," Marieke said.

"And to drink with dinner?" Marie asked.

"The Petit-Figeac Bordeaux," Melisende replied.

"An excellent choice," Marie said. "I will be back with your mezze."

They ate, they drank sparingly and made sure that they drank enough water, then they both tried to get some sleep. Lying flat is more conducive to sleep than sitting up, no matter how comfortable the seat is, so it was with delight that they accepted the mattresses that were offered and wrapped themselves in blankets and dozed and drifted off to sleep. Breakfast was served before landing, and they both opted for the classic omelette, eschewing the alternative of the steak and eggs. In Dubai, the sheer size of the place was almost overwhelming, but it was well-signed and they were able to find their way to the Business Class lounge, a truly huge place with all the amenities one could imagine.

"I have to say that so far Emirates has lived up to my expectations," Marieke said as they found themselves some seats in the lounge.

"It was rather nice, wasn't it," Melisende agreed.

"Now for the next leg," Marieke said.

"Which is our plane, do you think?" Melisende asked Marieke.

"Given that it's Lusaka, which is hardly a prime destination, my guess is that it's one of the parked planes somewhere over there," Marieke replied. "They'll take us out by bus."

"That's an adventure in itself," Melisende laughed. "Touring the outer reaches of the airport by bus."

"We don't have that long to wait, our Lusaka flight goes at about nine-thirty, so we've got just over an hour," Marieke said. "Time enough for tea or coffee and something to snack on."

"After the breakfast they fed us, I think all I want is coffee," Melisende said.

"If you just look after our bags, I'll get us some," Marieke said.

When the time came to take their Lusaka flight, they went downstairs to the tarmac level and were taken by bus to a stand off in the wilderness and boarded another Airbus, this one an A340. There was no jetway, they had to clamber up the stairs to the door.

"Here we are, 6A and 6B," Melisende said, pointing to the seats. "Do you want the window?"

"That would be nice," Marieke said. "I'd like to be able to see Africa when we get there."

"Well, since we're on the left-hand side of the plane, it'll only be when we actually fly over land that you'll see land; otherwise, you'll see a lot of water," Melisende pointed out.

"I hadn't thought of that," Marieke admitted. "How long's this flight?"

"Seven hours and ten minutes, so should be there by mid-afternoon, and Bridget said she'd pick us up at the airport. It will be nice to be back in Africa," Melisende said. "Don't you miss it terribly?"

"Sometimes," Marieke admitted. "But I'm happy with you in Paris, and if we can do this once in a while, then I'm more than happy."

"Perhaps now we don't have to worry about work, we could do this each year?" Melisende suggested.

"Only if there's not somewhere else you'd rather go," Marieke said. "I don't want us not to go somewhere you'd really like to go just to keep me happy going back to Africa."

"Don't worry, chérie," Melisende said. "If there's something I think we'd both like, I'll let you know."

The flight took them out over the Gulf of Oman to the Arabian Sea, then on down to the Indian Ocean, skirting the coastline of Africa, then made landfall over Tanzania and then on inland to Lusaka. The airport in Lusaka was less developed than Dubai, so it was down some stairs, then a walk across the tarmac to the arrivals building, where Commissioner Joseph Bwalya was waiting.

"Commandant Englebrecht," he said. "Welcome back to Zambia."

"Commissioner, this is *commissaire divisionnaire* Melisende Garnier of the *police nationale*; she and I have worked together for many years," Marieke said, making the introduction.

7

"Welcome to Zambia, Madame Garnier. I hope you will enjoy your stay. If you find at any time that you need help with anything, please do not hesitate to call me," Isaac said, giving her his business card.

"Thank you, Commissioner," Melisende said.

"So, Matshwane, off to the bush again," Isaac said, using the nickname that Marieke had acquired in her days in the Botswana Police, *matshwane* being the Setswana word for a ratel, an animal known for its tenacity and fearlessness.

"I am, Sir," Marieke confirmed. "Will and Bridget Martin have opened a new bush camp in the Kafue."

"I had heard that," Isaac said. "Are you flying out today?"

"No, we're staying overnight with Will and Bridget, and she wants us to drive a vehicle out to the park for her tomorrow," Marieke told him.

"Well, drive safely on the Great West Road, we do have some police checkpoints on that road, and there is a new toll booth, so take some Kwacha for the toll," Isaac told her.

"Thank you, Sir," Marieke said. "I hope you did not come out here just to meet us."

"I had other items to attend to," he replied. "It helps to keep an eye on things and see for yourself once in a while."

"That it does," she agreed.

"Come, let us get you through the formalities," he suggested. He led the way to the immigration desks and bypassed those to an office where the local chief of immigration was stationed. Marieke insisted on paying the fifty-dollar each visa fee, and for that, they received a rather nice-looking visa pasted onto a page of their passports. Isaac then led them to baggage claim, where they got some odd looks from other passengers, probably wondering why these two women should be receiving such attention. Marieke saw their bags and went to pick them up, but was forestalled by a policeman who grabbed them for her and carried them to where the others were waiting. As they walked out, Marieke saw Bridget and waved.

"Marieke, Melisende, so nice to see you again," Bridget said.

"Bridget, thanks for meeting us. This is Commissioner Bwalya, he and I have worked together in the past," Marieke said.

"Commissioner," Bridget said, shaking his hand.

"Mrs Martin, I gather from Marieke that you've opened another camp in Kafue," Isaac said.

"We have, we open in a few days, so we'll see how well it does," Bridget said.

"And Air Safari, is that doing well?" Isaac asked, displaying a knowledge of what was what around Zambia.

"It is, thank you, we're about to go to our winter timetable, so will see an increase in flights and traffic," Bridget replied.

"Good, good to hear of our local businesses succeeding, Matshwane, Madame Garnier, enjoy your stay," Isaac said. "I'll bid you a good day, I have matters to attend to."

"Thank you for coming to meet us," Marieke said. "It is really nice to see you again,"

"So, Marieke, good flight?" Bridget asked as they loaded their bags into her car.

"The best," Marieke replied. "I think if I had the option, I'd use Emirates in the future."

"Even more than Air France?" Bridget asked.

"I think so," Marieke said. "Emirates does a bang-up job. So, what's the plan?"

"We'll go home, and tomorrow we'll give you the Land Cruiser to drive out," Bridget said.

"You'll give us a map?" Melisende asked.

"You'll need it to negotiate the Lusaka streets and again when you get inside the park," Bridget said. "My advice is to leave early in the morning, before the traffic, so six if you can manage that?"

"We'll manage," Marieke assured her. "So, how is everyone?"

"We're all fine," Bridget replied. "As far as we can tell, two of the camps will open on time on the first of June and the Busanga one a little later, the rains were good and the roads are not all dry yet, so access is a little difficult, a couple of the other camps plan to open on the first of June, so we've got bookings on Air Safari for Ntemwa. We've had no reports of insurmountable problems at the camps, so now it's just a question of having guests show up."

"How's the airline doing?" Melisende asked.

"Very well," Bridget replied. "As I told your police friend, we're about ready to switch to the winter timetable, so more flights, two a day on the Kafue circuit and three a day to Mfuwe, three to Jeki and Royal, two to Royal, Jeki and Mfuwe, one each way for transfers between Luangwa and Lower Zambezi, and two a day to Livingstone, and we have the regular business to Ndola, Solwezi and Kasama as well, we're busy, bookings are good, so we're looking forward to a good season. Next summer we're thinking of perhaps Harare and Lilongwe, we'll see."

"How many planes do you now have?" Marieke asked.

"We've got the three new Twin Otters, built by Viking," Bridget replied. "That gives us 19 seats a flight, so we can meet the demand for our camps, plus for other camps, we've gone to a commercial seat rate, not a charter rate, unless it's a non-scheduled flight. If the traffic keeps up, we may have to add another plane."

"Does it pay?" Melisende asked.

"If we get at least 11 seats a flight," Bridget replied. "We'll also carry cargo for camps, and we charge for that. Sometimes people run out of things and just need it in a hurry, sometimes things break down and they need spares, so there's usually something extra on the flights. The two flights a day to Kafue bears looking at again, we may need three as other camps open on Busanga."

"What do you hear from Katrina?" Marieke asked.

"They're still enjoying life in Hawai'i," Bridget said. "Have you spoken to her lately?"

"Last month," Marieke said. "She had to go and settle up her Mum's estate in South Africa."

"Sussana lived to a good age," Bridget commented. "Ninety-two is a good age for anyone. OK, here we are, I'll just drop you, I need to go into town for a few things, I'll be back in about an hour. Make yourselves some tea, anything you want."

Bridget was back in an hour with more supplies to be taken out to the camp, or more properly, to two camps, the new one and the older one on the Busanga plain. Francesca, Alessandra's sister, who ran that camp, would meet them where they picked up the boat and take her share of the supplies. The third camp in the south of the park would be supplied by another run contracted out to a local man who did just that, ferry supplies. Will joined them at seven, done for the day, with the last flight in.

"Marieke, Melisende, how are you both?" he asked.

"Happy," Marieke replied.

"You don't miss your jobs?" he asked.

"We're actually both still on the rolls as consultants," Marieke replied. "We've been called in twice to give an opinion, so it's not a great inconvenience, and we still have badges to flash at officious junior officers."

"Thanks for driving the *bakkie* out for us," he said. "Dress warmly, though, I've put the windscreen up, but it still gets draughty under the canopy. The heater works, so you should be able to have warm feet."

"Here's a detailed map of how to skirt the traffic and get out onto the Great West Road," Bridget said. "You'll have to pay a toll at the new booth they put in, and when you get to the park gate, there'll be the park entry fee. Here's some Kwacha for that. This is a map for inside the park, with an inset of where to find the boat. I'll send you off with a couple of flasks of coffee, or tea if you'd rather, and a packed breakfast cum lunch. If you leave at six, you should be able to meet up with Fran and Alex at noonish. Stop at the mission at Nangoma for a loo break and a coffee and fifty-two kilometres further on pick up Stan, he's one of the staff going out to Mupundu, he'll be waiting by the side of the road, he'll recognise the *bakkie*. Fran and Alex should be waiting at the boat dock by the Lufupa River camp, Stan can direct you to it when you get close."

"Aren't you two thinking of retirement yourselves?" Marieke asked.

"We've set a date," Will said. "Five years from now, we're handing everything over to the girls and to a manager for the airline. We've got a place outside Livingstone that we'll move to, the biggest challenge is health care, we'll have to see how things work out, we may be forced to go back to the UK just because of that, fortunately, we kept making the National Insurance payments through the years, so we're eligible for an old age pension and for the NHS."

"We should have dinner and let you have a bath and get to bed if you're going to be out of here by six in the morning," Bridget said.

It was dark when Marieke and Melisende set off the next morning. Will pulled the Land Cruiser up to the door for them. It was a dull green with half doors at the front but no windows and no floor mats or other interior furnishings, just the seats and the canvas canopy that provided shade for the passengers and driver. It was set up as a typical safari vehicle with a frame fitted over the back that had three rows of bench seats, accessed by short ladders on each side. The benches could each seat three, so could easily accommodate eight guests, which was as many beds as the camp had. The whole of the back behind and under the seats was crammed with boxes of supplies, and there were even boxes on the seats, tied on with ropes. The sun was not due up until about six twenty-five, so they were well out of the city and headed west as it came up, which made things a little difficult seeing what was behind them as the rising sun shone right into the rearview mirror. Fortunately, traffic was light, so they had no issues with people coming up behind them unobserved. Marieke drove for the first leg to Nangoma, along dead straight stretches of road that dipped up and down at times, crossing small water courses. The road surface could have used some repair, and in places, the potholes were quite numerous. Once out away from Lusaka, the road was bordered by strips of red dirt, then low bush cover and fields of maize and other crops. There were some people walking along the road, many of them women with all manner of things balanced on their heads. They passed several lorries that looked really overloaded, that had broken down and were waiting either for parts and a mechanic, or a tow. After just over an hour, they were stopped at a police roadblock, and the officer asked to see Marieke's driving licence.

"This is not a Zambian licence," she said.

"No," Marieke agreed. "It is from France."

"Wait here," the officer said. She disappeared for a while and came back with another officer, this one more senior, judging by the insignia.

"This licence is not valid in Zambia," he said.

"I see," Marieke said. "If you have a telephone in your office, I believe we can clear things up."

"This way," he said. Marieke followed him and was shown the telephone. She dialled the number for Isaac, hoping that he was in his office at that early hour, and was gratified that he answered the telephone himself.

"Commissioner, this is Matshwane, we are at the first police block and I've been told by the officer here that my French licence is not valid," she explained.

"Put him on the phone," Isaac said. Marieke handed him the telephone and grinned to herself when he actually snapped to attention. He listened for a few minutes, then handed the telephone back to Marieke.

"So sorry about that," Isaac said. "Some of the police look to make some coffee money by coming up with bogus issues. There will be no further delays for you."

"Thank you, Commissioner," Marieke said. The officer then castigated the constable who had first questioned the licence, then escorted Marieke back to the Land Cruiser and saluted.

"Nice to know people in high places," Melisende commented as they drove off.

"I was hoping that he was actually in his office," Marieke said. "Otherwise, we would have been waiting there for a while."

They drove on until they reached the Nangoma mission, where they stopped for a loo break, a cup of coffee, and to top off the fuel tank. Will had been right, it was chilly in the Land Cruiser, but with the heater going full blast, and with gloves, hats and jackets, they stayed warm enough. They picked up Stan, he was where he was supposed to be and was aboard almost as soon as they stopped. Having Stan on board speeded things up at the park entrance, because he was known and they were sent on their way further down the main road until they crossed the Kafue bridge and then turned north into the park. The gate guard there knew Stan and knew where they were going, so saluted and raised the barrier. The next problem was tsetse flies. They were driving through a tsetse belt, and occasionally one would settle and bite. The bite hurt, so both Marieke and Melisende got good at spotting them and flicking them off before they had a chance to bite. The road was a fairly well-graded dirt road that wound its way generally northeast, with occasional detours around dambos and streams, one of them quite long before there was a dilapidated bridge that had clearly seen better days, probably from the sixties when the park was in its former heyday. For quite a while, they ran close to the Kafue River and got glimpses of it through the trees that lined the bank. When they got close to Lufupa, where the boat was, Stan guided them along the various small roads they needed to take and they finally came to the dock, where Francesca and Alessandra were waiting.

"Auntie Marieke," Alessandra said. "You made good time."
"We just wanted to get away from the tsetses," Marieke replied. "How are you both?"
"Busy," Francesca said. "How's retirement, Melisende?"
"We're happy," Melisende replied.
"Good, let's get all this stuff unloaded, I see Mum marked it, so Stan would you help load the Busanga stuff, and I'll start on our stuff?" Alessandra said. Marieke and Melisende helped by passing boxes down to Alessandra who stowed them in the boat, while Stan and Francesca transferred the rest into her Land Cruiser.
"I'll be off," Francesca said. "Enjoy your stay, and if you get bored with Alex, just come on over and take the old Land Cruiser and come on up and see me, we've not opened yet, won't until the fifteenth of the month, but if you're careful you should make it through, the track is drying out now, just try not to tear up the track too much, Alex can give you directions, or do you remember the way from when you were here before?"
"Thanks, Francesca, I think between us we can remember the way," Marieke said.
"Fine, I'll see you later, Alex," Francesca said.
"All set?" Alessandra asked. They climbed aboard the boat and Stan shoved it off and they drifted out into the Lufupa River, until Alessandra started the motor and spun them around to head out into the Kafue River. They avoided the pod of hippo that hung around at the confluence, then headed upstream towards the camp, a trip to the camp of about twenty minutes, and when they arrived. Grace, the camp manager, was waiting by the boat dock to help them unload.
"Grace, this is my Auntie Marieke and her partner Melisende," Alessandra said. "Grace Kachepa is our camp manager."
"Welcome to Mupundu," Grace said. "Did Bridget send out all that we asked for?"

"As far as I can see," Alessandra replied. "Let's get it all unloaded and to the camp, and we'll check."

"We've put you in this tent," Alessandra said, leading Marieke and Melisende to one of the staff tents away from the guest tents. "You've got two cots, a loo and a bucket shower, let me know if you need anything else."

"Thanks, Alex, we'll be fine," Marieke assured her. "If you need anything doing, just tell us."

"There is one issue if you could take a look at it," Alessandra said. "Our booking system is playing up, could you see what you can do?"

"We'll take a look," Melisende said. "Where's the computer?"

"I'll show you," Alessandra said and led the way to a small office behind the kitchen area. There, there was a large battery, the computer and a satellite uplink dish. "This is the log-on info that will get you into the system."

"What is the problem?" Marieke asked.

"We're having difficulty adding new bookings, sometimes they take, sometimes they don't," Alessandra said. "I'm not sure what's going on."

"We'll let you know if we find anything," Melisende promised.

"I like this place," Marieke said after Alessandra had gone to sort out all the supplies they had brought out with them. "It's quiet, it looks like it's isolated enough that there won't be fifty other Land Rovers all crowded around one poor leopard, just minding his own business and wondering why all the people don't go away."

"I hope we get the chance to take a drive around," Melisende said.

"I'm sure we will," Marieke said. "I'm sure that Alex will want to check on the tracks they must have put in. So, I'm into their system, let's just add a booking to see what happens."

"Look there, that field, what does it ask for?" Melisende said.

"Payment type, I would have thought that that was a repeat of that field there, I wonder why it's there twice?" Marieke pondered. "Let's see if we enter the same data in each field, if it clears the issue, does it print the invoices twice or once?"

"It clears the booking issue, and it does print the invoice twice, which could lead to problems if you're not paying attention," Melisende said. "Is there a contact us address?"

"There is," Marieke confirmed. "I'll send off a query to them and see if they can't just remove the extra field and the duplication of invoices. Good, let's just delete my test data. I wouldn't want to create issues."

"We may have fixed the issue, or at least found it," Melisende told Alessandra. "There was a duplicate field, and if you didn't enter the exact same data in both, it wouldn't accept the entry, but when it did, it gave you two invoices. We sent off a query to the software provider asking if they could do an update. In the meantime, we've posted a note telling you what to do to get the entries accepted and not embarrass yourself by billing people twice."

"Thanks," Alessandra said. "After lunch, I was going to take the Unimog out for a drive and finish putting the tracks in, and do any necessary cleaning up, would you like to come?"

"Absolutely," Melisende said.

They had lunch, then Alessandra led the way to the staff car park, where the vehicles were parked under some shade. The Unimog was there, with a small plough on the front. There was room in the cab of the Unimog for all three of them, and they climbed up into it and got comfortable. They drove from the camp along a track that had obviously been used recently, and Alessandra explained that it was the route in and that they would use it for game drives, and that it went quite far north until it reached a crossing over the Lufupa. She was more interested in the side tracks that she had been putting in recently and wanted to see if they still needed any attention. The grass on the sides of the road was still quite prolific, but it was not tall enough to affect the vehicles, and they did find a few places where the last of the rains had left some soft spots. Marieke was impressed with the skill that Alessandra had in shoving dirt around, to improve drainage in the future and to either fill in the soft spot or work around it.

"Are there many problems with poachers?" Melisende asked.

"There are some," Alessandra said. "This is a remote part of the park with almost no access, so although the Kafue, Lunga, Lufupa and

16

Ntemwa rivers form partially barriers to the south, east and west, to the very north there's nothing, so people will come in from the top side down almost as far as where the old Moshi camp used to be. We're trying, but it's a huge area, and to add to the problems from the north, the Ntwema to the west is not much of a barrier, not like the Kafue or the Lunga."

"What of the big mammals don't you get here?" Marieke asked.

"Giraffe and rhino," Alessandra replied. "We get almost everything else, but the rhino were shot out in the 1980s, and by 1998 they were declared extinct in Zambia, and giraffe have never really been here since the park was set up. There's a big push to get rhino back into the North Luangwa Park, we may look at that for another location in the future."

"What was the market for the rhino?" Melisende asked.

"Rhino horns for dagger handles for the Yemeni and traditional medicine for the Chinese, the prices were high enough that there were more than enough people who would risk the few game rangers that there were," Alessandra replied. "Elephant ivory is next, and there's a strong market for that among wealthy Chinese. The Zambians have sold their soul to the Chinese for infrastructure projects, and with that comes large numbers of Chinese and bought and paid for politicians."

"That's quite cynical," Marieke commented.

"Sadly, but that's how I see it, probably a good few in Lusaka don't see it that way, especially those in government, I'm careful where I voice my opinions and who might be listening," Alessandra said.

"How many visitors are due in on the first?" Melisende asked.

"Eight, four couples," Alessandra said. "All Americans, most of our clients are Brits, with a few Europeans thrown in for good measure, much easier for them to get here, we don't get too many Americans, they tend to go rather to Kenya or Tanzania, or if they do come here, they go to Luangwa or to one of the Wilderness Safaris camps here in Kafue, but we're working on that. The challenge for Americans is just getting here, it's either Delta to Jo'burg and then up, or one of the many carriers to Europe and then down to Jo'burg again, or what you did and take Emirates direct to Lusaka. There is the other American carrier, Ka Lei A Pele, that I was on twelve years ago, that does round-the-world stuff, but they go to Jo'burg as well." "Didn't you have an unpleasant experience with them?" Marieke asked.

"You mean twelve years ago when we got shot down over the Congo in 2002 when we were on their Flight 5 to Jo'burg," Alessandra said. "That wasn't the best, but we made it out, unlike most of the passengers who either died in the crash or were shot by the Congolese. That's an experience I don't need to repeat."

"I was amazed that you all survived that," Marieke said. "Katrina told me all about it one day."

"We were lucky to get away when we did," Alessandra said. "But it was a long trek from Angola to Mwinilunga, the last dash to the river and the border was rather hair-raising. I've no idea if the Angolans got all the Congolese involved."

"Of your clients, how many are repeat business?" Melisende asked.

"Probably 65% to 70%," Alessandra thought. "For some people, our camps are just what they're looking for, but for others, they're a bit too primitive; those are looking more for the lodge experience, so we don't see many of them back."

"This lot coming in, what do you know about them?" Marieke asked.

"Not too much," Alessandra admitted. "I know they're all from the States, they booked through one of the bigger agencies, I don't know if we're first or last on their list of places to go, we haven't seen their itinerary. We'll find out when they arrive, they're flying out from Lusaka on the morning flight of the first."

"We'll try and not get in your way," Marieke promised.

"You won't be in the way," Alessandra assured them. "You should join us for meals and meet and greet the guests."

"Sorry to interrupt," Melisende said. "What's that over there?"

"That's a Sharpe's Grysbok," Alessandra replied. "One of the dwarf antelopes, usually found on its own, browsers, can go without water for quite a while."

"Are there lots of antelope species in this park?" Marieke asked.

"Twenty all told," Alessandra said. "I won't bore you with the list, but the only big one we don't have is the gemsbok."

"I saw plenty of them in Botswana," Marieke said. "Particularly when I went out on a camel patrol."

"How was that?" Alessandra asked.

"Interesting," Marieke said. "If I had the choice, I'd stick to the Land Cruiser or a Land Rover, but the camels were quiet; they would go where we'd have problems with any vehicle, and they didn't break down."

"When did the Botswana Police stop using camels?" Alessandra asked.

"When I was still in Tsabong," Marieke said. "They finally disposed of the camels in 2001."

"What's that mongoose over there?" Melisende asked, pointing to the small animal rooting under some trees.

"A slender mongoose," Alessandra replied. "Eats rodents, birds and smaller snakes. You've got a good eye, Melisende. Maybe we should start back for dinner."

Dinner was the three of them, plus Grace, and Adam and Abel, who were the guides that the camp employed. Conversation was mainly about what each of them had seen that day, so that when the guests arrived, they would have a sense of where to take them to see various animals. Not that that was assured, the mammals moved around a lot and just because one was seen in a certain place, that did not guarantee that they would be in the same place the next day. Stories were told about past guests and their foibles, some of which were hilarious, some of which were sad. They were all curious to see what the Americans would be like; they got only a few, so to a great extent, they were an unknown quantity. Grace wanted to know about Paris fashions, so Melisende gave her the latest details of where the trends were going and who were the up-and-coming designers. Adam and Abel had heard stories from Alessandra about Marieke and her pursuit of villains, so pressed her for details of some of the cases she had worked on.

Showers were laid on after dinner, and Marieke and Melisende looked at the sleeping arrangements and considered what to do.

"What if we take all the bedclothes and set things up between the cots," Marieke suggested. "The floor may not be as comfortable as the cots, but at least we'll be together."

"That's probably a better idea than both trying to sleep in one cot," Melisende laughed. "We'd probably break it and then have to explain to Alessandra how and why."

"The floor's not too bad," Marieke said as she got down on the floor, stretched out and felt around for lumps and bumps.

"Fine, chérie, we'll just grab all the bedding," Melisende said. "What about the mosquito net?"

"We can hang one of them from there," Marieke said, pointing to a hook in the middle of the tent ridge.

"It's been a few years since we made love in the bush," Melisende said. "It's time to remedy that."

"It is," Marieke agreed. "But let's not scandalise the camp with too much noise."

"You're the noisy one," Melisende said.

"I know, I know," Marieke said. "I'll behave."

"Not too much, I hope," Melisende said.

If they had awakened anyone, there was no mention of it at breakfast the next morning, and Marieke had time to remake the beds before the housekeeping staff checked on their tent. A pattern they repeated each night and morning after that. For the next few days, Marieke and Melisende lent a hand when needed to help finish setting up the camp, but also took time off to drive themselves around some of the tracks that Bridget had put in. It was idyllic, no other people around, just the animals and birds. Marieke had a sketch map that Alessandra had given her that showed all the tracks that were fairly close to the camp, and she marked on that what they saw. On four drives, they took Adam and Abel with them and let them just look out for animals and birds and mark what, when and where. That would help them to establish patterns of animal movements so that they would have a reasonable chance of finding something if a guest had a real desire to see something particular. Marieke did discover that Abel spoke Setswana, as well as Bemba, Lunda and English. They saw lions, leopards, buffalo, elephant and myriads of antelope of many different species. The place seemed to be alive with animals, something that both Abel and Adam said was surprising because poaching had been rife in the past years, only dying out as they established the camp and started driving and walking in the area. They were sure that poaching would continue in the very far north of the park, but that was a huge area with no camps or lodges and very few roads. In days gone by, when the Moshi Camp had been thriving, there had been a lot less poaching as the game guards had been more active, and there had been more road traffic north of Moshi to the Kabanga post and the northern entry to the park.

Two days before the guests were due to arrive, Alessandra had a list of last minutes items to check on, beds to be made, plumbing for the loos to be checked in each tent, bucket showers to be tested, and then the kitchen and dining facilities to be reviewed, and finally vehicles and boats to be checked over to make sure they would run properly at least on the first day, after that, things happened, engines broke down, tyres punctured, all in the normal course of things. She left most of that to Grace, and she devoted her time to making sure that the tracks that they would use for game drives were nice and clear and that the various fire breaks they put in were clear of underbrush that would fuel a fire. Marieke and Melisende took advantage of her expeditions further away from the camp and went with her, driving around the bush, as far north as the Chibemba salt pan and other trips that either roughly paralleled the Lufupa, or ventured into the vast area that lay to the east towards the Lunga. They had a picnic lunch out and actually took a break from track maintenance to watch a herd of sable antelope. Dinner that evening was excellent, and they were joined at dinner by Mike and Ernest, the chefs who wanted to hear about French cooking. Melisende admitted that she was working on a cookbook and promised to print it out for them if Alessandra had enough paper for the printer. Alessandra told her to go ahead and print it, and she would get another box of paper out on the next plane.

The day before the guests arrived, Alessandra walked around with Grace with a checklist, and they checked the tents for bathroom supplies, the soaps and shampoos that they provided. They checked that there were coat hangers, hot water bottles, toilet paper, towels, solar lights, whistles, drinking water bottles, all the niceties that made tent living comfortable. They also checked for unwelcome visitors, rodents, snakes, wasp nests, all the things that could make tent life uncomfortable. Satisfied that they had done all they could, they sat down with the camp staff and went through the numbers of who would be arriving when. The kitchen crew then knew what to do in terms of menus and quantities of food to prepare, the housekeeping crew knew when the guests were arriving and departing, so knew when to prepare for linen changes.

"So, all ready?" Marieke asked Alessandra over dinner.

"As ready as we'll ever be," Alessandra replied. "We have a checklist that we've used before, and amended as time has gone on to catch the things that we missed before."

"How do you deal with all these guests?" Melisende asked.

"Some are a pleasure to have, some I'd like to see the back of as soon as possible, but for the most part, we manage," Alessandra replied. "It's the business that we're in, and if we didn't like meeting people, then we shouldn't be in the business."

"I remember my first trip to your camp in Botswana," Melisende said. "It was when Marieke was chasing after the man who was busy killing off all those he blamed for his prison sentence."

"We missed that," Alessandra said. "Fran and I were back in Italy at school. I do remember the first time we met Auntie Marieke, it was when you found the two headless corpses."

"Ah, yes, the two professors," Marieke recalled. "It was my first big case after I had been transferred to Gabs. I had had no idea until then how unpleasant the academic world could be."

"But you got your man," Alessandra commented.

"Both of them," Marieke confirmed. "It was quite a case, but it did get resolved, and they're still in prison, not a place I'd like to be."

"What time do you need to be up in the morning?" Melisende asked.

"Not too early," Alessandra said. "The plane will arrive at about nine in the morning, so I should leave here no later than eight-thirty, but maybe I'll go at about a quarter past, that will give me plenty of time."

"How soon before this park gets as busy as the Luangwa?" Marieke asked.

"I don't think for a while yet," Alessandra replied. "Although this was the first park, it has been rather neglected. Luangwa has had more development and has more lodges and camps, so is busier. It's also more open than here, there, spotting animals is easier than here, we've so much in the way of tree cover that the guides have to work to find animals. They're there, we know they are, but it's only on the Busanga and Nanzhila plains that things are relatively easy to spot."

"What are the other Zambian parks?" Melisende asked.

"Lochinvar and Blue Lagoon, two smaller parks not too far from here, well known for birds. Until not too long ago, Blue Lagoon was like a private hunting reserve for politicians and senior army officers. Then there's Liuwa Plain, Sioma Ngwezi and West Lunga to the west and north of us, Mosi-oa-Tunya at Livingstone, then to the east Lower Zambezi, South and North Luangwa, Luambe and Lukusuzi, generally off the Great North Road, there's Kasanka, Lavushi Manda, Isangano, Lusenga Plain, Mweru Wantipa and Sumbu, and in the far east on the Malawi border is the Nyika Plateau," Alessandra enumerated. "Some are well developed, others are struggling a bit, but things are improving as more people discover that Zambia probably offers the most authentic African experience."

"I suppose the government national parks department is typically underfunded," Marieke said.

"That's true," Alessandra confirmed. "There's more money in copper mining, so that typically takes precedence."

"Do those interests compete?" Melisende asked.

"They can," Alessandra confirmed. "Just to the east of the Kafue park are some of the oldest mines in Zambia, and there's always the possibility that better copper prices mean that they may become economic again. There's a controversy about a big new copper strike in the Lower Zambezi Park, the proposed Kangaluwi mine, it will be interesting to see what happens there, perhaps more concerning to us is another exploration site in the Kitumba Hills which are just east of the Kafue National Park boundary close to the old Sugar

Loaf and Lulu mines, between the Kafue and the Great West Road, that whole area of the park is big and wild with little access, so poaching could be a real issue."

"Katrina was telling me one day about trying to go to the Blue Lagoon park and getting turned away by the army, so finally camping out in an old building that had once been part of the Red Rose mine," Marieke said. "Then the next day they went on to Mumbwa and then back to the Copperbelt."

"They must have had fun exploring parts of Zambia back in the seventies," Alessandra said.

"Have you got a game scout assigned here?" Marieke asked.

"Yes, chap by the name of Henry, he's from the Copperbelt, so not local, but he's not bad, I went out with him and Abel to see what his tracking skills are like," Alessandra said. "He's not as good as Abel, but then that's not his job; his job is to carry the gun in case something goes really wrong."

"Have you kept up your shooting?" Melisende asked.

"I have," Alessandra replied. "We use the police range when they let us, and there's a range in Malawi that the guides use for qualifying, and I'll go out with a PH sometimes when there's a guided hunt in one of the concessions. I don't usually tell the guests that I will shoot things; most don't appreciate that. Once in a while, we get a guest who hunts in either the UK or the US and them I will tell, but I only shoot what we're going to eat. In Botswana, we shot and fed the meat to the guests, but here we don't do that, we buy chicken, lamb, pork and beef, no game at all. Have you kept up your shooting?"

"We have," Melisende confirmed. "But lately it's been mostly with handguns, we have both been out on the range recently to test fire new long guns that our police started using, Marieke's still the better shot."

"That's the product of a misspent childhood, or perhaps necessity in childhood," Marieke added. "Before I went to uni, Dad would give me a bullet, just one, and tell me to get food for the next few days, in that way he was very typical of the Boerjies, one bullet should be enough."

"What do you use in the police?" Alessandra asked.

"The standard sidearm issue is the Sig Sauer Pro SP," Marieke replied. "We've also used on different occasions the Ruger Mini-14, Remington shotguns, and the Heckler & Koch UMP and G36 guns and even the Italian Spectre M4."

"So, quite a variety," Alessandra said. "Well, if you two don't mind, I'm nodding off here, so I'll see you in the morning."

"She's busy," Marieke commented to Melisende.

"Not surprising with the first guests of the season arriving," Melisende said. "I suppose that even after all these years, there could be something that you've forgotten, and it will be the one thing that is remembered."

The first group

"Auntie Marieke, will you look at the water system for us?" Alessandra asked when they met for breakfast the following morning. "It looks like the bloody elephants have dug it up again. If you need to dig, Stan will show you where the backhoe attachment for the Unimog is."

"Of course, Alex," Marieke replied.

"I need to go and pick up this first batch of guests," Alessandra said. "I'll see you later."

"Go well," Marieke said.

Alessandra collected Adam and drove the short way back to their boat dock on the Kafue River, then they took a boat downstream back to the confluence of the Kafue and the Lufupa. Once there, she dropped Adam off to check on something that had cropped up on the old Land Cruiser they used for supply runs, and picked up the Land Cruiser that Marieke had driven out from Lusaka and drove the short distance to the airstrip. There she parked at the edge of the Lufupa airstrip, waiting for the plane to arrive with this first group of visitors for the year to the camp. The Lufupa airstrip was just that, an airstrip cleared out of the surrounding bush and then graded and surfaced so that it was usable in nearly all weathers. The strip offered little, apart from a small covered area by the hard stand and an old helipad, the markings of which were faded and barely visible; there was no terminal building, no shops, no restaurants or cafés, so she had brought water and damp towels for the guests. Because it was June, the morning was still quite chilly, but the African skies were clear and the sun was shining, and there was no inclement weather to worry about. They were well into the dry season, and the next rains were not expected until late October or early November.

Alessandra sat, wrapped up in her jacket, gloves and woollen hat and enjoyed the quiet of the bush, the sounds she could hear were birds, the repetitive calls of the ring-necked dove and the red-eyed dove and the deep booming call of the ground hornbill, the occasional raucous chatter of guinea fowl, and the cry of the fish eagles, and in the background the buzzing of insects, and from farther away different sounds, the whistles of puku and the occasional honk of a hippo in the nearby river, and once the faint roar of a distant lion. She also heard the odd tick tick as the engine of her Land Cruiser cooled down. Once or twice, she thought she heard a human voice, but they were probably just fragments of conversation from the nearby Lufupa River Camp carried in the wind. She heard a boat headed downriver and wondered which camp upriver it had come from, some of them bothered her as they had the tendency to race up and down river creating a wake and noise as they went, disturbing not only her guests but also animals that might be on the river bank, and also showing faint regard for the hippo that were in the river. The river offered so much: a convenient way to get to their camp, a great way to see game and birds, and for some, the opportunity to try their hand at fishing. In some ways, it was a shame that there were rapids in the river just upstream of the Kafue Bridge that carried the Great West Road, which would make an interesting alternative for transfers from camp to camp.

Her reverie was broken by the sound of another diesel Land Cruiser. It was from one of the lodges a little downriver and had also come to meet the flight. She watched it as it pulled up beside her. It was a light tan colour and had a canopy that ran the whole length and it had half doors at the front on which was emblazoned, Kamana Lodge, she smiled to herself as she thought about the diesel engine, it always seemed to her that when they were running at low speeds they sounded as if they were complaining.

"Hey, Alex," the driver said as she pulled up alongside.

"Howzit Tiffany?" Alessandra replied. "How are you?"

"Busy," Tiffany said. "I've got my eight here out on their way to Ngoma and four in, you?"

"I've got eight in," Alessandra replied.

"You're ready to open?" Tiffany asked.

"As ready as we'll ever be," Alessandra laughed.

"Folks," Tiffany said. "This is Alessandra, she runs a camp just up the river a little way from here."

"How did you enjoy your stay?" Alessandra asked of them.

"It was fabulous," one of the women said. "Tiffany is amazing, I can't believe I'm in the middle of Africa and yet still get hot showers, superb meals and animals as well."

"Will you come back?" Alessandra asked.

"Definitely," was the chorused reply.

"But," added one of the women. "Next time we'll probably come back later in the year when it's not quite so cold. I never imagined Africa as getting cold."

"It's the altitude," Alessandra said. "If you had been in the Zambezi Valley at one of the Lower Zambezi camps, you would have been warm enough, we're high enough up that overnight it will cool down a lot. If you do come back later in the season, I should warn you that late October and early November can get quite hot. Our peak season is probably August and September, when the weather is warm but not too hot, it's dry, with no rain, and the grass is down, so probably better game viewing."

"Maybe next time we come we'll check out the Lower Zambezi," the woman said.

"There's quite a few camps in the Lower Zambezi park," Tiffany added. "And you can fly into the Jeki or Royal strips, and it's only a short drive then to whichever camp you want. Some of them even offer canoe rides on the Zambezi."

"Aren't there hippos and crocs in the Zambezi?" a guest asked.

"There are," Tiffany confirmed. "But the guides know what to look for and how to keep you safe."

"If you want a real adventure, you could always try white water rafting on the Zambezi below Vic Falls," Alessandra suggested.

"What happens if you fall in or the raft gets upset?" a guest asked.

"They have safety kayaks and guides who know what to do," Tiffany added. "I've done it three times, once in October, which is when the rapids are really good."

"When's the plane due in?" a guest asked.

"Very soon," Tiffany replied.

Alessandra heard the plane before she saw it and looked around towards the north and found it as it flew over part of the huge Kafue National Park on its way to the strip. She watched as it flew towards her, then turned and went down the strip towards the north-west,

28

checking for any animals on the strip, before it turned and came back upwind to land. As she was sitting there, she would have been able to assure them that there were no animals on the strip, but the pilots survived by checking themselves as part of a routine. The plane, one of the Twin Otters that Bridget had mentioned to Marieke and Melisende, was the regular flight to Lufupa, operated by Air Safari. It had come in from the Ntemwa Strip near the Busanga Plains on the second leg of the circular Kafue Park run, a really short trip of only five to ten minutes, but which on the ground could be a couple of hours, depending on the state of the road. Alessandra waited for the plane to taxi over to the hard stand, then she and Tiffany drove out to meet their guests.

"Alex, Tiff," the co-pilot said as he got down from the plane. "How's things?"

"Good, thanks Chad, and you?" Alessandra asked.

"Good, we dropped off four at Ntemwa, and we've got twelve for here," he said. Alessandra waited while he helped passengers from the plane and then went over to greet them.

"Good morning," she said. "Welcome to Lufupa, I'm Alessandra Martin and will be taking some of you to Mupundu, and Tiffany Wilson here will take some of you to Kamana. Who's with me?"

"We are," a woman said, waving her arms at a group of eight. The others turned to Tiffany, who greeted them.

"I have some water and damp towels here for you if you would like to wait under the shade over there while we transfer your bags. If you'll excuse me, I'll just give the pilots a hand," Alessandra said, then joined Chad, who was busy pulling bags from the various compartments at the front and back of the plane. They were joined by the pilot, Phil, who came over to say hello and help with the luggage handling while the passengers milled around under the shade of the canopy by the hard stand.

"Hey Alex," he said. "Good to see you."

"Nice to see you again, Phil, how have you been?" she asked.

"Well enough," he said. "Let's just get these bags loaded into your Land Cruiser. I tagged yours with red and Tiff's with green."

"I see they've all got nice matching bags," Alessandra commented.

"It did make loading easier," he said. "They fit into the back nicely, better than some who come with huge hard suitcases, even after we tell them soft bags and what the size and weight limits are."

"Which bags are mine?" Tiffany asked as she joined them.

"These four, the green-marked ones," Phil said.

"I've got these bags to go," Tiffany said, pointing to the luggage she had taken from her Land Cruiser. "And these are the seat coupons for the passengers."

"Thanks, Tiff," Phil said. "When are you next in Lusaka?"

"I'm due two weeks off at the end of the month," she replied.

"Great," he said. "I've found a new place to go and explore."

"Look forward to it," she said.

"Are you two getting serious?" Alessandra asked.

"We are," Tiffany confirmed. "I'm thinking that a pilot's licence might not be a bad idea, then we could live in the same house and not have to just grab time together in the off-season and when I get breaks."

"Not a bad idea," Alessandra agreed.

Alessandra supervised the loading of her guests' bags into the back of her Land Cruiser and helped Tiffany pass bags to Chad and Phil as they loaded the outgoing luggage, continuing their conversation with the two pilots as they worked.

"How many through?" Alessandra asked.

"Twelve off at Ngoma and sixteen on, so it's sixteen back to Lusaka," Phil said. "Tiff, how did your other guests get out?"

"They did a ground transfer to Kaingu, we dropped them off at the bridge," she said, referring to the bridge across the Kafue River that carried the main road from Lusaka in the east to Kaoma and Mongu, in the west. "I'm not sure what they're doing after Kaingu."

"Let's get our outgoing pax loaded," Chad said. "Folks, if you're coming with us, let's get aboard, pick any open seat, there's water by the door there, grab a bottle as you go by." He stood by and helped those passengers leaving to get aboard and seated, then came to say goodbye to Alessandra and Tiffany.

"We'll see you in a day or so when your next group come out, we've got no one for you tomorrow," Phil said.

"Fine," Alessandra said. "We'll be waiting. You'll be bringing out four more for us on Friday, right? Will I see you then, Tiff?"

"I'll be here," Tiffany said.

"Right," Phil confirmed. "Is that it for you for this week, Alex?"

"No, we've got two ground transfers coming on that day too, they're coming up from Mukambi, we're meeting them by the Mukombo bridge at nine," she replied. "Well, have a good flight back."
"Thanks," Phil said. "We must be off, got the flight this afternoon and Chad's got a date tonight."
"Who with?" she asked.
"Not sure," Phil said. "He's been very cagey."
"Interesting," she said. "Chad, enjoy your date tonight."
"Thanks, Alex, Tiff, see you both Friday," Chad said. Alessandra and Tiffany watched as the plane taxied back to the other end of the runway, then turned and took off towards the south, on its way for the short hop to the Ngoma airstrip, before heading back to Lusaka.
"I'll see you, Tiff," Alessandra said.
"Bye, Alex," Tiffany replied.

Alessandra then turned her attention back to her guests.
"Again, welcome to Lufupa, please call me Alex, it's a little easier than Alessandra; if you're ready, we can all get aboard and I'll drive us to the boat landing," she said. There was some delay as they seemed to be sorting out who would sit where and next to whom, something that made Alessandra smile to herself as the drive to their next stop would be short. As she helped them aboard, Alessandra got each of their names, hoping, as she always did, that she would actually be able to fit names to faces by the time they reached the camp. They were all about the same age, mid-forties, she guessed, all looking very prosperous with elegant safari outfits and a fair amount of expensive-looking jewellery. The one poor soul looked as if he had caught something or was allergic to something, as he had a persistent cough and looked as if he had trouble breathing. Alessandra quickly thought through the names and came up with Alberto. She would have to keep an eye on him. The woman who had obviously nominated herself as the spokesperson of the group took the seat next to Alessandra and introduced herself, again, as Monica Davis, from Los Angeles. She explained that they were all from the US, something Alessandra already knew, but which Monica seemed to want to impress upon her. They had been planning this their first trip to Africa for some time They had already been to the South Luangwa and Lower Zambezi National

31

Parks, spending three nights in each, and this was their last stop before beginning their long trek home with the trip beginning with the hop to Livingstone, then the commercial flight to Johannesburg and onward from there. The two previous stays had been at lodges in the Luangwa and Lower Zambezi parks, among the many other camps and lodges scattered about the Luangwa and Zambezi rivers, so this would be a different experience, being more remote with no other camps around and under canvas.

"How was your flight out?" Alessandra asked.
"It was fine," Monica said. "It's an early start, early enough that it didn't get too bumpy. We got the guided tour from Phil, not that there was much to see, just lots and lots of farms and villages, then miles and miles of just bush, and the flood plains of the Kafue River. I didn't realise that the airstrips in this park were so close together."
"The strips may be close by air, but it can take quite a while to drive, depending on the state of the road," Alessandra said. "Where did you stay last night?"
"The Radisson Blu in Lusaka," Monica replied. "A quite nice hotel, but most importantly, close to the airport, so that we could make the seven o'clock departure without getting up at the crack of doom. We flew in from Jeki last night after our stay in Lower Zambezi."
"How was that?" Alessandra asked.
"Amazing," Monica said. "Different to the Luangwa park, but still amazing. The Zambezi is a big river, lots of hippo, crocs and eles."
"It is," Alessandra agreed. "The Kafue always seems to me to be a more relaxed river; you can shut off the motor and just drift, but we have our share of hippo and other animals in and around the river. How did you get to Luangwa?"
"We took a plane to Mfuwe, then they picked us up at the airport, then we took a plane from Mfuwe to Jeki," Monika replied.
"Did you fly with Air Safari?" Alessandra asked.
"We did, different pilots," Monica said. "Same story out there, some villages and farms, but lots and lots of bush."
"In the seventies, the population was only about 4.5 million, now it's almost 16 million, so imagine what it was like then," Alessandra said.

"Is this it?" Monica asked as they drove past buildings. "Are we there already?"

"No," Alessandra said. "This is the Lufupa River Camp. What you're seeing are the support buildings; all the guest accommodations are along the Kafue. We'll leave the Land Cruiser just past the Lufupa camp and take a boat from there to our camp. The Lufupa guys are kind enough to let us use their boat ramp and to let us leave a vehicle there."

"So, we all have to get out?" a woman, who Alessandra identified as Carol Davis, asked.

"We do," Alessandra confirmed. "The road to the camp would take quite a while to navigate, so it's far quicker by boat."

"How do you get all your supplies and everything in?" a man, whom Alessandra, after racking her brain for a few seconds, finally identified as James, asked.

"We put in a road to the north," Alessandra explained. "But, as I said, driving in would not be that much fun for visitors, it's a long way around, so we use this Land Cruiser for transfers to the strip and for excursions to the Busanga Plains, and that Land Cruiser over there for runs to town for groceries and then transfer everything by boat."

Alessandra pulled up at a boat launch ramp that had seen better days, but which was still serviceable. She waved to Adam, who was waiting by the boat, and he came to help transfer luggage. Alessandra introduced Adam as one of their guides, and then she and Adam loaded the luggage on board, and then helped the passengers board and get seated. The Land Cruiser she pulled off to the side and parked next to the old Land Cruiser.

"All ready?" Alessandra asked. "Good, we're actually in the Lufupa River here, but just over there you can see the Kafue, and we'll be going upstream."

"Is it far?" Monica asked.

"Not too far, just a few miles, so about twenty minutes, unless we see something on the way," Alessandra said. "We won't be racing up the river, it makes too much noise and we don't want to disturb things too much." Adam cast off the bow line and then jumped aboard, pushing the boat out away from the ramp as he did.

Alessandra started the motor and backed into the Lufupa stream, then started forward towards the Kafue. Where the two rivers met was obvious, the muddy green-brown Lufupa emptied into the much clearer Kafue, eventually merging and losing its colour and identity. Alessandra turned the boat into the Kafue stream and headed upriver.

"You just left your jeep there?" Monica asked. "You didn't lock it or anything?"

"There's not much to lock up," Alessandra laughed. "I put the key in the small box up under the canopy, but it'll be safe enough, the Lufupa people are not going to steal it."

"There was a Land Rover there," Monica said. "Who does that belong to?"

"One of the other camps," Alessandra replied. "Their camp is a little past Mupundu on the other side of the river in the big thumb that's created by the massive bend in the river."

As they went, she pointed out the types of trees that lined the banks of the river, and she also pointed out the birds that they saw. Her passengers seemed mildly interested, but not to the extent that she might have expected. Perhaps as this was getting towards the end of their trip, they had had enough of birds and trees and were now thinking of returning home to the traffic and bustle that is city life in the United States, or perhaps they were just not that interested in birds and trees. Alessandra slowed down and pointed. Just ahead of them, a group of elephant was crossing the river. They were in line astern and formed a barrier across the river. She waited until they had all crossed before proceeding and did note that that had warranted photographs.

"Can we offer you anything to drink, water, beer?" she asked. There were no takers, so she went back to the task of piloting the boat upstream. She noticed movement on one of the banks and slowed down and turned around to go back downstream, then came back up again.

"What do you see?" Monica asked.

"Lion," Alessandra said. "Just over there."

"Where? I can't see him," Monica complained.

"In that long grass over there," Alessandra said, pointing to a spot on the south bank. "You can see his ears, and if we drift back down a little, you'll be able to see him."

"Oh, I see," said Carol. "James, did you get some pictures?"

"He's not as close as those lions we saw in Luangwa," Monica complained.

"I'm sorry I can't get too close to the bank, it's a little shallow here, and I don't want to have to get into the water and start pushing. We can probably get you close to a lion," Alessandra said. "If we go out for a game drive, and we see one, we should be able to get really close. Shall we go on?"

"Yes," Monica said. "I need to find a ladies' room."

It was a relief to finally reach the landing that they used for the camp. Alessandra nosed the boat into the bank, and Adam jumped ashore with a line and secured the boat. Then he helped everyone disembark, and when they were all safely on the bank, he and Alessandra unloaded the luggage. They had two Land Cruisers at the boat dock, each arranged with six individual seats on the racks at the back, with a storage box between each pair of seats, and these differed from the one by the Lufupa airstrip in that they had no half doors in the front and no canopy. Adam loaded the luggage into the back of one of the Land Cruisers, and Alessandra asked the guests to climb aboard. There was again discussion about who would ride with whom, and Alessandra had to bite her tongue not to step in and assign seats. These people were worse than ten-year-olds; it looked like it was going to be a long few days.

When they were all finally loaded, Alessandra told Adam that she would go first, taking the Land Cruiser that had the luggage, and that he should follow in a few minutes.

"Why aren't they right behind us?" Monica asked after a few minutes.

"We want the dust to blow away or settle before they come along," Alessandra explained. "Otherwise, it's unpleasant for those behind."

"How far is it to the camp?" Carol asked.

"About ten minutes," Alessandra replied. "It's just back from the river here, a short distance and inland a little, behind the lagoon that's here. When the water is really high, we can actually use the boats to get right up to the camp."

"How long has this camp been here?" Monica asked.

"This is our first year here in full operation," Alessandra said. "We've had a camp on the Busanga Plains for over fifteen years, and we have another camp in the south of the park, on the Nanzhila Plains, which we've had for about six years. Before my folks moved to Zambia, they ran a camp in northern Botswana."

"So, you're not from Zambia?" Monica asked.

"No," Alessandra replied. "I was born in South Africa, my folks both worked there, and then they decided to change careers and took over an existing bush camp in the Linyanti area of Botswana."

"Is the Busanga camp still running?" Carol asked.

"It is," Alessandra confirmed. "My sister and her husband run that one, one of our long-time employees, Kossam and his wife, Charity, run the Nanzhila Plains camp, and my folks run the office in Lusaka. Well, here we are, welcome to Mupundu camp."

"What does Mupundu mean?" Carol asked.

"Mupundu is a tree, also known as the Mobola Plum, *Parinari curatellifolia*, to give it its taxonomic name, that is sought after for its fruit," Alessandra explained. "It's often found in the *miombo* woodlands that cover much of this part of Zambia, in fact, that tree over there is one."

They pulled up to the car park, and Grace and four of the staff were there to greet them.

"Welcome to Mobola," Grace said.

"This is Grace, she is our camp manager," Alessandra said. "And this is Joseph and Stan, they'll help you get settled in your tents. Please help yourselves to a cool towel to clean off the dust of the journey. Let's see, Monica and David, you're in tent number one, Carol and James, you're in tent number two. If you'll just show Joseph and Stan which are your bags, we'll get you settled. I'll wait for the others and get them settled, then perhaps you'd like to join us at the *boma* for a refreshing drink?"

"The *boma*?" Monica asked.

"The public area where we have our bar, sitting area and dining area," Alessandra explained. "You'll pass it on your way to the tents. The others will be in tents three and four, which are between here and the *boma*."

Alessandra watched as Grace led the way to the tents with Joseph and Stan carrying the bags and then waved to John and Rice to join her waiting for the next group. Shortly afterwards, Adam arrived with his Land Cruiser and the rest of the guests. Alessandra wondered what Adam made of it all, as what she heard was all in Spanish. As they pulled up, she stepped out of the shade of the trees to greet them.

"Welcome to Mupundu," she said. "We have moist towels here for you, to wash off the dust of the short journey. When you are ready, show John and Rice which are your bags and we will take you to your tents. I have put Sofia and Tom in tent number three and Catalina and Alberto in tent number four, does that sound agreeable to you?"

"That's fine," Sofia said. "Where are the Davises?"

"They are in tents one and two, which are the other side of the *boma*, the public area where we have the bar, dining area and sitting area," Alessandra explained. "None of the tents is too far from the *boma*, but at the same time, they are far enough apart to have some privacy. If you are ready?"

"Lead on," Sofia said. Alessandra picked up one of the bags and walked them to the first tent, number four.

"Catalina and Alberto, this is your tent, if you come inside with me, you'll see beds, with mosquito nets, there we have a rack for clothes and such, and if we go through this side entrance here you have your bathroom, flush loo there, washbasin and a bucket shower, just let us know when you want a shower and we'll fill the bucket with hot water for you. The bathroom looks out onto the lagoon here, but it is quite private, the other tents are that way, and the kitchen and staff tents are all behind us a little way to that side."

"Looks pretty nice," Alberto said. "Look, there are animals out on the lagoon there, what are they?"

"There are puku, impala, waterbuck, baboons, bush pigs and some kudu way over there," Alessandra replied, pointing out each in turn.

"If you'll excuse me, I'll just show Sofia and Tom to their tent and then perhaps you'd like to join everyone at the *boma* for a drink and introductions. Oh, before I forget, these solar lights, take them in at sundown and they will stay lit all night if you need them, we'll put them out again in the morning to recharge."

"What's the *boma*?" Alberto asked, apparently having missed the first explanation that Alessandra had given.

"It's the public area where we have our bar and dining table and places to sit," Alessandra explained again. "If you walk that way, past tent three, you'll see it."

Alessandra took Sofia and Tom to their tent and got them settled, then went back to the *boma* and joined Grace, Marieke and Melisende. She took off her jacket, hat and gloves, and hung them up. The temperature climbed quickly once the sun came up, so it was already a comfortable sixty-five degrees, quite a change from the overnight and early morning chill, which could dip almost to freezing.

"This looks like it's going to be trying," Grace said. "Monica and Carol were sniping away at one another. You know, I didn't hear one word out of the two men. I wonder why they came?"

"Probably paid the bills," Alessandra said. "I got the impression at the strip and in the boat that they've been together too long on this trip and are all looking for some time apart. Monica Davis seems to have put herself in charge; at the strip, they spent so much time talking about who would sit next to whom, I almost had to step in and tell them who was to sit where. It's not as if the trip from the strip to the boat landing is a long one."

"Well, they're only here for three nights," Grace said. "Imagine if they were here for ten days or more!"

"Perish the thought," Alessandra said.

"Alex, it's going to take us a little longer to fix the water supply," Marieke said. "There's enough in the header tank for a while, but the elephants ripped up the line between the borehole and the tank. We should have it fixed this afternoon."

"Thanks, Auntie Marieke," Alessandra said.

"We'll leave you to your guests, it sounds like they're going to be interesting," Marieke said.

"A lot of bitching and sniping, judging by the ride in from the strip," Alessandra said.

"Watch out," Grace cautioned. "They're coming."

"All settled?" Alessandra asked.

"We are," James said.

"This is a Malawi Shandy," Alessandra said. "Would you care for one?"

"Thanks," James said.

"What about you, Dear?" he asked of Carol.

"I'll try one of those," she said. Alessandra handed her a glass and then handed a glass to Monica."

"David said he'll be right along as soon as he's put some shorts on. Where are the others?" Monica said.

"The others are in tents three and four, which you passed on the way to your tents. I would expect them to be here momentarily," Alessandra said. She was right, it was no more than a minute when the other four came, dressed for the bush in matching outfits. Grace handed around glasses of the Malawi Shandy. David then made his appearance dressed in his shorts and very natty bush jacket from L. L. Bean, so Grace offered him a glass too.

"Welcome to Mupundu," Alessandra said. "I hope you enjoy your stay with us. If there's anything you think we may be able to do to make your stay more comfortable, please let us know, but please bear in mind that we are five hours by road to Lusaka. Sadly, we do have release forms that we ask you to sign."

"Waivers, right," Tom said. "We had to sign those at the other places as well. Where do I sign?"

Alessandra handed around the forms that indemnified the camp from suit should something untoward happen while they were out in the bush.

"Tell us a bit about this park, when and how it got started?" David asked. "Also, could I get some coffee?"

"Of course," Alessandra said. Grace scooted off and was back very quickly with Stan who brought coffee in urns, cups, sugar and milk and a plate of cake. David helped himself, then looked to Alessandra for an answer to his question about the Kafue park.

"It started back in the 1920s with the Kafue Game Reserve, and then over time the boundaries changed, and in the late 1940s the actual park was proposed and agreed upon and finally gazetted in the 1950s. Negotiations were held with various local chiefs, and there was some relocation of people," Alessandra said. "It's a pretty big park, larger than either the North or South Luangwa parks and much larger than the Lower Zambezi park, I think in overall area larger than your states of Massachusetts or New Jersey, but not quite as large as New Hampshire."

"That's huge," David said. "That's almost a small country, that's way bigger than Yellowstone."

"Well, we are larger than Swaziland and Gambia, and if we go outside Africa, we're larger than Israel and El Salvador," she said. "And, yes, we are larger than your Yellowstone park, more than twice as large."

"So, where are we in this park?" he asked.

"We are situated on the northern part of the park, on the north bank of the Kafue River, between the Lufupa and Lunga rivers," she explained. "When we built the camp, we had to put in our own road. There was part of a road that used to come close to the Chibemba Salt Pan, which is north of here, but it needed a lot of work. From the salt pan, we came south to here. We only really use the road extensively now when we open up the camp and close it again at the end of the season, but we do use the bottom part of it for game drives. We had thought about buying a 38-foot landing craft to move vehicles and materials up the river from Lufupa, but at $50,000 for quite an old used one, without shipping it here, the price tag was a little steep, so we bought a used Unimog, put a plough on the front and built our own roads."

"And the other way, what was it you said, the Lunga?" James asked.

"There's no crossing on the Lunga for a long way north," she replied.

"What does it take to set up a camp?" James asked.

"First, we had to get permission from the parks people, which meant submitting a business plan with estimated guest nights, which gives the Parks Department a forecasted revenue stream, then we had to spend money," she explained. "It takes quite a capital outlay to set up a camp. One needs tents for the guests and the staff, vehicles, boats, fuel, solar panels, generators, a large water tank, plumbing fixtures and supplies, furniture, linens, uniforms, crockery, cooking utensils, utilities, basic supplies and then the staff, which includes cooks and kitchen help, housekeeping, guides, maintenance and even a manager or owner! Then we had to build the camp, which took materials, and contractors to actually do all this work on the decks and platforms that we're on, and we had to install all the plumbing and put in the collection tanks, our Unimog came in handy there because we found a used backhoe attachment for it. Fortunately, we've done this before, so we had materials lists and basic plans for the guests' quarters; we just needed to decide where they would go."

"How long is your season?" James asked.

"From June until November," she said. "Essentially the dry season, but with some possible days of rain in November."

"What happens in the off-season?" Tom asked.

"Holidays, maintenance, taking care of bookings made, marketing to new potential clients, conventions, all the things that need doing, but which there is no time for in the operating season," she explained.

"Do you take the camps down in the off-season?" Alberto asked.

"We pack away the linens, the crockery, and anything that will not survive the rains and store them in a container," she explained. "We also have two people at the camps at all times to protect the sites; we rotate them in two weeks at a time."

"Where do you get your staff?" Carol asked.

"We knew the chefs; they had worked for one of the big hotels in Lusaka, but they wanted to come back out this way to be with their families," Alessandra replied. "The guides were with us at Busanga, and the rest of the staff we found locally between here and Mumbwa."

"Are they out here the whole season?" Carol asked.

"No, we make sure that they all have time off to be with their families," Alessandra explained. "So, we rotate them three weeks on

41

one week off, it means a larger roster than just simply coming for the season, but it's better for the staff to see their families regularly."

"Where does the Kafue start?" David asked.

"The Kafue is a wholly Zambian river. It rises about 45 miles or so northwest of Chingola, one of the big towns on the Copperbelt. It then winds its way around close to the Congo border, past Kitwe and Ndola and comes on out west towards us, then south of here, at the Itezhi-Tezhi dam, it goes back towards the east, past Lusaka to the south and then east of Chirundu it joins the Zambezi," Alessandra explained. "It's one of our main rivers, along with the Zambezi and the Luangwa."

"So, where do the Zambezi and the Luangwa start?" David asked.

"The Zambezi rises in northwestern Zambia, then runs through part of Angola, then back into Zambia and forms the border with Zimbabwe until it runs into Mozambique, then it eventually empties into the Indian Ocean. The Luangwa rises near Isoka, which is up on the Malawi border, then it runs roughly southwest through a remnant of the Rift Valley complex, until the confluence with the Zambezi at the Zambia, Mozambique border," Alessandra replied.

"What's the Itezhi-Tezhi dam used for?" Tom asked. "Is there a hydro plant there?"

"There will be," Alessandra confirmed. "When the dam was built in the 70s, it was to control water flow to the Kafue Gorge hydro plant, but we also started on a plant for electricity this year. When it's done, it will have a capacity of 120 megawatts."

"Do you have others?" Tom asked.

"We've got a couple more on the Kafue, in the gorge below Lusaka, then we've got a plant at Vic Falls on the Zambezi, we've got a station on the north bank of the Kariba dam, also on the Zambezi, there's a smaller one on the Mulungushi River, another on the Lunsemfwa River, and a few more even smaller ones," Alessandra replied.

"Is it enough, or do you need to burn fossil fuels?" Carol asked.

"We have some fossil fuel stations," Alessandra said. "There's the heavy oil plant at Ndola, and several small diesel stations. We also have the biomass plant by the sugar mills at Nakambala, and they're talking about a big new coal power station by the Maamba

Collieries. But most of our electricity comes from the hydro plants. We do export power to Botswana and Namibia, I suppose we get well paid for it, because we could actually use every kilowatt here."

"Any solar?" Carol asked.

"We have solar panels here, and for many who are not near the grid, it's an option, but we don't have any commercial-size facilities yet," Alessandra said.

"You don't run off a generator here?" David asked.

"We have one, but it's noisy and we prefer to use the panels and the battery storage if we can," Alessandra explained.

"You said something before about a copper belt," Sofia said. "What's that?"

"North and a little east of us here are a number of large copper mines," Alessandra replied. "They run in a line almost paralleling the Congo border, and there are mines on the Congo side as well. The area where the big Zambian mines were developed is known as the Copperbelt, and it's also one of our provinces. On a historical note, some of the earliest exploration for copper in Zambia was done not too far from here, between here and Mumbwa, there were mines with exotic-sounding names like, Hippo, Silver King, Blue Jacket, Crystal Jacket, North Star, Lulu and Sugar Loaf, to name just a few. There are some new prospects being explored, one in the Lower Zambezi National Park and one just to the east of the park here."

"And will those impact the parks?" David asked.

"Without doubt," Alessandra replied. "The Kangaluwi mine will actually be in the Lower Zambezi park, so it will be interesting to see what happens there. Supposed employment and investment in the mine will probably trump tourist income, so it may take a while, but look for that to happen. The one east of Kafue is not in the park but close enough that we'll see some activity, probably poaching and maybe even dust particles blown in the wind towards the park."

"Are there any other minerals in Zambia, apart from copper?" Tom asked.

"We have coal mines, emerald workings, we've had in the past a couple of gold mines, a lead and zinc mine, we've produced uranium and cobalt," Alessandra replied.

"What's the biggest one now?" James asked.

"The Kansanshi mine, north of Solwezi," Alessandra said. "It's interesting because it's where the first commercial copper production came from in 1908, before that, it had all been Zambian artisans smelting the oxide and even sulphide ores themselves and selling the copper in the form of crosses."

"Back to the Itezhi-Tezhi dam for a minute," David said. "Phil said something about sugar and the Kafue. Does that mean that the dam also controls water to irrigate the sugar?"

"I suppose it does," Alessandra said. "We grow sugar around the Mazabuka area, and the water does come from the Kafue; it is pumped out and distributed, but there's also a degree of seasonal flooding that occurs over the whole area known as the Kafue Flats."

"Who owns the sugar factory?" David asked.

"The company is essentially a sub of a South African company. It was started by Tate and Lyle back in the 60s and went through a period where it was nationalised, then bought back by Tate and Lyle, who then eventually sold it to Illovo, the South African company," Alessandra explained.

"We've never seen Zambian sugar in our markets," David said.

"Most of ours goes either to the EU or is consumed locally, I doubt that any goes to the US," Alessandra said.

"How big's Illovo?" David asked.

"Not huge by US standards," Alessandra replied. "And at the moment, the Rand to Dollar exchange rate is really poor, so the 13 billion or so Rand that is the Illovo Group converts to about 770 million dollars. Associated British Foods has a big stake in Illovo, so we see them as surviving. They had operations here and in Malawi, in South Africa and Lesotho."

"What else do you grow here?" Tom asked.

"Maize and tobacco are probably the other two big commercial crops," Alessandra replied.

"Where does the tobacco go?" Catalina asked.

"Most of it to Japan," Alessandra replied. "It's grown here by farmers and coops, with assistance and technical support from the Japanese buyers; it's a good cash crop for Zambia."

"Where does the maize go?" Monica asked.

"We consume most of it domestically, but we have exported to the Congo, Zimbabwe, Namibia, Botswana and Angola," Alessandra replied.

"Can I change the subject for a minute?" Alberto asked. "Where can I charge up my phone, my iPad, and camera?

"Over there, we have some outlets that you can use for charging. Did you bring the adapters for this voltage?" Alessandra asked.

"I did for my phone and the iPad, but I had to borrow an adapter for my camera," Alberto said. "Do you have one?"

"Probably," Alessandra said. "We've got enough to work with most things, we should have one for Canon, Nikon, Fuji, Sony and one for an Olympus."

"They're all there," Grace said. "If you need any help, let me know and I can usually fix most things, or set up an adapter."

"Is the water safe to drink?" Sofia asked. "I usually only drink bottled water."

"It is," Alessandra confirmed. "We put down a borehole and we have a header tank to supply the water to the kitchen and the tents, the water is really good here, we've had it tested and it's quite safe. As for bottled water, it gets bottled in Lusaka, so I'm not guaranteeing where the water actually comes from and how well it is filtered and treated before it's bottled."

"Where do you get your food and wine?" Sofia asked. "Is the food organic?"

"We buy our bulk supplies in Lusaka," Alessandra replied. "We also buy seasonal fruits and vegetables from the markets near Mumbwa. Wine we get from a wholesaler in Lusaka, and meat we get from another wholesaler in Lusaka. I would imagine that the fruit and veg that we get from Mumbwa is organic as the farmers can't afford much in the way of fertilisers, herbicides or pesticides, but I'm not sure if they belong to the Organic Producers and Processors Association, so can't guarantee that it's actually certified organic."

"Who does the cooking?" Catalina asked.

"Grace puts together the menu for a two-week period, and then Mike and Ernest are the chefs," Alessandra replied. "Donald, there mans the bar."

"Well, the food in Luangwa and Lower Zambezi was good," James said. "David is in the restaurant business, so he's always on the lookout for new dishes."

"What type of restaurant do you have?" Alessandra asked.

"Ours is upmarket in Beverley Hills, our parents started it a long time ago, and David and Monica took it over fifteen years ago. It's really more of a seafood restaurant and offers exotic dishes like fugu chiri, the soup made from puffer fish," James explained. "For the rest of us, Carol and I live in Dallas, where she's an anaesthesiologist and I work as a pathologist, Catalina's also in the medical field but, she's an epidemiologist with the CDC and Alberto works for the Atlanta Zoo and is a herpetologist, lastly Sofia is an entomologist, with a real interest in spiders and Tom is a botanist who works for the USDA in their poison plant lab in Utah, we all met at college and have stayed friends since."

"Well, I hope you're not disappointed with our cuisine, but trust that you will make allowance for the fact that all cooking is done over wood fires and baking is done in the ground," Alessandra said. "It would also seem that we'll have to brush up on our knowledge of things other than mammals and birds, it's not often we get experts in other disciplines staying with us. I hope we don't disappoint."

"You're telling me that this cake was baked in the ground?" David asked.

"Yes," Alessandra said.

"I need to get the secret," David said. "This is damn good."

"I'll tell Ernest," Grace said. "He'll be pleased that you like it."

"You said earlier that your folks worked in Johannesburg," Carol said. "What did they do?"

"My Mum was a chemical engineer at the explosives factory in Modderfontein, and my Dad worked for the ICI Paints Division," Alessandra replied.

"But, they left that and bought a bush camp in Botswana?" Carol asked.

"That's right," Alessandra said. "They told us that they got tired of the Jo'burg traffic and the constant locking up of their house and worrying about security, so they gave it up and moved to Botswana. It's funny, the camp they bought was run by a distant cousin of my aunt."

"Where does she live?" Monica asked. "The aunt, I mean."

"Hawaii," Alessandra replied. "She grew up here in Zambia, then they moved to the US and they've lived in quite a few places in the

States, including the LA Basin and Utah, but eventually moved to Hawaii. She said that the climate and everything else there is very much like Zambia, so she feels at home."

"And the cousin?" Monica asked.

"Calitzdorp," Alessandra said. "It's a small town in South Africa in the Cape, not far from Oudtshoorn, they grow grapes there and make a fortified wine, similar to port."

"Where did you go to school?" Monica asked.

"My sister and I went to a junior school in Botswana, then we went away to Italy for *liceo*," Alessandra replied.

"What, you went away to boarding school?" Carol asked.

"No, we stayed with another aunt and uncle and went to school with our cousins," Alessandra explained. "After *liceo*, we went to varsity in England, then came back here to be part of the family business."

"So, how long have you been guiding?" James asked.

"Since I was about fourteen, when I was tall enough to be in the bush without looking too much like prey," Alessandra said. "I grew up in the bush camps and learned from the Tswana guides and trackers in our Linyanti camp. Let me introduce our other guides," she said as two others joined them. "This is Adam and Abel. You met Adam earlier at the boat dock. They are our guides. Please don't think that you all have to go out together, we will be happy to take smaller groups, if that's what you prefer, and we can take game drives, boat rides or walks. If we walk, we have to take along the ZAWA game scout, for our protection and safety."

"We saw that in Luangwa," Carol said. "Grace, you're from here?"

"I was born and raised in Mufulira, which is one of the Copperbelt towns," she replied. "I got a degree in hospitality from the uni in Lusaka and have worked in lodges and camps in South Luangwa, Lower Zambezi and now here."

"Grace's husband is Adam," Alessandra added.

"We met in South Luangwa," Grace said.

"So, you get a two-for-one package?" Monica suggested.

"We do," Alessandra agreed.

"Are you going to go out with us?" Sofia asked.

"I will," Alessandra said. "We'll divide up the duties between us."

"What's a normal day here?" Tom asked.

"We'll give you a wake-up call about five-thirty, then breakfast, after which, take your pick, a game drive, a trip on the river or a walk, after which, lunch, then quiet time followed by tea and cake at three, then an afternoon drive, walk or boat trip, maybe a night drive, then dinner," Alessandra explained.

"What is it about these lodges and camps and the pre-dawn hours?" James asked.

"Many animals are most active in the dawn and dusk periods of the day, so the best chance to see things is during those hours," Alessandra explained. "The behaviour is known as crepuscular, as opposed to strictly nocturnal or diurnal, which is why we do an early morning drive or walk and an afternoon drive."

"Are things active at night here?" Catalina asked.

"There's always something," Alessandra said. "Predators like hyæna and lion often hunt at night, then there are the smaller predators like the genet and the civet, then there's also porcupines, aardvarks, pangolins, bush babies, springhares and foxes."

"I guess as I think about it, we saw the porcupine in Luangwa on our way back to the lodge after sundown," Tom said.

"Why do some drivers use a red filter on their spotlights on night drives?" Monica asked.

"It doesn't affect the night vision of animals as much as white light," Alessandra said. "We don't want to night blind antelopes and leave them more vulnerable to predators."

"What do we do this afternoon?" Sofia asked.

"I'll take you for a quick drive now if you like, then we'll have lunch at about 12.30," Alessandra said. "Then we'll go out later, about three, for a drive so that you can see the area, stop somewhere for a sundowner, and come back on a night drive in time for dinner."

"I need to check my e-mails. What's the service like here?" Monica asked.

"Almost nonexistent," Alessandra said. "We have a satellite link, but it's not the fastest. How important are your messages? If they are vital, we could go back to the Lufupa camp and ask them if we could use their system."

"Surely you can live a day without checking your e-mail?" David said. "Life goes on whether we're there or not. Juan is quite capable of running the restaurant without us."

"Oh, very well then," Monica said, huffily.

"Monica frets about their restaurant," Carol explained. "She's always worried about it, even when she's there."

"It's our livelihood," Monica snapped back. "We don't make our living knocking people out or cutting them up."

"No, you expose them to all kinds of risk when you feed them those exotic fish dishes," Carol said.

"Ladies, please," Tom intervened. "We're here to enjoy the serenity of the place, and we should revel in the fact that we'll be alone here with not twenty other jeeps all around us when we see something."

"What kinds of animals will we see here?" Alberto asked.

"Kafue is known for its diversity of antelope," Alessandra said. "We've got twenty species in the park, from duikers to kudu and sable antelope, we've also got lions, leopards, cheetah, elephants, buffalo, dogs, hyæna, wildebeest and zebra, plus a whole host of small mammals."

"So, no rhino?" Alberto asked.

"We have some in Zambia," Alessandra said. "But, not here. Back in the 60s, there were black rhino here and in both the Luangwa parks and in Lower Zambezi, but poaching knocked down the numbers quickly and by the early 90s, they were pretty much extinct in Zambia. We have been reintroducing, so now we have a population of black rhino in the North Luangwa Park and two white in the Lusaka Park. I saw some numbers that talked about 30 in Luangwa. We've had, on and off, white rhino in the Mosi-oa-Tunya park in Livingstone; we've lost a lot there to poaching, even recently, but last count was seven. Sadly, ZAWA have to put armed guards on the animals, or they'd disappear too. Also in 1963, two white rhino were brought here from the Umfolozi Game Reserve in South Africa and kept in a paddock at Ngoma, which is in the southern part of the park."

"And snakes?" Alberto asked.

"We have all the normal ones, you'd expect," Alessandra replied. "But, as I'm sure you're well aware, it's not often that our guests ever see any. If we're lucky, we might see a mamba or a puff adder."

"So, we won't see all of the big five mammals here?" James asked.

"Not in the Kafue park," Alessandra said. "If you want to see rhino and you have time, when you're in Livingstone, visit the Mosi-oa-Tunya park and see the white rhino there."

"We're going to Livingstone after here," James said. "We wanted to see the Victoria Falls before flying back to Johannesburg and the States, so we could do that."

"What about elephants?" Catalina asked.

"We have some good-sized herds," Alessandra said. "We saw a few crossing the river today, but we do have bigger herds."

"When we came up the river, you were pointing out birds. Are there lots in this park?" Tom asked.

"Not quite 500 different species, some of them not here now as they are migratory," Alessandra said. "If you have an interest, then Abel is the guide to go with; he's our in-house expert."

"So, what activities do you offer?" Carol asked.

"As I said, we can take you for game drives, or, if you prefer, you could take a trip up or down the river, or we can also do a walk," Alessandra said, repeating what she had explained earlier. "Or, you don't have to do any of that, you could just sit on the deck here and watch the world go by, from here you can see an amazing variety of animals and birds. There are bee-eaters that hang around in the trees here on the edge of the lagoon; it's probably a great spot for insects. We've also seen mongoose out on the lagoon, there's a pack that lives in the area and at the right time of day, they will venture out into the open."

"So, nothing else, no massages or spa treatments?" Carol asked.

"Sorry, no," Alessandra said. "We're focused on the environment and the animals. We like to think that we're part of the system, not just observers of it."

First excursion

"If you've finished your coffee, would anyone like to take a short drive before lunch?" Alessandra asked.

"I'll go," said James. "Carol, are you coming?"

"I think so," she said.

"I'll come with you," said Tom.

"I'll think I'll just stay and soak up and sun and the atmosphere," Monica said.

"How long will we be gone?" Sofia asked.

"Only about two hours, unless we run into something really exciting," Alessandra said.

"Sounds good to me," Sofia said. "Catalina?"

"I think I will," Catalina said.

"Anyone else?" Alessandra asked. Alberto shook his head, so she led her group to where the vehicles were parked and suggested that they climb aboard. Sofia elected to sit by Alessandra, leaving Carol, Catalina, David, Tom and James to climb into the back and find seats.

"I saw some other people when we came in," Tom said. "Are there other guests?"

"Which other people?" Alessandra asked, annoyed by the implied suggestion that the staff were not people and reminded of the expression furniture in the movie *Soylent Green*.

"There were two ladies in what you called the *boma* area when we arrived. I didn't see them when we came for coffee," Tom explained.

"Oh, that was my auntie and her partner," Alessandra explained. "They're staying with me for a couple of weeks and helping when I need it. Auntie Marieke is from Botswana and has spent years in the bush, and is a good maintenance person as well. Right now they're working on our reservation system and some other projects."

"Where are they staying?" Tom asked.

"In one of our staff tents," Alessandra said. "They're going home next week."

"Where to?" James asked.

"Paris," Alessandra said.

"What's that?" Sofia asked, pointing towards some trees.

"Those are kudu," Alessandra replied. "There are six there, females and young."

"I only see two," Sofia complained. Alessandra stopped the car and shut the engine off, and they just sat watching the antelope. Finally, Tom said, "I think I can see all six now, three to the one side of the big tree, one hiding behind it and two on the other side."

"Do you see the male who is over there to the right?" Alessandra asked

"No, where?" Sofia asked.

"Look at about two o'clock," Alessandra suggested.

"I still don't see it," Sofia complained. "Oh, wait, is that him with the big spiral horns?"

"It is," Alessandra confirmed. "And if you look at eight o'clock, there are some other antelope walking along the edge of the tree line, those are sable antelope."

"Those are amazing," James said. "We didn't see those before. Why are they different colours?"

"The male is much darker, almost black, hence the name, sable," Alessandra explained.

"I don't understand?" Sofia said. "How is sable black? I thought sable was a fur."

"Sable is a black fur, but in this case, it's a heraldic term, there are the five basic colours of heraldry, *sable* is black, *gules*, red, *azure*, blue, *vert*, green and *purpure*, purple, then we have the metals, *or*, gold and *argent*, silver," Alessandra explained.

"Heraldry, that coat of arms stuff in old England?" James asked.

"It is," Alessandra confirmed. "Look, something has spooked the sable, they're off. Ah, look back at about seven o'clock, you see those lions there?"

"Where?" Tom asked.

"Look in the grass carefully, you'll see the tips of their ears, and if you look at the monkeys in that tree over there, they're all looking down at that place, so the lions have been spotted," Alessandra said.

"I still don't see them," Tom said.

"Just wait a little while and they'll come this way," Alessandra said. "See, the kudu have also gone."

They waited another five minutes, then the lions showed themselves and walked past the car, giving it a quick glance, but basically ignoring it and the people in it and the shutter noises of the cameras firing away.

"Great shots," James said. "I'm not sure I like them being that close, though. Are you sure it's safe?"

"We're safe," Alessandra promised. "Shall we see what else we can find?"

"Well, that's closer than we got in Luangwa," Carol said. "When I asked if we could get closer, I didn't expect to be quite as close. But, I suppose if you've been doing this since you were a teenager, then if you say it's safe, it's safe. Have there ever been any accidents?"

"We had an incident in 2001 on the concession we had in Botswana, my sister had to shoot a lion because a visitor who thought he was more attuned to the bush than he really was, got into serious trouble when he wandered off from the camp on his own and irritated some lions, and the only solution was to shoot one of the lions, she had tried warning shots, shots across the top of the head, but nothing worked, so the only solution was to kill it, which she hated to do because we were the ones intruding. I remember that the investigation and paperwork seemed endless," Alessandra said. "We told him and his family to leave immediately and never come back. Apart from that, we've never had an issue."

"I thought I read something about people in a tent being attacked by a whole bunch of lions," Tom said. "Where was that?"

"That was in Zimbabwe in 1999, the story is that one of the guests had his tent open and the lions went in," Alessandra replied. "The protocol was to sleep with the tents closed up, and if you suspected trouble, then blow a whistle. Apparently, no one heard a whistle, but one of the guides heard his name being called and saw the guest running. There turned out to be twelve lions who surrounded the man, and flares, a vehicle and other noise didn't drive them off in time, and the man died of his injuries."

"What about the famous lions that are in the Chicago Field Museum?" Tom asked. "What was it, the Ghost and the Darkness?"

"The Tsavo lions, the names were not Patterson's but from the 1996 film," Alessandra said. "The Tsavo lions were probably the product of a whole series of events and circumstances, so were an aberration."

"Wasn't there another one that's also in the museum?" Tom asked.

"The Mfuwe lion in 1991," Alessandra confirmed. "That was another aberration; it was killed by a countryman of yours, chap by the name of Hosek."

"All this talk is making me nervous," Sofia said. "Can we talk about something else?"

"Look over there," Alessandra pointed.

"What are we looking at?" Sofia asked.

"Elephants," Alessandra said. "They're moving that way towards the river and should pass us over there, so if you want good pictures, then this would be a good time."

"Oh, I see them now," Sofia said. "Look, Carol, they've got some tiny ones there. How old would those be, Alex?"

"The really small one, about a month," Alessandra said. "This herd comes to this area quite regularly, and I had come across them when the baby was brand new. The matriarch was really uneasy then and was seeing everything off, but she seems a little more relaxed today."

"How cute," Sofia said.

"They are fun," Alessandra agreed. "I could watch them for hours as they learn how to use their trunks."

"They're quiet," James commented.

"They can move really quietly and quickly when they want to. There are times when the only way you know they're there is by the noise they make as they pull branches down to eat," Alessandra said. "Now that they've passed, shall we drive on a little and see what else we can find?"

They drove a little farther north with Alessandra pointing out birds and animals as they went. Finally, they came to quite a large clear area and standing staring at them was a sizeable herd of buffalo.

"Look at that," Tom said. "Three of the big five in just a short time. Pity you don't have rhino here, I presume there are leopards?"

"There are," Alessandra confirmed. "One of the best and easiest times to see them is late in the afternoons on the river banks.

Perhaps this afternoon, we'll see if we can spot one for you. We also get cheetah in this park, so you may be lucky and see them as well."

"We didn't see any in Luangwa or Lower Zambezi," Tom said.

"As far as we know, the only viable populations are here and in Liuwa, which is to the west," Alessandra said. "There was discussion about sightings in Luangwa, but the consensus was that the habitat is not the best for cheetah; the thinking was that the lion population is fairly high, putting pressure on any cheetah that arrives."

"I'd like to see one if we could," Sofia said. "They're such pretty cats. What's that over there?"

"That's a leguaan, a monitor lizard," Alessandra replied. "They're quite common here; they can get quite big, like that one."

"You said you get snakes here, I suppose some are venomous?" Carol asked.

"We have some," Alessandra confirmed. "But, generally, they'll get out of your way, in fact, most of our guests never see one while they're in Zambia."

"That would be fine by me," Sofia stated. "I know Alberto's dying to see some snakes, but they give me the creeps, for me, the only good one's a dead one."

"They're all part of the ecology, without them things would not be in balance, Alessandra said. "What did you see in Luangwa and Lower Zambezi?"

"Eles, buffalo, wild dogs, lions, lots of antelopes, hippos and crocs in the river," Tom replied. "Lots of birds as well, many by the rivers, oh, and we did see vultures, a whole flock of them on the remnants of a puku, I think it was."

"Did you take a canoe trip?" Alessandra asked.

"Some of us did," Tom said. "I have to admit to being a little nervous as none of us wanted to be croc bait, but the guides assured us that we'd be fine."

"We did see some people on the other side of the river," Sofia said. "The river's quite wide there, so they looked small, but they were there."

"The Zimbabwe park of Mana Pools is over there," Alessandra explained. "So, there's quite a few people go there. I don't know if the people at Lower Zam told you, but up until 1983, the Lower Zam was the private reserve of the President, so poaching there was risky and hunting was out, unless you went with the President's blessing."

"Who was the president then?" Carol asked.

"Kenneth Kaunda," Alessandra replied. "He was the first president following independence in 1964."

"Before independence, this was Rhodesia, right?" Carol asked.

"Not exactly," Alessandra said. "Zambia was Northern Rhodesia, and what is now Zimbabwe was Southern Rhodesia, which became simply Rhodesia after they declared their independence from Britain in 1965."

"Can't keep track of all the old African colonies and who had what until when," Carol complained. "You said you lived in Botswana, what was that before?"

"Bechuanaland," Alessandra replied."

They drove on a little further, then Alessandra asked if anyone would care for tea or coffee.

"That would be great," Catalina said.

Alessandra pulled into a clear area and parked in the shade of a huge tree that was on the edge of the clearing, a jackalberry, and after a quick look around, told her guests that they could get out and stretch their legs.

"I need to go," Sofia said.

"Let me just check the other side of this termite mound," Alessandra said. She walked around it looking for tracks, tracks of lions who liked to lie up on the mounds, tracks of snakes who often made their homes in holes in the mounds, and anything else that might not be so pleasant to run into.

"All good," she said when she came back. "Might I suggest ladies behind the mound here, and gentlemen over by that thicket. Before you all go, tea, coffee, water?"

"I'll take coffee," Catalina said.

"Same for us," Carol and Sofia echoed.

"I'll do tea," David said.

"Coffee, please," Tom said.

"Same here," James added.

Catalina was the first back.

"Is your husband unwell?" Alessandra asked. "He doesn't look as if he's enjoying the best of health."

"I think he's just under the weather a little, probably hasn't had enough sleep since we've been here," Catalina replied. "It seemed to start when we were at Lower Zambezi, and the cough has shown up since then, perhaps he picked up something down there."

"Has anyone else shown any symptoms of anything?" Alessandra asked.

"No," Catalina said. "I'm quite surprised, really, we've all done very well on this trip, no rushing to the bathroom, no horrible bites or itches, nothing, just Alberto."

"Let me know if there's anything you need," Alessandra said. "We do have a basic medical kit at the camp."

"I'm sure he'll be fine," Catalina said.

"What would you like in your coffee?" Alessandra asked.

"Everything," Catalina said.

"Including the Irish Whiskey?" Alessandra asked.

"Not Irish, but Scotch maybe, only joking, too early in the day for me," Catalina replied.

"What's that plant growing in this tree?" Carol asked when she rejoined them after her excursion behind the termite mound.

"That's a Leopard Orchid," Alessandra replied.

"It's really pretty," Carol said.

"What would you like in your coffee?" Alessandra asked.

"Just black, please," Carol said.

The others came back and got their tea and coffee and the biscuits that Alessandra handed out.

"It's really quiet here," James commented. "There's no other safari jeeps rushing around."

"Kafue may be the largest park we have, but it's probably one of the least appreciated ones," Alessandra said. "If you think about the Luangwa and Lower Zambezi parks, most of the camps and lodges are clustered near the rivers, here we have some of that, the stretch of the river that runs through the park is a good 150 miles, but access is not the easiest, so camps and lodges tend to be clustered where access is easiest. For Luangwa, there is the commercial airport at Mfuwe, but here we only have bush strips; the closest field is

Mumbwa, but that's an air force base and is closed to commercial traffic. So, here you either cluster around the easy access roads, or go farther afield like us or the camps on the Busanga plain, and try and use the bush strips to fly in when you can. Ground transfers are possible, but it's a good five hours from Lusaka."

"You can't imagine what our parks are like in the high season," Tom said. "It's getting so bad that they're probably going to have to limit access as the sheer pressure of numbers is affecting the ecosystems."

"How was your stay in Luangwa?" Alessandra asked.

"We stayed at the Lundwe Lodge," Carol said. "It was a great way to start the trip, excellent food, marvellous accommodations, good guides and good game viewing, in some ways it felt a little like a resort in the Caribbean or Hawaii."

"Then in Lower Zambezi, we stayed at the Mushika Lodge, a little more rustic than Lundwe, but not quite the same as here," Tom added. "We had our own rooms on platforms looking out over the river, and the dining and sitting areas were Ritz-Carlton style. Great food, magnificent game viewing and good guides. Our experience so far has been so good that when we get home, I'll be telling our friends that if they want a safari experience try Zambia, it won't be as crowded as Kenya and unless you absolutely have to witness the great migrations of animals, you'll see pretty much everything here."

"Are you glad you came, happy with your selection of places to see?" Alessandra asked.

"Absolutely," Carol said. "When we get back, I have to tell our booking agent that she did a great job."

"Who did you use?" Alessandra asked.

"April Grant, she goes by the name of Simba Safaris," Carol replied. "When I first checked on the name, I got confused because there's also a Simba Safaris in Arusha in Tanzania, but I figured out which one was April's. She told me that she's done safaris here herself, visiting the Lundwe and Mushika lodges, but never here, so you were an unknown for her, and she told me that the Mushika guys had recommended you. When I get back, I need to give her a report on what we found, accommodations, meals, guides, all that jazz."

"Well, I trust that we will make your stay memorable," Alessandra said. "Memorable in a good way, so you'll give us a good report."

"From what I've seen so far, I think that would be the case," Carol said.

"I was meaning to ask you, Alex, this trip we've mostly seen Toyotas, I thought the jeep of choice for these safaris was the Land Rover," Tom said.

"That used to be the case," Alessandra confirmed. "Since Tata bought Land Rover, things have changed. Tata has announced that it's going to stop production of the Defender at the Solihull plant, which is what we would use in its simplest form. In fact, when we did order them, we'd order them with the Africa package, which meant no electronics and stuff. Can't fix those things in the bush. The Defender doesn't sell enough to warrant the expense to keep up with safety and emission standards, so look for the model to be discontinued entirely in the next year or so."

"But, you don't buy these from Toyota like this," Tom said.

"No, we buy the most basic one we can, then ship it to a company we've worked with for years in Maun in Botswana to do the safari conversion for us."

"There's nobody here that would do it?" Tom asked.

"We're working with a shop in Lusaka, but they don't have the experience that our friends in Maun do, but they're getting really busy, so conversions can take time, so we need another plan. We might just have to set up our own company in Lusaka. If we did that, it would be an associated company with the one in Maun."

"I never thought about where you'd get these jeeps," Carol said. "I thought you'd just buy them from your local Toyota dealer.'

"We'd get the basic chassis through them," Alessandra confirmed. "But they're not in the business of conversions."

"I guess not," Carol said. "You've a lot to think about."

"I was commenting to Catalina just now that Alberto looks a little under the weather. Are you all feeling fine?" Alessandra asked as she handed around more biscuits.

"Feeling great," Tom said. "I haven't had the chance lately to do much fieldwork, so this is great. So many new plant species to see and try and remember."

"Is Monica feeling well, David?" Alessandra asked.

"She's fine," he replied. "I think she just wanted to sit on the deck with her bird book and see what came along."

"Well, that's worth doing," Alessandra said. "We've got bee-eaters in the bushes by the camp, then look for twin spots and blue waxbills on the ground and then all the water birds out on the lagoon. Plus, there's typically puku, waterbuck and bush pigs out there as well, and at certain times of the day, the vervets will move out into the open, followed by the dwarf mongoose, and there's always the chance of an elephant or two or a lion."

"It's amazing what's here," Sofia said. "I've even seen some spiders that I like. I saw a hermit spider just now the other side of this mound. So, what else might we see this morning?"

"Who knows," Alessandra said. "I think that's the beauty of trips like this, you really don't know what you might see, unlike going to a zoo. If you have a list of things you absolutely must see, you may be disappointed."

"I think we all came understanding that," James said. "For me, it's not just about the list of animals or birds we might see, but the whole environment, the wildness of the place and the closeness to nature you get."

"I hope Alberto starts to feel better," Alessandra said. "It seems to me that he's missing a lot."

"He is," Catalina agreed. "But he said this morning that he just wasn't up to anything and just wanted to stay in camp, relax, drink tea, soak up the sun and try and get over whatever it is he picked up. It's not often that he gets sick, but when he does, he can rather milk it and look for sympathy wherever he can find it. Monica's the only one who really falls for the act, which, sad to say, it often is."

"If you've all finished your coffees, we can go a little farther and see. There's a *dambo* close to here with water, so could be something there," Alessandra suggested.

"We're ready," Carol said, and the others nodded in agreement. Alessandra packed up the coffee cups and such, and they set off again, driving slowly through the bush, while she scanned the road ahead for tracks and the bush around for any animals. Once she stopped and got out of the Land Cruiser and studied the tracks, walking back up the road a little way, then ahead of them.

"Piccadilly Circus here," she told the guests. "There's been a leopard here this morning, plus lions and what looks like hartebeest and most recently some buffalo."

"You can read all that?" Sofia asked.

"It's quite clear," Alessandra said. "The leopard came first, then the hartebeest, then the lions and finally the buffalo. The leopard joined the road just back there and left again a little further on. The hartebeest have been walking down the road for a while, probably headed for the *dambo* ahead, the lions came in from that side, walked a short way down the road and left that way, and the buffalo crossed just ahead, quite a few of them."

"Why the road?" Tom asked.

"It's easier to walk down the road than through the grass, and if you're prey, then it offers some degree of safety because you can at least see what's in front and behind," Alessandra explained. "That's why roads are a good place to look for tracks. Shall we take a look at the *dambo* and see if there's anyone there?"

"Lead on," James said.

"Fine," Alessandra said. "If I see anything really worth stopping for, I will."

"Hartebeest," Alessandra whispered as she stopped the Land Cruiser at the edge of the woodlands.

"They're very wary," Sofia commented.

"I would be, too if I were one of them," Alessandra said. "Not much fun being lunch for a lion. I don't think they're about, the monkeys are not chattering, there's a couple of warthogs over there who seem fairly relaxed, but you never know."

"How many lions are in this area?" David asked.

"We know of thirty," Alessandra said. "One of the prides is quite big, ten animals in all, it takes a big group to pull down and consume a buffalo."

"Is that a snake?" Catalina asked, pointing to some bushes.

"It is," Alessandra confirmed. "A boomslang, quite a small one."

"Alberto won't be happy that he missed it," Catalina said. "What do they eat?"

"Other reptiles, snakes, frogs, lizards, small mammals and birds and eggs of birds and reptiles, they'll even eat each other," Alessandra replied.

"They're quite venomous, aren't they?" Sofia asked.

"Quite, it's a hæmotoxin venom, so if you get really bitten, bleeding internal and external can be a real problem," Alessandra replied.

"What are those birds over there?" David asked.

"The one on the left is a black-bellied bustard, and the one on the right is a hamerkop," Alessandra replied. "The noisy ones coming in now are hadedas, part of the Ibis family."

"They are noisy," Carol said. "The hartebeest don't seem bothered by them."

"They're no threat," Alessandra said. "The hartebeest are moving off now, no great rush, but they're definitely going."

They watched them go off into the surrounding woodlands, then laughed as the warthogs hauled themselves out of the mud they had been wallowing in and followed them, tails straight up in the air, like small wireless aerials. The hadedas quietened down and a peace and calm descended over the *dambo* and the waterhole. There were other birds in the trees somewhere, calling, and the insects had set up their constant background buzz, but to everyone, that was much better than the constant drone of traffic and roar of aircraft.

"It's amazing how much background noise there is in a big city," Carol said. "Even where we live in Dallas, which is surrounded by trees and some open space, there is noise, a constant drone of distant traffic, police and fire sirens, even aircraft. Tom, where you live in Utah, is it quiet like this?"

"Almost," Tom replied. "There's still some background traffic noise, and at night we can see the lights of the city. I imagine here that it's really dark and the stargazing should be great."

"It is this time of the year," Alessandra confirmed. "But after the harvests and after the farmers burn off the stubble and at the end of the dry season when we get bushfires, then there's a lot more dust and smoke in the air and the stars are not as visible."

"I should sit out one night and look at the stars," Sofia said. "That might be nice. I've studied the Southern Hemisphere stars and think I can pick out all the constellations."

Would you like to start back for lunch?" Alessandra asked.

"That would be great," Carol said. "What are we having?"

"I'm not sure," Alessandra admitted. "Grace makes up the menus, and she sometimes introduces new dishes, so we'll see what we have today."

The drive back to the camp was interspersed with occasional short stops to look at things of interest, and a longer stop to see what was attracting the attention of the vultures. Alessandra drove off the track for a short way until they could get a better view of what was happening.

"Lions, ten of them," Catalina said. "What are they eating?"

"That looks like a buffalo," Alessandra said. "I'd say they killed it early this morning. If you look over there, there are jackals waiting, and we've got quite a collection of vultures and marabou storks just waiting to step in and finish cleaning things up."

"They're not taking must notice of us," Carol commented.

"They know we're here," Alessandra said. "But, we don't represent a threat, and we're clearly not here to steal their kill."

"How much eating on a buffalo?" David asked.

"Depends on the age, anywhere from 1,000 to 2,000 pounds," Alessandra replied.

"Let's see if that were beef we'd be looking at between 630 and 1,260 pounds of a dressed-out carcass," David said. "That's a lot of eating."

"You also have to remember that all the organs and really soft tissues get eaten first," Alessandra said. "The predators know that the really nutritious part of the prey is all the stuff we would often ignore, perhaps use, like the stomach, the liver, heart, lungs and so on."

"Monica's going to be ticked off that she missed this," David said. "She's been on all week about wanting to see a kill, and this is the closest we've got. That's what comes of hanging out in camp and not going out and about."

"How much will eat lion eat?" James asked.

"They usually eat two to three times a week and can eat up to 15 to 20 per cent of their body weight at a single sitting," Alessandra replied. "So an average male lion of say about 400 pounds could eat as much as 60 pounds at one time, then they would be gorged and sleep."

"So this won't last that long," David commented.

"No, once the lions have gorged themselves and are sleeping, the others move in and tear away at the carcass, so probably in less than a week, there'll be hide and bones left," Alessandra said. "Then the insects take over, and in time all there'll be will be some bones bleaching in the sun. I need to get some pictures of these chaps so that we can keep track of who's in the pride. I know eight of these, but two are new to me, so we need to see if they're new to the area, or if they've switched prides."

"Do you keep track of what you've seen where?" Catalina asked.
"We do," Alessandra confirmed. "We try and count major predators as that gives us a pretty good idea of the ungulate population."
"I suppose predator-prey ratios will apply there," Catalina thought. "What you're making notes of, what does it include?"
"I'll record when and where we are, I've got a GPS tracker that tells me precisely where we are, then I'll note which lion pride this is and how many are here, and what they've killed, with a guess as to when," Alessandra replied.
"So, you're quite scientific about all this?" Catalina asked.
"If we're to understand the place, then we have to observe and not what we've seen," Alessandra said.
"You can identify the prides?" Catalina asked.
"We've watched them closely enough and taken mug shots, so we know who is who, this is the pride we call the Chibemba pride, their range is centred about the salt pan and this is towards the southern end of their range, almost to the range of the River pride, which are the ones closer to camp," Alessandra explained. "They all have to eat and sometimes compete with one another, but this pride is bigger than the River pride, so conflict is unlikely."
"All this talk about eating is making me hungry," Tom said. "I've got all the pictures I need, blood, gore and all."
"Shall we go on?" Alessandra asked.

They drove on, with the guests talking about what they had seen and how much lions could eat if given the opportunity. Alessandra made a quick radio call back to the camp when they were about five minutes out, and Grace and Joseph were there to meet the party with moist towels and cool water.

"Nice drive?" Grace asked.

"Great," Carol said. "Lots of animals and birds, even a snake, even a fairly fresh lion kill."

"What was that?" Grace asked.

"A buffalo," David replied. "They were all getting stuck in gorging themselves."

"So, said you had seen a snake, which one?" Grace asked.

"A boomslang, Alex told us, Alberto will be sorry he missed it," Catalina said.

"Lunch in fifteen minutes," Alessandra said.

"We'll be there," Carol said. "I just need to go and pay a visit before lunch."

"How was the drive?" Grace asked Alessandra when the guests had all wandered off.

"Fine," she replied. "Any issues here?"

"I'm not sure, Alberto doesn't seem too well, but I didn't see too much of him, or Monica, come to think of it," Grace said.

"Catalina told me that he seemed to get the sniffles a little in Lower Zam, but she said not to worry, he'll get over it, not a lot of sympathy there," Alessandra commented. "None of the others seem to be suffering any ill effects of anything, so perhaps he was just run down before they came and he caught some virus in Lower Zam or Luangwa."

"I talked to Marieke and Melisende, and they told me that they'll have the water fixed this afternoon. They had to dig up a little more than we thought, but they're putting the line deeper," Grace said.

"Thanks for checking for me," Alessandra said. "It's very nice to have someone to fix those things for us. It would have to happen right when we opened. Do we know who dug it up?"

"I think it's those two eles that hang around, the one with the one tusk and his friend," Grace said.

"We'll have to keep an eye on those two," Alessandra said.

'Which pride was it that had made the kill?" Grace asked.

65

"The Chibemba pride, they were at the southern end of their usual range," Alessandra replied. "I should tell Adam and Abel where it is, maybe they can check on it later and see who else is eating off it. I'll mark it on the map quickly and should probably let the Panthera folks know who I saw and where."

"I wonder if they're going to set up some camera traps in the area," Grace mused. "If I were them, I'd stick a couple around the salt pan to see who goes there and when."

"I'll talk to them about that," Alessandra said. "I was thinking that we'd put some of our own out there too, and there's another spot that's become a regular Piccadilly Circus, so a couple along the track there would be a good idea."

"I'll talk to Bridget and get her to buy some more and send them out to us," Grace said. "I'll get Adam to place them when we have them. "Did you get any good pictures of the Chibemba cats?"

"I did, bit bloody, but I did get good mug shots of eight of them, including two new ones," Alessandra replied. "I'll add them to the book."

Lunch was convened fifteen minutes later, and there was another long discussion about who would sit where. Alessandra wondered if it had been like this at the lodges they had stayed at in Luangwa and Lower Zambezi; if it had been, it must have driven the staff almost to distraction. Beer and wine were offered, and it was beer all around. Next, Grace went through the dishes of the day that were set out in a buffet to the side, so that they could help themselves to as much or as little as they desired. That day, they were having a chicken and beef stir fry with green onion rice and a green salad.

"Your aunt is not joining us?" Carol asked.

"No, they're off checking out our water supply," Alessandra said.

"Is there anything wrong?" Carol asked.

"No, it was just an elephant that tore up a couple of the lines, so now they're fixing them and burying them a little deeper, not that that will stop a determined elephant," Alessandra explained.

"What, they dig up water pipes?" James asked.

"They do," Alessandra confirmed. "I've watched them trace a line back and then dig it up at its shallowest. I've also watched them take water directly from a feed pipe that services an open tank, rather than the tank itself, almost as if they know the water will be fresher and cleaner."

"Who does the menu for your food?" Alberto asked.

"We had a consultant help us with menu planning, given the types of fresh fruit and vegetables we can get," Alessandra explained. "Then we took her suggestions and built on them to create a two-week cycle for the menu."

"Very good," Alberto said, between mouthfuls.

"How are you feeling, Alberto?" Alessandra asked.

"I've been better," he replied. "But, I'm sure I'll get over it. Did you all have a nice drive?"

"It was great," Catalina said. "And we saw a snake."

"You did," Alberto said. "What was it?"

"Alex said it was a small boomslang," Catalina replied.

"Ah, yes, *Dispholidus typus*," he said. "Interesting snake, very arboreal, goes after birds a lot."

"It was creepy, the way it moved around the bushes," Carol said. "I don't know why you like the things, Alberto."

"They have their place in the ecology," he said. "Without snakes, many places would be overrun with rodents. We have some nice specimens at the zoo. It's weird people say they hate snakes, but the herpetarium is one of the most visited areas of the zoo, and people spend more than the usual thirty seconds at each exhibit."

"Is that all the time people spend looking at things?" Alessandra asked.

"We've done lots of studies, and thirty seconds is about it, they come, they look, then they move on," Alberto replied.

"We also saw a lion kill, Monica," Carol said. "Quite a fresh one with the lions all with their heads buried in the carcass."

"Rub it in, why don't you?" Monica said. "Were there many lions?"

"Ten of them," Carol said. "Feeding on a buffalo they'd just killed."

"There were lions here, too," Monica said. "They were out on the grass over there, four of them, but they didn't kill anything, just drank and went off that way."

"Listen for them tonight," Alessandra suggested.

"You mean we'll be able to hear them?" Carol asked.

"Their calls carry a long way," Alessandra confirmed.

"I'll have to keep an ear open," Carol said.

"We have a dessert set out," Alessandra said during a lull in the conversation. "It's on the buffet, what are we having, Grace?"

"Today it's a passion fruit mousse," Grace replied. "Help yourselves, and there's tea and coffee as well."

"What would you all like to do this afternoon?" Alessandra asked. "You could take a walk, a game drive or a boat trip."

"You said on the drive before lunch that an evening boat ride is a good time to see leopards," Catalina said. "I'd like to take a boat ride."

"So, one for a boat ride," Alessandra said. "Any other takers?"

"I'll go," said Tom. "Sofia?"

"Yes, why not?" she said. "What about you, Carol?"

"I think I'll just take a drive," Carol replied.

"I'll go on a drive as well," James added.

"Put me down for a boat trip," David said. "Monica?"

"I think I'll just stay in the camp here," she said. "I want to see if those lions come back."

"Alberto, what do you fancy?" Catalina asked. "I'm going on a drive, are you coming too?"

"I'm going to do nothing, I'm not really feeling up to anything just now," he announced. "That's all right, isn't it?" he asked of Alessandra.

"Of course," she replied. "Sitting on the deck here is always fun, you never know what may go by. Please let me know if you think you need to see a doctor."

"Thanks," he said. "I just feel a bit off, but maybe a good rest and some sleep will fix things."

"As long as you're sure," Alessandra said. "For those going on an afternoon activity, if you could meet at the *boma* at three, we'll have some tea and cake, then we'll be on our way."

"For our river trip, what do we need to take?" Sofia asked.

"You won't need life jackets or anything like that," Alessandra said. "But take a regular jacket or pullover as it will get cool as the sun goes down. What does everyone want to drink as a sundowner?"

"I'm into this Brit thing of G & T," Tom said. "Picked it up in Luangwa and have to say it's very civilised."

"I'll go for some white wine," Sofia said.

"I'll take a Scotch and soda," David added.

"If we're on the drive, will we stop for a sundowner as well?" James asked.

"Of course," Alessandra said.

"In that case, G & T for me, too," James said.

"Red wine for me," Carol said.

"For me too," Catalina added.

"Fine," Alessandra said. "We'll take everything with us, bring cameras, binoculars, jackets for when the sun goes down. One more thing, in the morning, the protocol is that one of the staff will come with a wake-up call. These walkie-talkies we'll give you now, leave them in your tent. When you're ready to come for breakfast, call us on Channel 1 and someone will come a get you. We don't want you inadvertently walking into something."

"You get visitors then?" Sofia asked.

"At times," Alessandra replied. "We're very much in the environment, so we're the intruders, and we give them their space. All our staff are very capable of handling any situation that might arise. If you don't get a wake-up call at five-thirty, just sit tight and wait, we'll get you as soon as it's safe to do so."

"Will there be animals around the tents in the night?" Sofia asked.

"It's possible," Alessandra replied. "Keep the doors closed and they'll not bother you. A word of warning, if there are elephants around, they make a lot of noise breaking branches off trees, don't be alarmed, it's just them feeding. You may also hear them rumbling away; it's part of their communication system."

"We heard it at Mushika," James said. "I wondered what it was at first, but they explained, what they didn't tell us was that they can get very flatulent and there was one outside our room all night, kept us awake for a while."

"It got to be funny," Carol added. "Not too stinky though, just noisy."

The guests left, and Alessandra and Grace compared notes and decided that Alberto was perhaps ailing a little, but likely to get over it. So far as an opening day, things had gone remarkably well; apart from the waterline issue, there had been no reports of things not working, so it looked as if the year was off to a decent start. Then Alessandra went to check on the water line work.

"All done," Melisende told her. "Marieke's just parking the Unimog. Just a word of caution, watch out for Alberto and Monica, we both think there's something between those two, it might cause problems for you later."

"Great," Alessandra said. "That's all we need. It does explain the funny looks that I saw when we stopped for coffee and I commented on Alberto and Monica both being in camp."

"It may be nothing, it may be something," Melisende said. "But thinking like one of *les salles flics*, I'm always suspicious. He does seem to be genuinely ailing, though. Something isn't quite right."

"Catalina said that it started when they were in Lower Zam," Alessandra said. "I wonder if he didn't pick up something odd there, it doesn't look like malaria, so maybe something else."

"How was your morning drive?" Marieke asked when she joined them.

"Good," Alessandra said. "They saw plenty, a snake and a lion kill, and seemed to get on well enough. This afternoon, everyone's going out except for Alberto and Monica."

"We'll keep an eye on things," Marieke promised. "If Alberto gets worse, we'll see if there's anything we can do."

"I was telling Alex that it's our view that there's tension between him and Monica," Melisende added.

"We'll keep an eye on that too," Marieke promised.

"Would you like some coffee or tea?" Alessandra asked.

"Tea would be nice," Marieke said.

"Marieke and her tea," Melisende said, smiling at her partner. "Coffee for me, please."

"So, how is retirement?" Alessandra asked after they had tea and coffee in hand and were seated in the boma area.

"We're still on the books as consultants," Melisende said. "We've been called in three times since we officially retired to help solve a couple of cases, otherwise we've been enjoying life, travelling around France and visiting places we never got the chance to see before.

With both our pensions, we're financially sound, and already owning the flat was a great help there."

"And you're both healthy?" Alessandra asked.

"Very," Melisende replied. "We both exercise regularly and we watch what we eat and drink, so we're looking after ourselves."

"When we go out this afternoon, if you want to join either the drive or the boat, please do," Alessandra said.

"Which was most?" Marieke asked.

"I've got three on the boat and three on the drive, take your pick" Alessandra said.

"Maybe the drive today," Marieke suggested.

"Fine, so I'll see you both back here at three for tea, coffee and cake," Alessandra said.

Afternoon Activities

At three that afternoon, all assembled at the *boma* and had coffee or tea, and cake. Alessandra also confirmed the drink orders for sundowners. She then said that she was going to be the boat guide and that Adam would be taking the game drive. She also told Alberto and Monica that if they wanted showers, to just let Grace know, and it would be arranged, and she told the drive party that Marieke and Melisende would be joining them. Then she asked Alberto how he was and if he thought he needed medical attention.

"I'm managing," he replied. "I'll just take it easy and keep myself properly hydrated, and maybe I could get some tea with lemon and honey?"

"We can manage that," Alessandra promised. "Where would you like it?"

"At my tent, if that's doable," he said.

"I'll take care of that," Grace promised.

"Are you feeling better or worse this afternoon?" Alessandra asked.

"About the same, maybe a little worse, but that could be the end of it," Alberto replied. "I'm sure I'll get over it quickly enough."

Coffee and tea done, Alessandra and Adam led their respective parties to the vehicle park and loaded them up. Adam took off north to see what they could find and perhaps check on the lion kill and see what was happening, and Alessandra drove the short distance back to the boat dock. Without Monica, seating everyone was quick and efficient, and Alessandra then loaded the drinks cooler, cast off the boat and pushed it out into the stream.

"I thought we'd head downstream and then go up the Lufupa as far as we can," she suggested. "We'll have a sundowner up there and see if we can spot a leopard."

"That sounds great," David said. "What else could we see?"

"Plenty of birds, hippo and crocs in the river," Alessandra replied. "And, on the bank, could be impala, elephant, monkeys, it depends on who's coming to the river to drink, or hunt."

"There aren't many people about," Tom commented.

"There aren't," Alessandra agreed. "The Kafue is not that well known, despite the fact that it's the oldest and biggest park we have. It hasn't got the appeal yet of Luangwa. But, it does have a variety of habitats, from the river here to the plains in the north and the woodlands."

"What's that over there?" Sofia asked, pointing to some animals on the north bank of the river.

"Those are buffalo," Alessandra replied. "If you look, there's quite a sizeable herd of them, coming down to water in this lagoon."

"Are those the same ones that we saw earlier?" Sofia asked. "Can we get into the lagoon?"

"I'm afraid not," Alessandra said. "A month ago, we might have managed, but now there's a very good chance that we'd hang up and have to get out and push us out of there, and yes, it's likely that those are the same buffalo that we saw before."

"I don't fancy getting out into the water to push with crocs in the water," David commented.

"Nor me," Alessandra said. "If you look over there, there are a few good-sized crocs just waiting."

"They are big," Tom agreed. "Those things must be twelve to fifteen feet long."

"Look over there," Alessandra suggested, pointing off into the bush.

"What's there?" Sofia asked.

"Two bushbuck," Alessandra replied. "Looks like a ewe and a lamb."

"They're really pretty," Sofia commented. "We saw quite a few in South Luangwa and in the Lower Zambezi. We also saw giraffes in Luangwa, do you have any here?"

"We don't," Alessandra replied. "There is the Thornicroft's Giraffe in Luangwa, and you'll also find giraffe at Vic Falls, but we've none in this park."

"Pity," Sofia said. "I always associated Africa with giraffes, maybe it's all the movies made in Kenya and Tanzania."

"So, are we nearly at the Lufupa?" Tom asked. "That's where we picked up the boat when we landed this morning, that already seems like ages ago."

"You're right," Alessandra confirmed. "We'll just skirt around these hippo and then we'll go up the Lufupa and see what we can find."

"There's a boat," David said. "Full load of people too."

"They're the OAT folks," Alessandra explained.

"OAT?" Sofia asked.

"Overseas Adventure Travel, they do a deal that includes Botswana, Zambia and Zimbabwe," Alessandra explained. The two boats passed each other with waves and smiles, and Alessandra talked briefly to the driver of the other boat, who was also functioning as their guide.

They motored up the Lufupa slowly, stopping from time to time to look at birds, hippo, monkeys and impala, until they came to a largish pool, replete with water lilies, with jacanas walking around on them, and kingfishers flitting about. Alessandra stopped the boat and just let it drift slowly, while she attended to sundowner drinks, which she then handed around along with roasted peanuts.

"Keep your eyes open," Alessandra said. "There's a leopard about."

"How do you know?" Sofia asked.

"The vervet monkeys are alarm calling," Alessandra explained. "If they see a leopard, then they yell about it."

"What's that?" Tom whispered, pointing to something moving in the long grass.

"Good spot," Alessandra said. "You've just seen your leopard. If we stay quiet and just wait, he'll probably come out of the grass and walk along the bank there."

"Come on, move," Sofia whispered.

"All in good time," Alessandra said. "Now, cameras ready, he's starting to move this way along the bank."

"Here he comes," Tom said. "Oh, perfect shot, look, he's posing for us. That's a great shot, can they swim?"

"They can, they're actually really good swimmers," Alessandra. "But he's not going to come out here to the boat. He knows we're here, but he's not that interested. Ah, he's off, but he's in no hurry; we can probably follow him down the bank for a while." She lowered a small propeller into the water that was powered by an electric motor, which made it very quiet, and she then slowly followed the leopard down the river as he wandered in and out of the tall grasses by the river. Eventually, he scampered up the bank, and with one quick backwards glance at them, he was gone, into the bush beyond, possibly looking for his meal that night.

"That was great," Sofia said. "Tom, you must have got some great shots."

"I did," Tom confirmed. "I got so many that I just put the camera down and enjoyed just watching him, him or her, which was it, Alex?"

"It was a him," Alessandra confirmed. "Definitely male, if there were no other clues, like his size, head shape, general stocky build that that last view of him climbing the bank would have confirmed it. That one we've identified as Gamma two, we record who we see where and pass the information onto a research group who are studying large carnivores in the park."

"That was great," David said. "We didn't get such a good sighting in either Luangwa or Lower Zambezi."

"There was that one leopard in Luangwa," Sofia reminded him.

"Yes, but there were eight other Land Rovers all parked around the poor guy, here it was just us, thanks Alex," David commented.

"What's that over there?" Tom asked, pointing to activity near the riverbank that was mostly obscured by the long grass.

"More vervet monkeys, they've come down to drink now that the leopard's gone," Alessandra replied.

"Will the leopard eat them?" Sofia asked.

"They will," Alessandra replied. "It's interesting, vervets have different alarm calls for leopards and eagles, if they hear a leopard call, they'll scamper off up the trees, and if they hear an eagle call, they'll come down out of the canopy to lower branches."

"I suppose it's all about survival," Tom said. "So, what plants here are toxic?"

"The lucky bean creeper, *abrus precarius*," Alessandra replied. "It's said that one bean ingested will kill you, but if you don't break the hard outer skin, then it will just pass through. There's also the blackwood, *erythrophleum africanum*, a decoction from the roots will also kill."

"What about poisons used for fish?" Tom asked.

"The most commonly used is the fish poison bean, *tephrosia vogelii*," Alessandra replied. "It has other uses too, as a cattle dip for removing ticks. There are a few others that will make you sick, but there are probably more that will either have a beneficial effect, or no effect at all."

"Fascinating," Tom said.

"If you want to try something different, then a decoction made from the seeds of the sausage tree is supposed to increase the size of the male organ," Alessandra said. "You can believe that or not, but it is known that the fruits have been used for years as a treatment for eczema."

"I don't think I'll be trying it for either of those things," Tom laughed. "The sausage tree is what?"

"*Kigelia africana*," Alessandra replied.

"What's that tree over there?" Tom asked.

"That's a water berry, *Syzygium cordatum*," Alessandra replied. "The wood is good for boat building and for rafters of houses. It has a purple fruit that can be eaten; it is a bit acidic, but it does make good booze."

"And that one over there?" Sofia asked, a little more interested in trees now, now that she appreciated that they were used by the local people for all kinds of things.

"That's a jackalberry, *Diospyros mespiliformis*," Alessandra replied. "It also has edible fruits that are in high demand to eat, and you can also make beer from them. The wood is good for canoes, furniture and flooring. We parked by one this morning on our drive."

"They're huge trees, aren't they?" Sofia said.

"They certainly can be, the root systems stabilise the banks and provide all kinds of cover for birds and small animals," Alessandra said.

"There's just so much to look at and take in. How long did it take to learn all this, Alex?" Tom asked.

"There is much in common with Botswana, but there are species endemic to Zambia, so we had to add to what we already knew, and the guide exams are quite thorough," Alessandra replied.

"What grades of guides are there?" David asked.

"The most basic level is a transfer driver, someone who collects you from your hotel or the airstrip and drives you to the camp," Alessandra replied. "They have to be able to take care of the guests and fix a tyre, and know what to do if there are animals blocking the road. Then there's the Grade 2 guide, which is a driving guide, they drive the guests around and point out animals, birds, trees and such and finally, there's the Grade 1 guide who are walking or canoeing guides, they have to know what to do if confronted with animals who may become aggressive if they feel threatened. There are exams for each level, and they are tough."

"And the guides you have?" David asked.

"All of us are qualified as walking guides," she replied. "And we have three younger members of our staff who are studying for their Grade 2 certificate. If you take a drive tomorrow, one of them may be with you as a spotter."

"So, you can't just set up shop and claim to be a guide?" Sofia asked.

"I suppose you could, if you were outside the park on a private reserve, but you wouldn't last long," Alessandra replied. "Word would soon get out, and you'd be out of business. There's a couple of places in South Africa that I'd call factory photo safaris catering to the mass market, and I gather their standard of guiding leaves much to be desired."

"Apart from knowing animals, birds, reptiles, trees and stuff, what else are the guides supposed to know?" Sofia asked.

"Basic mechanics, how to change a wheel, basic engine things, so if we have a breakdown, we've some chance of getting going again, first aid, and the ability to not get lost," Alessandra explained.

"The wheels on this truck must weigh a ton," Sofia commented.

"They're not the lightest," Alessandra agreed. "But we manage."

"I'm beginning to appreciate more now of what we saw in Luangwa and Lower Zambezi," David said. "The guides talked about all kinds of things, but there was just so much to take in."

"We would have the same experience if we came to the States and went to Yellowstone," Alessandra said. "Everything would be new and different, plus you've got volcanic things going on there."

"Right, *Old Faithful* for one," David said. "Is there any volcanic activity in Zambia?"

"We have no active volcanoes; the closest are in Tanzania. We get small earthquakes once in a while. If you live on the Copperbelt, you can often feel the underground blasts, which feel like earthquakes. We've got a few hot springs, the closest to here is Gwisho, which is in the Lochinvar Park. When you were in

Luangwa, there was one fairly close in the Nsefu Park at Chichele," Alessandra replied.

"You said Zambia has about 16 million, what do they all do?" David asked.

"Subsistence farming, mining, commercial agriculture, tourism, and government are the main areas," Alessandra replied. "Our two main industries are mining and agriculture, with tourism lagging behind, but building."

"Got to be a problem here, being landlocked," David said. "Must make imports and exports difficult."

"It does," Alessandra confirmed. "It's better now than it was in the seventies, now we have the railway links to Cape Town and to Dar es Salaam, and road links as well."

"Still, it's a long way to the nearest seaport," David said. "Which is closer, Dar es Salaam or Cape Town?"

"Dar is closer than Cape Town, but the closest seaport is Beira, and there is a rail link that connects through Zim," Alessandra replied.

"At least there's some air service," Tom added.

"We don't have the number of flights that Jo'burg has, but we've enough for now. We used to have BA and UTA, but they both dropped out, probably not enough traffic for them."

"You know, I really like this place," Sofia said. "I think I'll come back, we had taken this trip as a once-in-a-lifetime, but I'm thinking that over."

"What is that?" Tom asked, pointing towards a bush on the bank, he had been staring at something through his binoculars for a couple of minutes.

"Good spot," Alessandra said. "Alberto will wish he came out with us this morning and this afternoon, what you're looking at is a twig snake, they look just like twigs and are ambush predators feeding on frogs, chameleons and small birds."

"Wait 'til I tell him," Sofia crowed. "Maybe it'll be an incentive for him to get well and start going out again."

"Shall we start on our way back?" Alessandra asked, getting no reply, she unshipped the small electric-driven propeller and lowered the

78

main motor back into the water, and they set off downriver towards the Kafue. On the way down, they saw several groups of hippo, crocodiles on the banks, and a few impala here and there, often in close association with vervet monkeys. Once in the mainstream of the Kafue, Alessandra headed back upstream towards the camp. They saw all kinds of birds and small antelopes coming down to the water to drink, and even a herd of elephants off in the distance headed away from the river. By one rocky outcrop in the river, Alessandra slowed down and pointed to some birds.

"Those are skimmers," she said. "If you look at their beaks, the mandible is longer than the culmen; they feed by lowering the mandible into the water as they skim over the surface."

"Where do they live?" Sofia asked.

"The rivers and coasts of Africa," Alessandra replied. "You can find them on the Zambezi, obviously here on the Kafue, the Okavango, Lake Ngami and Lake Dow."

"Pretty, aren't they," David said.

"There's a breeding colony up the river," Alessandra said. "We could take a ride up there tomorrow if anyone is interested."

"That might be nice, to go the other way," Sofia said.

"What's that funny-looking duck over by the bank there?" David asked, pointing to a bird on the south bank.

"That's a finfoot," Alessandra replied. "It doesn't have webbed feet, but big lobes on its feet to help with swimming, they're often hard to spot, so good spot, David."

"I like the setting sun on the water," Sofia said. "Makes for great photos."

"Did you get many sunset pictures in Luangwa or Lower Zam?" Alessandra asked.

"Probably way more than I'll ever look at again," Sofia replied.

"I remember when I was just a kid, my dad had a film camera and he didn't take that many pictures because he never had enough film, so our vacation pictures were maybe three or four 36-exposure films, now we'll take more than that in ten minutes," David added.

"Photography sure has changed," Tom agreed. "What I like about the new digital cameras is that I can fit them to a microscope easily and get great shots."

"Hey, what's that bird got over there?" Sofia asked, pointing to the bank.

"That's a goliath heron with a green water snake," Alessandra said. "Bringing Alberto with you must be the reason we've seen the snakes; normally, we don't see any, or on rare occasions maybe one, but that's three so far."

"Alby will be pissed when we tell him that we saw two just on this boat ride," Sofia gloated. "Serves him right for getting sick."

"I doubt that he did that on purpose," Alessandra said. "It can't be much fun to go on a safari and spend half your time laid up."

"I suppose so," Sofia relented.

"Look at those crocs over there," Tom said. "They're huge, what do they eat?"

"Almost anything unwary enough to get too close to the water where they're hiding," Alessandra said. "They'll take antelope, birds, even people."

"Wouldn't want to be taken by a croc," David said. "Can you eat them?"

"They are edible," Alessandra replied. "I haven't tried them myself, but those I know who have, say that the meat is very lean and tastes very much like various bird meats."

They were almost back to the dock when Alessandra received a radio call from Adam, who told her that there was a male lion lying among the trees quite close to the boat dock. He gave her a precise location, so when she nosed the boat into the dock, she told her passengers to wait in the boat until she had checked out the area. The lion was still where Adam had seen it, but she was able to get the guests into her Land Cruiser without disturbing it. They spent a few minutes watching the lion, then the light started to fade, and he finally stood up, stretched, roared a few times, then took off at a slow walk through the trees.

"That was a great sight," Tom said. "He didn't seem at all bothered by us."

"He's had enough to eat, and we're just not on the menu," Alessandra said. "Did you hear the answering call?"

"I thought I heard something," Sofia said. "But I wasn't sure."

"There are four females that typically hang around with this male, this is the River Pride, their territory runs from here to almost where we saw the buffalo kill, that's where we sometimes see altercations between the prides," Alessandra explained. "These chaps are going to get together soon and start their hunt for the night. Shall we go back to the camp now? It's only a few minutes, anyone for showers?"

"I'll have one," Sofia said.

"Me too," Tom and David added, almost in unison. Alessandra made her call on the radio and told Grace that showers were asked for tents one and three. At the camp, they were met by Grace and Joseph, who had warm towels to wipe away the dust of the ride.

"Dinner at seven-thirty," Alessandra said. "Come to the boma early and have a drink before dinner."

Tom was the first to show up at the boma for a drink, and Donald was by his side quickly asking what he would like.

"Scotch and soda, please," Tom replied.

"So, how was your first day?" Alessandra asked.

"Great," Tom replied. "It's quite different to Luangwa or Lower Zambezi, for one thing, it's quiet, we haven't seen anyone else yet, apart from those OAT guys, and they were down the river away from here."

"We think that's one of the selling points of this park," Alessandra said. "We like it and have done well here. What does your poison lab do?"

"We run it for the US Department of Ag," Tom said. "We're mostly concerned with plant species that are toxic to grazing animals."

"What about browsers?" Alessandra asked.

"Them too, but the only domesticated browser we have is the goat. We may have to expand things in time, as we're seeing more alpaca farms now, so we need to know what they eat. With the goats, those things will eat anything and not seem to come to any harm," Tom laughed. "Say, here's Carol and James, so Carol, how was the drive?"

"Amazing," Carol said. "I don't know how Adam sees these things, but he stops and points and, eventually, with some clues, I see what he's showing me. I thought our guides in Luangwa were good, but for me, Adam's the best we've had so far, sorry Alex."

"No, that's fine," Alessandra assured her. "I learned all I know from the Tswana guides in Botswana and am still learning. So, what did you see?"

"A wonderful leopard," Carol said. "He was just sitting in this tree looking at us, if Adam hadn't pointed him out to me, had I been driving, I would have driven right by him. Then there were the sable, the hartebeest, the oribi, the kudu, the waterbuck, buffalo, I forget what else, but all kinds. Here comes Alberto and the rest. How was the lazy afternoon, Alberto?"

"This place is amazing," he replied. "You just have to sit here, or by your tent and just stay quiet and all kinds of things wander by, I watched baboons and mongoose until I took a nap, I seem not to be able to get my breath, I'll have to go and see about it when I get back."

"What would you like to drink?" Alessandra asked, nodding to Donald, who was hovering nearby, unwilling to interrupt.

"I'll just have a beer," Carol said.

"I'll take a gin and tonic," Alberto said. "Catalina said she'd be here as soon as she's had her shower."

Catalina did join them after about five minutes, and she asked for a brandy and soda.

"You missed all kinds today, Alby," Tom said. "We saw a twig snake and a green water snake. The twig snake was waiting for dinner, and the water snake was being eaten by a heron."

"Did you manage to get pictures?" Alberto asked.

"I did," Tom replied. "So did Sofia and David, so between us, we'll probably have everything you might want."

"What else did you guys see?" Alberto asked.

"Great leopard sighting," Sofia replied.

"We had one too," Carol said. "He was sitting on this tree branch just looking at us. I was telling Alex earlier that if I had been driving and not Adam, I would have driven right by it."

"How are you feeling, Alberto?" Alessandra asked.

"I've been better, not feeling so good tonight," he replied.

"Do we need to get you to a doctor?" Alessandra asked.

"I'll make it until we get to Livingstone," Alberto said. "I've got enough medications to keep things at bay for a while."

"Please don't think that you have to stay," Alessandra said. "We can get you medical help."

"No, I'll be fine," he said.

"Don't feel you have to be brave about this," Alessandra cautioned.

"No, it's fine," he said. "I've been worse."

"Excuse me," Ernest said. "I would like to tell you about tonight's menu."

"Please do," Monica said. Ernest then went through the menu, describing each course. That done, they all repaired to the dining table and found seats. They were joined by Marieke and Melisende, who had been on the drive with Carol and James.

"Alex tells us that you're from Paris," Monica commented. "Have you always lived there?"

"No," Marieke said. "I grew up in Namibia and went to uni in Lyon, which is where we met. I worked in Botswana until I moved to Paris."

"What did you do there?" Monica asked.

"I had a minor functionary job with the government," Marieke said.

"And you, Melisende?" Monica asked.

"I also worked for the government, the French government, but in a slightly less minor rôle," Melisende replied.

"What kind of work did you do?" Sofia asked.

"Analysis," Melisende said. "Marieke and I worked together a lot."

"I like Paris," Tom said.

"Me too," added Catalina.

"Where do you live in Paris?" Monica asked.

"We have a flat opposite Notre Dame," Melisende replied. "It is very central and convenient."

"Can you see Notre Dame from your apartment?" Monica asked.

"We can," Melisende confirmed.

"So, now you are plumbers," Tom commented.

"There's always something that needs fixing," Marieke said. "And, we enjoy coming here and are happy to help Alex."

"What is there to see in Botswana?" Tom asked.

"There are several major national parks," Marieke replied. "They vary from Chobe and the Okavango to the Central Kalahari, that is semi-desert, quite different to here."

"Are you a French citizen now?" Carol asked.

"I am," Marieke confirmed. "I was a South African, then became a Botswanan, now I'm French."

"What did your family do in South Africa?" Carol asked.

"We actually lived in South West, Namibia, and my folks had a farm, but they were both killed when their car hit a landmine, so I sold the farm and moved to Botswana," Marieke replied.

"That must have been terrible for you," Carol said, horrified.

"It was what it was at the time," Marieke said. "There was always risk in South West, a lot less now that it's Namibia."

"Would you mind taking a group shot of us having dinner?" Monica asked, handing Marieke her camera.

"Not at all," Marieke replied. She took a few shots, and then took one with her iPad as a memorial of the trip.

Stan and Joseph came with plates, soup dishes actually, and served everyone. They followed that with dinner rolls, then water and wine or whatever people wanted to drink. The main course followed the soup and was a chicken dish.

"This is good," David said. "I'm going to have to up my game a bit in LA, the three places we've been all had great food, and none of you have the resources that I do."

"It's just necessity," Alessandra said.

"What's the plan for tomorrow?" Alberto asked.

"It's up to you," Alessandra replied. "Take a drive, go out on a boat, take a walk, or sit here and do nothing and watch the world go by."

"I'll stay here and watch the world go by," Alberto said. "Donald told me that he has seen a mamba close by occasionally, perhaps I'll get lucky and see it, but mainly, I think I'll just take it easy, maybe I can shake off whatever it is that I've got. After you guys told me all about the snakes you saw today, I'm looking forward to seeing one myself."

"I think I'll take a walk," Tom said.

"That sounds like a good idea," David added.

"Anyone else?" Alessandra asked.

"No, I think a boat ride," James said.

"A boat ride," Sofia said.

"I'll stay in camp," Monica said.

"A drive for me," Catalina said.

"A drive for me, too," Carol added.

"Right," Alessandra said. "I'll take the drive, I thought we might take a packed lunch and go on up to the Chibemba Salt Pan and see what we could find. Adam will take the boat trip, and Abel will do the walk with our game scout, Henry. If we meet for breakfast at about six, then we can get going before it gets too warm. If you have hats and gloves, I'd wear them; it could be chilly when we set out."

"It's much cooler here in the mornings than it was in Luangwa," Sofia commented.

"We're quite a bit higher up, and the higher altitude means cooler nights and mornings," Alessandra explained. "In May and early June, we can even get an overnight frost, especially on the Copperbelt."

"Could we get some coffee?" Tom asked.

"Of course," Alessandra said. She got up from the table and went quickly to the kitchen, and came back with the promise that coffee would follow. Joseph and Stan came over shortly afterwards with coffee, cups, milk and sugar. Tom and Monica were the only takers, but the others all indicated that an after-dinner drink would be welcome. Marieke took the orders and went to the bar to get things, and she and Donald came back with the requested drinks.

"It's so peaceful here," Catalina said. "This has to be the nicest location we've been to on this trip."

"We think we picked well," Alessandra allowed.

"You did indeed," Tom said.

"So, no Mr Martin on the horizon?" Sofia asked Alessandra.

"Not at the moment," Alessandra replied. "It is a little difficult out here."

"I can imagine," Carol said. "How often do you get into town?"

"In the season, perhaps two or three times," Alessandra replied. "Unless something comes up that requires attention in Lusaka that my folks can't deal with."

"Must be a lonely life at times," Monica said.

"I stay busy," Alessandra said. "There really isn't time to get lonely, there's always something happening and new people to meet, and in the bush, you never know what you may see each day. I've been

85

guiding for some years now, and you'd think it would become old hat, but each day brings something new and exciting."

"I've been going through lists of all that we've seen," Sofia said. "I can't believe how long it's getting, loads of animals and birds, now snakes and other reptiles, and I've added spiders to my list. Now all we need are a few more things like terrapins or tortoises."

"We'll keep an eye out for them," Alessandra promised. "Excuse me a minute, did you hear that?"

"What was it?" Catalina asked.

"There's a leopard about," Alessandra said. "It sounds like he's out on the lagoon there. Let me get a spotlight and we'll take a look."

She quickly went to the office and came back with a spotlight and red filter and played it over the lagoon.

"There he is," Sofia said. "What's he after?"

"Probably one of the impala that's out there," Alessandra said. "But, look over there, the River Pride is moving over here, and there he goes."

"That leopard left in a hurry," David said.

"He knows that he's no match for the lions," Alessandra said. "So discretion is the better part of valour here."

"Well, I think I'm for bed," Tom announced. "I'll see you all in the morning."

"Is anyone else going now?" Alessandra asked.

"I am," Monica said.

"I'll walk you back to your tents," Alessandra said. "We wouldn't want you to encounter something on your way."

"Is that the protocol?" Tom asked.

"It is," Alessandra confirmed. "And, in the morning, you'll get a wake-up call. If you don't, please stay in your tent until we come and get you, as it means that there's something around."

"What is most likely?" Monica asked.

"Elephant, lion or even hyæna," Alessandra replied.

"Really, right in the camp?" Tom asked.

"We don't bother them, and they don't bother us, but we don't wish to antagonise them, so we give them a wide berth and we each go about our business," Alessandra said.

"And you've not had any problems?" Monica asked.

"None, not here, not in Busanga or on the Nanzhila plains," Alessandra assured her.

After the guests had been seen back to their tents, Alessandra and Grace sat for a few minutes with Marieke and Melisende, discussing the day and the plumbing issues. The problem had been fixed, but there were supplies that needed replenishing. Grace made lists to add to the list for the next trip to town. If things were dire, they could always contact Lusaka and have bits and pieces put on the plane and flown out on the daily run, but none of them saw things as that urgent.

"So, what do you think of this crop?" Marieke asked.

"There's tension," Alessandra said. "There's something going on between Monica and Alberto."

"You are quite right," Grace said. "You'd hardly been gone five minutes when I saw Alberto slinking off to Monica's tent, and they both asked for showers about fifteen minutes before you came back."

"God, that's the last thing we need," Alessandra said. "Why couldn't they wait until they got to Vic Falls?"

"As I recall, neither Alberto nor Monica is going out tomorrow morning," Grace said.

"We'd better warn Joseph and Stan in case they go to make up the tents and stumble across the two of them shagging away," Alessandra thought.

"I'll do that," Grace said. "They probably have it already worked out anyway, but I'll see what they have to say. I have to say, though, Alberto doesn't look too happy; he really does look like he's come down with something."

"I do rather wish that he'd agree to cut his trip short and go and get medical help," Alessandra said. "I don't want to have to medevac him out."

"I suppose if you've paid a lot for the trip, you don't want to have to cut it short," Grace said.

"I suppose not," Alessandra admitted. "But I'm concerned about him, I think he's sicker than he admits, but Catalina doesn't seem that concerned, and I suppose if she's not, then I shouldn't be."

Anyway, I'm off to bed, I'll see you in the morning."

"So, Auntie Marieke, how's Paris?" Alessandra asked. Conversation then switched to Paris, fashions, retirement, current events, the escapades of François Hollande, civil unrest due to same-sex marriage discussions, something of real interest to Marieke and Melisende, and civil unrest due to construction projects and other issues.

"So, where should I send Adam tomorrow, upriver or down?" Alessandra asked.

"I'd send him upriver to see the skimmer colony you mentioned before and whatever else is up there, I heard from Abel that there's a new lion up there, a chap with black markings on the top of his ears," Marieke said.

"Good idea," Alessandra said. "And Abel for the walk?"

"Along the bank towards Lufupa," Marieke suggested. "There'll be plenty to see."

"Good, we'll do that, I'm for bed, I'll see you in the morning," Alessandra said.

"It's a long day for them," Melisende commented after Alessandra had left. "They've got to be up before six, and they can't go to bed until the last guest is seen off to his or her tent."

"She seems to enjoy it," Marieke said. "Not my idea of an ideal job, but to each their own. Do you think there really is something going on between Alberto and Monica?"

"*Oui, certainement,*" Melisende said. "Notice the looks between them, the guilty starts as the others look their way. I hope they don't create problems for Alex."

"So, what shall we do tomorrow?" Marieke asked.

"Maybe we could tag along with Alessandra," Melisende suggested. "See what the salt pan looks like."

Early morning

In the morning, breakfast was eaten in comparative quiet; it was only Alberto who really talked, waxing lyrical about the chances of seeing a snake or two. Marieke and Melisende joined them for breakfast and asked Alessandra if they could go with her that morning, which she agreed to readily. Alessandra wondered, cynically, if Alberto's talk was all just a cover to try and throw others off about his true condition, and she also wondered if the others were taken in by it all. Catalina pulled her aside and asked if they could get on a flight that afternoon, or failing that, the morning after. She was not happy with Alberto's condition, no matter how many assurances he gave her that he only had a mild viral infection and he would treat the symptoms, and it would go away in time. Alessandra checked with the office and came back and told Catalina that they were on the afternoon flight. She asked Catalina if she still wanted to come on the drive, and after some obvious soul-searching, she said she did. She felt that Alberto could manage for the day, particularly after Monica joined them and said that she would keep an eye on him and feed him honey and lemon tea and food as well. Alessandra promised to have them back well in time to get the boat to Lufupa and the afternoon plane. Monica said that if Catalina packed her bag, then she would make sure that Alberto had his bag packed and ready to go.

That done, Alessandra made sure that she had provisions for the day, and when all had finished their breakfasts, she suggested that they start out in fifteen minutes, which would give them all time to use the loos if they needed to, collect their binoculars and cameras and generally get themselves ready for the morning, or day. Alessandra herself took her camera and binoculars, her water and went out and checked on the Land Cruiser. The fuel tanks were full, all the tools and equipment they would normally carry were safely stowed and in the in-between seat boxes were blankets. She watched Adam leave with Sofia and James, off to get the boat to see what they could see from the river. Then she saw Abel leave with Henry, the ZAWA scout, and Tom and David off for a walk along the riverbank. Finally, her four arrived, keen to go and make a day of it.

With only four passengers, loading was quick and simple, particularly as Marieke and Melisende knew that, as non-paying guests, they should take seats last, giving the paying guests the choice of seats. Alessandra drove east and then north, away from the river and into the generally untravelled lands beyond. The track generally stayed along the edge of the wooded areas, so that they could usually see *dambos* and clear areas on at least one side. It was not long before she stopped.

"What do you see?" Carol asked.

"Roan antelope," Alessandra said, pointing. There was quite a large herd walking towards them; she counted at least thirty.

"They're pretty, aren't they?" Catalina said.

"They are," Alessandra agreed.

"What are those birds on the antelopes?" Catalina asked.

"Ox peckers," Alessandra replied. "They pick off the parasites like ticks. If you look past them on the other side of this *dambo*, you'll also see some hartebeest."

"Oh, I see them," Carol said. "What about lions?"

"Lions generally lie up in the daytime," Alessandra said. "We may see some, but they may not be the most active."

"We saw some yesterday and they were close," Catalina said. "I'm happy to see them at a distance, but without fences or glass, they just look a lot bigger than those you see in the zoos."

"What are those birds on the other side of this *dambo?*" Carol asked.

"Those are red-necked francolins, and over there are some guineafowl, and you can hear the flappet larks above us," Alessandra replied.

"What's that funny noise that sounds like running your fingers across corrugations?" Carol asked.

"That's him," Alessandra confirmed.

"I always thought that larks had pretty songs," Carol said.

"Some do," Alessandra confirmed. "We have the monotonous lark, and believe me, it is, it's a nice enough song, but it seems that they don't know anything else, so there's no variation."

"What's the best songbird here?" Catalina asked.

"I'd hesitate to say, my favourite is the black-collared barbet," Alessandra replied. "But in the early morning, it's nice to hear the doves and out on the river, the fish eagle."

"So many to choose from," Carol said.

"Shall we go on?" Alessandra asked.

"Please do," Catalina said. "This is wonderful, there's no other people, it's quiet when you shut the car off, it's so different to Luangwa or the Lower Zambezi. They each have their attractions, but it seems to me that here you really have to go looking for things, but when you do find them, it's so rewarding."

"We think so," Alessandra agreed. "Why put yourself somewhere where there are tons of other people. Imagine what it's like in Kenya or Tanzania, where your private safari is private as far as the edge of your car, but you're not alone watching a poor leopard in a tree, who's probably wishing that all these people in their *bakkies* would go away."

"I never thought of that," Carol said. "Private only means that it's you in the car, not that the reserve is your own domain. Here it feels like it is your domain, there just aren't any other people around to intrude on your viewing."

"What's that over there?" Catalina asked.

"That's an oribi," Alessandra replied.

"He's a pretty little guy," Catalina commented.

"He is," Alessandra agreed. "Shall we stop for some coffee?"

"Great idea," Carol said. "I could use some coffee right now."

"We're almost to the Chibemba Salt Pan, and that's a good place to stop and see who comes for the salt," Alessandra suggested. They came out of the trees, and there was a plain in front of them, and centred on it was the pan. Alessandra negotiated her way to the pan, then drove back south a short way and parked under some trees in the shade.

"Now, we wait," she said. She poured coffee and handed it around, then handed around biscuits. They sat and watched and waited and were rewarded after about fifteen minutes by a family of wild dogs that came trotting up to the salt pan.

"They're really pretty, aren't they?" Carol whispered.

"They are," Alessandra agreed. "This family has been here a while, and they've been very successful in raising their pups. They have a den a little to the east of here."

Eventually, the dogs moved off, and then the herbivores moved back in. They clearly were not going near the place while the dogs were there. There were impala, puku, waterbuck, kudu, and some sable antelope, then the elephants came, a whole herd of them, probably about sixty in all, all ages and sizes and after them the buffalo.

"This is amazing," Carol said. "Absolutely amazing."

"I can't get over how many animals there are here," said Catalina. "It's like they were all waiting in the wings for those dogs to go, then they showed themselves."

"They all recognise predators," Alessandra said.

"Even the elephants?" Catalina asked.

"Even them," Alessandra confirmed. "I know of lions that have taken elephants, and there have been cases of dogs going after calves, but usually the herd moves to defend, so it's a tough chase, even if it's a big pack."

"I suppose life is like that," Carol said. "Some have to kill to live."

"True," Alessandra agreed. "Nothing survives except at the expense of something else."

"I suppose that's true," Carol thought. "Even the herbivores kill something when they eat plant matter."

"What's that?" Catalina asked, pointing off into the distance.

"Cheetah," Alessandra replied. "They're moving this way, so we'll just stay quiet here and watch."

"They're coming really close," Carol said. "Are we safe?"

"They're curious," Alessandra said. "They may actually come up to the truck and look at us, just stay still."

"This one's right here," Carol whispered. "I can hear him purring."

The cheetah stayed long enough to look over the Land Cruiser and the people in it, then went off to investigate the salt pan.

"That was amazing," Catalina said. "I could have reached out and touched him."

"It was actually a her, but they were just curious," Alessandra assured her. "We're a little big for them to consider us as easy prey; impala and small duikers are more their size."

"Wait until I tell Alberto," Catalina said. "We'll be sorry he stayed in camp, even if he did think he'd see a snake."

"Perhaps," Carol said, with a small private smile to herself.

"Alessandra, I really need to go," Catalina said.

"Let me just check around, then I'll tell you where it's safe," Alessandra said. She got out of the Land Cruiser and walked to a nearby termite mound, walking all around it looking for tracks on the ground that would tell her if anyone had taken up residence in the recent past. She found nothing untoward, no lion tracks, no hyæna tracks, nothing that would be a threat to Catalina. It needed to be checked because the termite mounds were favourite spots for lions to lie up in the daytime and survey the scene, looking for opportunities that might arise for an easy kill. She also tracked the cheetahs to see where they had gone, and saw them off in the distance, headed away from them on some mission of their own. Marieke volunteered to go with Catalina and keep cavey, looking out for any threat that might come her way. When Catalina and Marieke had gone, Alessandra looked at Carol and asked what was uppermost in her mind.

"Is there something about Alberto that we should know?"

"We all, well, most of us, suspect that Monica and Alberto have a thing," Carol replied. "The only two who don't or don't want to know are Catalina and David."

"Should I be concerned?" Alessandra asked.

"I don't think so," Carol said. "We're a mixed-up group, I think in college each of us dated all the others, and we are where we are."

"Alberto seems quite sick to me. Why is Catalina not more concerned?" Alessandra asked.

"He's got a history of getting convenient sprains and ailments when we're all together, I think so he and Monica can fool around while we go off and ski, or play tennis," Carol replied. "I don't know how much the others have put together, but it seems obvious to me."

"Should I be concerned about fireworks?" Alessandra asked.

"I wouldn't think so," Carol said. "I think this has been going on for a while, and David and Cat just either ignore it or convince themselves that it's purely platonic and that Monica is truly the nursemaid of the group."

"Catalina and Alberto are on the afternoon flight out," Alessandra said. "I've also arranged for a hotel for them and a doctor to visit the hotel. I think Alberto really does need to seek medical attention, and I think Catalina has finally come to the same conclusion."

"That's good, because this time I don't think he's faking it," Carol said. "And Monica actually looks concerned."

"That's better," Catalina said, as she and Marieke rejoined them.

"Carol?" Alessandra asked.

"I think I will," Carol replied. Marieke went with her as well, and they were back quickly enough, and Carol asked what the cat-like animal was that she could see stalking through the grass on the other side of the termite mound.

"It's a serval, they eat rats, birds, lizards, frogs, just about anything they can catch. They're typically a little more active in the daytime than most of the other cats," Marieke said.

"Are they like lions? Do they live in prides?" Carol asked.

"No, lions are the only cats that are social; all the others are basically solitary, usually with a territory," Alessandra replied. "So, you won't see prides of leopards, servals or caracals. Let me know when you're hungry, I brought lunch, so we can just sit and watch and see who comes next."

"What kind of animals did you see in Botswana, Marieke?" Carol asked.

"It depended where you were, but very much the same as here," Marieke said. "Towards the north in and around the Chobe park, elephants were common, in the central part of the country, lots of antelope and the associated predators, plus the gemsbok, which we don't get here."

"That's the guy with the black and white striped face, right?" Carol asked.

"That's him," Marieke confirmed. "People think of the Central Kalahari as a wasteland, but it's actually teeming with life, the gemsbok among it."

"Will you come and keep cavey for me as well?" Melisende asked Marieke.

"Your aunt knows her way around the bush," Carol commented to Alessandra.

"She grew up on the farm in Namibia, from what she told me, it was a long way out of any town, so there were lots of animals around, apart from the cattle they kept," Alessandra replied. "She's a really good tracker and a good shot too, her dad used to give her one bullet and tell her to go out and get dinner for them, so she learned to shoot really well, but that's the old Afrikaner way."

"Afrikaner, so she's a Boer?" Carol asked.

"Her dad was," Alessandra replied. "That's why she's Englebrecht."

"So, she speaks Afrikaans?" Carol asked.

"That, English, French, Setswana and San," Alessandra confirmed. "Actually, she's part San herself, from a long time ago."

"San, that's what they used to call the Bushmen, isn't it?" Carol asked.

"Right," Alessandra confirmed. "She was sent away to uni in France because it was safer for her there than in South Africa."

Melisende and Marieke came back, and all of them sat and watched as the world went by, as zebras wandered up to the pan, licked at some salt, then left, to be followed by warthogs, hartebeest, impala, roan antelope, and another huge herd of buffalo.

"You said earlier that all the rhino had been shot," Carol said. "If there were any here now, where would they be?"

"Actually, in the sixties, this was one of the better areas for rhino," Alessandra replied. "I'm guessing that they liked the salt pan, and there is plenty for them to browse on."

"Why browse?" Carol asked.

"In Africa, we have two types of rhino," Alessandra said. "The white rhino is a grazer. If you look at its mouth, it's got a wide mouth that is adapted for grazing. The black rhino has more of a browsing mouth, almost prehensile lips adapted for browsing."

"I know I said this before," Carol commented. "But this is like having your own private reserve. Why is it that Kafue is not better known?"

"I think Luangwa offers a lot in a smaller area, so it's possible to see what most people want to see fairly quickly," Alessandra said. "There are times here when we have to go really looking, plus there aren't other vehicles from other camps and lodges calling sightings in."

"We noticed that," Carol said. "Our guide was on his phone a lot, talking to others, and that often led to us driving directly to where they had seen something."

"I'm glad we added this to our trip," Catalina said. "Do you want us to spread the word when we go home?"

"That would be great," Alessandra said. "Publicity is always good for us; we get a lot of return visitors, but new ones are always good."

"All the animals seem to have gone," Catalina observed.

"It's the heat of the day, most lie up somewhere in the heat of the day and then get more active again when it starts to cool off a little," Alessandra said. "What is it, only mad dogs and Englishmen go out in the midday sun?"

"So, what do we do?" Carol asked.

"Why don't we have lunch, then relax for a while?" Alessandra said.

"What do we have for lunch?" Catalina asked.

"I'm not sure, let's take a look," Alessandra suggested. She put down the tailboard of the Land Cruiser and took things out of the picnic basket and the coolers. There was food enough for five, or more, and she let the others help themselves before she got hers. They ate and looked around, watching birds soaring high in the sky and others scratching around on the ground, looking for insects, seeds, whatever they could find. They heard in the distance a fish eagle, probably sitting on one of the trees that lined the banks of the Lufupa. It was as peaceful as the wild could get, the only sounds being those of birds, insects and the wind in the trees. When lunch was finished, Alessandra packed everything away and then looked around the area for anything they may have dropped. She picked up orange peel and put it in a bag.

"Isn't that biodegradable?" Carol asked.

"It is," Alessandra confirmed. "But it's not native. We've taken the position that if vervets or baboons find the peel and eat it, then they'll be on the lookout for more, so in time, they might raid our camp. We haven't gone as far as some places where the mantra is you feed them, we shoot them, but we don't want anything to become habituated to human food or waste, so we're very careful about what we do."

"That makes sense," Catalina said. "Marieke, what was it like where you grew up?"

"South West, Namibia, is hot, a lot of semi-desert, and a lot of grasslands, and some spectacular scenery" Marieke replied. "My folks had a farm there, which I suppose would equate more to a ranch in the US."

"Was the rest of your family from Namibia?" Catalina asked.

"No, they're South African. Mum and Pops lived in South West because Mum was Tswana, so the marriage was illegal in South Africa," Marieke explained. "In the wilds of South West, no one took any notice, but if they'd lived in the Cape, where the rest of the family was, they would probably have been arrested."

"I suppose much like the southern states in the US," Catalina commented. "It wasn't that long ago that that would have been the same there, even now I wouldn't give a mixed marriage much chance without a lot of problems."

"And you said they were killed by a landmine?" Carol asked.

"They were," Marieke confirmed. "It was during the struggles for independence from South African rule, so chaps would come south from Angola to take part. It was a fairly brutal bush war, in some ways similar to the one in Zim."

"But you were not part of that?" Carol asked.

"No, I went away to uni in France, and when my folks were killed, I sold the farm and moved to Botswana, which was where my mother was from," Marieke replied.

"And you, Melisende, where does your family live?" Carol asked.

"We were from Lyon, but my parents were both killed in a traffic accident, so now I live in Paris," she replied. "I've got some distant relatives in the Lyon area, but we are not close, and you?"

"I grew up in Southern California, in Orange County, went to USC and met all the others there," Carol replied.

"So, Alex, what do we do now, wait for the animals to wake up and come back?" Catalina asked.

"That's about it, make yourself as comfortable as you can," Alessandra suggested. "And if you can, take a nap. I'll wake you if anything comes by."

They were awakened by the radio; it was Grace calling from the camp.

"Base to Alex, base to Alex, come in," Grace said.

"Alex to base, go ahead," Alessandra replied.

"Base to Alex, we need you here," Grace said.

"Something wrong?" Alessandra asked.

"We've a situation," Grace said. *"Lo muntu ena fili."*

"OK, Grace, we're up by the salt pan, we'll be back as soon as we can," Alessandra replied. "Sorry, ladies, it looks like we'll have to cut our trip short."

"I wonder what could have happened to make them call you back?" Carol said.

"We'll find out when we get there," Alessandra said, keeping to herself, for now, the news that a man was dead, which was what Grace had said, using a now almost completely unused pidgin language of the mines in Zambia, that she knew that Alessandra also spoke as it had a lot in common with the Fanagalo that was used in the South Africa mines. Alessandra made sure they had everything secure in the Land Cruiser, then started back for the camp. They were held up for a few minutes by the elephants they had seen earlier, but they eventually wandered off, leaving the track clear again. It was only a little more than twelve miles to the salt pan, but it still took almost an hour to get back. Grace was there to meet them.

"Grace told Alex that they have a death," Marieke quietly told Melisende in Breton, betting that neither Carol nor Catalina spoke Breton, had probably not even heard of it. "Look at all the vultures there in the trees, amazing how they can spot death and then all congregate."

"Thanks for coming back," Grace said.

"What's up?" Alessandra asked.

"We've got a death on our hands," Grace said quietly. "You'd better get ready for a reaction from Catalina, it's Alberto, looks like a mamba."

"I'm so sorry, Catalina," Alessandra said. "But Alberto seems to have had some kind of incident, at first blush it looks like a snake, and he's dead."

"Dead, how can he be dead?" Catalina said. "Where is he? I want to see."

"We've moved him to the storage container," Grace said. "I've sent Adam down to Lufupa to contact ZAWA and the police. I thought it best to move the body; we don't want predators and scavengers prowling around while we wait for the police to show up. I hope I did the right thing."

"I'm not sure what else we could have done. I see the vultures had this one spotted; there must be every vulture in a five-mile radius sitting in those trees now," Alessandra said. "We don't have any protocols for this."

"Maybe we should think about some," Grace suggested.

"Maybe, does anyone else know about the death?" Alessandra asked.

"Everyone," Grace said. "James Davis introduced himself to me as a pathologist, and he's taking a look at Alberto right now."

"Catalina, if you'll come with me, we'll go and see Alberto," Alessandra suggested. She led the way to their storage container, and they saw James closely examining Alberto.

"Alberto, qué pasó, qué pasó?" Catalina cried.

"I am so sorry," James said. "It appears as if your husband was bitten by a snake, probably a mamba."

"No, no no, no es posible," Catalina cried. She reached out and took his hand, not quite stiff from rigour mortis. Then she flung herself down on the floor and cried, deep, wracking sobs. Alessandra took her hand and helped her up and took her off to the *boma,* where all the others were gathered. As she left, she asked James if he would continue to look into things.

"I'll have a preliminary report soon," James said. "But, it seems fairly clear to me, looking at his body and the respiratory distress that he was clearly in, classic signs of a snake bite. Obviously, I can't be certain without a full PM, but the signs seem fairly clear to me."

"Do you mind if we take a look?" Marieke said.

"If you're sure it won't upset you," James said.

"I think we'll manage," Marieke said. "Can you uncover him for me?"

"There you are," James said.

"Who reported it?" Marieke asked.

"The housekeeping guy called Joseph, I guess he was on a laundry run, saw the body and ran to the *boma* to tell Grace," James replied.

"Where was he found?" Marieke asked.

"On the path near his tent," James said. "It looks like he walked a little way from his tent and collapsed. My guess is that the snake was in his tent. Grace said that she'd try and get more ice, or in this heat, we'll have a ripe corpse on our hands before too long. Seen enough?"

"Thank you," Marieke said.

"I'd better go and see how everyone is doing," James said.

"What do you think?" Melisende asked Marieke after James had gone.

"It's meant to look like a snake bite, but there's a lot that bothers me," Marieke said. "If it's supposed to be a mamba, there's only one apparent strike, that's not typical for a cornered mamba. The bite site doesn't look quite right to me. If you looked closely, the supposed fang marks went up, not down, and mamba fangs go down, almost as if it's been created with a thorn or something like that. The condition of the body isn't quite right for a mamba bite. He was found on the path from his tent to the *boma*, so did he stagger that far after being bitten?"

"So, you're thinking this is not snake bite at all, but something else?" Melisende asked.

"Definitely something else, he got here with respiratory issues, so the chances are it was something he picked up elsewhere. If it was a mamba bite, then that just finished it for him. We should go and take a close look at his tent, and where he was found. I've got a new chip for my camera, I'll take pictures of where he was found and the tent and its surrounds," Marieke said. They collected Henry, who had been hanging around watching things and went to the path where Alberto had been found.

"Alberto left his tent and walked down the path here, you can see he starts to get unsteady, now he's weaving, now he falls, then he dies," Marieke said, following his tracks and taking pictures as she went. "There are a lot of other tracks here, Joseph and then Stan, here Grace, then two others, we'll need to get their footprints to sort out who is who, this one here was here before Joseph."

"That one, the guest that was with us on the walk," Henry said.

"Which one, Tom or David?" Marieke asked.

"The one called David," Henry said.

100

"Interesting," Marieke said to herself. "And the other?"

"Not sure, not one I've seen, so perhaps the lady who went with Adam," Henry replied.

"No, this one's Monica," Marieke said. "I saw her this morning and followed her for a short way. This is Monica. I should get a look at all their tracks so that I know who's who."

"No snake, though?" Melisende asked.

"No snake," Marieke confirmed.

"No snake," Henry confirmed.

"Look, you can see here where Monica kneels by the body, then David arrives and she leaves," Marieke said. "He kneels by the body, then gets up and walks over there and comes back and kneels again, then he leaves and then Joseph and Stan arrive. What's over there?"

"Nasty-looking thorn bushes," Melisende said.

"One of the acacias," Marieke said. "This one has got nice long straight thorns, I wonder if there's any chance of finding a thorn near where the body was."

"I think a slim chance," Melisende said. "Looking around, there's a lot of ground cover, and unless you can grid the area and do a centimetre-by-centimetre search, it would be pure chance."

"You're right," Marieke agreed. "Do any of these bushes have curved thorns?"

"What about that one there?" Melisende asked, pointing to a bush.

"Wait a bit, that would work," Marieke said. "Short, curved and very sharp thorns. Don't get mixed up with one of them."

"Let's take a look inside the tent," Marieke suggested.

At tent number four, Marieke and Henry first circled the tent from the outside. "No tracks of a snake here," she said, and he nodded in agreement. "Let's see if he's still inside."

"Is that safe?" Melisende asked.

"We'll be fine," Marieke assured her, after picking up a stick and creating a fork in the end. They opened the door and looked inside, under the bed, up at the rafters, by the clothes hanger, in the bathroom, in fact everywhere. "No snake here," Marieke said.

"Could it have come up through the drain?" Melisende asked.

"No, the grid openings are too small," Marieke said. "The bite mark, or ersatz bite mark, is on the thigh, so if it was a snake, it had to be in the room and a pretty big snake, the height of the apparent bite mark is 65 cm. The height would work if a two-metre mamba reared up to strike, then that would fit, but even then, the angles of the fang marks look wrong to me. No, I think something or someone did him in, and then things were staged to look like a snake bite. Let's go and take another look at where they found him."

"So, someone knew of the hanky panky between him and Monica and killed him?" Melisende asked.

"It looks that way to me," Marieke said. "I don't see one of the staff doing this, so it's got to be a guest. The question is, what with. Where were they all this morning?"

"Catalina was with Carol and Alex and you and me," Melisende replied. "Tom and David were with Abel and Henry, and Sofia and James were with Adam."

"So Catalina has the best alibi," Marieke thought. "We were called back after they found the body."

"Perhaps she had a confederate?" Melisende suggested.

"Yes, and the initial review of the body by James Davis was no apparent foul play, no obvious injuries, so no reason not to move it," Marieke mused.

"We should try and get some more ice on the body soon," Melisende said. "Or, as James Davis said, we'll have a ripe corpse on our hands. Henry, can you go to the kitchen and see how much ice they can spare?"

"Yes, Madame," he replied.

"How long before the Zambia Police arrive?" Melisende asked.

"If there's space on the afternoon flight, they could be here by four," Marieke thought.

"Any thoughts?" Alessandra asked as she joined them.

"First thought, it wasn't a snake," Marieke said. "Henry and I found no evidence of a snake where they found the body, or in and around his tent. There are marks on his thigh that look like bite marks, but they can be easily put there with a thorn."

"Adam's just back, ZAWA has deferred to the Zambia Police, and there's two officers on the flight out this afternoon," Alessandra said.

"Apparently, the Zambia Police want all the guests to stay here until the officers have seen the place where we found the body and talked to all the guests and the staff. Adam told the Zambia Police that you were here, and they asked if you would sit in on the interviews. You're quite famous with the Zambia Police, Auntie Marieke, is that because of the commissioner that Mum said met you at the airport?"

"It all goes back years ago when we were looking for killers of the two profs, the killers landed in Zambia, then stole a mekoro and crossed the Zambezi and left that way as well, the Zambia Police helped us a lot with that, so I got to know one of the senior officers quite well, since then I've worked with the Zambia Police on a number of cases, most recently with Commissioner Bwalya and several of his senior officers," Marieke replied.

"I remember that we were back from school and Dad found the Land Rover and then called the police and you rode up with us on the plane from Maun," Alessandra said.

"When was this group supposed to leave?" Marieke asked.

"Thursday from here, then Friday morning, SA flight to Jo'burg," Alessandra said.

"Will the Zambia Police let them go if the death is suspicious?" Marieke asked.

"Not if it's suspicious," Alessandra said. "For sure, we're shipping Alberto out of here as soon as we can, we'll wrap him up as best we can and ask the police to send a body bag on the flight this afternoon, and we'll put him in it. I'm sure the Zambia Police will want details of what you found, or didn't find, where the body was and in the tent."

"I'd better write up my notes now so that I don't forget anything," Marieke commented.

"How is Catalina?" Melisende asked.

"A bit more contained, less hysterics," Alessandra said.

"Is it real, or theatrics?" Melisende asked. "I'm sorry, but once a policewoman, always a policewoman. Any byplay with the others?"

"Odd looks from Monica at the rest, particularly Catalina, but other than that, this lot is going to be hard to shake," Alessandra said.

"What do they do for a living?" Melisende asked.

"Alberto, would you believe was a herpetologist," Alessandra replied. "Catalina is an epidemiologist at the America Center for Disease Control and Prevention, Monica and David Davis run a restaurant known for serving puffer fish, Carol is an anæsthetist, James, as you now know, is a pathologist, Sofia is an entomologist specialising in spiders and Tom runs the poison plant lab for the US Department of Agriculture."

"Wonderful, any one of them could engineer a poisoning and know how to cover it up," Marieke said. "We'll have to see who is the best poker player."

"Have you any ideas about the toxin or poison?" Alessandra asked.

"As I think about it, Alberto reminds me of a few cases I saw in Botswana. There was an old lady who breathed in a lot of dust that had abrin in it. She had difficulty breathing; eventually her lungs filled up with fluid, and she died. Her skin had a bluish tinge and her eyes were red, Alberto's got the same look about him, There were four others as well that all had a similar look about them, all with the same eye redness and bluish tinge to the skin, and all of whom had had difficulty breathing," Marieke said. "The beans are easy enough to find, creating a powder would be easy enough, if a little risky for the person grinding the beans, getting him to breathe it in would take a little thinking out, but could be done. How was he when he arrived?"

"He was coughing a little, and it has got worse over the past day, and he was complaining this morning about not being able to breathe," Alessandra replied.

"So, best guess, the toxin was introduced somewhere else, if I recall correctly, symptoms in as little as 8 hours, but could be as long as 24 to 48 hours, death in 36 to 72 hours depending on the dose and how it was administered and how healthy the person is," Marieke said. "Where were they 36 hours ago?"

"The Radisson Blu," Alessandra said. "And before that, they were at a camp in the Lower Zambezi. You're sure this wasn't accidental or something he picked up along the way?"

"Yes, but proving that will be the challenge," Marieke said. "If I'm right and this is abrin poisoning, that can only happen if the bean is opened up, you could swallow a whole bean and just poop it out with no ill effects, but break the aril and you're in deep trouble."

"Why do you think it's abrin?" Alessandra asked.

"As I said, it looks very like the case I had in Botswana," Marieke replied. "It's probably bad luck for whoever did this that there is someone here who has seen a death from abrin before. How likely is that?"

"Not very," Alessandra said. "So, if there's the possibility of a plant-based toxin, does that point to Tom as a good suspect?"

"Perhaps," Marieke said. "But let's not leap to conclusions."

"Sorry to keep you all waiting," Alessandra told her guests when she and Marieke, Melisende and Henry arrived at the boma. "The Zambia Police are sending a couple of officers out to investigate on the afternoon flight. They have requested that everyone stay here until they have conducted their preliminary interviews and prepared the report they will need to do."

"When can we leave?" Catalina asked. "I don't want to stay here any longer now that I have to."

"That will be up to the Zambia Police," Alessandra said. "I'm sure that they will make every accommodation they can for you, but they are bound by the rules and laws, so they must investigate."

"Even if it's clearly accidental?" James asked.

"I'm sure that even in the US that deaths must all be investigated and the coroner will rule on whether or not it is accidental," Alessandra said.

"Coroner's court?" Tom asked.

"We follow the British style of coroner's court here," Alessandra explained. "The coroner has the responsibility to hear all evidence pertaining to the death, including police reports, post-mortem examination results and anything else he or she considers germane. The coroner will rule on the cause of death: accidental, misadventure or something else."

"So the coroner doesn't do the autopsy?" James asked.

"No, PMs are typically done at the Teaching Hospital or another regional centre," Alessandra explained. "The coroner here is more like a magistrate than a medical person."

"Interesting," James commented.

"Auntie Marieke, will you take the boat and go to the Lufupa strip and meet the police officers?" Alessandra asked.

"Of course," Marieke said. "Should I leave now?"

"That would give you more than enough time," Alessandra thought.

"Coming Melisende?" Marieke asked.

"Of course," she replied. "Unless Alex needs me for something?"

"No, we're fine," Alessandra said. "Grace and I will take care of things. I need to get a tent ready for the coppers when they get here."

Marieke and Melisende took one of the Land Cruisers and drove to the boat dock, then went downriver to Lufupa and got the other vehicle and drove to the airstrip. There were two other vehicles waiting for the plane, and the drivers were curious about Marieke and Melisende. Marieke introduced herself and explained where she was staying, and that led to all kinds of questions as the bush telegraph had been active and they all knew about the death. All Marieke could and would tell them was that it was an apparent snake bite and that the Zambia Police were sending an officer out to investigate. Conversation stopped as they saw the plane come in, do its fly by, then land.

"Hey guys, you from Mupundu?" Chad, the co-pilot, said as he got out of the plane.

"We are," Marieke confirmed.

"Heard you had issues," Chad said.

"We did," Marieke confirmed.

"We've got a body bag for you," Chad said. "Let me get it for you, then I can unload the rest of the luggage."

He busied himself, and Marieke saw the pilot helping passengers leave the plane and saw the uniformed officers get out. She knew them; they had been on two of the teams she had worked with in the past.

"Commissaire Englebrecht," one of them said. "How nice to see you again, even if it's not under the best circumstances.

"Superintendent Felix Zimba, Chief Inspector Ernest Mwewa, this is Commissaire Divisionnaire Melisende Garnier, whom I work with in Paris," Marieke said, making the introductions.

"So, Matshwane, what do we have?" Felix asked.

"We've a death, that some have suggested is from a mamba," Marieke replied.

"But, you have your doubts?" he asked.

106

"I suppose it's the policewoman in me," she said. "My review of the area where the body was found and the tent where he stayed showed no snake tracks."

"Ah, excuse me, there are our bags," he said. They retrieved their bags and went to the Land Cruiser, and Marieke drove them to the boat dock.

"So, you were saying about tracks?" he asked.

"Right," she said. "I looked around the area where they found the body and saw evidence of a man in distress, but not snake tracks. I had Henry, the ZAWA game scout and Adam and Abel, two of the guides from the camp, also look, and they concurred, no snake, but there were marks on his thigh of an apparent strike."

"Just one?" Felix asked.

"Just one," Marieke confirmed.

"That would be unusual," he commented.

"My thought exactly," she agreed.

"Who is the dead chap?" Felix asked.

"Dr Alberto Juarez, a herpetologist at the Atlanta Zoo in the States," Marieke replied.

"There's irony for you," Felix said. "Who are the other guests?"

"Dr Catalina Juarez, wife of the dead chap, epidemiologist at the American Center for Disease Control and Prevention, Dr James Davis, a pathologist from Dallas, Dr Carol Davis an anæsthetist, wife of James, Dr Sofia Macmillan, entomologist specialising in spiders from Utah State University, Dr Tom Macmillan, spouse, works for the US Department of Agriculture poison plant lab also at Utah States, David Davis, restauranteur from Los Angeles and Monica Davis, his spouse, also with the restaurant," Marieke enumerated.

"Wonderful," Felix said. "All well educated, many of them with skills to cover up a death."

"I forgot to mention, the restaurant that the Davises run is known for serving puffer fish, which, if not done right, will kill," Marieke added.

"Just gets better," Felix said. "Anything I should know before I interview them?"

107

"Monica Davis and Alberto Juarez had a relationship," Marieke replied. "We haven't been able to pick up whether David Davis and Catalina Juarez knew or suspected, but the others certainly knew and commented on when we were alone."

"You are full of good news," he said. "Who decided it was a mamba?"

"James Davis did a preliminary gross examination," Marieke replied. "We were not there when they found the body; we were at a salt pan to the north and were called back by the camp manager, Grace Kachepa. By the time we arrived back in camp, they had moved the body to a container, and Davis was looking it over. He said that he had experience with snake bites from Texas, and was confident that that was what we were looking at."

"Who actually found it?" Felix asked.

"Two of the housekeeping staff, Joseph and Stan," Marieke replied. "One of them stayed, and one went to fetch Grace. She called in James Davis, and he said to move the body."

"Pity that you didn't see it in situ," Felix said. "I suppose they had to move it fairly quickly, or you'd have every predator and scavenger from miles around all paying a visit."

"I agree, I have taken a lot of photographs," Marieke said. "I'll give you the camera chip."

"How long a boat ride?" he asked as they boarded the boat.

"Twenty minutes," she replied.

"Good, now any suggestions as to how to proceed?" he asked.

"That's up to you," she said. "This is your case, we're just here as observers."

"That's true, but I value your opinion and would appreciate your help," he said. "Should I take the guests first or the staff?"

"I think I'd do the guests first," she suggested. "Get their stories before they have too much time to agree on a common response."

"Where are they now?" he asked.

"We left them all at the *boma* with Alex and Grace," Marieke replied.

"You suspect one of them?" he asked.

"I don't see this as a snake bite," she said. "In many ways, it reminds me of cases I had in Botswana where the victims had inhaled abrin dust and died. Alberto has what I see as the same presentation of the results of the toxin."

"So, start with the spouse, Catalina, how's she doing?" Felix asked.

"Not quite as hysterical when we left," Marieke said. "When she was told of the death, I saw it as a genuine surprise, and she seemed really distressed, or else she'd get an Academy Award for Best Actress."

"When you were at the salt pan, who was with you?" he asked.

"Alex Martin, Carol Davis, Catalina and the two of us," she replied.

"And the others," he asked.

"Alberto has not been doing well since he arrived, showing signs of respiratory distress, so he's been staying in camp, taking no excursions at all. Monica Davis also stayed in camp, ostensibly to watch game on the lagoon from the deck," Marieke replied. "David Davis and Tom Macmillan went with the guide, Abel, and Henry the ZAWA scout for a walk, and finally, Sofia Macmillan and James Davis went for a drive with the other guide, Adam, who by the way is married to Grace Kachepa."

"Any idea of when they all got back to camp?" Felix asked.

"No," she replied. "We had taken a picnic lunch, so expected to be out for most of the day, but normally walks and drives get you back by eleven or so."

"And they called you when?" he asked.

"Twelve-thirty," she replied. "Lunch is normally served about noon, so either during or just after lunch."

"You said that Alberto hasn't been doing well since he arrived. What were his symptoms?" Felix asked.

"He had a light cough when he first got here, and that has worsened, and this morning he was showing real signs of distress," she replied. "His wife had made arrangements with Alex to get them on the flight you came in on to go to Lusaka and seek medical help."

"Pity she didn't do it sooner," he said. "Now, when I interview all these people, I'd like you both there, take note of what they say and how and if you see or hear anything that warrants more questions, just ask. I'll tell them that we've worked together in the past and that you're assisting me with the approval of the Commissioner. Do they know you're with the French Police?"

"They know we live in Paris and they know that we both work for the French government, we just said that we did analysis," she replied.

"Analysis, I like that," he laughed. "Where were they before they came here?"

"We understand that they were first in South Luangwa, then the Lower Zambezi," she replied. "I don't know which camps or lodges, I gather from what Alex said, three nights in each, and they're due to leave here Thursday for Livingstone, then on Friday for Jo'burg and back to the States."

"Is this it, are we here?" he asked, as Marieke nosed the boat into the bank at the boat dock.

"Just a short drive from here," she said.

"Before we get there, let's make things easy for me when I introduce you to these people. How do your ranks equate to ours?" Felix asked.

"Commissaire would be superintendent and divisionnaire would be chief superintendent," Marieke explained.

"That makes it easier to say," he said. "This is unfortunate for Ms Martin that a guest died, not good for the camp, I hope it does not affect bookings and mean a loss of revenue for ZAWA."

"I doubt that will happen," Marieke said. "He didn't die in the tent, so there's no association there. If we can show he either died of natural causes or something more nefarious, then it really won't reflect on the camp. It's clearly not food poisoning, which would drive people away."

"Quite," Felix said.

When they arrived at the boma, Marieke and Melisende stood back while Felix introduced himself.

"Good afternoon," he said. "I am Superintendent Zimba, and this is Chief Inspector Ernest Mwewa. We are here to investigate the unfortunate death of one of your friends. We will be interviewing each of you in turn to understand more about Dr Juarez and what may have occurred here. We will be assisted during this investigation by Chief Superintendent Garnier and Superintendent Englebrecht of the French national police. We have worked with Commandant Englebrecht before, and she is well known to us both from her work with us and before that, when we assisted her in an investigation when she was with the Botswana Police. We have made arrangements for everyone to fly to Lusaka tomorrow. We regret cutting your stay here short, but this rather takes precedence. Do you have any questions for me?"

"Do we need lawyers?" James asked.

"If you feel the need, that can be arranged, but that would likely not be until late tomorrow or the day after," Felix said. "Why would you think that you needed a lawyer?"

"I thought this was a simple snake bite issue," James said. "I don't understand the need for lots of interviews."

"This is what you I believe would call an unattended death, and the law requires that we investigate so that we may present those findings to the coroner's court for official determination of cause of death," Felix explained.

"Just cooperate, James," Carol said. "The sooner we can get all this done, the sooner we can get the hell out of here."

"How do you want to handle this, Superintendent?" Alessandra asked.

"I'd like somewhere quiet where we can talk to you," he replied. "What about the dining table there?"

"That's fine," Alessandra replied. "I presume you'd want privacy?"

"That would be good," Felix said. "And I would ask the rest of you to remain here. Chief Inspector Mwewa will keep you company. If you'll excuse us for a few minutes, we'll get ourselves set and then ask for our first interviewee."

"I'll have some tea and coffee sent down for you," Alessandra said.

They walked down to the dining area and looked to Felix for their leads.

"Ernest, I want you to keep an eye on these people, engage them in general conversation, take special note of any byplay between them, we don't want them concocting a story if one or more of them had any hand in this, perhaps before we start we should view where the body was found, view the tent where he stayed and also the body. Matshwana, if you please."

Marieke led the way to where Alberto was found, and Felix and Ernest looked around a nodded. Then they looked in and around

111

the tent and finally went to the container where the body was. Felix uncovered it and looked carefully at the leg where the apparent snake bite was, and also took note of the general condition.

"That's no snake bite," Ernest said. "The puncture marks of the fangs go the wrong way; they should be angled down, these are angled up."

"I agree," Felix said. "The question is, was it done just to confuse or to mislead?"

"That we will only find out in the interviews," Ernest said.

"I agree," Felix said. "I think we'll take the widow first."

"I will scribe for you," Melisende volunteered. "I have a laptop computer with me and can record the interviews as they are done and print out the documents later. The camp does have a printer and plenty of paper. We could also print the photographs if you'd like."

"Thank you, that would be most helpful," Felix said.

Catalina's account

"Thank you all for being patient," Felix said. "We are ready to begin. We don't anticipate that this will take too long. Dr Juarez, would you be so kind?"

"I don't understand," Catalina said after she sat down at the dining table. "I thought that Alberto died from a snake bite?"

"We're sorry for your loss," Felix said. "Is there anyone in the States that you should contact, children, his parents?"

"I can do that as soon as we can get to a phone in Lusaka, we have no kids, but I should call his parents and let them know," Catalina replied.

"I'm sorry to have to do this, but as I'm sure you will understand, there are things that we do need to ask," Felix said.

"I guess I understand," Catalina said. "I still can't accept that he's dead, and I'm not sure how much help I can be. I thought we were dealing with a snake bite."

"I have some experience with snake bites. I grew up on the Copperbelt and have seen many snake bites in my career, and while it seems possible, it may also be something else, or may be a combination of things," Felix said. "We're concerned that his death may have been something he ingested or inhaled on the trip here or since he's been in Zambia, or an underlying condition that was exacerbated by something here. We understand that Alberto was a herpetologist. Tell us about him, was he in good health?"

"He had the usual colds and flu over the years, but nothing major, no surgeries or anything like that," Catalina replied. "We skied, played tennis a lot, we jogged regularly, he was mildly asthmatic, he had an inhaler for that, but he didn't have to use it that often. I think the jogging and hiking we did helped a lot."

"No underlying conditions, no weaknesses of the lungs?" Marieke asked.

"No, just the asthma," Catalina said. "He was healthy, ran almost every day, kept his weight in control, I'd say better than most of the rest of us."

"Has he always been a herpetologist?" Felix asked.

"His first degree was biology, that's how we met, we were at USC together, in fact we were all at USC for our bachelors', then he went on to study snakes with a master's then a doctorate, then he got a job at the Atlanta zoo, and has been there ever since," Catalina said.

"Do you know if he had even been bitten by a snake?" Marieke asked.

"I think a few times, but I don't think ever by what I would call a really venomous snake, mostly constrictors that were upset about something," Catalina replied.

"Do you know if the Atlanta Zoo has a wide collection of snakes?" Melisende asked.

"I think pretty wide, I know they have Cape cobras, gaboon vipers and other African snakes," Catalina replied.

"Has he ever been anywhere else in the world?" Felix asked.

"He went to Brazil a couple of times to look for anacondas and for other nasty snakes, like the Lancehead viper, which he went to some little island to see. I gather that the place was alive with snakes, and their bite can be lethal really quickly," Catalina said.

"Do you know if he was ever bitten by them?" Felix asked.

"No, he told me that they'd been really careful and the Brazilians actually sent a doctor with his team in case," Catalina said. "By the sound of it, not somewhere I would ever want to go."

"So, no probable build-up over time of a reaction to venom?" Marieke asked.

"You mean like when people who are allergic get stung by bees and the next time is way worse, no, I don't think he had any issues like that," Catalina said.

"What about scorpions, spiders, centipedes or other things?" Melisende asked.

"Don't think so," Catalina said. "We don't get too many of those creepy crawly things around the house, the zoo might get some, but I'd guess that there's plenty of things at the zoo that would eat them."

"Who organised the trip to Zambia?" Felix asked.

"I think Carol first suggested it," Catalina said. "It was last year at Christmas, we had all met up at a cottage that Monica and David have at Lake Arrowhead to go skiing there. We were talking about things we'd all like to do, and Africa came up, a first for most of us but a return for Alberto, who had been to South Africa once before."

"Did you all have a good time skiing?" Marieke asked.

"We did at first, then Alberto sprained his ankle, so Monica took care of him while the rest of us went skiing," Catalina replied.

"Why Zambia?" Felix asked. "Not many people even know where Zambia is; most people think of Kenya and Tanzania first for safaris, then maybe South Africa."

"Probably my suggestion," Catalina said. "I track outbreaks around the world, even though I've never been sent out of Atlanta, so the Congo is familiar to me. at least on the map, and I knew that Zambia bordered the Congo and was probably a safer bet than the Congo. Also, not as risky as Rwanda or Congo Brazzaville or Gabon. I thought about Kenya and Tanzania and have some friends who have been to both, but hearing stories of ten or more jeeps all parked around the same tree watching a leopard soured me on them a little so it was Zambia or Zimbabwe, and one of me colleagues just visited Zambia on an official trip and got to go to Luangwa and he told me how great it was, so, I settled on Zambia."

"Your education is a doctor of medicine?" Felix asked.

"No, my bachelor's is biology, then I have a master's and a doctorate in public health," Catalina replied. "My doctoral thesis was infection spread mechanisms."

"Who put the trip together?" Felix asked.

"Carol found a travel agent in Dallas who specialises in Africa, and she put it all together, everything from Johannesburg on, we had told her that we'd all make our own ways to Johannesburg," Catalina said.

"How did you get to Jo'burg?" Marieke asked.

"Delta to Amsterdam, then KLM to Johannesburg," Catalina replied. "We could fly non-stop to Amsterdam from Atlanta, and I'm sure you know that KLM is partnered with Delta, so it was one ticket all the way. As I said, the others were all going to make their own way to Johannesburg. Then from Johannesburg to Lusaka, it was South African."

"Sorry to ask this, I know it's not relevant, just curiosity, was it expensive?" Melisende asked.

"At first I thought so, then when I looked at it all, everything is included, it's not like a hotel, where there's the room rate, but then you've got meals, laundry service, activities, all extra, so that adds up to quite a bill. A trip to Hawaii would have cost us almost as much; the only real difference was the airfare."

"Thank you," Melisende said, filing away the information for their personal use at a later date.

"You said that you all met at Christmas?" Felix asked. "Did you all meet again before Johannesburg?"

"We met again at Easter, in Dallas at Carol and Jim's place to finalise all the details," Catalina replied. "We were all getting quite excited by then, looking forward to the trip, Alberto was full of snakes and what we might see, I think he must be the only person I know who really is into snakes."

"What did you do at Easter?" Melisende asked.

"Oh, we played tennis, we took a trip to Austin to listen to good music, it was fun, we drove down together, Monica and David came with us, and Jim and Carol went with Sofia and Tom," Catalina replied. "We had a great time, and it was a fun weekend. The next time we met in person was in Johannesburg."

"Did you all play tennis?" Felix asked.

"For the first day, then Alberto complained that his ankle was acting up and Monica volunteered to be nursemaid, which suited me as I was on a roll and even beat James and David," Catalina said. "The other thing we discussed was shots, pills and prevention. I got the latest reports from work, and we went through all the recommended shots and decided on Yellow Fever and a Polio booster. As the one guy at work said, get vaccinated for that which will kill you and treat other things symptomatically. We debated Malaria pills and hunted around for something that wouldn't have weird side effects. I've heard of people having anxiety attacks, hallucinations, all kinds of unpleasant things, just shows how the mosquitoes and the parasites have adapted to the older medications that no longer work."

"How was the flight over?" Marieke asked. "Was Alberto all right on both the flights?"

"He was," Catalina replied. "He was excited to be coming, we had a great flight to Amsterdam, then there was quite a long layover until we got the flight to Johannesburg."

"What did Alberto eat and drink on those flights?" Felix asked.

"I've tried to remember all that he has eaten and drunk over the past couple of weeks. Let's see, on the flight from Atlanta, Delta served dinner, Alberto had chicken, as far as I could see, it looked fine, it certainly smelled good. I had beef. If there had been anything wrong with the chicken, I would have expected a reaction a lot quicker," Catalina replied. Marieke noted that the scientist in Catalina was now coming forward, and she was trying to remember details that might help.

"And to drink?" Melisende asked.

"Nothing out of the ordinary, some white wine with dinner, coffee, a Diet Coke, water," Catalina replied.

"And at Schipol?" Marieke asked.

"We went to the airline lounge there for KLM and they served all kinds, I'm not really sure what Alberto tried, but he gave me samples of everything he had and I've had no reactions," Catalina said.

"Did he have any known allergies?" Felix asked.

"A couple of minor ones that trigger asthma, too many onions will do it, no contact dermatitis, no bee sting allergies, nothing that's cropped up over the years," Catalina replied.

"Did you manage to get any sleep on the Amsterdam flight?" Marieke asked.

"You mean, did we get run down because of lack of sleep? I don't think so, we both managed a few hours after dinner," Catalina said.

"What did KLM serve on the Jo'burg flight?" Felix asked.

"Let's see," Catalina said. "The usual champagne and nuts after take-off, then for lunch smoked salmon, then braised lamb with pasta and vegetables, for dessert we had the cheese plate, we both had the same meals, so unless Alberto had an allergy to something I didn't know about, then unlikely to be that meal."

"Any other meals before landing?" Melisende asked.

"We had a light meal in the afternoon," Catalina said. "Chicken with mashed potatoes and more vegetables, followed by a chocolate mousse, again, we both had the same."

"To drink?" Marieke asked.

"An Argentinian red," Catalina replied. "After lunch, coffee, black, and a Cognac. Water, the bottles that KLM served, mostly Evian."

"And when you landed in Jo'burg, what then?" Felix asked.

"It was late, so we checked into a hotel, there's one right by the airport, you can walk there easily, through the multi-storey parking lot," Catalina explained. "We had nothing more to eat that night, and for breakfast, we both had muesli, yoghurt and coffee, then headed back to the airport for the South African flight to Lusaka."

"Is that when you met up with the others?" Felix asked.

"We saw them all at breakfast at the hotel," Catalina said. "They'd flown in on Qatar, Emirates and South African."

"What about the South African flight to Lusaka?" Felix asked.

"They served us a breakfast, omelette, we all had pretty much the same," Catalina said. "Once we got to Lusaka, we found the charter people and left straight away for the airport by Luangwa."

"Mfuwe, right," Marieke said. "At Mfuwe, then what?"

"The lodge people met us and drove us to the park to the Lundwe Lodge, where we checked in, then had lunch," Catalina said. "We all felt like a nap after lunch, so we didn't get back together again until the afternoon game drive."

"And you were with Alberto that whole time?" Felix asked.

"I was," Catalina confirmed.

"How did Alberto seem, any cough, any obvious signs of respiratory distress?" Marieke asked.

"None, no cough, no shortness of breath, nothing," Catalina said.

"What did they serve for lunch?" Felix asked. "No, rather than answer that, did Alberto have anything that you did not?"

"As I think about it, no," Catalina replied. "We all had the same lunch, all eight of us and the other guests, the guides and owners of Lundwe."

"What were the accommodations?" Melisende asked.

"We had a chalet, concrete floor, stone walls, wooden rafters and a thatched roof," Catalina replied. "Nice bath and shower, both, full-sized bed with mosquito net."

"No plants, trees, or bushes in flower adjacent to the chalet?" Marieke asked.

"Not that I remember," Catalina replied.

"No insects, or what you referred to as creepy crawlies in the tent?" Melisende asked.

"None that I saw," Catalina replied. "I think the staff sprayed for bugs while we were out on game drives."

"You all went on the game drive?" Felix asked.

"All in the same jeep," Catalina confirmed. "It was great, not much dust, lots of animals, we got back about six, visited the bathroom, had another sundowner, then dinner."

"You all stayed in the jeep except for the sundowner?" Marieke asked.

"We did," Catalina confirmed. "We stopped near the river, by some big trees and had our drinks. Alberto had a Scotch and soda, from the same bottles as Tom."

"He didn't go wandering off to use the facilities?" Felix asked.

"Thinking about it, no, he didn't," Catalina confirmed.

"No reactions to the dinner?" Marieke asked.

"None," Catalina said. "We had beef for dinner, beef done with red wine, roasted potatoes, glazed carrots and broccoli, for dessert a fruit salad, papayas, mangos, passion fruit and bananas, a South African red with dinner and Amarula afterwards. Have to say it was really good, even Dave and Monica, who have the fancy restaurant in LA, commented on the quality of the food."

"How long were you in Luangwa?" Felix asked.

"We had three nights there," Catalina said.

"And you all did very much the same things, ate the same things and didn't handle or touch any plants?" Felix asked.

"Not really," Catalina said. "They offered walks like they do here, and Tom and David went out on two morning walks, while the rest of us took drives. In the afternoons, we all went on the same drives.

119

As for plants and such, neither Alberto nor I touched or handled anything."

"And during that time in Luangwa, Alberto showed no signs of respiratory distress?" Marieke asked.

"None, he was as chipper and chirpy as ever, going on about snakes, and how they are misunderstood and how they balance the ecosystem," Catalina said.

"Could you sketch for me the layout of the Lundwe Lodge?" Felix asked.

"I'll try," Catalina said. Marieke gave her some paper, and Catalina drew.

"Which of these chalets was yours?" Marieke asked.

"Let's see, Alberto and I were here, Tom and Sofia were here, Monica and David here, next to our chalet, and Carol and James here, and the bar and dining area here, then there were more chalets over here and the staff quarters must have been over here somewhere," Catalina explained.

"Did Alberto spend any time in the camp on his own at any time?" Felix asked.

"Not there, it was all so new, we did everything together," Catalina said. "There was so much to see, we were right on the river, we could look out and see animals and birds right out the door, if you can call it a door."

"And the sleeping arrangements, the usual mosquito nets?" Marieke asked.

"That's right, there was one hung from the roof and we tucked it in around the bed," Catalina said. "First time I've slept under a net, bit weird at first, but I got used to it."

"And nothing of note got in under the net?" Melisende asked.

"No buzzing mosquitoes, if that's what you mean," Catalina said. "I hate it when you can hear the stupid things buzzing around your ears, and I can imagine that if one gets in under the net, it would drive you up the wall. But nothing that I recall on any of the nights we were there."

"While you were at Lundwe, you all ate the same food, and no one had any issues?" Felix asked.

"Apart from eating too much, no," Catalina said. "I've wondered if there was something in the food, but as far as I could see, it was all pretty much unprocessed stuff, so no odd additives, nothing that might cause a reaction. Alberto was never the only one to eat something specific."

"I hate to be indelicate, but bowel movements?" Marieke asked.

"Bit stopped up after the flights, but that's a hydration issue, once in Zambia with regular water, that cleared itself up, and I was fine and Alberto didn't complain at all," Catalina said. "He seems to do better than I when it comes to that, if all else fails, I resort to Senokot, and nothing the other way either, no Montezuma's Revenge, or anything that would further dehydrate."

"Did Alberto have to use his inhaler much in Luangwa?" Marieke asked.

"Come to think of it, he did," Catalina said. "I think it was the dust when we went out for game drives. Although we were close to the river, it did surprise me how dry it was and how hot, at least in the daytime; it cooled down nicely at night, though, so we slept well."

"So, you don't think lack of sleep could have weakened Alberto's immune system?" Marieke asked.

"No, we slept really well, as soon as we went back to the tent after dinner, we were both out and didn't wake until the guy came by in the morning with the wake-up call."

"And from there you went to the Lower Zambezi?" Felix asked.

"Yes, we drove back to the airport and flew to Jeki. I didn't know it was going to be just a dirt strip, but it was fine, a longer flight than I would have thought, an hour and a half," Catalina said.

"And during that time, Alberto was fine?" Felix asked.

"Oh yes, happy smiling, laughing," Catalina said.

"No coughing, no runny nose?" Melisende asked.

"No, none," Catalina said. "You think he inhaled something and that made him sick?"

"We're still just trying to understand what he may have been in contact with," Felix said.

"This is a delicate subject," Melisende said. "But was all well between you and Alberto?"

"Yes, I've never looked anywhere else, since Alberto and I got together at college," Catalina said.

"And Alberto?" Melisende asked.

"I'm beginning to wonder if there wasn't something between him and Monica," Catalina replied. "He seemed to have issues of one type or another when we were all together, and I don't know why it was always Monica who played nursemaid. I hesitate to confront her, I wouldn't want to accuse her of something she didn't do."

"Do you know if things are well between Monica and David?" Felix asked.

"I've wondered about Dave and his sous chefs," Catalina replied. "He picks really good ones but they don't seem to last that long and he's bitched in the past that he's just getting them trained up when Monica finds something to pick on and they're gone."

"Where did you stay in the Lower Zambezi?" Felix asked.

"The Mushika Lodge," Catalina said. "The staff from the camp met us in a jeep at the Jeki strip, and it was a fairly short drive to the camp. We had a chalet on the river, a little different to Luangwa, but really nice."

"And you were there three nights as well?" Felix asked.

"We were," Catalina confirmed.

"What was the layout of the Mushika Lodge?" Felix asked, pushing another piece of paper over towards Catalina.

"Let's see, they had three nice chalets and one a little larger that would probably be good if you had kids, we were here, David and Monica were next to us here, then there was the dining, sitting and bar area, then Tom and Sofia here, and Carol and James here in the bigger room," Catalina said, making her sketch. "The place is right on the Zambezi, built up on stilts, I guess because the river must come up after the rains, all the rooms were connected by wooden walkways that went back to the *boma* they called it, we looked out over the river."

"Mosquito nets there too?" Marieke asked.

"Right," Catalina confirmed.

"And no creepy crawlies?" Melisende asked.

"Not really, there were these millipedes, black things that the guides told us were harmless, but other than them, nothing unpleasant in the chalet," Catalina replied. "A few more mosquitoes around, but I suppose, as we were on the river and it was warmer and more humid and there was a lot more water everywhere compared to Lundwe, that that was not surprising."

"What were the activities at Mushika?" Felix asked.

"I suppose the usual," Catalina said. "Wake up call at five-thirty, then breakfast, then your choice of walk, ride or boat."

"Do you remember what everyone did each day?" Felix asked.

"Let's see, the first afternoon we all went on a boat trip up the Zambezi, saw tons of hippos and crocs, some elephants and some people in canoes," Catalina said. "We stopped on some little island for a sundowner, then went back as it was getting dark, got back about half an hour after dark. Had dinner that night, then went back to the tent and crashed."

"And the next day?" Melisende prompted.

"Well, I wanted to do a walk, so did Sofia, I think Sofia was hoping to see some spiders," Catalina said. "So after breakfast, we went off with one of the guides and the ZAWA guy, Tom and David wanted to try their hand at fishing, so they went off in a boat, Carol and James went for a drive and Alberto stayed behind spotting things from our room with his binoculars and camera."

"And Monica?" Marieke asked.

"Come to think of it, she stayed back for a massage," Catalina said. "Told me afterwards that it was great and that I should get one."

"Did you?" Marieke asked.

"Didn't have or make the time," Catalina said. "We all got back together for lunch, then us girls hung around in the bar talking until the afternoon drive, and the guys went off to do guy things or nap, don't know, all I know is that Alberto showed up at three for afternoon tea, then we all went for a drive, we split up into two groups, mine was me, Sofia, Monica and Jim, Monica made a big thing about organising everyone."

"Dinner that night, anything stand out?" Marieke asked.

123

"Not really, it was fish, really good, I think Monica and David were keen to know more about it as they wanted to know what the recipes were, I think for their restaurant," Catalina said.

"And the next day?" Felix asked.

"Alberto and I went with the ZAWA guy and Joy, one of the guides, for a walk, looking for snakes," Catalina replied. "The others split up, and four went in canoes on the river and David and Monica took a drive."

"Did you see any snakes?" Felix asked.

"We did actually, Alberto said it was a puff adder, nasty-looking, fat thing," Catalina said. "Alberto took loads of pictures, and if the rest of us hadn't been there, I'm sure he would have gone a lot closer, but the ZAWA guy and Joy said no way."

"Did Alberto come into contact with any plants, trees or bushes on your walk?" Marieke asked.

"I can't really remember, we drove out a short way somewhere, then left the jeep and walked, I suppose in a wide circle, because we came back to the same spot and picked up the jeep to go back for lunch," Catalina replied. "I know we brushed through some long grass in a couple of places, but other than that, no bushes or trees."

"Did you see any vines or creepers on your walk?" Marieke asked.

"I suppose we did," Catalina replied. "Joy was forever pointing things out and telling us what they were and what they were used for. I confess I wasn't as interested as Alberto."

"Lunch that day?" Melisende asked.

"The usual, salads and cold meats, really good, then the guys all went off again to nap or do guy things, and us girls sat in the *boma* area comparing notes and discussing what we wanted to do next, as a big trip I mean, go to China, or Paris, Australia, New Zealand, or wherever," Catalina said. "We didn't go back to our tents at all that afternoon. Alby joined us at about two, and the rest of the guys joined us at three, and after coffee, we all took a boat ride up the Zambezi."

"What kind of inhalers did Alberto use for his asthma?" Marieke asked.

"The dry powder type with capsules that he dropped in," Catalina replied.

"Did Alberto use his inhaler much in Lower Zambezi?" Felix asked.

"He did on the last morning we were there before we left for Lusaka," Catalina said. "Thinking about it, we had had avocado in a salad the night before, I should have told him not to eat it as it does affect him."

"Then the day you left for Lusaka?" Felix asked.

"Right, there was a morning drive, then had lunch and got an afternoon flight from Jeki to Lusaka, on the morning drive there was Alberto, Carol and James and me, the others went for a walk with Joy and the ZAWA guy," Catalina said. "Come think of it, Alberto was coughing a little on the drive, not too much but more than he had before the whole trip, you don't suppose he picked something up at Mushika?"

"Have there been any outbreaks of disease of note this year?" Marieke asked.

"There's an Ebola outbreak in West Africa, and there have been a couple of cases of MERS reported in Saudi," Catalina said. "But nothing here or in the Congo."

"How have you been, Dr Juarez? Any coughing, difficulty breathing?" Marieke asked.

"Not a bit," Catalina replied. "Whatever Alberto had, it isn't catching, or I would have shown symptoms by now."

"How was the flight to Lusaka?" Felix asked.

"Just great, pretty short, only about thirty minutes, so up then down," Catalina said. "We had a bus laid on for the Radisson Blu and all had dinner together and had an early night. It seems to me now that I think about it that Alberto was coughing a little more through the night. In the morning, we grabbed an early morning breakfast, then had the bus take us back to the airport in time to get the flight out here. You saw Alberto here, complaining about not feeling great and saying that he would probably go and see about it when we got home."

"And since you've been here, we've eaten what you've eaten, so if Alberto picked something up, it was probably before you got here," Marieke thought.

"How could we find out?" Catalina asked.

"We will want to do a post-mortem examination," Felix said. "We have to establish definite cause of death."

"That's fine," Catalina said. "I want to know now, I want to know what it was. But how did he get that apparent bite mark on his leg?"

"That's a good question, perhaps it is a bite mark, and because your husband was already having problems, the effects of the toxin were quicker," Felix agreed. "We'll also need to go back and look where he fell and see if there are any thorn bushes there that he might have hit."

"Is there anything you can think of that might help us understand what happened to Alberto?" Melisende asked.

"Not that I can think of," Catalina said. "Alberto really wanted to come on this trip. I think he was disappointed that he'd started to feel bad and didn't feel up to any activities."

"Do you know what he did when he stayed in camp?" Felix asked.

"I suppose slept, sat on the deck, either just outside our tent or there by the dining table," Catalina replied. "I don't think he did a lot, he complained more and more about not feeling well, and he was coughing more and using his inhaler more, we both thought he had picked up a bug somewhere."

"Thank you, Dr Juarez," Felix said. "We may wish to talk again in Lusaka. Let me walk you back to the *boma*."

"Just drop me at the loo that's over to the side of the *boma* there," Catalina said. "If I think of anything else, I'll let you know, but right now, all I want to do is go home. I'll see when I can get Alberto from you and then work with the embassy to ship him home."

"I think it would be a good idea for us the take the inhaler and the capsules that Alberto had and have them tested to make sure they were delivering the correct doses," Felix said.

"Of course," Catalina agreed. "Let's go to my tent, you can take the inhaler and all the capsules, and I'll use the loo there."

"Let's stop at the office and pick up a couple of plastic bags," Marieke suggested. "We'll need to protect the inhaler and capsules."

"What do you think?" Felix asked Marieke and Melisende after they had dropped Catalina at her tent.

"I've an idea, but it's going to need a lot of confirmation," Marieke replied. "I suspect that it was an inhaled toxin, either abrin or

126

something very similar, but that is only a suspicion; there could also be other explanations. I wouldn't want to become so focused on the one idea that we would miss other solutions."

"I agree," he said. "But instincts are often right, we won't ignore other possibilities, but we will make sure we look for evidence of all kinds. If this was deliberate, what about Dr Juarez?"

"Don't think she did it or had a part in it, but I think she's beginning to put two and two together and now she's got her ideas of what, who, when and perhaps even how," Marieke replied.

"I agree," Melisende added. "She knew all about Alberto and Monica, and I'm sure that there were other women that he was involved with, but for all that, she loved him and was prepared to accept him for what he was. Not many women would tolerate that; in fact, most would leave or take action of some kind, but not her. She now has her list of suspects, and at the top of that list is David Davis, but she doesn't think he is smart enough to put it together himself, so in her mind, he had at least one confederate."

"You concluded that just from what she said?" Felix asked.

"That plus what I have seen over the past two days and her body language, she would make a poor card player; she gives too much away."

"How do you think it could have been done, if this were actually a homicide and not accidental?" Felix asked.

"Do your research before you come, take advantage of the fact that he suffers from asthma and uses a dry inhaler, pick a plant that is common and that will yield a toxin that can be inhaled, bring some empty capsules of the right colour, fill them here with the powder and add them to his supply," Marieke replied.

"So, it would be random chance when he actually used it, it could even have happened on the flight back to the States," Felix thought.

"If I wanted to remove a rival or an enemy this way, I would have waited until we were in Jo'burg and substituted the capsules there so that I wouldn't be anywhere around when the toxin took effect," Marieke added.

"You have a devious mind," he laughed. "But, that makes sense, we need to talk to the rest of these people and see if this could have been an accident. I wonder if we test these capsules, if one or more of them will contain abrin, I'll have to caution the lab, don't want one of our people exposed, there could still be some toxin in the inhaler itself and possibly one or more of the capsules. So, where was he found, between here and his tent, wasn't it?"

"It was," she concurred. "I took a look at the bushes earlier, and he couldn't have fallen into a thorn bush; the closest ones are the wait-a-bits over there, and the only tracks there are mine and Melisende's."

"I would have thought there would have been risk in preparing the powder," he said.

"That's true," she agreed. "But all these people are used to dealing with labs and toxins, from puffer fish to spiders, to PMs and even anæsthetics."

"So, if, and it still is a big if, it was done this way, that suggests that they brought protective clothes, masks and gloves, if it had been me, they would have been discarded already and the best place to do that in Lusaka, doing that in a bush camp or lodge is too risky," he thought. "So, who next?"

"Take your pick," she said.

"I think David Davis, the cuckolded one," Felix said. "I have to say, Madame Garnier, that your typing skills are far, far better than mine."

"I try," Melisende said. "But, I will have Marieke edit what I have written before printing it for you, I want to be sure that the idioms and language are properly reproduced."

David Davis

"Dr Juarez has been most helpful," Felix told the others when they got back to the *boma*. "We'll get through all this as quickly as we can, and to that end, I will take Mr Davis. Would you come with me, Mr Davis?"

"You mean me?" David asked.

"You and Monica are the only ones not doctor something," James commented.

"Mr David Davis," Felix confirmed.

"Rub it in, will you," David commented to James.

"Hey, you could have gone on and got your doctorate in food science," James replied. "All you had to do was stick it out for another year and submit that thesis I know you've written."

"Someone had to take over the restaurant," David said. "And you made it clear that you wanted no part of it."

"Guys," Carol interrupted. "Focus here, we've got Alberto's death to think about, not your constant sibling bullshit."

"Don't know what I can tell you," David commented as he followed Felix to the dining table.

"You may be surprised," Felix said. "Tell me, whose idea was it to come on this trip?"

"Carol's," David replied. "We'd all spent Christmas at the cottage we have up in Lake Arrowhead, and we got to talking about things we'd done and not done, and an African safari came up. Alberto had been to South Africa before, to a snake thing, but for the rest of us, it would all be new."

"Why Zambia, why not Kenya or Tanzania?" Felix asked.

"I guess it was Catalina who suggested Zambia; she tracks all kinds of nasty outbreaks around the world, so she'd at least heard of Zambia, so we took that as a suggestion and then Carol contacted a booking agent in the US to set it up for us," David explained. "I did some internet searches of my own as well."

"And all was well at Lake Arrowhead?" Marieke asked.

"Everything went well at Christmas, except Alby sprained his ankle so stayed home while the rest of us went skiing, Monica volunteered to play nursemaid," David said.

"Was the skiing good, or was it mediocre and not a great loss for him not going?" Marieke asked.

"Skiing was great, we'd just had a really big fall, so snow was deep and fresh, not beaten down to ice," David replied. "So, I guess Alby must have really twisted things to miss out on that."

"How many days were you at Lake Arrowhead?" Felix asked.

"Eight in all, skied every day," David replied.

"On which day did Alberto sprain his ankle?" Felix asked.

"Second day we were there, so he missed most of the skiing, Monica stayed back with him at the cottage, and I guess ran after him and did the nursemaid bit," David said.

"Is she good at that?" Marieke asked.

"I guess so," David replied. "When I get sick it tends to be suck it up and deal with it, unless it might affect the food, then I'm banished from the restaurant until I get a clean bill of health, if I sprained my ankle, she'd have me in the kitchen directing things and maybe even cooking if I could stand, ankles don't affect food."

"Otherwise, all was well between Alberto and Catalina?" Felix asked.

"As far as I could see," David said. "Cat's a pretty good skier, so she was excited about the new snow and wasn't going to let Alby's ankle problems ruin her vacation."

"Did you meet again before coming to Zambia?" Felix asked.

"We got together at Jim and Carol's place in Dallas," David replied. "Played tennis, went to Austin to a concert, it was funny Alby was still complaining about his ankle, so he sat out the games with Monica applying ice while Cat cleaned the floor with the rest of us."

"How many days were you there?" Marieke asked.

"Four in Dallas and two in Austin," David replied. "We all drove down there for the concert, stayed at the Hyatt on the waterfront, which was good because it was right over the road from the arts centre."

"And you all went to the concert?" Marieke asked.

"Sure did," he replied. "Country and Western concert, shit-kicking music as it's known at home."

"Did you talk to any of the others in the months between Christmas and Easter?" Felix asked.

"Oh sure," David replied. "Phone calls, emails, lots to talk about where we were going, what to wear, what we might see, oh, and Cat had all kinds of information from the CDC about what shots to get for Zambia and what medicines to take for malaria. That gave us time to get our shots before we left."

"And then Johannesburg," Felix said.

"Right," David confirmed. "We flew Emirates from LAX to Dubai, Airbus A380, huge, great thing, amazed that it actually flies. Fairly short layover in Dubai, then dropped down to Jo'burg on another Emirates flight. Have to say our own airlines could take lessons, we've forgotten what it means to be a world-class airline."

"Johannesburg is where you all met again?" Marieke asked.

"Right, saw them all at breakfast before we took South African to Lusaka," David confirmed.

"And Dr Juarez, Alberto, seemed fine then?" Felix asked."

"Chipper as ever," David. "Kept on about hoping to see snakes."

"And at breakfast and on the plane, did Alberto eat anything different from the rest of you?" Marieke asked.

"No, breakfast at the hotel, just a light thing, then on South African standard airline food, no choice, we all ate what we were given, it wasn't bad though," he replied. "Not too long a flight, safety talk must have been given in three or four different languages, don't rightly remember exactly how many. Interesting coming into Lusaka, sharing the runway with really small light planes. Terminal's a bit antiquated, but I doubt that Zambia's got that much money to throw around on a new terminal, and it didn't look like that were that many flights. Did surprise me a little to see a South African Air Force plane there, I guess some visiting dignitary."

"And at Lusaka, you just took the plane out to Mfuwe?" Felix asked.

"Right," David confirmed. "We went to the Air Safari counter and they had everything ready for us, checked our bags in, then went through the security screen to the gate. Short enough flight, like Southwest in many ways, you get a drink, water, tea or coffee or a soda and a bag of peanuts, that's it. The lodge guys from Lundwe met us and drove us out there. Monica did her usual thing of organising everyone and who should sit where. At the lodge they assigned chalets and we were in number two, as I recall Alby and Cat were in number one, James and Carol in three and Tom and Sofia in four, with the bar and dining area at the other side of one, then there were a bunch of other chalets the other side of the bar. I guess Alby and Cat were closest to the bar on our side."

"What was your first day at Lundwe?" Marieke asked.

"They fed us lunch, then we all took a nap, which I think we all needed, big time change for us, nine hours ahead, then we met again at about three, had coffee and cookies, then took a game drive," he replied.

"During the game drive, did Alberto show any signs of distress?" Felix asked.

"Not a bit," David replied. "We were out until about six, had sundowners near the river watching the hippos and the crocs, back for cocktails and dinner. I'm thinking of trying to poach their chef, can't believe what he turned out with what must be the minimum of resources and facilities. I think we all crashed that night, long flights, time change, fresh air, I know I did, showered quickly, then into bed, dropped the mosquito net and out like a light."

"And the next day?" Felix asked.

"Guy came by the chalet at some God-awful hour to get us up," David said. "Grabbed some breakfast, then Tom and I went for a walk in the bush with Ephie the guide, a guy from ZAWA with the cannon, and a young kid carrying coffee and cookies."

"What did you look at on the walk?" Marieke asked.

"All sorts," he replied. "Animals, birds, trees, plants, even ants," he replied.

"Where did you go, near the river or away from it?" Felix asked.

"Don't rightly know, we could have been near the river, but couldn't see it," he replied. "We drove some distance, left the jeep, then walked and came back to the jeep. These guys must really know the bush or have an amazing sense of direction, if they had asked me how to get back to the jeep, I wouldn't have had any idea."

"Did you see any interesting trees, bushes, vines or creepers on your walk?" Marieke asked.

"I guess we did," he replied. "Tom's more into that; he's the plant guy. Ephie, the guide was good, anything Tom or I, asked, he could answer, and I got the impression that it was straight answers, not an invented story for the tourists."

"Did Tom have any special interest in any of the plants?" Marieke asked.

"Didn't seem that way to me, looked at everything and asked about a few," he replied. "Suppose that's natural, he's the plant guy after all."

"When you got back for lunch, was Alberto there, and how did he seem?" Felix asked.

"Fine," David replied. "The others had all taken a game drive and I guess they'd seen buffalo, zebra, impala, and kudu, things we'd seen but only at a distance, I guess walking is very different to being in a car."

"So, I presume then lunch and quiet time?" Marieke asked. "Did you stay in your chalet during that time?"

"You got it, went and crashed," David said. "Then a game drive in the afternoon, sundowner and dinner. As I recall, Alby had the same as me. Next day was a repeat. Tom and I went for another walk with Ephie and Isaac, the ZAWA guy and Banda the kid with the coffee. I like the walks, as I said, you get a different perspective, and you see more of the small stuff that you'd miss from a car. There was this one time we stopped and Ephie asked us if we could see it and damned if I could see anything, then he showed us this praying mantis, small guy, no idea how he spotted that."

"Did you see any of the others moving about during the quiet times?" Marieke asked.

"Can't say that I did," David replied.

"And that last evening at Lundwe, how was Alberto?" Felix asked.

"Chipper as ever, no obvious signs of distress or anything," David replied. "Telling us all about how important snakes are to the ecosystem as a whole and what snakes eat and who eats snakes, including other snakes, that struck me as creepy."

"Did anyone leave their chalets after dark?" Felix asked.

133

"I didn't," David replied. "Can't answer for the others, but that would break protocol, and I don't know about you guys, but I would be afraid of running into something unexpected. They warned us that there could be lions, hippos or eles around, so don't go out after dark without a staff member."

"Then it was Lower Zambezi," Felix prompted.

"Right," David confirmed. "Up again at the crack of bloody dawn, breakfast, pack, jeep to the airport, then the flight down to a place called Jeki of all things. I say place, it's just a dirt strip, better make sure you've got enough gas to get out of there, no facilities there at all. We all did well on the flight down there, even though we didn't go that high, and it got a little bumpy as we dropped down into the Zambezi Valley. The Mushika guys were waiting for us, and we drove to the lodge, nice place right on the river, chalets up on stilts, we had number one, then Alby and Cat, then the bar and stuff, then Sofia and Tom and Jim and Carol out at the other end."

"How high up off the ground were the chalets?" Marieke asked.

"Maybe ten feet," he replied. "They all had wooden walkways out to them from the *boma* area and a platform all around, so nice balcony to sit and watch the world go by."

"And there, Alberto seemed fine?" Felix asked.

"I guess he'd been using his inhaler a bit more, maybe some of the dust we kicked up on the game drives," David commented. "But thinking about it, he was fine, as soon as we got out of the dust, he settled down again and didn't have to use his inhaler. Alby was asking the Mushika guys about snakes, what they had around and what he might be able to see. They were at pains to point out that it was only going to sheer chance that they might see a snake; they reminded him that snakes generally get out of the way of something really big."

"What were the activities while you were at Mushika?" Felix asked.

"Let's see," David thought. "First day, drive from the strip to the lodge, actually saw all kinds just on that drive, then lunch, then quiet time, then tea, coffee and cookies, then we took a boat ride on the Zambezi, lots of eles, hippos, crocs, even some canoeists, stopped on some tiny island for a sundowner, then came back down the river to the camp, for dinner. As I think of it, Alby was doing fine then, snorting on the inhaler a bit, but nothing dramatic."

"And the next day?" Felix asked.

"Another God-awful time for a wake-up call, then Tom and I went to try our hand at fishing, not bad really, caught some mega tiger fish," David replied. "I think Sophia and Cat went on a walk and Jim and Carol went for a drive, Monica stayed for a massage and I'm not sure now what Alby did, probably just hung around his chalet or the bar, as I recall they had a pretty good library of books on Africa and even some on Zambia, wildlife books, birds, trees, and reptiles."

"And in the afternoon?" Marieke asked.

"The girls all hung out in the bar gossiping, and us guys went back to our tents to nap," David replied.

"Could you draw me a quick plan of the layout of the camp?" Felix asked.

"Sure," David replied. He drew quickly and even added trees and the like.

"So, each chalet was apart from the rest and quite private?" Marieke asked.

"Quite," he confirmed. "Although we had the chalet next to Cat and Alby, we couldn't really see it, must be 100 feet or so between each of the chalets. If you wanted to go from chalet to chalet, you had to go to the *boma,* then back out again."

"As far as you know, you all stayed in your chalets until afternoon tea?" Felix asked.

"I did, don't know about the others," David replied. "But the girls and the bar staff would have seen anyone, as I said, to get from chalet to chalet, you had to go back to the bar area and then out to another chalet. Don't know what you're getting at here."

"It's possible that Dr Juarez handled something that he would have been better leaving alone," Felix replied. "We're trying to pin down movements so that we can determine if that happened."

"You're thinking maybe he got into something that didn't agree with him, that makes more sense to me than a snake, I thought Jim was too quick to jump at that," David said. "Almost like Jim wanted us to look that way and nowhere else."

"And that afternoon?" Marieke asked.

"Let's see, that afternoon we took a game drive, split up into two truckloads, mine was me, Tom, Alby and Carol, and found a whole pack of wild dogs, really cool. Sundowner by the river, then back for fish for dinner, not the ones I caught, but some bream, really good too," David replied.

"Then bed and as far as you know, no one left their chalets after that?" Felix asked.

"That seems risky to me," David said. "Protocol at the lodge was that after dark, the camp staff escorted you, same as in Luangwa. I know I didn't leave, took my shower and crashed. If any of the others went walkabout, I don't know."

"Tell me, so you happen to know if Dr Juarez sleepwalks at all?" Felix asked.

"No idea," David replied. "You should ask Cat."

"She's never mentioned it at all?" Felix asked.

"Never," David confirmed.

"And the second full day at Mushika?" Felix asked.

"Let's see, Cat and Alby went for a walk looking for snakes, Monica and I went for a drive, the others tried canoeing," David replied.

"Do you know if they saw any?" Marieke asked.

"Alby and Cat you mean, puff adder, according to Alby, I think he would have picked the damned thing up if the guide and the ZAWA guy hadn't been there," David said. "After lunch that day, the girls stayed in the bar plotting our next trip while us guys went off to nap."

"Did you see anyone at all when you were in your chalet?" she asked.

"Saw a couple of guys go by in canoes, saw a boatload of tourists going up the river, never saw them come back down, so don't know where they went, maybe they were doing a transfer from the Jeki strip to a camp or lodge up the river somewhere," he replied. "Didn't nap much that day, just sat out on the balcony and watched the world go by, hippos, birds, a couple of lizards, even a croc or two in the river. Didn't see Alby at all, no idea if James and Tom stayed put or went visiting."

"And that afternoon?" Felix asked.

"That afternoon we did another boat trip up the Zambezi, and I'd have to say that Alby was using his inhaler a bit more," David said. "Stopped on a different island for a sundowner, more trees and vines on that island."

"And at dinner, you all had the same to eat?" Felix asked.

"All of us, no choices there, not that I'm complaining, food was good, well prepared, interesting presentation, well plated, like the chef had training somewhere," David replied. "After dinner sat for a while around their campfire and shot the breeze, told them about what we'd seen in Luangwa and they wanted to know about game and such where we live, probably Tom and Sofia are the only ones that live out in the woods and could see stuff, not sure what they get in Utah."

"And your last day at Lower Zambezi?" Felix asked.

"Up with the larks, before the bloody larks, breakfast then a drive before lunch, then the flight from Jeki to Lusaka, really short flight, up then down, then bus to the Radisson Blu and a decent shower before dinner and an early night," David said.

"And would you say that Alberto was showing the same or more signs of breathing problems?" Felix asked.

"Thinking about it now, maybe a little more, maybe it was all the trees and bushes around, who knows what they might have been giving off that Alby reacted to," David replied.

"Was he using his inhaler much?" she asked.

"I guess he was," David confirmed. "I didn't take that much notice, that's Cat's department."

"While you were at the Radisson Blu, did you see any of the others?" Marieke asked.

"We all met in the bar, then had dinner together, but other than that, no socialising," David replied. "Monica and I pretty much stayed in our room, except for dinner and breakfast."

"And then the flight out here," Felix prompted.

"Right, up early the next day, breakfast, then the flight out here, noticed that Alby was starting to not look great on that flight. Looks to me like he caught a bug or something at Lower Zambezi, and maybe the snake just finished him off," David suggested. "Mind you, just because Jim says it's a snake, doesn't mean it is, he's got snakes on the brain since he had to deal with a couple of deaths in Dallas from one of those religious cults that like to mess with snakes."

"That's what we're trying to confirm," Marieke said. "Tell me, did Dr Juarez get on well with you all?"

"I'd say yes," David said. "We all met at USC, I was there doing food science and met Monica there who was a business major, Alberto was a biologist, Carol was doing biochemistry as a pre-med, and Jim was taking biology as his pre-med, Sofia was also a biologist and Tom was the botanist, who does that leave, Cat, right, she was another biologist."

"So, you and Monica were rather the odd ones out, not taking the natural sciences," Marieke commented.

"Right, but Tom and I roomed together from freshman on, so I got to know all the others pretty well," David said.

"I'm sorry to have to ask this, but do you know of any issues between the doctors, Juarez?" Felix asked.

"You suspect Cat?" David asked.

"No, but it helps to have a complete picture of the people involved," Felix replied.

"Well, Cat was really into Alby," David said. "Never knew of or heard anything to the contrary."

"And Dr Alberto Juarez?" Felix asked.

"I'd guess that she was more invested in the relationship than he was," David replied.

"Have you travelled before as a group?" Felix asked.

"Sure, did a couple of Vegas trips, did a Napa Valley booze trip once, went to Alaska fishing one time," David replied.

"And there was no tension on those trips?" Felix asked.

"Monica tends to get a bit bossy, she's the manager at our restaurant, I'm the chef, so I cook and she does everything else, so I suppose she's gotten used to bossing," David thought. "The others take it in good part, but it can get a little annoying at times, you must have heard that when we arrived and were going to take that really short jeep ride to the boat that it took forever to figure out who was going

138

to sit where, I think Alex was on the verge of saying, you here, you there and so on."

"Catalina said something about dating others at college, did you?" Marieke asked.

"Went out with her once, same with Sofia, but that was all," David said. "Never really sat down and constructed a matrix of who dated who."

"Are you aware of any health issues Dr Juarez may have had?" Felix asked.

"Apart from the asthma thing, no," David said. "Far as I could tell, Alby was in better shape than the rest of us. I gathered from him that he got nipped a couple of times by constrictors, but I don't think any of the nasties ever got him."

"Do you know if he had any food allergies?" Marieke asked.

"Not that I ever saw," David replied. "Whatever I put in front of him, he ate, he did have to watch the onion family, too much would trigger an attack, but it had to be quite a lot."

"Were any of the meals served you in any way overdone with the onion family?" Felix asked.

"I wouldn't have thought so," David said. "I found the food to be good, better than good in fact, picked up some ideas and recipes to take home and try out on my clientele."

"Is there anything else that you can think of that would help us understand what happened to Alberto?" Marieke asked.

"No," David replied. "I figured that he saw a snake, got too close for comfort, and a bite finished him off because he'd already picked something else up."

"Thank you, Mr Davis," Felix said. "We may conduct another interview to satisfy ourselves and your embassy that we've properly investigated his death."

"Piss poor way to end a vacation," David commented. "Never expected anything like this."

"Do you know what your wife did when she stayed in camp?" Felix asked.

"Never bothered to ask," David replied. "She can get prickly at times, wants to be the boss of everything and doesn't like being asked what she's up to."

"That begs the question, is all well between you two?" Marieke asked.

"We rub along well enough," David replied. "She's been a little distant and preoccupied this past year, but we're looking at expanding to another location, so I'm sure she's distracted by that."

"Along those lines, and sadly, it is a question that will get asked, have you had any involvement outside marriage?" Marieke asked.

"Don't let on to Monica, but I've had a couple of one-night stands with my sous chefs; they are all so keen to impress and progress that they'll do pretty much anything," David replied.

"Your confidences will stay with us," Felix promised. "You said that your wife has been distant, and you think it's because you're looking at another location, could it be more than that?"

"I guess it could," David agreed. "You mean with Alby?"

"That is a possibility," Felix said. "From all you have told us, they have had many opportunities in the past to be together for extended periods of time."

"Right, thinking about it now, I could see that," David said.

"From what you've told us, they have been on their own a few times," Marieke remarked.

"They have, maybe we need to sit down together when we get home and see where we are," David said.

"That could be a difficult conversation," Felix sympathised.

"Before you go, Mr Davis, what did you do when you found Dr Juarez by the path?" Marieke asked.

"I didn't find him, the housekeeping guys did," David said.

"That's not quite accurate," Marieke pressed. "Monica Davis found him first, then you came, then the housekeeping staff came."

"No, that's not how it happened," David said. "I saw one of the housekeeping guys come back to get Grace, all excited too, went to see what the issue was, saw the other one there with Alby and checked on him, he was dead."

"You're sure Mrs Davis did not come to you with the information?" Felix asked.

"No, I was wondering what the issue was, so went and had a look and saw the housekeeping guys, then once I had figured that he was dead, left and saw Grace and James coming," David said.

140

"I see, why did you walk over to the thorn bushes?" Marieke asked.

"I was checking around to see if there was anything like a snake there," he said.

"What did you check on when you knelt by Dr Juarez?" Marieke asked.

"I checked on him and found that he was dead, knew that James, as a pathologist, would be better qualified than I to make some assessment of the cause of death, so left them all to it," David said.

"I see," Felix said. "Let me walk you back to the *boma*."

Felix was back in a few minutes and sat down with Marieke and Melisende.

"Any thoughts?" he asked.

"Very polished at talking a lot and saying little," Melisende said. "He's not exactly lying because we did not ask him directly if he were involved in the death of Alberto, but he has left a lot out, his movements at each of the camps, what he actually did in the quiet times, and what he was doing when when Alberto was in extremis."

"You think he had a hand in this?" Felix asked.

"He did," Melisende replied. "He knew about Monica and Alberto, and for all he tried to project an image of what I believe is called an open marriage, whereas it is fine in his mind for him to have liaisons outside the marriage, the same did not apply to his wife. He may have been getting comments from his friends, and I believe he decided to do something about it."

"How?" Felix asked.

"It seems to me that the lodge in the Lower Zambezi Park is where the toxin was introduced, if that is what happened," Melisende said. "Although he said that access to the chalets could be observed from the bar area, we would need to see the actual place and see how easy it would be to go to another chalet unobserved, or climb up from the ground, all of the men here are in good condition, they ski they play tennis, I'm sure they're all quite agile."

"I would agree that the respiratory ailment seems to have worsened since they left Lower Zambezi," Felix said. "Perhaps there is a plant there that is blossoming that Dr Juarez was allergic to."

"It's a possibility," Marieke agreed. "But I would have thought that an allergic reaction would show itself sooner."

"It also struck me that he was trying to direct our suspicions, if we were to have any, to his brother, James," Melisende added. "There is also no real record of their individual movements while they were in camp. Any one of them could have visited and talked to another without the rest knowing."

"I noted that," Felix said. "Let's take the brother next and see what his story is."

James Davis

While Felix went to collect James, Marieke mulled over what David said and not said and decided that he knew more than he was prepared to say. She noted that whereas he had commented on Catalina's feelings for Alberto, he had really just glossed over any comment about Alberto's feelings for Catalina, just the more invested remark. He had also glossed over and talked around what Monica had been doing on her days in camp, and had also glossed over what he and Tom had looked at on their walks in the Luangwa park. Following up with Ephie and Isaac might be useful. If she was right about the abrin, then they would have had to collect the beans, and then carefully process them to produce an inhalable dust, making sure that whoever did it did not inhale the stuff themselves, that suggested planning and some research into what plants could provide the raw materials to make the toxin from. It also suggested that whoever may have created the inhalable form had brought some protective gear with them, which, if they had, she was now sure would have been disposed of already, something that Felix had already commented on. She strongly suspected that the toxin may have been added to one of the capsules that Alberto used for his asthma inhaler, but proving that would mean finding the one that had been tampered with, and that could be anywhere from the Lower Zambezi to Lusaka, and small enough that it would be looking for the veritable needle in a haystack.

"I don't know what else I can tell you," James said when they sat down at the dining table.

"You may be surprised," Felix said. "Dr Davis, I gather you all first met at USC."

"Right, University of Southern California in LA," James confirmed. "I did my pre-med there, then stayed on for my medical degree, did a short residency there, then went to Johns Hopkins for pathology, been practising for 15 years now. Met Carol at USC, she also did her medical there, we actually shared an apartment, then when I did my residency, she did hers at CHOC, Children's Hospital of Orange

County, then moved back with me to the East Coast and started as an anaesthesiologist there, then we both moved to Dallas."

"Your brother David also went to USC, was that at the same time?" Felix asked.

"It was, Dave, had taken a couple of years off and bummed around the world learning about food and cooking styles, then he came back and did the food science bit at USC before taking over the family restaurant. All eight of us spent a fair amount of time together while we were at USC and actually did study," James replied. "It was a grand time, and LA was a great place to go to college. Having Dave as one of our clique was great too, because he could not only cook, but he enjoyed doing it, so we ate well, we pooled money and let Dave just buy what he needed and prep it for us. Some of the meals were experiments, and some of them were awful, but for the most part, they were successes."

"Tell me, whose idea was it to come on this safari?" Felix asked.

"Carol's," he replied. "We'd all been up at David and Monica's place at Lake Arrowhead for Christmas skiing and got to talking about things we'd never done. Carol suggested an African safari, Alby's the only one of us who's been to Africa, so for the rest of us it was a new adventure."

"Did you all ski?" Felix asked.

"We all did until Alby said that he'd sprained his ankle, so he stayed in the cottage with Monica nursing him," he replied. "That put him out of the skiing for most of the stay, come to think about it."

"Who did the actual bookings for the trip?" Felix asked. "And why Zambia?"

"It was Cat who suggested Zambia, she knows the African countries, at least on the map, she tracks outbreaks, so she's usually on top of what's going on," David replied. "Carol got a booking agent in Dallas to do it all for us. They did everything except getting to Jo'burg."

"Did you meet again before coming to Zambia?" Felix asked.

"They all came to our place in Dallas for Easter," James replied. "We played tennis a lot and then went to a C and W concert in Austin."

"And you all played tennis?" Marieke asked.

144

"Alby bailed, saying his ankle was playing up, and Monica took charge as usual and applied ice and TLC," he replied. "But he did come with us to Austin, and I saw him doing the Texas Two-Step, so there wasn't that much wrong with his ankle, or Monica did a miracle cure. Easter was also when Cat gave us the latest from the CDC about health risks in Zambia and what shots to get and what to take pills for. As I recall, the biggest debate was the malaria pills, I guess some can give you pretty nasty side effects."

"And between Christmas and Easter, and coming here, did you have much contact?" Felix asked.

"Phone calls, e-mails, Carol was organising everyone, making sure we had everything we needed, the booking agent gave us a list of what to bring, what to leave at home, so that was useful," James replied.

"How did you and your wife get to Johannesburg?" Felix asked.

"We took American to O'Hare, then Qatar to Doha and Qatar to Jo'burg," James replied. "Met everyone else for breakfast at the hotel that's right at the Jo'burg airport."

"Did Dr Juarez seem in good health to you on this trip?" Felix asked.

"He was until maybe the last day at Lower Zambezi, then he started coughing a bit and using his inhaler more; it seemed to get worse when he got here," James replied.

"David told me that he went on walks in the Luangwa with Tom," Marieke said.

"Those two have always been as thick as thieves," James said. "It would be interesting to know what they were up to on their walks."

"Why do you say that?" Marieke asked.

"Well, Alby clearly got into something he shouldn't have, and I think that pushed his immune system way down, so a mild snake bite, that I still think he got, would just finish him," James replied.

"As a doctor, would you have advised Dr Juarez to seek medical help?" Felix asked.

"He was, I thought, holding his own, and I thought he'd be good until we got home, then I was going to tell him, not advise but tell, to see his primary care guy and figure out what he had," James replied.

"Do you know if Alberto had any allergies or sensitivities to any foods or beverages?" Marieke asked.

"His asthma could be triggered by too much onion or leeks, but I wouldn't have said that any of the meals were too oniony," James replied. "I never came across any other allergies that he might have had."

"You have had experience with snake bites?" Felix asked.

"Quite a few, Texas has got rattlers and they'll have a go at you if cornered," James replied. "Fatalities occur, but they're not that common; the eastern type of rattler seems more deadly than the western we have in Texas."

"Have any of the others shown any signs of illness or sickness?" Felix asked.

"Not a bit," James said. "Alby was the only one. I did wonder whether he'd done something really dumb and tried to pick up the puff adder that he told us that he and Cat had seen on their walk at Mushika, but I don't think that he's that crazy."

"I think the guide and the ZAWA scout would have stopped him if he had tried to," Marieke said.

"Probably right about that," James agreed.

"What was the layout of the Lundwe Lodge in Luangwa?" Felix asked.

"Let's see, can I draw on this? Great, Tom and Sofia here, then me and Carol, then Dave and Monica and Cat and Alby at the end with the bar and dining beyond them, then past that the other chalets that the lodge had," James explained.

"How far apart were the chalets?" Felix asked.

"I'd say 50 to 75 feet, maybe more," James replied. "Close enough that you know there's someone else around, far enough apart that it's private city."

"And at Mushika?" Felix asked.

"We were at the one end, then Tom and Sofia, then Cat and Alby and Dave and Monica at the other end, all the common areas were up the bank a bit," James replied. "And we got to our chalets by wooden walkways that led from the *boma* out to each chalet."

"Did you see anyone moving about between chalets at Lundwe?" Marieke asked.

"Nope," James replied. "When I went back to nap in the afternoon, I did just that, and at night I wasn't going out of the chalet without an escort."

"What did you do at Lundwe?" Felix asked.

"First day, nap then game drive," James said. "Next day, Tom and David did their walk thing while the rest of us did a game drive."

"And Alberto seemed fine then?" Marieke asked.

"He did," James confirmed. "Lunch, nap, then afternoon game drive. Next day just a repeat of the first. Alby looked and sounded fine. Then we drove back to Mfuwe and flew down to Jeki, whoever dreamed up that name? The Mushika guys picked us up at the strip and drove us to the camp. Anyway, lunch, then nap, then a boat ride up the Zambezi."

"If someone went from one chalet to another, they would have been seen by someone?" Felix asked, pointing to the drawing that James had done.

"That's right," James confirmed.

"So, anyone in the bar would have seen if someone was moving about?" Felix asked.

"They would," James confirmed.

"And the first full day, what did you all do?" Felix asked.

"Sophia and Cat took a walk, Tom and Dave went off fishing, Carol and I took a game drive, Monica stayed in camp for a massage, and Alby stayed too, wouldn't mind betting that he gave her another kind of massage," James said. "Afternoon, we all went on a game drive, two jeeps, me, Cat, Monica and Sofia in one, the rest in the other. Next day, Alby and Cat took a walk looking for snakes, Dave and Monica went for a drive the rest of us tried canoes. That afternoon, we all went on another boat trip, this time downriver. Amazing to think that there's only a couple of bridges over the river."

"What did people do in the quiet times?" Felix asked.

"The girls sat in the bar on the first day, probably bitching about us, and the second day they were planning the next big adventure, us guys went and napped," James replied.

"And you didn't leave the chalet except to go out on the afternoon activity?" Felix asked.

"No," James replied. "No idea if anyone else did either, you should ask the girls, they would have seen."

"And when you left for Lusaka?" Felix asked.

"Game drive in the morning, then they fed us lunch and sent us on our way to Lusaka and the Radisson Blu," he replied. "We had dinner together, thinking about it, Alby was showing a bit more distress, but I didn't think it too serious at the time. Flight out here was nice, kind of roundabout, but I guess with the air force base in the direct line you can't fly over, so must fly around. After we got here, Marieke here has probably seen as much of or more of Alby than we have. Something tells me that any romantic notions that he and Monica might have had were dropped as he got sicker, then I guess the snake did him in."

"At the Radisson Blu, did you see the others?" Marieke asked.

"We met up for drinks and dinner, then breakfast the next morning before getting the flight out here," James replied. "Carol and I didn't leave the room otherwise, too busy enjoying the shower, bath and comfort of the place, if you get my meaning."

"Does Mr Davis suspect anything between Dr Juarez and Mrs Monica Davis?" Felix asked.

"David may be my older brother, and I suppose he's bright enough, but he's either got his head in the sand or he's dimmer than I thought," James replied. "It's been obvious to the rest of us that Alby and Monica have a thing going, but Cat and David seem oblivious."

"We suspected that might be the case from their interaction with each other here," Marieke said. "Do you think Catalina knew the situation?"

"Don't rightly know," James said. "She might be like David, head in the sand, or she may have known and just decided to ignore it."

"Does Alberto have family in Atlanta?" Marieke asked.

"I don't think so," James said. "I think his parents live in Houston, and he's got a younger brother, lives in Galveston. I guess Cat will be calling them when we get to Lusaka this afternoon."

"And Catalina?" Marieke asked.

"Whole mob of them, in Las Cruces, New Mexico, must be a dozen all told, parents, brothers, sisters-in-law, nieces, nephews, even a grandmother, I think," James replied.

"Is there anything else you can think of that would confirm your initial view?" Felix asked.

"No," he said. "It looked pretty straightforward to me, classic symptoms of snake bite."

"Thank you," Felix said. "We may request another interview in Lusaka; we have reports to file to satisfy the coroner's court and your own embassy that we have properly investigated this tragic death."

"You know, I used to swear I could pick out cops a mile away, how did I miss you and Melisende?" James asked Marieke.

"We do try and be inconspicuous," she replied.

"What was policing in Botswana like?" James asked.

"I suppose much like police work elsewhere," she said. "A lot of paperwork with an occasional very interesting case."

"I guess that's police work everywhere," he said. "Are we done?"

"For now," Felix confirmed. "As I said, we may wish to talk to you further when we are in Lusaka."

"Better get it done quick, we're out of here on Friday to Jo'burg, then home, or I suppose most of us will be, Cat may need to stay a bit to work with the embassy to ship Alby back to the States," James said.

"Does Zambia have many unattended deaths?" James asked.

"By unattended, I presume you mean with no doctor present," Felix said. "We do, there will be accidents, ingestion of poisons, animal attacks, deliberate killings and others. Some we are able to follow, some just go unreported, we are limited in the resources we have, as I'm sure many smaller communities are where you live."

"What about cross-border crimes?" James asked.

"We have those too," Felix confirmed. "It is several of those that have led Superintendent Englebrecht and me to work together."

"I guess ivory poaching could be one," James thought.

"That certainly came up," Felix agreed. "Those cases were usually delicate in that there was almost certainly some political figure involved."

"So, I guess that you'll be talking to Tom next, remember he and Dave have always been as thick as thieves," James said. "They roomed together at college and pretty much did everything together except take the same subjects."

"What does Tom, Dr Macmillan, actually do?" Felix asked.

"The USDA runs a poison plant lab in Utah, at Utah State in Logan, they look at plants that can affect grazing and browsing livestock, can't afford to have too many cows, sheep or goats die, or horses, I suppose," James explained.

"The USDA?" Felix asked.

"US Department of Agriculture," James explained. "Sometimes they're called upon to recommend a solution for a new invasive weed that is taking over pastures, and the farmers and ranchers don't want to spend a fortune on herbicides or put their stock at risk by too much spraying."

"I see, thank you," Felix said. "Why Utah?"

"Don't know," James said. "It's often the case that the government puts its labs and other offices in states away from the East Coast, usually to get the vote of the local representatives and senators."

"Before we finish, this may be indelicate, but are you aware of any extramarital interests that David or Catalina may have had?" Felix asked.

"Dave, I think Dave has had eyes for his current sous chef for a while, and the one before her, maybe that's why Monica gets rid of them," James replied. "The current one, Aubrey, redhead, stunning, and fawns over Dave sickeningly."

"Would Monica be aware of things between David and these others?" Marieke asked.

"Damn straight, which is why she gets rid of them," James replied.

"And Catalina?" Marieke asked.

"She's hard to read," James said. "She's mega smart, so wouldn't surprise me if she knew all about Alby and his antics, but she's really into him, so maybe she just accepted that as the price for having him."

"Can you envisage a scenario where that affection and devotion would be challenged?" Felix asked.

"I guess if it got too obvious, or she felt publicly humiliated, then she might do something, but I would see her more the lawyer type than the bump off your husband type," James said.

"Tell us, Dr Davis, what did you do when Grace came to you with the news that Dr Juarez was dead?" Marieke asked.

"I went with her to where Alby was, checked on him, he was dead all right, quick look showed the snake bite marks on his thigh, so I suggested that we move him somewhere where I could do a quick gross examination, which confirmed my original thought, snake bite. That plus the evidence of respiratory failure," James explained.

"Did you see any evidence of a snake around where Dr Juarez was found?" Felix asked.

"Not there, so figured he got it in his tent and went to look for help," James said. "I never figured that Alby, of all guys, would let himself get bitten by a snake."

"Did you see anyone else other than the housekeeping staff and Grace anywhere near Dr Juarez?" Felix asked.

"No, figured there were enough there as it was," James said.

"Thank you for your candour," Felix said. "This has been most interesting, but I'm afraid leads us no closer to unravelling the situation."

Felix walked back to the *boma* with James, leaving Marieke again mulling over the import of James's comments, particularly those about Tom and David. Was that just an observation, or was he trying to deflect attention from himself onto either Tom or David. Of all of them, probably Tom would be the most likely suspect in terms of knowledge of poison plants, but with the internet, anyone could quickly research what was out there and what might be found where, and probably even instructions as to how to prepare decoctions or powders. Gone were the days of digging through dusty tomes in libraries; now all it took was a computer, a connection to the internet and some patience. With that happy thought, she knew that the suspect list was back to seven; any and all of them were clever enough to do the research and take the precautions necessary to create the inhalable toxin and find a way to deliver it. They all knew enough about Alberto and his health to know what his vulnerabilities were. Clearly, some of them knew about relations between Alberto and Monica, but did Catalina and David really know and understand and did they choose to just turn a blind eye, or did one of them, possibly with the help of others plan to correct the situation, and did that make Monica the next target. As far as she knew, Monica had no vulnerabilities, unlike Alberto, but that did not make her safe. But then again, perhaps she was wrong, perhaps this was just an accidental death and for whatever reason, someone, she guessed David, decided to muddy the waters. When the interviews were all done, they needed to sit down together and compare notes. Melisende had this uncanny ability to pick out someone who was lying, even the best of them, so she would know if those she talked to told all they knew, or wanted to tell.

Felix came back briefly and asked for views.

"It would seem that the affair between Alberto and Monica was common knowledge," Melisende said. "That begs the question, did he think that David and Catalina really not know, or were they oblivious, either deliberately or otherwise, or did he think that they knew and either just accepted it or were biding their time to take action. Why did he try and muddy the waters by confirming the supposed snake strike in a place where the guides and the scout would probably have experience of such, that bespeaks spur-of-the-moment action to draw attention away from something he suspected. Finally, was the ersatz snake bite strike a contrivance of David and James, or did David do it and James saw it for what it was and played along?"

"A lot to consider," Felix said. "We should test the waters to see if Drs Davis and Catalina Juarez spent much time together."

"Although I know I am the one who raised the spectre of a deliberately introduced toxin, but we should still be open to other explanations," Marieke said.

"We will be," Felix assured her. "When we do the PM, we'll be doing a tox screen and looking for whatever we can find, including but not limited to the abrin."

"I'm not aware that there are any reliable tests for abrin," Marieke said.

"Nor am I, but that doesn't mean there isn't one," Felix said. "We'll need to consult with the university teaching hospital to see if they have any ideas."

"As far as I'm aware, there's no cure either," Marieke commented.

"Again, that is my understanding too," Felix said. "That's what would make it the perfect toxin, particularly if inhaled in quantity, undetectable and untreatable."

"It does pose questions, though," Marieke said. "If this was done, whoever did it had to be really careful or they would expose themselves, and potentially the housekeeping staff of a lodge if it was done there."

"Good thought, we should ask if any of the Mushika staff have shown any signs of respiratory problems," Felix said. "I think we'll talk to the plant expert next."

Tom's tale

"Will this take long?" Tom asked as he trailed after Felix to the dining table.

"It shouldn't," Felix replied. "Dr Davis and Mr Davis told me that you all met at the University of Southern California?"

"That's right," Tom confirmed. "I was there doing botany, met Sofia there, who was doing biology. We got together after graduating and both went to UC Davis for doctorates, mine in botany and hers in entomology, particularly spiders. She teaches now at Utah State, where I work for the USDA."

"While you were all at USC, did you all get on well?" Felix asked.

"Surprisingly," Tom replied. "You'd expect that eight people with different interests would fall out now and then, but we didn't, went to concerts together, studied together, even took some spring and summer breaks together."

"David mentioned that you roomed together at USC," Marieke commented.

"We did, it was great because he could cook, we probably ate better than 99 per cent of the students there, he would cook for all eight of us," Tom said. "I missed the cooking when he graduated and went off to run the restaurant, but we did get to eat there a few times when they weren't that busy and they could comp us some meals."

"What took you to the USDA?" Felix asked.

"I knew some cattle ranchers and they were often looking at plants that were, as they would put, less desirable grazing, and wanted to know more about new invasive species and what could be done about them, so a job came up with the USDA, I applied and got it," Tom replied.

"Tell me, whose idea was it for this safari?" Felix asked.

"I'd say Carol was the one pushing for it," Tom said. "We were at David and Monica's place at Lake Arrowhead, and places to go came up. Nepal, Bhutan, Peru and Antarctica were all thrown out as well, but Carol pushed for Africa, only Alby had been before, and his trip was all snakes in South Africa, so he hadn't seen much of anything else."

"Why Zambia?" Felix asked. "It's not usually the first country that comes to mind."

"That was Cat," Tom explained. "I guess she'd been doing some work on outbreaks in Africa, and she told us that Zambia had nothing going on to concern us and that some guy in her office had just been on an official trip that included a side trip to Luangwa, so Zambia it was."

"Who made all the arrangements?" Marieke asked.

"Carol found an agent in Dallas who asked us if we wanted them to do everything, including air from the US, but Carol told them that we'd all make our own way to Johannesburg, and asked them to do everything after that," James replied.

"Did you meet again between the Christmas gathering and meeting in Johannesburg?" Felix asked.

"We got together at Easter in Dallas, Alby had one of his famous ankle sprains, and Monica did the mother hen bit, plus we emailed and talked on the phone a lot," Tom replied. "I'd say that Alby's ankle problems were contrived because we went to this concert in Austin, and Alby was up there line dancing and doing the Texas Two-Step with everyone else."

"What kind of research did you do on Zambia?" Felix asked.

"I guess I looked at what animals and birds were found here, I looked a bit at the history of the country, I checked on how many national parks there were, and even tried to find something about trees and plants, not too successful there, there's a lot about South Africa and much of it will apply, but not all," Tom replied.

"How did you get to Jo'burg?" Felix asked.

"We took Delta from Salt Lake to Miami and then South African," Tom replied. "Talking to the others, I think we'd have been better off either doing the Delta KLM thing, or picking Qatar or Emirates."

"You said that Alberto had one of his famous ankle sprains. I gather from that that he has had them before," she said.

"A few times," Tom said. "First time was on a Vegas trip, then again in Napa, then at Christmas, each time Monica does her thing.

Dave's been a friend since college days, but there are times when he's either looking the other way deliberately, or he's not as bright as I thought he was. It's been obvious to the rest of us that Alby and Monica have this thing going."

"Obvious to Catalina as well?" Felix asked.

"Not sure about that," Tom replied. "She's a hard one to read."

"When you met the others at Johannesburg, did Alberto seem in good health?" Marieke asked.

"Fit as a fiddle, apart from his asthma," Tom replied. "We all met for breakfast before getting the SA flight to Lusaka, and he was chowing down on his muesli and stuff."

"Did they serve breakfast on the South African flight?" Felix asked.

"Omelette, not bad for airline food," he replied. "We all had the same, and no one had any ill effects. Alby was smiling and happy, happy, I think, at the prospect of seeing a snake or two in the wild and not in a herpetarium. Can't get over the crew on the South African flight to Lusaka, same girl gave the safety briefing in three languages."

"From Lusaka, you flew to Mfuwe?" Felix asked.

"Right," Tom confirmed. "We collected our bags from South African, then found the Air Safari desk, checked our bags and then found the gate. Egg beater plane, comfortable enough, landed at Mfuwe, and the lodge guys met us there."

"I'm sorry, egg beater plane?" Felix asked.

"Prop job," Tom explained.

"Ah, I understand," Felix said. "Then what?"

"Drove to the lodge and got settled, then lunch, a quick nap, then a game drive in the afternoon," he replied. "Cat was right to pick Zambia, animals everywhere, on that first drive we saw eles, lions, buffalo, leopard, impala by the hundreds, zebras, giraffes, you name it, plus more birds than I've ever seen. Had a sundowner by the river and back for dinner. Dinner was great, don't know how these guys do it, maybe it's just the food that is fresh enough that we're not eating things that have been on the shelf for days or weeks and not doped up with pesticides and herbicides."

"And Dr Juarez showed no signs of respiratory distress then?" Felix asked.

"Not a bit," Tom replied. "Ate the food, drank the wine and went off to bed like the rest of us, and I'm sure slept."

"What did you do for the first whole day there?" Felix asked.

"We'd seen so much on the drive that Dave and I thought it would be interesting to see things from a different perspective, so after breakfast, we went on a walk, with Ephie the guide and Isaac the ZAWA guy," Tom replied. "They also sent along a young kid with the backpack and the coffee, Banda, I think his name was. We were right, it was different, couldn't get that close to animals, but Ephie also talked about trees, plants, bugs, you name it."

"Was anything of particular interest?" Felix asked.

"Everything," Tom said. "The guides here are really good, tell you all about the plants, the folklore, uses that plants are put to, what eats them, what doesn't."

"Did anything strike you as really interesting?" Felix asked.

"It struck me that cattle grazing wouldn't do well, didn't see many grasses that I recognised," Tom said. "Goats maybe, but, apart from the predators, the cattle would have a hard time with the grasses I saw."

"Was David as interested as you in the plants and trees?" Felix asked.

"Probably not," Tom said. "But Ephie pointed out birds and smaller animals as well, so he had plenty to grab his interest, probably looking at birds and antelopes and thinking about how he'd cook them. He did ask Ephie a few times if things were good to eat, and how the local people cooked them. I gathered from Ephie's reply that pretty much all the antelopes are good to eat, with maybe the exception of the waterbuck that apparently has an aftertaste that's not the best. Some of the antelope are pretty big, like eland and kudu, so one of them would do for quite a while."

"Do you know what Dr Juarez did that morning?" Felix asked.

"The others all went on a game drive," Tom replied. "From their reports, they got to see some huge kudu and a bunch more buffalo."

"And Alberto was in apparent good health then?" Marieke asked.

"Full of it," Tom said. "Chatty, joking, chowing down on lunch like it was his last meal."

157

"Do you know what triggers his asthma?" Felix asked.

"Pretty much too much of any of the alliums," Tom replied. "But none of the meals we had, I would have said had too much in them. After lunch, nap time, then coffee and cake at three."

"And the afternoon?" Felix asked.

"Another game drive, along the river, hippos, crocs, millions of birds," Tom said. "Oh, eland too and waterbuck. Had a sundowner among some humungous trees, that Ephie said attracted antelope because they like to eat the seed pods. There was even a strangler fig there, and he picked some figs for us; if you could get around the bugs inside them, they tasted pretty good. I remember Alby tried some, but then so did I and I had no bad effects. Dinner was good, Alby did well with that, no issues that I saw."

"With the layout of the chalets at Lundwe, was it possible to see people moving about?" Marieke asked.

"I guess so," Tom said. "The chalets were in pairs on either side of the bar and dining, so from one pair to the other, you'd have to pass the bar, and there was usually someone there, within the pairs, the only ones who would see were those staying there."

"And the second full day in Luangwa?" Felix asked.

"Pretty much a repeat of the first," Tom replied. "Dave and I went for another walk, looking at trees that have uses from building to furniture to medicines. The others all took another game drive, this time away from the river, quite a ways in fact, lots of zebra and giraffe doing their eating upwind thing on the acacias, from what Sofia told me. They had morning coffee by this waterhole that was teeming with birds. Sofia said it was as noisy as hell."

"And in the afternoon?" Felix asked.

"We all went on a game drive, actually saw some other people too, they were looking at some lions who were doing the cat thing of sleeping under the bushes before they got ready for the afternoon hunt," Tom replied. "To answer the next obvious question, Alby seemed fine then, maybe coughed a little when we got behind this other jeep for a short while and ate his dust, but Ephie pulled off that track and went another way, and things got better. Dinner was great, we all ate the same and no ill effects at all."

"And in the quiet time, you saw no one moving about?" Marieke asked.

"I was looking out at the bush and was watching some eles, so didn't see much else," Tom replied.

"Then you went to Lower Zambezi?" Felix prompted.

"Right, up early, breakfast, pack, drive to the airport, then another puddle jumper to Jeki," Tom said. "Mushika guys met us at the Jeki strip and drove us to the lodge. Cool place, right by the river. Warmer and more humid than Luangwa. Only realised it when the guides pointed it out to us, but the other side of the river is Zimbabwe. They fed us lunch, then nap time, then a boat ride up the Zambezi. Lots of hippos, crocs and eles wouldn't want to fall in."

"And Alberto seemed fine then?" Marieke asked.

"Wanted to know all about water snakes," Tom said. "I guess there are a couple that hang out in swamps and wetlands."

"Activities in Lower Zambezi?" Felix asked.

"Let's see, first full day, Sofia and Cat did a walk, I went with Dave to try some fishing, Jim and Carol took a drive, and Monica stayed in camp for a massage, and no big surprise, Alby stayed as well," Tom replied. "Lunch, then the girls all hung out in the bar solving life's big mysteries, while us guys went for a nap. Then, game drive that afternoon, two trucks, Monica did the boss bit and told us who to go with, so it was me, Dave. Alby and Carol. That must have been the drive when we saw the dogs."

"And the second full day?" Felix prompted again.

"Up at the crack of doom, Cat and Alby went for a walk looking for snakes, Monica and Dave went for a drive, the rest of us tried our hand at canoes," Tom replied. "Maybe Alby picked up something he shouldn't have on the walk, I've heard of guys getting really sick after picking up lion, or baboon poop without wearing gloves."

"That is a possibility," Marieke agreed.

"I figure that's more likely than a snake bite," Tom said. "Also explains why he started to get sick after we left Lower Zambezi. I know Jim's had experience with snake bite, more than me, but for me, the jury's still out on that. He's got this thing about snake bite now after he did a couple of PMs on people from one of those religious cults that mess with snakes. That afternoon, the girls stayed in the bar again, talking about our next trip, while we went off to nap. Then in the evening, another boat ride, this time downriver to some little island for a sundowner, I suppose it was in Zambia, no idea where the international border runs."

"As a matter of interest, it is usually along the *thalweg*, which is the line most likely to allow navigation, or the *medium filum*, which is the middle of the river, providing of course the two countries agree on which are the actual banks, that's made complicated where there are numerous islands and water courses," Marieke explained. "I had to research that for a case I had in Botswana to see if things were in our jurisdiction or in Namibia."

"I'll add those two words to my lexicon for Scrabble and provoke challenges that I can then rebut," Tom said, almost gleefully.

"Can you sketch for me the layout of the two lodges?" Felix asked.

"Sure," Tom said. "Let's see, at Lundwe, Sofia and I had this one, then it was Jim and Carol, Dave and Monica and Cat and Alby at the other end, chalets probably 100 feet apart, so plenty of privacy, at Mushika, Jim and Carol at this end, then Sofia and me, Cat and Alby and Dave and Monica at the other end. Again, chalets a good 100 feet apart, all up on stilts with wooden walkways that connected to the *boma* area, lots of bush so almost impossible to see the next chalet."

"So, you would not have known if Monica had, for example, visited Alberto in his chalet?" Felix asked.

"Not at Lundwe, no way to see, but at Mushika you'd have to go back to the *boma* and then back out again, so anyone there would see you, but as far as I know she was never on her own to sneak off, except for the day she got the massage and the times here at this camp," Tom replied.

"When did you first see Alberto start to look less than healthy?" Felix asked.

"I guess that last morning at Mushika when we were getting ready to fly to Lusaka," Tom said. "Then he got worse as time went on. I was just hoping he'd get over it before the flight home. Flying when you're sick is really bad, done it once, don't need to do it again."

"Is there anything else about Alberto's health, things he may have done or been exposed to that may have sickened him?" Marieke asked.

"Not that I can think of," Tom said.

"You mentioned before about the relationship between Alberto and Monica," Felix said. "May we explore that a little more? You said that you were not sure if either David or Catalina was really aware of what was going on. Do you really think they were that oblivious, or did they both choose to ignore it?"

"Thought about that a lot," Tom said. "Like I said, I've been close to Dave since college days, and I think he was somewhat afraid of Monica, didn't want to ever offend her, told me once that he wouldn't want to cross her. Cat, like I said, hard to read, but if she was pissed off enough, I wouldn't put anything past her. Alby was a nice enough guy, but he did play around a bit, usually outside our circle, so Monica was an anomaly."

"This may be indelicate, but any rumours or outright knowledge of extra-marital entanglements with David or Catalina?" Felix asked.

"Dave often wondered about him and the sous chef he has, Aubrey, redhead, great at chopping stuff up and hangs on every word that Dave utters," Tom said. "I grant that she's a looker, but so's Monica, but who knows what attracts. Cat, don't know, don't see too much of them, but I always got the impression that she was really into Alby, for all his faults."

"You've commented that Monica and Alberto had a relationship. Do you know if Monica looked elsewhere apart from him?" Marieke asked.

"Not that I'm aware of," Tom said. "But, who knows, we live in the wilds of Utah and they live in LA, so who knows?"

"Thank you for your time," Felix said. "We may wish to conduct another interview in Lusaka to be sure we properly report our findings to the coroner's court and your embassy."

"No problem," Tom said.

"Let me walk you back to the *boma*," Felix said.

He was back quickly for his review before the next interview.

"Thoughts?" he asked.

"Very glib," Melisende said. "Glossed over what they looked at on their walks and what they actually did. I would suggest that you talk to the guide, Ephie, and the ZAWA scout, Isaac; they will have seen things that neither Tom nor David mentioned."

"I had had the same thought," Felix said.

"Those we have talked to so far have been remarkably composed," Melisende commented. "If Alberto were a friend of long standing, one would expect a little more emotion."

"It's also apparent that all was not well in the Davis household, the Monica and David household," Felix said. "As you said earlier, Madame Garnier, perhaps things had reached the point where Mr Davis felt that he had to take action or appear an absolute fool in front of his friends."

"If against one, why not both?" Marieke asked.

"This one is easier to hide, go to a far-off place, where the policing is assumed to be less than diligent, engineer something that looks like it could be natural causes and leave. Even if we are able to prove after the fact that a particular individual actually murdered Dr Juarez, how would we get them back from the States. Extradition treaties are all very well, but the procedures take forever, and often nothing ever really happens. Matshwane, how did you get the two back to Botswana who had killed the professors, the case that Chief Superintendent Kossam Phiri told me about?"

"I had help from the daughter who arranged a memorial in Gaborone and invited all those they had known and worked with," Marieke replied. "Once in the country, I picked up two suspects and charged them with the murders. I had had conversations with the British Home Office, and they had told me that because Botswana had the death penalty at the time, the chances of us ever extraditing them were slim to none, so artifice was called for. We were lucky the two perpetrators were arrogant enough that they thought they could get away with it because they thought they had covered their tracks well."

"From what Kossam told me, you had a complete day-by-day, hour-by-hour record of their movements," Felix said.

"I did, but that took time, time that we don't have," she replied.

"No, we don't, do we, so Monica Davis is next," he said.

Monica

Felix went and got Monica and brought her to the dining table and held the chair for her while she seated herself.

"Mrs Davis, we'll try and not keep you too long," he said. "We're trying to understand all that may have occurred to Dr Juarez that may have contributed to his sad demise."

"I'm not sure how I can help," Monica said.

"Help often comes from unexpected directions," Felix said. "Tell me, whose idea was it to come on this trip?"

"I suppose we all agreed to it, but I guess it was Carol who first suggested it," Monica replied. "Dr Juarez had been to Africa before, but only to South Africa and only to a herpetologists meeting. We were all at the place that David and I have in the mountains for a skiing trip and got to talking about what trips might be fun."

"We gather from your husband that you are all friends from days gone by at university," Felix said.

"That's right," she replied. "We were all at USC at the same time, most of the others were doing natural sciences, but I was taking business and David food science. I had known Carol from before we even went to college, we went to high school together in Anaheim."

"Anaheim, that's in California, isn't it?" Felix asked.

"Right," she confirmed. "Home of Disney Land."

"When you were in the mountains we understand that it was a skiing trip?" Felix asked.

"It was," she confirmed. "Started off great then Alby sprained his ankle, he's done it before, so I volunteered to be nursemaid."

"His wife wouldn't want to do that?" Marieke asked.

"Cat is super competitive," Monica said. "When I mentioned that I'd baby Alby, she jumped at the chance and took off. She's probably the best skier of us all, and she wanted to show up the guys."

"Why Zambia?" Felix asked. "Sadly we're not the first country that people think of when considering an African safari?"

"I suppose that was Cat, she's up on all the countries in Africa, tracks them for outbreaks of nasty diseases, and I guess one of the

163

guys in her office had just been here and recommended it," Monica explained.

"Who made all the arrangements?" Felix asked.

"Carol found this woman in Dallas who said she'd take care of us, and I've got to say that she didn't disappoint," Monica replied. "We each said we'd make our own way to Jo'burg, so I researched fares and airlines and came up with Emirates. Huge great Airbus out of LA non-stop to Dubai, long flight though, sixteen hours in the same metal tube. We should have gone to Chicago and picked up Qatar like Carol and Jim did. Still would have been a long flight, thirteen and a half hours, but marginally better than sixteen. From Dubai, another flight to Jo'burg."

"And you all met up in Johannesburg?" Felix asked.

"All stayed at the same airport hotel, but got in at different times, so met up for breakfast before flying South African to Lusaka," Monica confirmed.

"The others were in good spirits when you met?" Felix asked.

"We were all keen to go and see," Monica replied. "Had another breakfast on the plane, plane was full, but they did a nice job. In Lusaka had to queue for a while to get through immigration, but by the time we did, our bags were there, so we picked them up and went back into the terminal to find Air Safari. Funny little plane out to Mfuwe, bit like flying Southwest, bags of peanuts and a soda, that's all you get. The Lundwe Lodge guys picked us up at Mfuwe and drove us to the lodge, fed us lunch, went through the activities we could pick from, gave us all the protocols and safety chat, then we pretty much all crashed."

"You slept?" Felix asked.

"Damn straight," Monica confirmed. "I was tired, David was tired, I guess we all were. Woke up just before three, they had told us tea or coffee at three, so we went. Then we took a drive, all eight of us in the one truck, still can't believe all the animals we saw."

"Did you do the usual thing and stop for a sundowner?" Felix asked.

"We did," Monica confirmed. "G & Ts all round, plus some chips, I guess you guys call them crisps. Got back just after sunset, had dinner then shower and bed."

"And during all this time Dr Juarez seemed in good health?" Felix asked.

"He was just fine," she replied. "Talking about snakes, the one thing I could never bring myself to like about him, this thing about snakes."

"What did you do the next day?" Felix asked.

"Got up to David bitching about being woken up early, quick breakfast then I opted for a drive, David went off with Tom on a walk," Monica replied. "Does the game scout ever have to shoot anything?"

"Very rarely," Felix said. "Usually at the worst, it's a warning shot."

"Any tourists ever been killed on these walks?" she asked.

"There have been a few in other countries," Felix admitted. "But the circumstances of each point to the fact that they were probably quite preventable if the right precautions had been taken and the guides and scouts better trained. The rest of you all went on another game drive?"

"We did," Monica replied. "Saw more animals, tons of birds as well. God knows how many photos I've taken."

"Did your husband make any comments about his walk when he returned?" Marieke asked.

"Bitched about Tom collecting seeds," Monica replied. "But mainly bitched that the animals were far away and took off when they tried to get closer, but he did say that they'd seen a ton of birds."

"On your drive, did you observe Dr Juarez coughing or sneezing when you were near trees?" Felix asked.

"You think maybe pollen allergy, hadn't thought of that," Monica replied. "Not that I recall, he seemed right as rain when we were at Lundwe."

"After the game drive you had lunch then I presume quiet time before the afternoon activity," Felix said.

"That's right, lunch was really good, made notes so that we can start offering a different kind of menu at the restaurant," Monica said.

"Your restaurant has a focus now?" Felix asked.

"We do a lot of fish, including the exotics like fugu, what people usually call puffer fish, it draws in some, but to my mind, it's too much trouble for the revenue we see from it," Monica replied. "We're one of the very few places that serves fugu, and that's because

165

David went to a special training course in Japan to learn how to prepare it and not kill off the clientele."

"It's very toxic?" Felix asked.

"Very, it's a tetrodotoxin which essentially paralyses the muscles while you remain conscious, so you basically die of asphyxiation, not a good way to go," Monica explained. "Mess up the prep and you've got a real situation on your hands."

"Fortunately we do not have that here in Zambia," Felix said.

"I know," Monica said. "From what David told me, the fish doesn't create the toxin, it comes from bacteria that can also be found in octopus and other sea species."

"Your second day at Lundwe?" Felix asked.

"Basically same as the first," Monica said. "David went off with Tom to commune with nature and the rest of us took another drive, bit further afield than the first, but still with tons of animals. Lunch, nap, coffee, afternoon drive with all eight of us, sundowner, dinner, shower, crash."

"From Lundwe you then went to Lower Zambezi," Felix said.

"Right, up at the crack of doom, breakfast, pack, drive to Mfuwe, plane to Jeki, then jeep ride to Mushika Lodge," Monica said. "They gave us lunch, then nap, then coffee and a boat ride on the Zambezi, big river, nice one though, not like the concrete rivers we have in LA."

"What was the layout of the Mushika camp?" Felix asked.

"Four chalets, all up on stilts, I guess to stop them from being flooded when the river is up, to get to the chalets, you had a wooden walkway that led from the central hub," Monica explained. "We had number one, next to us were Cat and Alby, then on the other side were Jim and Carol, and last, Tom and Sofia."

"Could you see the next chalet from yours?" Marieke asked.

"Just about," Monica said. "It was mostly hidden by the trees, but if you knew it was there you could make it out."

"Was the ground between the chalets clear?" Marieke asked.

"You mean underbrush, I guess it was," Monica said. "The trees made a nice shady canopy, but down below it was pretty bare, saw animals from time to time going either to the river or back from it. I would imagine from a fire point of view good to have no thick underbrush that could burn, our place in LA is like that, have to bring in goats to eat down all the underbrush or we'd have a huge fire hazard."

"And during this time Dr Juarez seemed fine?" Felix asked.

"He was, used his inhaler a bit in Luangwa, but I think that was dust, in Lower Zambezi he seemed fine," Monica said.

"Your first full day at Mushika, what did you do?" Felix asked.

"I treated myself to a massage," Monica said. "It felt good, really good."

"And the others?" Felix asked.

"David and Tom went fishing, why God alone knows, maybe it's a guy thing, Jim and Carol took a drive and Sofia and Cat went on a walk," Monica replied.

"And Dr Juarez?" Felix asked.

"Alby stayed in camp, did see him in the *boma* a couple of times, reading mainly," Monica said. "That afternoon us girls sat and solved the problems of the world while the guys went off to the chalets and did whatever guys do when they're on their own."

"You all met then at three?" Felix asked.

"Yes, coffee, cookies then a drive, two jeeps four in each, had to sort them out to get them to decide who wanted to go with who," Monica replied.

"Who was in your vehicle?" Felix asked.

"Me, Sofia, Cat, and Jim," Monica replied.

"Why not just spouses?" Marieke asked.

"I was just looking to mix things up a little," Monica replied. "It helps when you've been together for a while."

"Your second day at Mushika?" Felix asked.

"David and I went for a drive, Cat and Alby went off on a walk, I think he was hoping to see a snake, the others all tried their hand at canoeing," Monica replied. "The rest of the day followed the pattern of the others, except us girls sat in the bar and planned our next trip."

"Did you decide?" Marieke asked.

"It's between Australia and New Zealand," Monica said. "Outback of Oz or glaciers of New Zealand."
"And during that time your spouses were all in their chalets?" Felix asked.
"I guess so," she replied. "Have to confess wasn't watching that closely. They were all supposed to be napping, but I suppose could have come and gone without me seeing. Alby did join us at about two, came before the others who showed up at three for coffee and cake before going out for the afternoon."
"That afternoon?" Felix asked.
"Boat ride, other way that time," she replied.
"And during that time Dr Juarez seemed fine?" Marieke asked.
"Didn't see him use his inhaler at all in Lower Zambezi, except the last day when we got up, took a drive, all together, lunch, then to the airstrip and flew to Lusaka and the hotel. Took a good, long shower, then drinks and dinner. Next day, up early, quick breakfast, then the puddle jumper out here," Monica replied.

"When you landed Alex commented that Dr Juarez seemed to be having difficulties," Marieke commented.
"He was," Monica confirmed. "Like he'd picked up something in the last couple of days, maybe a virus or something."
"I gather that you skipped the afternoon drive on the first day you were here," Felix said.
"Right," she said. "I've had enough of driving around looking at animals, so stayed in camp, just watching them from the deck of my tent and from here, there's so much here you don't need to go around looking for it."
"Did it strike you that Dr Juarez was getting worse?" Felix asked.
"He was, I watched him go from poorly to downright sick," she said. "I was glad when Cat told me that she'd booked to get her and Alby to Lusaka to see a doctor."
"What did you do when you found Dr Juarez on the ground?" Marieke asked.
"I didn't find him, the housekeepers did," Monica said.
"That isn't quite true, is it," Marieke said. "You found him and knelt by him, probably checked his pulse then called David."
"How could you possibly know that?" Monica asked.

"We have the guides here and the ZAWA scout," Felix reminded her. "They make their living understanding what they see on the ground."

"All right, I was going to check on him to see how he was doing, and there he was, lying by the path, I couldn't find a pulse, David was the first person I saw at the *boma*, so asked him to check as well," Monica said.

"Tell me, how long had the affair between you and Dr Juarez been going on?" Felix asked.

"It wasn't an affair," she said. "He was a convenient entertainment."

"Did your husband know?" Felix asked.

"He was too busy running after his various sous chefs to notice or care what or who I did," she complained bitterly. "I get rid of them as soon as I can, but then he seems to find another quickly enough and it's not long before they're running after him."

"Did Dr Catalina Juarez know?" Felix asked.

"I doubt it," Monica said. "She sees herself as this great scientist and athlete but worships Alby from the ground up, oblivious to all the other women that he fools around with."

"There are others?" Felix asked.

"One at the zoo I know of, one at a bar he likes, and another at the law office they use," Monica replied.

"How do you know this?" Felix asked.

"Because I hacked his emails a few times and scrolled through all what he gets and hides from Cat," Monica replied. "But, I didn't kill him if that's what you think, he was too much fun to do that. None of this happened in Zambia, so you've got nothing on me, look at Jim and Tom, they're ones with the expertise to do this and know how to cover it up, maybe even Carol, she's probably got access to all kinds of knock out drops."

"You say that as if you know this was not an accident?" Felix asked.

"You can't think Alby, the snake guy, would let himself get bitten by a venomous snake, no, one or more of them had a hand in this, don't ask me how, but I don't see this as an accident. I would prefer that you didn't tell them what I've just told you, I'm going to be protecting my back from now on," Monica said.

"You see your life as being in jeopardy?" Felix asked.

169

"I do," she replied. "Somehow they got to Alby, and I'm afraid that I'll be next if I don't watch myself. I'm pissed that my playmate is gone, so I'm going to look to the rest of my life and probably make some changes."

"The allegations you make are very serious," Felix said. "They could lead to your own legal problems if you repeat them."

"I'm not going to say anything in front of any of them, I wouldn't trust any of them now, even Carol, and we've known each other for years," Monica said. "It's a pity I was sitting the wrong way at Mushika, so I couldn't see if anyone came and went down the walkways to the chalets, it would have been interesting to know if anyone paid a visit to Alby those afternoons when we were there."

"When you knelt by Dr Juarez did you see any tracks of other people or animals?" Marieke asked.

"I don't know," Monica admitted. "I don't think so, the path had been swept that morning, so the only obvious tracks I saw were Alby's. As for animals and snakes, I wouldn't know what to look for."

"Is there anything else you can tell us that may help us understand what happened here?" Felix asked.

"Not at the moment," Monica said.

"We may wish to conduct another interview in Lusaka," Felix told her. "We have an unexplained death here and we have to investigate and then submit our report to the coroner's court for an official ruling on cause of death."

"No problem," Monica said. "But unless you arrest us, I'm out of here on Friday, things to plan when I get home."

"Thank you for time and candour, Mrs Davis," Felix said. "Let me just walk you back to the *boma*."

"Well that was unexpected," Felix said to Marieke and Melisende when he rejoined them.

"It was rather," Melisende agreed. "I see her as an aggrieved person who is annoyed that her arrangement has been interfered with. Far from fearing for her safety, I would be watching my back if I were one of the others. I see her as calculating and capable of just about anything. I noted that she glossed over things until asked the direct question about Alberto, then she protected herself with a plausible account of what she did and why."

"Do you think she knows who did it?" Felix asked.

"Not yet," Melisende said. "But she will be churning over in her mind all that has happened in the past few days, who did what and when. I see her as very organised and she will have in her mind at least her equivalent of our murder board."

"If we are able to confirm it is murder," Felix reminded her.

"That is true," she concurred. "But you and I and Marieke all believe that that is what this is, our challenge is to first prove that it is and then to work out who and how."

"That is the challenge," Felix agreed. "So, who's left?"

"Dr Carol Davis, Dr Sofia Macmillan and the staff from here," Marieke replied.

"We'll take Dr Davis next," Felix said.

Carol's account

"Please sit, Dr Davis," Felix said as he brought her to the dining table.

"I'm not sure what I can tell you," Carol said. "As Marieke and Melisende know as was with them when Alex got some kind of message that brought us back here as quickly as we could get here."

"I understand that," Felix said. "What I am trying to do is learn all I can about Dr Juarez and his movements up to the time of his very unfortunate demise. I understand that the idea of a safari came from you?"

"That's right," Carol confirmed. "We'd all gone for a skiing trip at Monica and David's place at Lake Arrowhead. We got to talking about our next trip and I suggested a safari, I confess I'd been going through old movies, *Hatari, Out of Africa, White Hunter Black Heart, King Solomon's Mines,* and thought that I'd like to see for myself."

"Why Zambia?" Felix asked. "Normally, people would think in terms of Kenya and Tanzania or one of the private reserves in South Africa."

"Cat suggested Zambia," Carol said.

"Cat?" Felix asked.

"Sorry, Catalina, Dr Catalina Juarez," Carol explained. "Apparently, some guy in her office had been here and had made a trip to Luangwa and recommended that we give it a whirl."

"Again, I understand that you found the booking agent," Felix said.

"Right," Carol confirmed. "Simba Safaris, April Grant, not to be confused with a company with the same name in Arusha. April knew all the Zambian camps and operators and put the whole thing together from when we hit Jo'burg. I'd told her that we'd all make our own way that far, and that after that, it was all her show."

"You said that you were on a skiing trip. Did you all ski?" Felix asked.

"I'm sure that the others have told you that Alby sprained his ankle, or said that he did, and Monica volunteered again to be nursemaid,"

Carol said. "It's got to be an open secret that those two had a thing, why David or Cat didn't break things off with Monica or Alby beats me."

"Do you think they knew?" Felix asked.

"I ask myself that a lot, if they didn't know they had to be stupid, and neither of them is, so it had to be they didn't want to know," Carol said.

"How would you have reacted if James had been having an affair?" Marieke asked.

"I'd have dumped all his crap on the lawn, changed the locks and got a really nasty bitchy lawyer," Carol replied. "But, we're not them, and they have to live with what they are."

"You also met again at Easter?" Felix asked.

"We did, our place that time, tennis and a concert in Austin, Alby sat out the tennis but did the Texas Two-Step in Austin," Carol said.

"The Texas Two-Step?" Felix asked.

"Country and Western dance, simple steps done in four-four or two-four time," Carol explained. "I figured he didn't want to play tennis so that he and Monica could play different games. Cat was busy mopping the floor with everyone, so she didn't care."

"And you had other contact before you came?" Felix asked.

"April sent us a ton of stuff on Zambia and Africa, websites to look at, movies to watch, books to at least look at if we didn't read them, and Cat also got the latest from the CDC where she works on what shots to get, so we all talked and e-mailed back a forth a lot," Carol replied.

"To get here, your husband said that you flew Qatar?" Felix asked.

"Right," she confirmed. "Qatar is a partner with American, so we booked a ticket with American, Dallas to Jo'burg, so American from DFW to O'Hare, then Qatar to Doha, then Jo'burg. Got to say, Qatar was a real step up from the American flight."

"And you all met in Johannesburg?" Felix asked.

"Yes," she said. "There's a hotel right by the airport, so we all stayed there and met for breakfast before taking the South African flight to Lusaka. In Lusaka, we found the Air Safari desk, checked in our bags and flew to Mfuwe where the Lundwe guys met us."

"We have heard that at that time Dr Juarez was in good spirits and apparent good health," Felix commented.

"He was," Carol confirmed. "Eager to get out and see animals in the wild and not behind the barriers they have at his zoo. The Lundwe guys fed us lunch, went through all the protocols, then we took a nap until three. I'm betting that all of us just faded, it's quite a time change for us, and although Qatar had these great lie-flat seats, pyjamas, the works, I don't think we slept that well."

"On your afternoon drive, Dr Juarez seemed fine, no coughing or other respiratory distress?" Felix asked.

"Not a bit," Carol replied. "He was fine at dinner that night and breakfast the next morning."

"What did you do the first full day at Lundwe?" he asked.

"I went with most of the others on a drive, Tom and Dave went on a walk," she replied. "I should get back to April when we get home and tell her that she was spot on for the choices. Tom and Dave were full of their walk when they got back, all about trees and stuff, not too much about animals, but then I guess if they see you coming on foot, they beat a fast retreat. Alby did well on the drive. I think the dust got to him a bit as he used his inhaler a couple of times. He's got one of those dry ones that you drop the capsules in, first time I'd seen one, most of the ones I've seen have been the propellant type, pressurised canister, you must have seen them."

"I'm familiar with them," he said. "Can you draw for me the layout of the Lundwe lodge and the chalets?"

"Sure," she said. "Main buildings here, chalets here and here, four one side of the bar, then some more on the other side, staff quarters, I guess over here, tough to see anyone going from chalet to chalet."

"Do you think anyone did?" he asked.

"I did," she replied. "I went to Monica's chalet to borrow, beg, steal some lip gloss, I'd forgotten to bring mine."

"Was Mr Davis there?" Felix asked.

"Come to think of it, he wasn't," Carol replied. "Maybe he was in the bar, didn't see."

"That afternoon?" Felix asked.

"Another game drive," she replied. "It amazes me, each time you go out, it's different, it'd never get boring or become mundane."

"Since high school," she confirmed. "I've learned to let her stuff just slough off my shoulders; she's tolerable in small doses, but it can get a little wearing at times. We usually land up screaming at each other, then a week later we're over it and talking again. Dinner that night was fish, not the ones Dave and Tom caught; I gather they tossed them back. Alby was fine, no coughing, no real inhaler use."

"Your next full day at Mushika, you tried your hand at canoeing?" Felix asked.

"I did," Carol confirmed. "I was nervous at first, but the guides were good and it was fun. Alby and Cat went for a walk, and Alby came back over the moon because he'd finally seen a snake in the wild and not behind glass. Monica and David finally did something together and went for a game drive."

"They hadn't spent that much time together?" Marieke asked.

"When we all were, otherwise, he was off with his bosom buddy Tom doing something," Carol said. "We had lunch, then us girls sat in the bar again planning the next big trip, came down to the outback in Australia or the glaciers in New Zealand, me, I'd prefer New Zealand, but the Spider Queen will probably vote for Oz, so will Tom and Alby would have, not much in the way of snakes in Kiwi land. Guys were out and about again, a lot of coming and going, I'm surprised they got any naps in. I'm pretty sure Alby didn't because he came and sat with us at about two."

"You saw them?" Marieke asked.

"I had the best view," Carol explained. "Cat and Monica had their backs to the river again, so me and Sofia saw it all. Another boat trip that afternoon, down river this time, the Zambezi is really a big river, we're on the Trinity but it's not the same, to start with we don't have crocs and hippos."

"And then you went to Lusaka?" Felix prompted.

"Up early, breakfast, game drive, then lunch, then they shipped us all back to the airstrip and the flight to Lusaka," Carol confirmed. "Alby was coughing a bit more that morning and sucking on his inhaler. I thought there was something in the air, like a pollen that had got to him. We flew to Lusaka and bussed over to the Radisson

177

Blu, had a long soak in a tub, then drinks and dinner with the gang. Our room wasn't that close to the others, the hotel's a bit like a rabbit warren, corridors leading all over, so don't really know where they stayed, other than room numbers that didn't mean anything to me. Up early the next day, breakfast, then bus out to the airport and Air Safari out here, Alby seemed to me to be doing a little worse, but he brushed it off as something he'd picked up in Lower Zambezi."

"I gather he opted out of all the possible activities here?" Felix asked.

"He did," Carol confirmed. "I have to confess that the uncharitable side of me thought that was just so that he and Monica could get together, but now I think it was because he really wasn't doing that well. He skipped the morning drive when we arrived, then the afternoon drive or boat ride. I have to say now that he seemed to be going downhill, and Cat finally took an interest and got him booked on an earlier flight to Lusaka to see a doctor, a day late as it turned out. They should have stayed in Lusaka and sought medical help instead of coming out here."

"Dr Davis, did you see the body?" Felix asked.

"I didn't," she replied. "Jim's the pathologist, so I left it to him, and they had him moved and looked over before we made it back to camp."

"Do you have any thoughts about your husband's thesis that this was a snake bite?" Marieke asked.

"Jim's got snakes on the brain since he dealt with that mad snake cult in Texas and did three PMs in a row on idiots that had played with too many rattlers," Carol replied. "I think he picked up a virus or something, either at Lower Zambezi or maybe even before that, my inclination is Lower Zambezi, but incubation periods of a week are not uncommon, so it could have been Luangwa or even before."

"And the apparent snake bite marks?" Felix asked.

"One of the guys is being an idiot," she replied. "Or he fell into a thorn bush and spiked himself, that's probably more likely as I think of it, I don't think even our guys, as dumb as they can be at times, are that stupid."

"How did you all get along?" Felix asked.

"We managed," she replied. "I was Monica's friend and as you know I married Jim, but lately we've been drifting apart, different interests, different aims and goals in life, maybe we should have all had kids, then we'd have something in common to bitch about."

"Is there anything else you can think of that might help us find out what caused Dr Juarez's death?" Felix asked.

"I'd get a good PM done, check for viruses if you can," she replied. "I'm not sure how good your facilities are, but better to get it done as quickly as you can before any possible viruses die off."

"We will be taking his body on a charter flight tomorrow morning, first thing," Felix replied. "The plane should have arrived right at dusk and will be waiting for us at Lufupa in the morning."

"We can't all go tonight?" Carol asked.

"Lufupa is not a lit strip, so safety dictates that we wait for full daylight, as we're all going on the same plane, we do not want further issues," Felix said. "Let me walk you back to the *boma*. Thank you for your time and insights. There will undoubtedly be a more formal interview when we are in Lusaka, we have to present our findings to the coroner's court, and your embassy will want assurances that we have properly investigated this unfortunate death."

"Well, that was interesting," Felix said to Marieke and Melisende when he rejoined them. "Thoughts?"

"Apparently, all our males just became, what is it that the Americans say, persons of interest," Melisende said.

"They all lied through their teeth," Marieke said. "My money is on Tom to collect the seeds and prepare the powder and load the capsules, then David to make the substitutions. That way, Tom can say that he did not kill Alberto, and David can say that he had no idea what was in the capsules. We will need to talk to the chaps in Luangwa and get confirmation that they did indeed collect the right seeds. It would be nice if we could find something that points to the grinding of the seeds, but I think that's an outside chance."

"Sadly, I see these people all leaving the country before we can put together enough evidence to convince our prosecution service to act," Felix said. "But, we must try. Shall we take the Dr Macmillan now, what was it Dr Davis said, the Spider Queen?"

"A little dig there, I think," Marieke said. "Perhaps those two don't like each other that much."

The Spider Queen

"I'm not sure what I can tell you that you haven't already heard from the rest of us," Sofia said as she took a seat at the table.

"We never know what may be of interest or use to us," Felix said. "We have been given chapter and verse about your activities since arriving in Zambia. What has been your observation about Dr Juarez and his health?" Felix asked.

"I'd say he was normal until the last day in the Lower Zambezi, then here he got worse," Sofia said. "I was pleased to see that Cat finally decided that enough was enough and that they would leave early and find a doctor in Lusaka, pity she didn't do that before we all flew out here."

"We know that your speciality is spiders, do you know much about species we get here?" Felix asked.

"I researched things a bit before we came," she replied. "I know that a few can give you a nasty bite, the black and brown button spiders of the *Theridiidae* family among them. The button spiders deliver a neurotoxin that causes pain, muscle rigidity, vomiting and sweating. I didn't see any signs of that with Alby. There are others that deliver cytotoxins, and the six-eyed can actually cause internal bleeding. From what I saw of Alby, I'd say that his condition was more respiratory, which to me suggests something he inhaled, perhaps ate, but more likely inhaled, rather than a bite or sting."

"So, you don't see his condition as being likely to have been caused by a spider bite or even scorpion sting?" Marieke asked.

"Not that I could see," Sofia replied. "Most of the nasty scorpions are more desert living and are found south of here in Botswana, Namibia and parts of Zimbabwe and South Africa. There's some discussion about the granulated thick-tailed scorpion, *Parabuthus granulata,* being found in dry desert sandy parts of Zambia, but there's no real evidence yet that they're found outside Namibia and Botswana. Most scorpion stings are usually associated with numbness, and Alby said nothing about that. Spider bites here, I believe, are typically not fatal; they may be painful, but unless you had an underlying condition, you'd be in the record books if you died."

"Tell us about the interaction between all of you at the Lundwe and Mushika lodges," Marieke said.

"Not too much to tell," Sofia replied. "Lundwe, we were getting over the flight and the jet lag, so did sleep quite a bit. The chalets were far enough apart that it was difficult to see anyone moving about, unless they walked right in front of your chalet. Our chalets were on one side of the bar, and there were some more on the other side. At Mushika, the chalets were in pairs on either side of the bar, less people there, only eight of us, not like the twenty all told at Lundwe. At Mushika, there was quite a bit of coming and going between chalets. Two afternoons we were there, us girls stayed in the bar and tried to solve the problems of the world and decide where to go next, and the guys were supposed to be napping, but I saw Dave and Tom a couple of times and Jim and even Alby, all very furtive, but I figured they were just plotting a trip of their own. Alby must have had a hard time sleeping because he came to the bar long before the others."

"How is it that Dr Catalina Juarez said that she saw no one?" Marieke asked.

"She and Monica had their backs to the walkways, and the guys weren't exactly making their presence known, not creeping or tiptoeing, but walking quietly and quickly, as I said, almost furtively," Sofia said. "Carol and I saw them and we raised our eyebrows a couple of times, but as I said, we thought the guys were working on their idea of a trip. We'd done this one, so they probably thought they should get to say where we went next."

"And it's between New Zealand and Australia?" Felix asked.

"It is," Sofia confirmed. "I know they'll all think I'd vote for Oz because of their spiders, but I'd rather go and look at glaciers on the South Island."

"Did you know about the relationship between Mrs Davis and Dr Juarez?" Felix asked.

"I'm pretty sure that the only ones who didn't were Dave and Cat," Sofia replied. "Not even sure about that, they may have just chosen to look the other way."

"What about Mr Davis?" Felix asked. "Did he have any extramarital entanglements?"

"He seemed to go through sous chefs pretty quickly," Sofia replied. "I think he found one, had a fling, then Monica stepped in and canned them, she was the business head, all Dave did was the food and the cooking. Cat, don't know, I doubt it, but you never know."

"What will you do now?" Marieke asked.

"I guess we're all going to Lusaka tomorrow morning, then I suppose a formal statement, then we can leave and see if we can't get an earlier flight home, if we can't, then an extra day in Livingstone, if we can find a hotel there," Sofia replied.

"You wouldn't stay to offer support to Dr Juarez?" Felix asked.

"The Ice Queen doesn't need my support," Sofia replied. "She's ultra rational and looks at things very objectively, not much emotion there outside of her adoration of Alby and all things Alby."

"Thank you for your time, Dr Macmillan. There will be a formal interview in Lusaka so that we can pass on to the coroner's court the results of our investigations, and convince your embassy that we have done all we can," Felix said. "Allow me to escort you back to the *boma*."

"It would seem we should have interviewed the ladies first," Felix commented as he rejoined Marieke and Melisende.

"You will certainly have many questions when you interview them all again in Lusaka," Marieke said. "I get the impression that she's been perhaps most straightforward of them all. All is not sweetness and light between them; they all have flaws, their relationships are not as simple as we have been led to believe, and I get the sense that most, if not all of them, are downright devious."

"I wonder if they all have nicknames for each other," Melisende said. "Nicknames often tell us a lot, the Ice Queen, for instance, paints a picture for us, one who is largely detached."

"So, so far we have means, the abrin, motive, infidelity, opportunity, perhaps at Mushika," Marieke commented.

"But who is the prime suspect?" Felix asked.

"David Davis," Marieke replied. "He had the motive, he could be given the means, and we should investigate further the opportunity."

"You see any of the others having a hand in it?" Felix asked.

182

"I see Tom as the most likely to help," Marieke replied. "He is the plant man, he, I am sure, did his research before they came, he knew what seeds to look for and gather, and he could have easily ground some into powder, placed it in empty capsules and then given the capsules to David to do with that he would."

"And the others?" Felix asked.

"I don't see any of the women helping, but James at least muddied the waters with his snake bite hypothesis, why I don't know," Marieke admitted.

"We should see what Alessandra Martin and the staff have to say," Felix said. "I'll have Ernest join us for that, do you speak Lunda, Bemba or Tonga?"

"I'm afraid not," Marieke said. "The best I can do here is Setswana, but I doubt that is spoken here."

"We should see what Chief Inspector Mwewa has to tell us about their behaviour and demeanour," Felix said. He signalled Ernest to join them.

"That is an interesting group," Ernest said as he sat down. "While you were talking to the widow, Dr Juarez, the rest made small talk about the animals they had seen and how good the trip had been until now. When Dr Juarez returned, she sat apart from the rest and glared at them, particularly Mrs and Mr Davis."

"And for subsequent interviews?" Felix asked.

"There was body language, between the men particularly, but no words exchanged about what they had said, the only thing asked was was everything OK, and the answer was, in all cases, no problem," Ernest replied. "I would say that they're hiding something."

"It'll be interesting to see how much the story changes when we interview them again tomorrow," Felix said.

"You see a need?" Ernest asked.

"We should have interviewed the women first," Felix said. "They gave us different accounts than those of the men, so we have some questions to ask."

Next steps

The guests dealt with, Felix, turned to the staff. They were, probably quite naturally, quite nervous about being interviewed, but he and Ernest managed to put them at ease and just get them talking about what they had seen and not seen. First and foremost in the not-seen category was a snake or evidence of a snake, so no tracks on the ground, no alarm calls from birds or bush babies, nothing that would indicate that a snake was even in the area. Their story was quite straightforward. They had been doing housekeeping chores at each tent and had come across Alberto lying near the path. While Stan had stayed to check on Alberto, Joseph had gone to get Grace so that she could take charge.

It had not taken Grace more than a few seconds to ascertain that Alberto was quite dead, and she had seen the apparent strike marks of a snake, so she had had Stan and Joseph move the body to one of their containers and she had fetched James Davis who she knew was a pathologist. Neither Stan nor Joseph could offer much more. They had seen Alberto after breakfast and had seen him go back to his tent and had thought that he might not be feeling well, so had given him peace and quiet, thinking that he might want to just sleep. They commented on the people tracks near and around the body and identified those of David and Monica, Monica first, then David afterwards, so surmised that Monica had found Alberto first, checked on him, judging by the tracks on the ground, and had then left, possibly to inform the others, as David arrived next. Their reading of the tracks was that David also knelt by the body, possibly to see if he had signs of life. Privately, Marieke thought it more likely that he knelt to use the thorn to make the ersatz strike marks. In her view, if he had done it, he had done a fairly credible job, getting the spacing right, but he had missed the angle. In that both Adam and Abel concurred. Their reading of the tracks coincided with that of Stan and Joseph. That did not mean that David had killed Alberto, merely that he had muddied the waters somewhat with the thorn.

Interviews done, Melisende handed her laptop computer to Marieke, who edited her notes and put them in order, then used the printer that the camp had to produce a paper copy that she gave to Felix. Marieke also took the chip from her camera that had photographs of the body, where it was found, and the surrounds, and the tent and its surrounds, and also gave that to Felix, who handed it back with the request that she print out the pictures. That done, there was not much else to do that evening except have dinner and retire before getting the plane in the morning to Lusaka. Alessandra had juggled things around a bit and accommodated Felix and Ernest and thanked her lucky stars that the pilots who had flown out had sent a message that they were staying at the Kamana camp, or she would have had two more to accommodate. None of the guests had brought a computer with them, and only Alberto had brought an iPad, so checking for internet search history looking for local plant poisons was not an option and Felix doubted that anything his department asked the US authorities to do would be acted upon, or if it was it would hardly be done in a timely manner. He doubted that anything would be resolved before the guests were due to leave to return to the US, so wondered if one or more of them would actually get away with murder. That was, of course, if in fact one or more of them had had a hand in introducing the toxin to Alberto. It was always possible that he had inadvertently done it to himself by messing about with the lucky bean seeds. He thought that unlikely, but one never knew. Catalina did give Felix that access code for Alberto's iPad, and he was able to confirm that there was nothing on it that would have relevance to the investigation, but he did hold on to it for the moment.

Alessandra served dinner a little later than usual and then suggested that they all retire to their tents and pack. She promised an early breakfast and said that they would be leaving at six-thirty the next morning to go to the airstrip and their return to Lusaka. She then asked Marieke and Melisende what their plans were.

"We're going to fly back to Lusaka and see the Commissioner," Marieke said. "I'm sure he'll have questions, maybe even a task or two."

"I'm sorry you have to cut short your trip," Alessandra said. "When you're done with the Zambia Police, you can always come back. When was your return flight?"

"Not for another ten days," Marieke replied.

"Well, then, do what the Zambia Police want and then come back," Alessandra said.

"Will you refund anything for this group?" Marieke asked.

"Only if they really press," Alessandra said. "They were all for leaving anyway, and our refund policy is no refunds inside the thirty-day window and none if the trip is cut short while they're with us.

Everyone assembled at six the next morning, and after quick tea and coffee and something to eat, they all left for the airstrip, with Marieke, Melisende, Felix and Ernest going with Adam and the wrapped body of Alberto while Alessandra and Abel took the guests. At Lufupa, Alessandra took the guests to the airstrip in the Land Cruiser that Marieke had driven from Lusaka, while Marieke and the others in their boat used the old Land Cruiser that was there. The pilots were already there, doing their pre-flight checks and took charge of the body bag. They then loaded the body bag and all the rest of the luggage and looked to the passengers to board.

"Right, folks," Daryl, the pilot, said. "Let's get you all loaded, and we can make our way back to Lusaka. We should be in Lusaka before nine, so look for a smooth ride, not warm enough yet for thermals."

While they were all boarding, Marieke took the opportunity to identify whose tracks were whose and cement them in her mind for possible future reference.

The flight back to Lusaka was quick enough. There, they were met by Inspectors Chikonde and Kachepa, who drove them to the police headquarters. Felix and Ernest took the guests to a waiting area while Inspector Chikonde took Marieke and Melisende to see the commissioner.

"Matshwane, thank you for your help," Joseph Bwalya said. "It is a pleasure to see you again, Madame Garnier. I should wish it would have been under better circumstances. So, Matshwane, before I join

186

Superintendent Zimba and interview these people, give me your impressions and what you and he learned when you talked to them all yesterday."

"They have been a tight-knit group since college days; they all went to the University of Southern California in Los Angeles at the same time. Six of them have either medical degrees or other doctorates, a pathologist, an anæsthetist, an epidemiologist, a poison plant expert, an entomologist with a speciality in spiders, and two restaurateurs who serve up fugu dishes, the type that will kill you if not done right. So all in all, a well-educated and bright group. The dead man was a herpetologist. Although they have been a tight-knit group, my sense is that cracks are forming, particularly with the women. I don't think Dr Carol Davis much cares for either Dr Sofia Macmillan or the widow, Dr Catalina Juarez," Marieke started.

"And the death?" the commissioner asked.

"Supposed to be snake bite, as determined by Dr James Davis, the pathologist," Marieke replied.

"But, you see issues with that?" the commissioner asked.

"I do, the supposed strike mark is in the right place for a mamba hit, but there's only one, and the fang penetration is angled up, not down," Marieke explained.

"Your reading of where the body was found?" the commissioner asked.

"Unfortunately, the camp staff had already moved the body when we got there," Marieke said. "Not because they were trying to conceal, but merely because it needed to be out of the sun and well away from predators and scavengers, they moved it to a container and brought ice to help slow deterioration, and Dr James Davis did an examination and gave his opinion. Dr Alberto Juarez was found on the path that leads from his tent to their *boma*. It's a sandy path, regularly raked clean and smooth by the camp staff, so tracks all tend to be very recent. I saw his tracks coming from the tent and could see that he was in distress. He fell and died. The tracks of the camp staff were there, the ones that found the body, there were also the tracks of Monica Davis and David Davis, who both knelt by the body, then more of the camp staff who then moved the body."

"And if not snake bite, what is your thesis?" the commissioner asked.

187

"I looked over the area where he was found, and there was no evidence of a snake, neither on the path, nor in and around the tent where he had been staying. The camp staff heard no bird or monkey alarm calls, so there probably wasn't even one in the area," Marieke said. "To me, he had all the signs of abrin poisoning. I had seen a few cases while I was with the Botswana Police, and this reminds me of those."

"Abrin, tell me more about that," the commissioner asked.

"Abrin, from the lucky bean creeper, *Abrus precatorius*, known in some countries as rosary beans or peas for the obvious reason, far more toxic than ricin, which comes from castor beans," Marieke said. "Can be ingested or inhaled. If eaten and well chewed before swallowing, one bean is enough to kill, so if you ever have the itch to put one in your mouth, spit it out, or swallow it whole without breaking the aril. If in a powder form and inhaled causes fever, cough, airway irritation, leading to respiratory failure and death, usually within 36 to 72 hours, also leaves the skin with a bluish tinge."

"So, when did Dr Juarez first start exhibiting symptoms?" the commissioner asked.

"According to all the statements, the last morning they were in Lower Zambezi at the Mushika Lodge," Marieke replied. "They all said that he seemed to get progressively worse so that by the time he was in the Kafue, he was quite sick."

"And he never thought to get medical help?" the commissioner asked.

"His wife finally decided to do something at the end of their first full day in Kafue, and she arranged for an early flight for her and Dr Alberto Juarez to Lusaka to seek medical help," Marieke explained.

"If it was respiratory, how is it that he and only he seemed to have a problem?" the commissioner asked.

"I have a theory," Marieke said.

"I'm all ears," the commissioner said.

"Dr Alberto Juarez was an asthmatic and used an inhaler, the type that uses disposable capsules," she replied.

"Go on," the commissioner urged.

"I believe it would be possible to gather the lucky beans, they're common enough, grind them to a powder and then fill an empty capsule and secrete it into the supply he had," she elaborated.

"I suppose taking care not to kill yourself in the process," the commissioner joked.

"Indeed," she agreed.

"Who's the best candidate for the seed gathering and such?" the commissioner asked.

"They all have the intelligence to do so," Marieke said. "But of note is the fact that Dr Tom Macmillan and Mr David Davis both went for walking safaris on two days in Luangwa."

"So Macmillan sorts it out and gives the capsules to Davis, and then it's just chance when it happens," the commissioner thought.

"I believe they slipped up there," Marieke said. "If the substitution had been done when they were on their last day together in Livingstone, he may have died on the plane or when he got home, and no one would have known what to look for."

"So the question is, is there any proof that we can uncover to prove that?" the commissioner mused. "I'll make sure that when we do the PM, we look for whatever we can find. Is abrin detectable?"

"That I don't know," Marieke replied. "While I was in Botswana, there were no reliable tests available to us, but that was some years ago now, so perhaps there are today. Even if we are able to show that abrin was the issue, that does not automatically suggest that it was administered deliberately. Alberto Juarez could just have easily done something foolish like try and make a rosary and not be careful enough when he was piercing the seeds to string them."

"That is always a risk," the commissioner agreed. "It amazes me that we do not have more deaths, perhaps any doses they get are small enough that although they may get a cough and some other issues, it is rarely serious enough to cause death. I'm going to crave your indulgence and ask you both to go with Inspector Chikonde and see what you can learn in Luangwa and Lower Zambezi."

"I'm sure that Inspector Chikonde does not need my help," Marieke said.

"I am the one who asked for your help," the inspector said. "We will be looking for needles in haystacks, and your eyes are as good as mine, and you are of the bush, whereas I am of the town, for all I grew up in Chipata, I never visited the Luangwa park."

"We picked Inspector Chikonde because he is from Chipata and speaks the language commonly used in that part of the country," the commissioner said. "We have arranged a charter flight for you to be at your disposal for the next few days and have places for you to stay that are close to the two lodges. In some sense, this is a race against time. We know that most of this group is due to leave the country on Friday, and we have nothing to hold them here, so we need something, it could be quite small and eventually lead to nothing, but we need something."

"We will do what we can," Marieke promised. "While we are off gallivanting around the country, it would be useful to check the rubbish from the Radisson Blu. If I had brought gloves and masks to protect myself while I ground the beans, I would want to get rid of them, and Lusaka is a safer bet than Lower Zambezi."

"We will make discreet enquiries," the commissioner promised.

"How is it that you have the visit to Luangwa already arranged?" Marieke asked. "We have only just arrived."

"Superintendent Zimba sent me a private message ahead of your arrival. He was up half the night at Lufupa on their radio sending me details," the commissioner explained.

"That's why the outboard on the boat was already warm," Marieke said. "He'd taken it down to Lufupa and come back before dawn."

"So, Matshwane, your plane awaits, and I await," the commissioner joked. "We must press on, me to my interviews and you to your hunting and tracking."

The charter flight to Mfuwe was in a small plane operated by Sky Trails, and there were just the three of them, plus the pilot, so there was room enough for their luggage on the back seats. The Zambia Police took care of the departure tax, payable at the airport, and which Marieke presumed went towards maintaining the airport, and hopefully not either into the general fund of the government or, in the worst case, the pockets of politicians. None of them had been to the Luangwa National Park before, not even the inspector, as they had learned, so this was all very new and exciting. They were met at the Mfuwe airport by Inspector Mwanza, who was in charge of the Mfuwe station. He gave them a dilapidated Land Rover that had seen much better days to use while they were there, he assured them

190

that it still ran, and most importantly, it had a full tank of petrol. Accommodations had been arranged at the Munga camp, which was a tented camp a mile or so downriver from the Lundwe Lodge. Inspector Chikonde consulted the map that his colleague had given them and drove them to the camp, where they checked in and dropped their luggage. Marieke wanted to see the layout of the Lundwe Lodge before the light failed, so they drove there and found the manager, Robin Hopkins. She had been notified that they were coming and was most helpful, and gave them the tour, pointing out which chalet had been used by which couple. Marieke dutifully recorded with her camera all that they saw.

"We would like to talk to the staff who would have interacted with the American guests," the inspector said.

"Of course," Robin said. "That'll be Anel who manages the bar, and Joy and Felix who look after those chalets. I'll get them for you."

She was back quickly with the three, and the inspector talked to them all in Nyanja, the language commonly spoken in that part of the country. They did not learn too much, only that all had seemed perfectly healthy while they were they, and there had been no odd comings and goings between chalets. As far as Anel could tell, they had all been very amicable, and there had been no harsh words or exchanges. He would have been in the best position to see that as his station behind the bar placed him so that all in the *boma* was visible to him.

"Would it be possible to interview your guide Ephie and the scout, Isaac?" Marieke asked.

"Of course," Robin replied. "Do you want them at the same time?"

"It might be better if we did them separately," Marieke thought.

"You should take Isaac first before he disappears for the evening," Robin said. "Unlike Ephie, who has to stay in camp to mix with the guests, we have no say what the scouts do when they're not called upon for duties. Our guests are all out right now on a drive, so why don't you set up in the *boma*, and I'll get Isaac for you. Give him a beer and you won't be able to stop him talking."

Robin brought Isaac to the *boma* and introduced the inspector. Isaac had been informed by his ZAWA supervisor that they were coming and had been instructed to answer any and all questions. He spoke

191

some English, but Inspector Chikonde spoke to him in Nyanja, and he was much more comfortable with that. Inspector Chikonde gave him the beer he was expecting, and they got from Isaac a brief history of his career with ZAWA. He had been a scout for twenty years and was thoroughly familiar with the Luangwa parks, both South and North. Inspector Chikonde and Isaac traded family histories, then the inspector looked to Marieke for her lead, and Marieke asked Isaac to tell them about the two walks that Tom and David had taken.

"We took one of the usual routes," Isaac replied in Nyanja and interpreted by Inspector Chikonde. "We drove to near the Luwi camp, parked there and walked in a wide circle around and back to the Land Rover."

"What did the guests look at or show a real interest in?" Marieke asked.

"They were very interested in almost everything," Isaac said. "The one they call Tom was very interested in plants and asked us a few times which one was the toothbrush tree, which was the best tree for fish poisons and more."

"This one?" Marieke asked, showing him the group shot she had taken at dinner and pointing out Tom."

"That's him?" Isaac confirmed.

"Did he collect any seeds?" Marieke asked.

"Many," Isaac replied. "At any tree that we stopped at, he asked which were the seeds and collected some; he had a lot of small plastic bags with him that he wrote the name on."

"Did you find any lucky bean vines?" Marieke asked.

"Not on the first day, but we did on the second day, he collected enough to make a rosary or a necklace," Isaac replied. "Ephie told him to be careful if he pushed a needle through them when he was stringing them together, and he said he would do it when he was at home."

"Did the other one, David, have any interest in all this?" Marieke asked.

"Some," Isaac replied. "But he was more interested in the birds and the small mongoose and voles that we saw."

"Did Tom know much about the trees?" Marieke asked.

"He knew names from a book and sometimes identified the tree properly, but not all the time," Isaac replied. "He must have found a book with pictures and names and read it, but it did not make him very good at naming the trees."

"Did the two men talk much on their walks?" Marieke asked.

"Some," Isaac replied. "But it was mainly about the animals that they saw, the one, David, was very interested in which ones we ate and how we cooked them."

"He has a restaurant in America," Marieke explained. "I am sure that if he could find a source for bush meat, he would add it to his menu and charge high prices for it."

"Ephie did tell him that waterbuck is not always the best choice," Isaac said. "But also reminded him that we are in the national park and hunting is forbidden."

"Is there a game management area close by?" Marieke asked.

"Around South Luangwa, there is Mumyamdzi, Lumimba, Lupande, Sandwe and Chisomo," Isaac replied.

"Thank you for that," Marieke said. "It has nothing to do with the current investigation, but of interest to me. The ones called Tom and David were the only ones from that group who walked?"

"They were," Isaac confirmed. "I heard that one of them died in Kafue?"

"That is correct," Marieke said. "We are trying to find out why."

"I heard that it was reported that it was a mamba," Isaac said.

"It was reported," Marieke confirmed.

"How many strikes?" Isaac asked.

"One," Marieke replied.

"One?" Isaac asked.

"One," Marieke confirmed. "That is why we are investigating."

"Never in my time with ZAWA or before did I hear of a mamba only striking once," Isaac said.

"Quite," Marieke said.

"The place where the man was found was it outside?" Isaac asked.

"It was," Marieke confirmed. "There was nowhere where a snake would have been cornered and provoked to attack, and in the tent, there was no evidence of any disturbance caused by a man trying to avoid a snake, and there was no snake in the tent."

"And the birds and monkeys made no warning?" Isaac asked.

"Not that anyone heard," Marieke confirmed.

"Thorn bushes in the area?" Isaac asked.

"Wait-a-bit close by," Marieke replied.

"I see," Isaac said, nodding his head. "So, human, not reptile."

"Possibly," Marieke said. "Thank you for your time, Isaac. You have been most helpful."

After Isaac had gone, Marieke looked to Inspector Chikonde for his impressions.

"Isaac wasn't that impressed with the bush lore of the Americans," he said.

"I agree," Marieke said. "I would have thought that the US would not welcome people bringing seeds in from a foreign country, but perhaps if there's no soil present, so no nematodes or other organisms, the seed would be harmless enough."

"Should we ask Robin to arrange for us to go out with Ephie and Isaac to take the same walks they did?" Melisende asked.

"I think that would be a good idea," Marieke agreed. "Isaac said that they gathered lucky beans on the second walk. I wonder should we just do that one, or both?"

"I would suggest both," Inspector Chikonde said. "We need the best picture we can get of these people and their movements. If we can get Ephie and Isaac for the day, we can do both walks tomorrow. How are your tracking skills?"

"Rusty," Marieke admitted. "It has been a few years since I had to track anyone down."

"All done with Isaac?" Robin asked as she joined them.

"Yes, thank you for arranging that," Inspector Chikonde said. "Would it be possible for us to take the walks that Tom and David took?"

"Why not?" Robin said. "I've got two guests who want to go on a walk tomorrow, so just tag along, be here at six and Ephie will drive you to close to Luwi camp and walk from there, take the second walk in the afternoon, we're scheduled for drives then, and I've got enough drive qualified guides for that."

"When is Ephie due back tonight?" the inspector asked.

"Soon," Robin said. "He just called in with shower orders, so he should be here in under ten minutes. We've got twenty guests here at the moment, so I've got four groups out for drives. Ephie's just one of our guides, one of two who are walk-qualified. Been with us for ten years now, he's a good guide and gets on well with guests. So, Alessandra lost a guest, happened to me once, that was a massive heart attack, chap just keeled over on his way to dinner, and we couldn't revive him. They medevaced him out, but there was nothing they could do. Forgive the question, but, Inspector Chikonde, I understand, but Marieke and Melisende, where do you fit in this?"

"We were there," Marieke replied. "And we're both with the French *police nationale*, and I have worked with Commissioner Bwalya before, so he asked us to assist Inspector Chikonde."

"I also asked for that help," the inspector added. "Nominally, I am in charge of this investigation, and I will use all the resources I can to try and close it."

"So, while you wait for Ephie, what may I bring you from the bar?" Robin asked. "We've got a pretty wide selection of wines, beers and spirits."

"Ladies first," the inspector said.

"What whites do you have?" Marieke asked.

"We've got a reasonable selection, you might want to try the Hamilton Russell Chardonnay, it's really quite good," Robin suggested.

"Let's try it," Marieke agreed. "Melisende?"

"*Moi aussi,*" she replied.

"Inspector?" Robin asked.

"A Mosi, please," he said. Robin went to the bar and was back with the drinks that she handed around. Marieke and Melisende both took tastes and told Robin that it was excellent.

"Are you based in Lusaka, Inspector?" Robin asked.

"I am now," he replied. "I started in Chipata, then was transferred to Chingola, then Kabwe and now Lusaka."

"Ah, here's Ephie and the other guides and our guests," Robin said. "Excuse me, I should go and greet them."

195

When everyone had showered and cleaned themselves up, they all congregated in the bar and were obviously curious about Inspector Chikonde.

"Ladies and gentlemen, we are joined tonight by some guests from the Munga camp; they are in the park on business," Robin said.

"Police business?" one of the guests asked, indicating Inspector Chikonde's uniform.

"Indeed," Robin confirmed. "But there is nothing that need concern anyone here, their's is business from a previous time. This is Inspector Chikonde of the Zambia Police, and we also have Marieke Englebrecht and Melisende Garnier of the French *police nationale* with us."

"Must be ivory or rhino horn poaching," another of the guests commented.

"I'm sure if they want to tell us why they're here, they will," Robin said. "But if they cannot, we should respect that."

"Marieke Englebrecht, that doesn't sound very French," a guest commented.

"No," Marieke confirmed. "I was originally from Namibia and served with the Botswana Police before moving to France."

"Botswana must have been interesting," a guest said. "Was it like the *No. 1 Ladies' Detective Agency?*"

"In some ways," Marieke confirmed. "But for quite a while I was stationed in Tsabong, which is out along the South African border, many miles from Gaborone, while I was there, we patrolled at times on camels."

"Camels?" Robin asked.

"Camels are good in the desert," Marieke explained. "They don't need roads or petrol, so we could go to places that would otherwise be inaccessible."

"What fun," a guest said.

"Sometimes," Marieke said. "But camels can be cantankerous at times and need careful handling."

"How long was your longest stint out on camels?" Robin asked.

"A month," Marieke replied. "I was chasing a cattle thief, and he was very good at evading me, but I did catch up with him eventually."

"Like *Inspector Bonaparte* in one of Upfield's novels," a guest commented. "Always gets his man, or woman, come to that."

"We call her Cibuli," Inspector Chikonde said. "Cibuli is the Bemba for the honey badger, which is a very determined little animal."
"Fearless, too," Robin added.

"Have you been in Africa before, Madame Garnier?" a guest asked.
"I have," Melisende replied. "Botswana, here in Zambia, but also Chad, Mali and Niger."
"Right, old French colonial territories," the guest said knowingly. "So now you're chasing down ivory traders, good thing too. Is there much of it here?"
"There is more than we would like," the inspector replied. "We work closely with ZAWA and foreign police forces to try and stop the flow of not just ivory but also other products that are banned, or come from species that are endangered here."
"I suppose that includes rhino horns, pangolin scales, and such?" a guest asked.
"It does," the inspector confirmed. "We lost most of our rhino population some years ago, and we are trying to build it back up, but protecting them takes money. Pangolin scales are the latest problem, the scales themselves are just keratin, like the rhino horn and your fingernails, but there are beliefs in China that they have magical healing powers and are used in traditional medicines, they've just about killed off the endemic population they have in the south of the country, so are now looking elsewhere. There is also a problem with trophy horns from species like sable antelope being poached and sold outside the country, and in country, we have the ever-present issue of bushmeat, part of which is simple economics and part a growing fashion to eat bushmeat."
"I didn't think there were any rhinos left in this park," a guest commented.
"There aren't," Robin confirmed. "There are some in the North park, but they are in a heavily patrolled and protected area. There are also some white rhinos in the Mosi-oa-Tunya park near Livingstone, and they have guards on them night and day."

"Ladies and gentlemen, dinner is served," the chef said. Robin made the introductions to Ephie and told him that they would be joining his walk the next day and wanted to see where the Tom and David walk had gone. He sat by them at dinner, and they made small talk, not wanting the other guests to learn why they were really there. The guests were an interesting mix, mostly British, with two Germans, four French and two Swiss. The French wanted to know where Melisende and Marieke were stationed. They, the guests, were from La Rochelle on the west coast, so a long way from Paris. Dinner was excellent, and both Marieke and Melisende felt that they had eaten far too much. After dessert and before coffee, Inspector Chikonde thanked Robin for her hospitality and said their good nights to the guests and drove them back to Munga, where Amanda was waiting to escort them to their tents and arrange hot water for showers.

"This is a nice camp," Melisende commented to Marieke as they took late showers. "Less crowded than the Lundwe Lodge."

"Probably caters to a different market," Marieke thought. "I'm sorry you got dragged into this. I had been hoping for a quiet holiday, not a possible murder investigation."

"It is of no matter," Melisende assured her. "We are together in this, which is what matters."

"I hope we can get this done quickly so that we can go back for a few days with Alex," Marieke said. "Alex did mention that she's got an empty guest tent for the next week, so we could have more comfortable beds."

"The floor was fine," Melisende said. "But, I'm not sure for how many more years I could manage that."

"I wonder where they've put us in Lower Zambezi," Marieke said.

"Have you ever been there?" Melisende asked.

"No," Marieke replied. "I've crossed the Zambezi a few times, but that was up above Vic Falls where the Botswana-Zambia border is."

"I suppose we should get some sleep to be ready for the walk in the morning," Melisende said. *"Bonne nuit chérie."*

"Bonne nuit chérie," Marieke echoed.

The five-thirty wake-up call seemed to come very quickly, not that they had a late night, but it is still early in the morning. They grabbed a quick bite to eat and told Amanda that they would be back for dinner, then left for Lundwe. Marieke and Melisende had on light tan trousers and shirts, with broad-brimmed hats and light boots, and they noted that the inspector had changed from his uniform to similar attire. Ephie was waiting for his walking guests when they arrived at the *boma*. Just before six, the two guests, Graham and Ellen Wilson, arrived, so Ephie led them to the car park where Isaac and Banda were waiting. They loaded up the Land Rover and left for the environs of the Luwi camp, where they would walk. When they parked, Ephie asked for a volunteer to carry the second pack that had extra coffee and water; as they were the extras, Inspector Chikonde said that he would take it. Ephie then set out the rules, single file with Isaac in the lead and Banda bringing up the rear. He told them to stop him at any time with questions and also to let him know if he needed a break for water or anything else, which Marieke interpreted as meaning use the loo, or bush as it would be. Looking at the ground, Marieke could see old tracks and recognised that this was a walk that Ephie often used, perhaps with minor detours now and then, but always in a large arc around that would lead back to where they had parked. She even recognised the tracks of Tom and David; there had been no rain to wash them out, and the wind had obviously been light enough that it had not blown soft soil and sand over them completely.

Isaac set off, leading the way, while Ephie pointed out trees, birds, the occasional small reptile and lots of what he called sign, what others would call poop. He pointed out impala, kudu, baboon, wildebeest and zebra tracks and sign, and guessed ages. They had been walking for about twenty minutes when Marieke saw Tom's tracks go off to the right a little.

"Ephie," she said. "What did you stop and look at here?"

"A tamarind and a kudu berry tree," Ephie replied. "This is a really nice example of a tamarind, and that's not a bad kudu berry either."

"Is this the same tamarind that is used in Indian cooking?" Graham asked.

"It is," Ephie confirmed. "We gather the seed pods and make a paste from them for use in cooking, and we also make a drink with them, and a hefty dose can be used as a laxative."

"So, they're edible?" Elizabeth asked.

"They are," Ephie confirmed.

"And the kudu berry?" Graham asked.

"We don't eat the fruit from them," Ephie said. "But antelope and elephants do, and the seeds are then dispersed when they defecate."

"Are the seeds toxic?" Graham asked.

"Not that I'm aware of," Ephie replied. "We do inhale the smoke from burning some roots as a cure for pneumonia, and a bark extract is said to cure diarrhoea. When we were here before, some other guests picked up some of the seeds to take with them."

"I remember them, the Americans," Graham said. "They were here at the end of their stay when we first arrived, two of them talked a lot about the seeds they had collected, and I heard the one ask the other if they had enough."

"Did they happen to mention which one?" Marieke asked.

"No, they both seemed to know which one they were interested in," Graham replied. "When we asked them about seeds, they said they were taking them for study to see what germination rates were."

"I wonder if that was just a blind to cover what they were really after, or if they genuinely were gathering all kinds of seeds for study later," Marieke said in a quiet aside to Melisende. "I'd better get a picture of these trees and this place to record where they stopped."

"We should see what else they were interested in," Melisende said.

They walked on, stopping every now and then to look at trees, admire animals from a distance, study tracks on the ground, and Ephie asked them to speculate what they were and how old. Marieke was actually very good at that, but she kept quiet; it was, after all, the experience of the paying guests that mattered. They stopped at ten more trees where Tom had gathered seeds, and Marieke made notes to herself, recording what species, and took pictures. They walked on, then stopped and Ephie held us his hand. He and Isaac both studied the surrounding grass carefully, then Ephie pointed, and they saw moving out of the grass into the dry riverbed beyond a dozen wild dogs. The dogs stopped and all turned around and looked at them, then trotted off around a bend and out of sight.

"That was amazing," Graham said. "Is it true that they're cruel and ruthless hunters?"

"I wouldn't say that," Ephie replied. "They are successful because they do hunt as a pack, and they cooperate. Their success rate is probably well over 60 per cent, while lions are lucky to hit 30 per cent. In the past, they have been hunted to the point of extermination in some places, and for years, many farmers regarded them as the ultimate pest and shot them on sight. They do get distemper, so contact with domestic dogs is not always good. Let's go on a little further, there's a nice spot ahead for coffee."

They stopped at a *dambo* and had coffee. Ephie had been right, it was a nice place to stop, shade from some big trees and a great view of the *dambo*, on which were a group of zebra, not quite a herd, which suggested a larger number. The zebra watched them warily, eventually moving off into the longer grass beyond.

"It's quiet here," Ellen commented. "No traffic noise, no aeroplanes, just birds and insects."

"It can get quite noisy first thing in the morning, when everything wakes up," Ephie noted.

"What nocturnal species do you get here?" Ellen asked.

"Porcupines are the ones that come to mind first, then there are the pangolins and the aardvarks," Ephie replied. "We also get the usual rodents and other small animals, and hyaenas and lions will hunt at night too, and there are owls and other birds active at night."

"Bats, do you have many bats?" Ellen asked.

"We have over 60 known bat species," Ephie replied. "Forty-five of those are insect eaters. If you want to see something truly amazing, you should visit the Kasanka National Park between October and December to see the annual bat migration from the Congo. There are millions of them that come and then go back. It's not the largest mammal migration in the world in terms of biomass, but it is in terms of individuals. Estimates put the number at about ten million."

"Are they insect eaters?" Ellen asked.

"No, they're fruit-eating," Ephie replied.

"Probably just as well you have all those insect eaters, though, or we'd be eaten alive by bugs," Graham commented.

"They do help balance things," Ephie agreed. "Some bat species will eat their body weight of insects in a single night."

"You've been stopping where someone else has been to look at trees," Ellen commented. "Is the Zambia Police interested in someone?"

"We are checking on the activities of certain individuals," Inspector Chikonde confirmed. "It is a long process and probably typifies the mundane nature of most police work."

"It's those Americans, isn't it?" Ellen asked.

"We would like to know a little more about what they've been doing," the inspector admitted.

"I knew those chaps were up to no good," Ellen said.

"You don't carry guns," Graham noted.

"When they are needed, we have them," the inspector noted. "But out here we have Isaac with us, and there is no need."

"Does Zambia have witch doctors?" Ellen asked of Ephie.

"I wouldn't say that," Ephie said. "We do have traditional healers who use medicines from plants and trees to cure things. I believe there is a proverb that says for every ill a herb is growing, for every disease a cure can be found."

"Do the cures work?" Ellen asked.

"I would say that some definitely do," Ephie replied. "We have to keep in mind that aspirin originally came from willow bark and was used by the Egyptians thousands of years ago. The very word aspirin tells us a lot, as it comes from Spiraea, the plant group that includes jasmine and others from which salicylic acid can be derived. In common use in Zambia is the word, *muti*, which is medicine, but is also the word for tree, so clearly people recognised the association between trees and medicines."

"I suppose quinine falls into the same category?" Graham asked.

"Right," Ephie agreed. "Quinine comes from the cinchona tree native to South America, and it kills the malarial parasites."

"So the gin and tonic of the colonials was not a bad idea," Graham commented.

"Indeed," Ephie agreed. "The quinine in the tonic water would have had a beneficial effect."

"Are some of the trees poisonous?" Ellen asked.

"Some of the trees and shrubs can be used to get toxins," Ephie confirmed. "In some cases, it's a matter of dose amount, in others, it's something to stay well away from. One we have, we call, *Mukoso*, comes from the *Erythrophleum africanum,* or Ordeal Tree, its roots are used to make a digitalis-like glycoside, which in small doses is used for chest trouble, but in larger doses is fatal."

"So, if I wanted to get rid of my noisy neighbours, I should get hold of some of this root and feed it to them?" Ellen asked.

"I wouldn't recommend that or advise it," Ephie laughed. "But it was said that in days past, if you took sun-dried scrapings of the roots and poured them into your enemy's beer, it would eliminate him for certain."

"I'll keep that in mind if our neighbours start keeling over," Graham said.

"Shall we go on?" Ephie asked.

"Let's," Ellen said. "I'm interested in these trees and bushes now. There's more to see than just large animals."

"That's one of the nice things about a walk," Ephie said. "You see things that are sometimes missed from the back of a vehicle."

"What are those birds over there?" Graham asked, pointing to a large number of them swirling around some water.

"Those are red-billed queleas," Ephie said. "They're often referred to as feathered locusts. They are seed eaters and can devastate a cereal crop."

"There's certainly a lot of them," Graham commented.

"It's probably one of, if not the, most numerous birds in Africa," Ephie said.

"What else did the Americans look at?" Graham asked.

"One of them was most interested in the trees and bushes, and the other birds, small mammals and anything else we could see," Ephie replied. "If you look over there, there are puku and vervet monkeys, they often can be found together, they have a kind of symbiotic relationship, the puku warn of any predators as their field of vision is better as they're taller."

"Don't you see the same with ox-peckers?" Ellen asked.

"We do," Ephie confirmed. "The ox-peckers get the external parasites to eat, which helps the host by ridding it of the pest."

"Ephie, what did the other guests go over there to look at?" Marieke asked, pointing to the tracks.

"You've a good eye," Ephie commented. "We went to look at the apple-ring thorn tree, our guests wanted some of the seed pods."

"Why are they called apple-ring" Ellen asked.

"If you look at the seed pods, they look like apple rings," Ephie said after he went over and got a couple. "Animals love them and in some places people gather the pods for fodder.'

"Any medicinal uses?" Graham asked.

"A decoction is used for eye problems in cattle, and the bark is used in some traditional medicines," Ephie replied.

They walked on and Marieke soon recognised that they were almost back where they started, there was a false baobab tree near where Ephie had parked, and she could see it.

"Here we are," Ephie said. "We'll run back to the lodge now for lunch."

"Thank you, Ephie," Ellen said. "That was fascinating."

"Thanks, Ephie," Marieke added. "That was most useful."

"Will you be having lunch with us?" Ellen asked Marieke.

"We are invited," Marieke confirmed.

Ephie drove them back to the lodge, and Marieke, Melisende and Inspector Chikonde waited in the bar area until lunch.

"Did we learn anything?" the inspector asked.

"We did," Marieke confirmed. "We should see if we can find out if Tom Macmillan has any seeds still in his possession. He may have just discarded them all with the excuse that he could not take them back to the US. I'm interested to see what they collected on their second walk, because there were no lucky bean vines on this walk."

"Do you know if any of the other seeds they collected were toxic?" the inspector asked.

"Quite a few could make you sick, but I'm not sure if any would be fatal," Marieke replied. "We'd really need a good *ngaka* to tell us. I don't know any here, and the one I knew best in Botswana is dead now, plus the trees and bushes here are not quite the same as in Botswana."

"*Ngaka?*" the inspector asked.

"Traditional healer, *sangoma*, witch doctor," Marieke explained.

"How did you know an *ngaka?*" the inspector asked.

"Old family relationships through my mother," Marieke explained. "Plus, I knew one because I had arrested him after trailing around the desert after him for a while. The one I knew best was able to tell me much about one death that had been engineered with *zwezwe*, the arrow poison that comes from the *Strophanthus kombe* vine; it will mimic a heart attack, but I don't see that used here."

"No, this is respiratory," the inspector confirmed.

"Ready for lunch?" Robin interrupted.

The afternoon walk was very focused on where Tom and David had gone and what they had looked at, and which trees, bushes and vines they collected seeds from. They had indeed collected lucky beans. Ephie showed them the tracks and Marieke recognised them at once.

"How many seeds did they collect?" she asked Ephie.

"I would say more than they would need to make a rosary, probably 150 to 200," Ephie replied. "I thought that was what they wanted them for. Where did you learn your tracking skills?"

"From the San who lived on our farm in Namibia," she replied. "I don't claim to be very good. In Botswana, I used a San tracker a couple of times to follow people. I could do it myself, but from an evidence point of view, my testimony would be treated as indicative, whereas the San tracker's testimony was definitive in our courts."

"So, now we know that the Americans had bags of seeds from thirty-two plants, that's a lot of bags, even the small plastic bags they were using. Someone had to see all those," Ephie thought.

"We will be checking," the inspector said. "This has been most useful, thank you for your time and patience."

"I am happy to help," Ephie said. "Should we return to the lodge?"

"Robin, thanks for the help and for letting us drag Ephie off," Marieke said while Inspector Chikonde said their thanks and goodbyes to Ephie and Isaac.

"Hope you get your man," Robin said.

"We've yet to show that this wasn't just a terrible accident," Marieke cautioned.

"Maybe, but cops the world over get a sense of when things are not quite right," Robin said. "Where next, Lower Zam?"

"That's right," Marieke replied. "We'll stay the night at Munga, then take off early tomorrow morning."

"You're welcome to eat with us," Robin invited.

"Thank you," Marieke said. "I think the inspector wants us to eat there to thank them for giving us a place to stay. I'm not sure who paid for it, I'm sure somebody did. I doubt they'd give up two tents for free even if we are only at the beginning of the season."

"If we can help in any way further, give us a bell," Robin said. "Will you be going back to Mupundu?"

"If we can," Marieke replied.

"Say hi to Alex for me," Robin said. "Go well."

"Stay well," Marieke replied.

Lower Zambezi

Dinner at Munga was good, not quite the elegance of Lundwe, but still good. There were some other guests, and they skirted around telling those guests why they were there. In the morning, they grabbed an early breakfast and left to get their flight down into the Zambezi Valley. It had been arranged for them to meet Luke Botha, the manager of Mushika, at the Jeki strip at ten, so were ready to leave the Mfuwe airport by eight.

"Where did you stay the night?" Marieke asked Vernon, the pilot.

"I've got a mate in Mfuwe," he replied. "He flies out of here, too, so he put me up."

"How long is the flight down to Jeki?" Marieke asked.

"Hour and forty-five minutes," Vernon replied. "Good weather for flying today, so don't see any problems. "Who wants the front seat?"

"Why don't you take it, Inspector Chikonde?" Marieke suggested.

"Thank you," he replied. "This will be the first time I've sat in a co-pilot seat."

As Vernon had predicted, it was good weather for flying, and after waiting for a scheduled flight to leave Mfuwe, they were off following it to Jeki. Vernon talked to the pilot of the Air Safari flight, and they coordinated who would land first. When they got to Jeki, Vernon overflew the strip and they watched the Air Safari land and taxi off to the hardstand where vehicles were waiting, then he went back around and came in and landed and also taxied over to the hardstand.

Vernon helped them get out of the plane and unloaded their bags, and introduced Luke as he joined them.

"Welcome to Mushika," Luke said. "You'll be with us for the one night, will that be enough?"

"It should be," Inspector Chikonde replied. "I'm Hippo Chikonde, and this is Marieke Englebrecht and Melisende Garnier of the French police; they're helping us with this case."

This was a departure from the formality at Lundwe, so now Marieke knew Inspector Chikonde's first name.

"Englebrecht doesn't sound very French," Luke commented as he loaded their bags into his Land Cruiser."

"My folks were from South Africa and Botswana," Marieke explained. "Pops was a *regte* Boer and Mum was Setswana, we lived out in the wilds of South West."

"Ah, I understand," Luke said.

"How long have you lived in Zambia?" Hippo asked Luke.

"All my life," Luke replied. "I was born in Ndola, and the folks had a farm near Mkushi. They sold up a couple of years ago and live down by Livingstone now. They came up to Zambia in 1948 from South Africa and had a small farm for a while outside Ndola."

"How long to the lodge?" Marieke asked.

"Depends who's in the way," Luke replied. "Anywhere from thirty minutes to an hour. So, the chaps in Lusaka said that you were interested in the movements of some recent guests."

"That's correct," Hippo said. "We're interested in the recent party of eight Americans that you had."

"All the doctors," Luke laughed. "Doctor of this, doctor of that, they seemed harmless enough. What's the issue?"

"One of them is dead," Hippo said. "He died of apparent respiratory failure, and we're trying to discover if that was natural causes or something else."

"Which one?" Luke asked.

"Dr Alberto Juarez," Hippo replied.

"Right, the herp *ouk*, badly wanted to see a snake while he was here, went out on a walk and saw a puff adder, all my *ouks* could do to restrain him from getting too close," Luke replied. "Don't tell me a snake got him?"

"That was the first report," Hippo said. "But Marieke doesn't think so."

"Why's that?" Luke asked.

"The apparent strike is right for a hit on the thigh," she replied. "But, there's only one strike and the fang penetration is up, not down, plus there were no tracks around the body or his tent, and there were no warning calls from birds or the monkeys heard."

"Thorn job," Luke mused. "Easy to do, wait-a-bit thorn, should have pushed it down, not up. So, what caused the respiratory failure?"

"My thesis is abrin," Marieke replied.

"That would work," Luke agreed. "Seen three cases myself, sadly, all fatal. Accident or deliberate?"

"That's the question," Hippo said. "That is the question."

"Well, we'll get you to the lodge, get you settled, if you're not superstitious I've put the two ladies in the chalet where the Juarez folks were, and you Inspector in the one that the Macmillan couple had, and Vernon, we've got a pilot's tent for you," Luke said. "Hope you ladies are comfortable bunking together, we can't pull that bed apart."

"Do you snore?" Marieke asked Melisende.

"No, do you?" was the retort.

"I'm sure you'll let me know," Marieke laughed.

"Tell me, Luke, have any of your staff shown any signs of breathing difficulty or coughing?" Marieke asked.

"Not a bit," he replied. "If it was abrin, then it was restricted to him. I've not seen anything in my staff. Hold on, bit of a traffic jam here, ah, I see, dogs, whole pack of them."

"Are there many packs in the Lower Zambezi park?" Hippo asked.

"We've got the one big pack," Luke replied. "They're growing as a pack, so they're doing well. Let me just call my chaps and see where they are and if they've seen the dogs already this morning."

He talked on the radio for a few minutes, then announced that his guests had seen the dogs earlier and were now off following some lions.

"I wonder why it is that most visitors want to see lions," Melisende pondered.

"Probably because where they come from, they don't have the really large predators," Marieke suggested. "In Europe, there are cats like lynx, in some places there are wolves, even bears, but most of the people never see them."

"I suppose that's right," Melisende said. "We have all three in France, but you only see them if you go to the Alps and even then the right places in the Alps. We have been lucky, we've seen all three."

"Looks like the dogs have moved off and traffic is moving again," Luke said. "Not too long now."

He drove for another twenty minutes to the lodge.

"We're here, we'll park here and I'll walk you to your chalets and then maybe you would like a look around," he said.

"Thank you, Luke," Hippo said. Luke led the way, and two of his people appeared and took their bags, and followed along. Luke took them first to where Hippo was to stay, and then to where Marieke and Melisende would be.

"These are very nice accommodations," Marieke said to Luke.

"Do what we can," he said. "I'll show Vernon where to stay, and shall we meet at the *boma* in ten minutes?"

"I wonder why Hippo opened up to Luke where he didn't to Robin," Marieke said. "And why now did he finally tell us his name, Hippo, I wonder if that's a given name or one he adopted or was given by his friends?"

"Perhaps he'll tell us in time," Melisende said.

"Let's take a quick look here and then go for the tour," Marieke suggested.

"This chalet is really nice," Melisende said. "Look, there's even a bath on the balcony there, and such a nice view of the river."

"So, if I stand in the bathroom here where medicines would probably be put, can you see me from the bed?" Marieke asked.

"No," Melisende replied. "Move towards the river, now, now I can see you."

"So, there's quite a large blind spot there," Marieke said. "What's down below?"

"We should take a look after Luke has shown us around," Melisende suggested.

They joined Hippo and Luke at the boma, and he took them on a tour of all the facilities and chalets. The other guests were out on a walk, so they trespassed briefly in their chalets just to get a feel of what they were all like, took notes and pictures, then they repaired back to the *boma* for coffee and discussion.

"So, what can I tell you?" Luke asked.

"We have statements from the American group that detail their activities while they were here," Hippo said. "As I recall, you picked them up at Jeki, brought them here for lunch, then in the afternoon took them on a boat ride up the Zambezi."

"That's right," Luke said, consulting his logbook. "The drive from the strip to the lodge had taken a while as it became a game drive in itself. After lunch, they all went off to their chalets to nap."

"Who guided the boat trip?" Hippo asked.

"That would have been, Willie," Luke replied. "He'll be back later if you want to ask him about those folks."

"The next day?" Hippo asked. Luke consulted his logbook briefly.

"Two *ouks*, Tom and David, went with Willie to try their hand at fishing, Rice took James and Carol for a drive, two were walkers with Simon, Catalina and Sofia, Monica wanted a massage and Alberto just hung around his tent, afternoon, two drives, one with Willie, that was David, Alberto, Tom and Carol, the others with Rice," Luke read out.

"And your guides reported nothing apparently wrong with Alberto?" Marieke asked.

"Nothing," Luke replied. "Next day, Alberto and Catalina were walkers, the chap wanted to see a snake, they found one for him, as I said before, puff adder, Simon did the walk again, Rice took David and Monica for a drive, and the rest tried canoeing with Willie and Kingfrey."

"On the walk, did Simon report that Alberto had picked up anything he shouldn't have?" Marieke asked.

"No, I think he wanted to get closer to the puff adder than Simon and George, the ZAWA scout would have liked, but they made it clear what the limits were," Luke replied.

"Do you have a masseuse on staff?" Marieke asked. "I'm just curious, it would seem like quite an expense."

"There's an itinerant in the Valley," Luke replied. "She works between four lodges, and we can usually work it between us not to double book, sometimes it happens, but we've been able to work around things so far."

"It has been reported to us that in the afternoons the ladies stayed in the bar, while the men went off for naps or something," Hippo said.

"Or something, I think," Luke said. "According to Gibson, our barman, there was quite a bit of coming and going among the men on both afternoons. Those ladies could drink, though, lost count of how many bottles of wine they went through."

"On their last day here, we have heard that Dr Alberto Juarez started to cough and had some breathing issues," Hippo said.

"I suppose he did, but only on the last morning they were here," Luke said. "I just put it down to the change from Luangwa to the more humid Valley, affects some people. They took a boat ride down the Zambezi, that last night they were here, then a game drive in the morning before I took them back to Jeki and the plane. I noticed that Alberto had one of those inhalers that asthmatics use. He was puffing on it a bit at the plane."

"May we take a closer look at the chalet Dr Tom Macmillan was in?" Marieke asked.

"Of course," Luke said. "Let's see that would be number three, this way."

"Are any of your guides here at the moment?" Marieke asked.

"Simon and Rice," Luke replied.

"I think it would be advisable if they joined us to confirm anything that we see and find," Marieke said.

Luke picked up Simon and Rice and led them down the walkway to the chalet, and they looked it over.

"What's underneath?" Marieke asked.

"Not much," Luke replied. "A couple of times in the season, we knock the growth down so that there's no fire hazard and no cover for beasties to hide in, we cleaned it out before we opened, and did the same about ten days ago, so just before your chaps arrived. That usually entails knocking back all the growth and raking the sand smooth so that we can see snake tracks if there are any, standard village practice."

"How do we get down there?" Marieke asked.

"The best way is back to the *boma*, then around the side over there and down, the quickest way, if you're agile enough, is climb over the rail and use the supports to climb down," Luke said.

"I think for us the longer way around," Hippo said. Luke led the way back and around, and they were soon at the base of the posts that supported the platform on which the chalet stood.

"Have you ever climbed up or down?" Marieke asked Luke.

"A few times," he replied. "When we were building the lodge, there was quite a bit to do, so I was up and down a lot."

"Is that some fibre trapped on that post there?" Hippo asked, pointing to something trembling in the breeze.

"Let's get a picture of that before we remove it," Marieke suggested. "We may need to show where it came from."

"I'll take a look," Luke said. He climbed up to where the fibres were, retrieved them and came back down and handed them to Hippo.

"What do you think?" Hippo asked, handing it to Marieke.

"Wool," she replied. "Has the feel and texture of wool, what do you think, Melisende?"

"Wool," Melisende confirmed. "Right denier size for knitted goods, so my guess, socks, colour, I'd say fawn or tan."

"What colour socks do your staff wear?" Hippo asked Luke.

"We have a standard green, darkish green," Luke replied.

"This doesn't look very weathered," Melisende said. "If it had been there a while, I would have expected more bleaching of the dye; it must get most of the midday sun here."

"It would," Luke agreed.

"I don't see any recent prints around or leading to the base here," Marieke said. "Just ours, Simon, Rice?"

"No recent ones, there are some from a while ago when we cleared the area of brush, but they are quite old and there are no signs that tracks have been made and brushed out," Simon said, and Rice nodded in agreement.

"Will you take a look underneath?" Hippo asked.

"Do your thing," Melisende said to Marieke.

"I see footprints, they are the same as some of those at Mupundu, Tom, he was down here," Marieke replied. "In fact, he was here twice. I'll get some photos of the prints before I go tramping around and confuse things."

"Are they agile enough to climb down?" Hippo asked.

"They all ski and play tennis," Marieke replied. "So, I'd say yes, they're agile enough."

"So, what was Tom up to down here?" Hippo asked.

"Do you have gloves, a mask and some evidence bags?" Marieke asked.

"Here you are," Hippo said. "I anticipated something like this and came prepared. I've enough for you, Simon and Rice."

Marieke moved under the chalet, and Simon and Rice followed in her footsteps, so as not to confuse things.

"He came over here," Marieke said. "He knelt down here and was busy doing something. Luke, do you have something like a rake, or some kind of tool that I can sift through the sand here?"

"I'll be right back," he said.

"Do you see something?" Hippo asked.

"The sand has been disturbed here and here," Marieke replied, pointing to two places, and Simon and Rice both nodded in agreement. "I see no prints of small mammals, so nothing dug up or buried by an animal. I'll get shots of these areas too before I dig."

"Would this work?" Luke asked when he came back with a kitchen utensil that was normally used with a wok.

"Let's try," Marieke said. She sieved through the sand and placed all that she had sieved out onto an evidence bag. "Well, well, what do we have here?"

"What have you found?" Hippo asked.

"Believe it or not, four capsules that would be used in an inhaler," Marieke replied. "I'll photograph them as well."

"I wonder how they got down here, I know a rhetorical question," Hippo said. "Luke, how do you manage rubbish from the chalets?"

"There's a waste basket in each one, and we empty it daily and bag it all up and once a week transfer it all out by road to Lusaka, it goes out on the same lorry that brings supplies in," Luke explained.

"And you know it gets to Lusaka and isn't dumped at the side of the road on the way?" Marieke asked.

"I'm pretty sure it does," Luke replied. "The office has commented from time to time about how much rubbish people generate."

"Did we miss this week's run?" Marieke asked.

"Goes out tomorrow," Luke replied.

"Could it be delivered to Police Headquarters?" Hippo asked.

"I'm sure it could," Luke said. "There are two bags which are from the chalets, two from the bar and four from the kitchen."

"I think we'd be most interested in the two from the chalets," Hippo said.

"I wonder if there's anything resembling a mortar and pestle," Marieke said, casting around for anything that looked out of place.

"What would you need to grind the seeds?" Luke asked.

"Something to bash them with, a stone would be fine for that, then something to bash them on," Marieke said. "You'd want to be able to constrain the fragments, you wouldn't want to lose what you're grinding into the surrounding soil, and you certainly wouldn't want to breathe it in."

"Is it safe for you to be digging around there?" Melisende asked.

"I'm masked and gloved," Marieke replied. "I've seen no evidence of lucky beans yet."

"How toxic is it?" Hippo asked.

"3.3 micrograms per kilo when inhaled," Marieke replied. "When ground finely, it's a yellowish white powder that's quite stable, so doesn't lose its effectiveness over time. So, let's say that Alberto was about 75 kilos, a lethal dose would be 250 micrograms or so, each seed is about 75 milligrams, so crushing up only a few would give you a massive dose, these are size 0 capsules, so they'd take about 500 milligrams, so for four capsules you'd have to grind up about 30 seeds, and be bloody careful doing it."

"Well, you just be careful too," Melisende warned. "We don't need another death."

"Ah, what have we here?" Marieke asked, mostly of herself. "Plastic bags, looks like one inside another inside another, the outer one is quite a bit larger than the inner two. They show some damage from being struck, and there's what looks like fragments of seed arils in the innermost one, then is the next one a pair of long tweezers and what looks like a splint, the kind we used to get in the chemistry labs at school, where you're using a lighted split to test for flame colour. Looks like some wet wipes, gloves and tape as well. Hippo, do you have a larger evidence bag?"

"Here," Hippo said, handing her the largest one he had.

"Not big enough, Luke, do you have a couple of large rubbish bags?" Marieke asked.

"Be back with them now, now," he said. He was indeed and handed the bags and some tape to Rice, who passed them to Marieke.

"Good, seal that up," Marieke said. "Let's see if there's anything else."

After scratching and sifting for another fifteen minutes or so, Marieke did not uncover anything else that should not have been there, so she stopped looking.

"What I should do now is shower, clothes and all and make sure I wash off anything that I may have picked up," she told the others.

"Make sure you wash thoroughly," Hippo said. "I don't want to have to report to the commissioner that something unfortunate has taken place."

"You think that's what was used to smash up the lucky beans?" Luke asked.

"It may be," Marieke agreed. "But we cannot say for certain yet. If not, it begs the question of what is in the bag and why is it buried under the chalet. I'll go and shower and join you all in the *boma* when I'm done."

"None of your housekeeping staff have shown any signs of coughing?" Hippo asked. "I know I asked that before, but seeing this, I have to ask again."

"No one," Luke said. "How long after exposure do symptoms show?"

"Anywhere from eight hours on, death in 36 to 72 hours," Marieke replied. "Our man who died probably inhaled the stuff the last full day they were here. Then he compounded the dose each time he used his inhaler."

"Could it be accidental?" Luke asked.

"Accidental would more likely be chewing one and swallowing it," Marieke said. "That's the more common way that people die from this toxin. To inhale dust, you'd have to be deliberately creating it, so hardly accidental. I'm off to shower, I'll see you all in a few minutes. Luke, do you have a plastic bag that I can put this face mask and gloves in?"

"I'll get you one," he promised. He was back in a few minutes with two bags that would normally line a small waste basket.

"Simon, Rice, do you agree that these things were buried recently?" Hippo asked.

"Less than a week," Simon said. "And the prints that were here match those of one of the American guests who went fishing with Willie."

"I agree on the age of the burials," Rice added. "Less than a week."

Marieke went to the chalet, turned the water on in the shower and stood underneath it. She then took off the face mask she had and dropped that into the plastic bag that Luke had provided. The gloves followed. Then she undressed, washing out each item of clothing as she went. Satisfied that she had removed any possible traces of dust that may have been lingering, she got dry clothes and dressed. The wet items she strung out along the balcony to dry in the sun. That done, she joined the others in the bar.

"Could this be added to the rubbish bags that are going out?" she asked of Luke.

"Sure sure," he said. "What can I get you, tea, coffee, beer?"

"Tea would be fine, thank you," she replied. He poured tea, then left them to their own devices while he went off to attend to lodge matters.

"So, what have we?" Hippo asked.

"Capsules that we should test for the asthma medicines," Marieke replied. "And what looks like the means to reduce beans to powder."

"That may, of course, be quite unrelated," Hippo said.

"It may," she agreed. "But it seems unlikely that someone on the staff would bury something under one of the chalets."

"Unless it was some kind of drug trafficking," Hippo suggested.

"True," she agreed. "We should ask Luke if there's a problem with that here. The tracks I saw under the chalet match those of Tom Macmillan, and I saw no others and the burials are quite recent, less than a week."

"Is this too simple?" Melisende asked.

"Perhaps," Marieke agreed. "But what was the risk, the chances of someone going below the chalet and digging around are very slim, why would anyone want to?"

"That's true," Melisende agreed. "So, if we take the thesis that it was Tom who ground the beans and filled the capsule, it was still a huge risk for him to fill the capsules with the powder and seal them."

"Looking at the bags, I'd suggest something like a transparent camera bag, something you could get your gloved hands in and seal up and do your filling and cleaning up in comparative safety,"

Marieke said. "That all bespeaks planning and practice, learning how hard to hit the bags to break the seeds up but not puncture the bags, it would take time and gentle hits rather than heavy bashes. There were a couple of stones down there, flat river-worn stones that were smooth, and one would have made a great surface to use as a base while hitting with the smaller one."

"How do you clean off the capsules once they're filled and out of the bag?" Hippo asked.

"The capsules are typically gelatine and that's insoluble in alcohol, so use a wet wipe that is alcohol based to remove any dust on the outside," Marieke suggested. "All those things would have had to have been brought here, but nothing would weigh that much, so not a big weight penalty."

"How is it that you know so much about capsules?" Hippo asked.

"Melisende and I worked on a drug smuggling case," Marieke replied. "The gang we were after was moving cocaine into France as vitamin capsules, I know a very inefficient way to do it, but it did mean it could be directly sold without having to be split into saleable packages in France."

"Should we gather the stones as evidence?" Melisende asked.

"It wouldn't hurt," Hippo said.

"Give me another pair of gloves, a mask and two of the large evidence bags, and I'll get them quickly," Marieke said.

"Here you are," Marieke said when she handed the evidence bags to Hippo. "Two rocks, my guess is that if we examine them under a microscope, we'll see plastics from the bags."

"That takes care of the how," Hippos said. "Or at least part of the how, it still begs the question of the substitution."

"If I were Tom, I'd give the capsules to David and tell him that that was his department," Marieke said. "I might be prepared to make the means, but I wouldn't be prepared to deliver the means."

"What do we know about the movements of Dr Alberto Juarez and Mr David Davis while they were here?" Hippo asked.

"According to all the ladies, Alberto joined them about two in the afternoon of their last full day here, and David didn't join them until three, so he had a whole hour to swap out the capsules," Marieke said.

"We need to interview the staff here and see if we can pin down the movements of the victim and our two prime suspects," Hippo said. "We should start with the barman."

Gibson was asked to join them, and Hippo talked to him about the visitors, showing him the iPad that Marieke had brought and the picture of the group. They talked for about forty minutes in all, going over all that Gibson could remember. He struck Marieke as the perfect barman, the type that would remember what everyone drank and not have to take any notes at all, and also be aware of what the guests were doing and who was likely to want more to drink and who not, and yet stay unobtrusive. Gibson was very observant and had an amazing recall, placing people at times and places. After he had gone, Hippo gave Marieke and Melisende a quick version of what he had learned.

"Gibson confirmed that the ladies spent the afternoons in the bar, with visits to the loo that is over there," he said. "He also confirmed that on the last afternoon, Dr Alberto Juarez came and sat with them at about two and the other men not until three. He did see David go to Tom's chalet twice that afternoon, the first time about two-fifteen, the second two-thirty and that between those visits he went down the walkway to Alberto's chalet."

"Do you need a formal statement?" Marieke asked.

"We may if there is a prosecution," Hippo conceded.

"What about James?" Melisende asked.

"He went to see David about two," Hippo replied.

"So, the ladies were right, a lot of coming and going," Marieke said.

"So much for quiet time and naps," Hippo said.

"In their various statements, the men all claimed not to have left their chalets at all on either afternoon until it was time for afternoon tea," Marieke said.

"So, I wonder if they have modified their tale now?" Hippo said. "The commissioner had their statements that you took, and I'm sure will be asking questions."

"Everything all right?" Luke asked as he joined them.

"Fine," Hippo said. "Gibson has been helping us."

"He's a good man," Luke said. "The drives are due back soon. Do you wish to talk to Willie and Rice?"

"We do," Hippo said. "Thank you."

"I'll go and see them in, and then we can have lunch and you can talk to Willie and Rice," Luke said.

"Should we be going back to Lusaka this afternoon?" Marieke asked Hippo.

"In the morning would be fine," Hippo said. "If we leave here at first light, we'll be in Lusaka by seven and at the office before most get there. I'll let Vernon know."

"If you have to detain someone, then I wouldn't want you to miss them as they skip the country," Marieke said.

"We can always pick them up at the airport, either Livingstone or Lusaka," Hippo said. "That would be a first for me, picking someone up at the airport."

"Is there enough evidence to detain?" Melisende asked.

"That's up to the commissioner," Hippo said. "I would, but there's the politics of picking up Americans, their State Department will want chapter and verse, and I'm not sure we want to give them that."

"How are relations with the Americans?" Marieke asked.

"Not bad," Hippo said. "They're working hard to counter the Chinese influence, they've had a late start as the Chinese have been here essentially since the 70s when they built the TAZARA line. Lately, the Chinese have been buying up the copper mines and other industries. Anyway, I want to hear from the guides here what they saw and or heard."

"What about the housekeeping staff?" Melisende asked.

"Them too," Hippo agreed. "Ah, it looks like people are arriving."

"Hello," a man said. "Doug Robertson, my wife, Robin."

"Hippo Chikonde, and this is Marieke Englebrecht and Melisende Garnier," Hippo replied, making his introductions.

"George and Matilda White," the other arrivals said. "Are you staying long?"

"Only the one night," Hippo said.

"Hey folks," Luke said. "I see you've met. This is Inspector Chikonde of the Zambia Police, and the two ladies are with the French *police nationale*. They're here investigating."

"Not us, I hope," George said.

"Not you," Luke assured him. "Guests that were here before you came."

"Someone must have really queered the pitch to have the Old Bill from two countries asking about them," Doug commented.

"Inspector, this is Willie and this is Rice, Inspector Chikonde from Lusaka," Luke interrupted.

"Hippo Chikonde," Willie said. "It's been a few years."

"Willie Mwanza," Hippo said. "You're right, it has been a few years. How is your family?'

"Doing well," Willie replied. "Still living out at Chizongwe, I saw that your parents both died. I'm sorry."

"They were both ageing and not doing well," Hippo said.

"The inspector has questions for you and Rice about a previous guest," Luke explained. "Perhaps we should have lunch and then you can sit together and answer the questions they have."

"Thank you," Hippo said. "Perhaps we could also talk to the rest of the staff, those who are housekeeping and anyone else who may have had contact with the guests."

"I'll arrange it," Luke promised. "As soon as you're done with Willie and Rice, I'll bring the other chaps over."

Lunch was served and eaten with general conversation, mainly about what the guests had seen and done that day and the day before. They had been lucky and had seen the dogs, plus the lions they had been following, as well as leopards, buffalo, elephants, and a host of smaller species. The guests were full of praise for Willie and Rice and said that they were far better than other guides they had had in the past. Marieke wondered where that had been and asked.

"We took a trip together to South Africa, to what I now see as a factory safari, pushing through as many guests as they can, ten to twelve per vehicle and what seemed like very structured drives," George replied. "This is miles better. We've seen more in the day and a half we've been here than we did in six days there, and it hasn't been rushed, it's been very relaxed with time to just stop and stare."

221

"Have you been on a safari?" Robin asked Marieke.'

"I grew up in Namibia," Marieke replied. "On a farm away from town, so in many ways, my childhood was all a safari. We've also spent time in northern Botswana at a tented camp there."

"If you're from Namibia, how are you with the French police?" Doug asked.

"I went to university in France, did some time in the Botswana police, then moved back to France and joined the force there," Marieke replied.

"If you'll excuse us," Hippo said. "Duty calls, we must press on with our investigation."

Hippo excused himself to Marieke and Melisende and had a long conversation in Nyanja with first Willie, then Rice. The interaction between them was interesting; it told a lot about their personalities. Hippo was analytical, Willie was very outgoing and was therefore probably a good guide with guests, particularly new ones; he seemed to have an instinct for things. Rice, on the other hand, was more academic and even scientific; the two made a good combination. After the conversations with Willie and Rice, Hippo gave Marieke and Melisende a quick review of what he had learned. Alberto had been fine on all the outings until the last morning when they were going out to the airstrip, when he was seen using his inhaler, something he had not done before. Rice thought it might be the dust in the air from the traffic that had gone before them; whatever it was, he seemed to be having some difficulty breathing. They both suggested he seek medical help in Lusaka rather than go on to Kafue. He had told them that he was fine and that he would get over whatever was bothering him. They had not interacted with the guests except for the activities and at meal times, so could not comment on whether they had been out and about at all during the quiet times.

The housekeeping staff filled in some gaps about movements and confirmed what Gibson had told them. One of the staff, usually tasked with weed control, told them that he had seen Tom under his chalet and presumed he had seen something interesting to look at.

That had been on the afternoon of the first full day they had been at Mushika. The staff that had cleaned the chalet of Alberto had noticed a used capsule in the rubbish on the last morning when they left for Lusaka, but before that none. There had been nothing of particular note in any of the other rubbish bins. Hippo thanked them all for their time and gave Marieke and Melisende the essence of what he had learned.

"So, Tom was seen under his chalet," Melisende said. "And David was seen to visit Tom twice while Alberto was in the bar. How good a card player is your commissioner or the superintendent?"

"That's probably what it'll come down to," Hippo admitted. "We've got circumstantial evidence of activities and comings and goings, but unless we can lift fingerprints from those plastic bags or inside the gloves, we've got nothing concrete."

"So, do we change plans and fly to Lusaka this afternoon?" Marieke asked Hippo.

"I've given that a lot of thought, by the time we get to Lusaka, it will be after four, so I still think it would be better to arrive first thing in the morning and report what we've found to the commissioner then," he replied. "It will be up to him how to proceed."

"I can't see you wanting us after we've briefed the commissioner," Marieke said. "If we're not needed, we'll go back out to Mupundu."

"I can't answer for the commissioner, but my view is that we take it from here," Hippo said. "I am very grateful to you for your help. I doubt that I would have been able to uncover the buried items under the chalet, I wouldn't have known that the sand had been disturbed recently, my bush skills are not that good. So, this afternoon, let's just make sure we have done all we can to get our notes in order."

"You can take the camera chip that has all the photographs on it," Marieke said.

"Thank you," Hippo said.

"I wonder if the lodge has a printer we could use," Melisende said. "If they do, I could print out all the notes I have taken and you could have them now."

"I'll ask Luke," Hippo said.

By the time dinner came, they had put in order all they could; they had printed out not only the notes that Melisende had recorded on her computer, but also copies of the pictures that Marieke had taken. Hippo was satisfied that they had done all they could; the rest would be up to the team in Lusaka to determine just what was in the plastic bags and if there were any fingerprints that could be lifted from the bags or the gloves.

"Will you join us for dinner?" Luke asked.

"That would be most appreciated," Hippo said. "I want to thank you for everything. Your staff has been most helpful."

"Hope you get your man," Luke said.

"So do I," Hippo said.

Dinner was probably better than the one that had had at Lundwe, and that was saying something. The guests wanted to talk about Zambia, and its history, so Luke, Willie and Hippo were kept busy answering questions and talking about everyday life. By the end of dinner, Marieke just wanted to soak in the bath that was on their balcony and get some rest.

"This is luxury," she commented to Melisende as she submerged herself in the water.

"Isn't it unusual to have a bath in the chalets?" Melisende asked.

"I would have thought so," Marieke agreed. "But I'm not complaining. I wonder how the water is heated."

"There's a big gas cylinder outside the chalet on the one side," Melisende said. "And I saw an on-demand water heater, so providing there's gas, you'll get hot water."

"I wonder how long each cylinder lasts," Marieke said.

"A few months, I would think," Melisende thought. "Perhaps even long enough for a season. Are you going to lounge there all night, or can I get a wash before the water gets cold?"

"All yours," Marieke said. "I hope we can get back out to Kafue tomorrow afternoon. When we're done at the police station, I'll call Will and see if there's space on the afternoon flight."

Debriefing

Five-thirty seemed to come very quickly, but both Marieke and Melisende were already awake, listening to the dawn chorus of birds and animals. It might still be an hour before the actual dawn, but everything was waking up and getting ready for the day.

"Do you hear those lions?" Melisende asked.

"Across the river, I'd say, in Mana Pools," Marieke suggested. "There's the answer from this side of the river. Let's go and get some breakfast and be ready to go when Luke takes us back to the plane."

"Morning, ladies," Hippo said when he joined them for breakfast. "I've talked to Vernon and he tells me that his pre-flight checks will take a few minutes, but once that's done, we can be off. We'll ride out to the strip with him, no need to take more than one vehicle."

"That's fine with us," Marieke said. "We're ready when you are."

"Morning all," Vernon said as he joined them. "Ready for the quick flight up to Lusaka?"

"Just let us know when we need to go, we're ready," Marieke assured him.

"If you're done, we can go now," Vernon said. "Willie's driving us to the strip. It's not yet six, but it'll be six-thirty by the time we're there. so off at probably six-forty-five, seven at the latest, put us in Lusaka at seven-thirty."

"That's good," Hippo said. "We can be at the police station by eight and start our debrief."

"You chaps get everything done you wanted to?" Vernon asked.

"We hope so," Hippo said. "I don't think we missed anything of consequence, but there are times when it's the smallest thing that is the most important."

"Are you all ready?" Willie asked as he joined them.

"We are," Hippo replied. Willie drove them at what some might have thought as breakneck speed out to the airstrip, and they were fortunate that there were no animals on the road to impede their progress.

"If you'll just stay here with Willie a few minutes," Vernon said when they reached the strip. "I'll do my pre-flight and give you a yell when I'm ready."

"It was good to see you again, Willie," Hippo said.

"And you," Willie echoed. "You should look to get a transfer out here to Chipata."

"I might even do that," Hippo said. "Thank Luke again for us, this has been most useful."

"I'm ready, we can load up," Vernon said.

"Go well," Willie said.

"Stay well," Hippo replied.

"Do you want the front seat again?" Vernon asked Hippo.

"That would be nice," Hippo said. "That is, if you ladies are agreeable to sitting in the back?"

"We're fine," Marieke said.

"Right," Vernon said. "All buckled in, good, we'll take off to the south, climb out, then turn to the left and come back around for Lusaka. Flight time about thirty minutes, so we'll have you in Lusaka in time for a second breakfast."

"You think we're Hobbits?" Marieke asked.

"Hadn't thought of that," Vernon laughed. "OK, here we go."

The takeoff and climb out went smoothly enough but there were a few bumps as they turned left and flew up and over the hills that formed the northern side of the Zambezi Valley. On the ground Marieke could see bush, with the occasional road and the even more occasional vehicle on the road, until they were within ten to fifteen minutes from Lusaka, then the development was more pronounced, with roads, houses, fields and all the signs of human habitation. Their arrival into Lusaka was delayed while they waited for a South African Airlines plane to land, then they went in and taxied over to the hardstand.

"That was a nice flight, thank you, Vernon," Marieke said.

"Any time," he replied.

"Shall we go?" Hippo asked.

"Lead on," Marieke said. They trooped out through the terminal to the car park where Hippo had left his car. Traffic was already a mess as people started their days at work or school. Hippo actually resorted to using his lights and siren a couple of times to move laggards out of the way, and also to move those trapped by others jumping lights and blocking intersections.

"This is almost as bad as Parisian traffic," Marieke commented. "It's like Italy, there are lines on the road, signs and all kinds, that people seem to regard as suggestions, not rules."

"I thought it was just us that had these problems," Hippo said.

"Oh no," Marieke assured him. "We get gridlock often as we have more cars on the roads than they were ever designed for."

"Well, we're almost there," Hippo said. "Just down Independence a short way."

They parked and made their way into the headquarters to an office that Hippo was using.

"Let me just check and see if the commissioner is in yet," Hippo said. "Would you like some tea or coffee?"

"Coffee would be delightful," Marieke replied.

"I'll be back," Hippo promised. He left and was as good as his word and was back in a very short time with coffees for all, and news that the commissioner was in a meeting but would be available at nine.

"While we wait, let me get all this stuff to the forensics people to see what they can get from it," he said. "Fingerprints would be really good. I wonder if we have been able to get prints from the Americans. I'll also get extra copies of the pictures you took printed out so that we can show where we went, what we looked at and what we found."

"I doubt that they would volunteer to give their fingerprints," Melisende said. "Most people will only consent if there's no real choice, and until now, what reason could we have for asking for prints?"

"Quite," Hippo agreed. "I'll be back in fifteen minutes or so."

"Should we have done more to help?" Marieke asked Melisende after Hippo had left.

"I don't see what else we could have done," Melisende replied. "We went out to Luangwa and Lower Zambezi, we interviewed the staff and the guides, we looked over the chalets where they stayed, and you found where stuff had been buried, how did you know where to dig?"

"The ground has a different look when it's been disturbed," Marieke explained. "When we found the decapitated bodies, it was the flies that showed us where to dig. In this case, there was nothing to attract flies, so it was the soil itself we had to look at."

"It's interesting," Melisende said. "Looking around, police stations must be the same the world over. The same cheap desks and chairs, the same files of case files, the same coffee."

"It's not the best, is it," Marieke laughed. "But then until we got our own things for making coffee, ours was nothing to write home about."

"It was downright awful," Melisende corrected.

"Are we ready?" Hippo asked when he returned. "The commissioner can see us now."

They walked the halls to his office, which was markedly better than that of Inspector Chikonde, but befitting a high-ranking officer. They were met by his assistant, who announced them. Joining the commissioner for the meeting was Superintendent Zimba.

"Matshwane, Madame Garnier, Inspector, welcome back, tell me what did you find out there?" Joseph asked.

"We made our way to the Lundwe Lodge and saw the chalets where the Americans had stayed, and we interviewed the staff and the guides," Hippo started. "They noted no apparent animosity between the guests, and all seemed healthy to them."

"What about the walks that Dr Macmillan and Mr Davis took?" Joseph asked.

"They went out both times with the guide, Ephie, the scout, Isaac and a staff member by the name of Banda who carried the refreshments," Hippo replied.

"Anything of note on those walks?" Joseph asked.

"Tom, Dr Macmillan collected seeds, 32 small bags in all," Hippo replied. "We followed their trail and saw where they had stopped and what trees, bushes and vines they gathered seeds from. We have pictures of all the places where they stopped and gathered seeds."

"Any of interest to us?" Joseph asked.

"They did collect quite a lot of lucky beans on their second walk," Hippo replied. "The guide cautioned them to be careful if they were making a rosary."

"Who did the collecting?" Felix asked.

"Dr Macmillan," Hippo replied. "That was confirmed by both the guide, Ephie, and the ZAWA scout, Isaac."

"Do we know if Dr Macmillan still has all these seeds?" Joseph asked.

"I do not," Hippo replied. "I have had no occasion to meet them, except at the airport, and he had his luggage there, but there was no reason for me to search his luggage. I have to say that Commissaire Englebrecht did us a great service by pointing out where Macmillan and Davis had left the normal path that the Lundwe people take on their walks. Ephie, the guide, remarked on her tracking skills."

"Was there anything else of note at the Lundwe Lodge?" Joseph asked.

"Not that we could determine," Hippo replied. "All reports were that they left the lodge in good spirits and flew to Lower Zam and the Jeki strip, where they were met by Luke Botha, the manager of the Mushika Lodge."

"I know him," Joseph said. "Knew his folks when they had their farm outside Ndola before they moved to Chipata. Where are my manners, may I offer you tea or coffee?"

"Tea for me," Marieke replied.

"I would prefer coffee," Melisende added. Commissioner Bwalya buzzed his assistant and gave the orders for tea and coffee, and added his own and that of Felix and Hippo.

"So, as far as anyone can tell, Dr Juarez was in apparent good health in Luangwa?" Joseph asked.

"There were no symptoms of any kind observed or reported," Hippo confirmed.

"So, on to Lower Zambezi," Joseph said. "Ah, thank you, Paula, tea and coffee and even biscuits, wonderful."

"The layout of the chalets at Mushika is unique," Hippo said. "To get from one to another, you essentially have to walk back to the boma then out again."

"Unless you're quite agile and are prepared to climb down and back up again," Marieke added.

"That's correct," Hippo said. "The chalets are on raised platforms, perhaps three metres above the ground."

"But you found something?" Joseph asked.

"We found fibres that look like wool, possibly from a sock; they were caught on one of the cross bars that form part of the support for the chalet," Hippo said. "I have taken them to forensics so they can confirm what they are. You can see in this picture here where they were. There were no tracks of people between the chalets at the ground level, but beneath the chalet number three, which was where Dr Macmillan stayed, we saw evidence of his tracks as confirmed by two of the guides from Mushika."

"Could Dr Macmillan have dropped something off the balcony of his chalet and climbed down to retrieve it?" Felix asked.

"Unlikely," Hippo replied. "His prints were under the chalet, not around the perimeter. Anything falling from the balcony would not have gone underneath, the ground is soft, so it would not have bounced underneath, but stayed just where it fell."

"Go on," Joseph instructed.

"Commissaire Englebrecht, accompanied by Simon and Rice, went under the chalet and investigated the tracks left by Dr Macmillan. They all agreed that the ground had been disturbed recently in one spot and dug and retrieved a plastic bag with four capsules of the type typically used in inhalers. Those capsules have been given to forensics to determine what they contain," Hippo said. "And to see if there are any fingerprints on them."

"Very good," Joseph said. "Anything else?"

"Quite a lot," Hippo said. "There was another burial site, and that contained a group of nested plastic bags with fragments of seeds in them and other items, you can see in this picture. There were also two stones recovered that showed evidence of plastic on them that would be consistent with one being used to strike a plastic bag placed on the other."

"Could they have been buried by a member of the staff or a previous guest?" Felix asked.

"That's always a possibility," Hippo admitted. "However, the guides at Mushika were adamant that there were no recent tracks around the chalet, and the burial was less than a week ago, so that rather excludes prior guests. As for staff, I suppose that's a possibility if they had climbed down from the balcony, but why?"

"I'm thinking like counsel for the defence," Felix said. "Could the bags have been washed downriver and deposited?"

"That would seem highly unlikely," Marieke replied. "Along the edge of the river, there were indications of prior water heights and some debris, but none as high as to reach under the chalet. Does not the Kariba Dam largely control the flow these days?"

"It does," Felix confirmed. "There have been problems though caused by the dam, large water releases in heavy rainfall years have eroded the banks of the river below the dam, and I understand that whereas in the past there was silt borne by the water that would settle out in the side channels of the river, that no longer happens as the silt drops out above the dam, so what is released is clean water. Sadly we also have problems with the dam itself, the outfall is eroding back under the dam wall, failure of the dam would be catastrophic for those downstream, including the Cabora Bassa dam, which would also fail and then the whole of the Zambezi delta in Mozambique, but that is another matter, not something for today."

"So, the theory is that Mr Davis and Dr Macmillan hatched a plan for the despatch of Dr Juarez, they gathered lucky bean seeds in Luangwa and Dr Macmillan prepared the powder in Lower Zambezi and filled the empty capsules, which he then gave to Mr Davis, how did he, Davis, manage the substitution?" Joseph asked.

"In the second afternoon that the party was at Mushika, Dr Juarez was in the bar from two on, whereas the rest of the men did not go there until three," Hippo replied, consulting his notes. "Mr Davis was seen going to the chalet of Dr Macmillan twice in the period between two and two-thirty, and between those visits, he was seen by Donald the barman going down the walkway that led to the chalet of Dr Juarez."

"So, the first time to get the capsules, then make the substitution, then take the ones he had removed back to Macmillan for disposal," Joseph mused. "Why not dump them himself?"

"I think that was part of the plan," Marieke said. "Keep things nice and separate, no capsules anywhere near Davis, so that there's no suspicion attached to him. I think things went a little awry at dinner that night, apparently avocados trigger his asthma, so he had need of the inhaler, he used up the capsule that was in it, and had to add a

231

new one; it was just chance that he picked an adulterated one. Once inhaled, the toxin would start to show in eight hours or less, then as he used the inhaler more to counter his breathing problems, he made it worse. Then it was just a matter of time."

"Thank you," Joseph said. "We have been busy here as well. We formally interviewed the seven and got somewhat different accounts than they had first given. I surmise that one of the women spilt the beans about seeing the men out and about during quiet time at Mushika. They all had plausible reasons for being out and about, and all had had convenient memory lapses when they spoke to you at Mupundu."

"Has the PM been done?" Marieke asked.

"It has," Joseph confirmed. "The conclusion of the pathologist was no snake bite, but severe respiratory failure likely caused by a toxin, which was probably abrin."

"They can't be more specific than that?" Marieke asked.

"Sadly, no," Joseph replied. "As we had both suspected, there is no reliable test for abrin yet. The university has been researching and has found scholarly articles from the 70s and even one as recent as 2012. That one was from Switzerland and uses DNA tests to check for ricin and abrin, but we don't have the equipment here in Zambia to be able to do that."

"So, our villains picked the right toxin," Marieke said. "Not one that is commonly used, difficult to detect and fatal."

"These photographs you took are most helpful," Joseph said. "I will be interested to see if our forensics people can find anything we can use to build a case against the two prime suspects."

"Can you bluff them, bully them, coerce or cajole them into breaking ranks and have one tell on the other?" Marieke asked.

"We've been looking at that," Joseph said. "Who, in your opinion, would break first?"

"Dr Macmillan," Marieke said. "They are both very glib when it comes to accounting for their movements, but David Davis, I would say, is the more accomplished liar, whereas Macmillan makes a living by dealing with data and facts. He could also claim that he had no idea what Davis planned to do with the capsules he gave him. I suppose Macmillan could also claim that he was interested in the traditional medicine uses of the lucky beans."

"Madame Garnier?" Joseph asked.

"I would agree with Marieke," Melisende replied. "David would make the better card player; he holds his cards close to the vest, he throws out, what do you call them, red herrings, he deflects questions with inconsequential answers."

"Where are the Americans at the moment?" Marieke asked.

"All but Dr Catalina Juarez are in Livingstone; they have a flight out tomorrow on South African," Joseph said. "We had no real evidence to hold them in Lusaka. Dr Catalina Juarez is working with their embassy to sort out the procedures for transporting the body back to the States."

"Is the US Embassy satisfied with the PM conclusions?" Marieke asked.

"They have to be, there's nothing else," Joseph said. "Unfortunately, the coroner's court doesn't meet until Monday, so we won't have an official cause of death and the circumstances surrounding the death; the only definite conclusion to date is that the death at Mupundu was not caused by food poisoning there or any other agent."

"What does the prosecution service have to say?" Marieke asked.

"You know them, they want everything nicely sewn up with a big red bow, which we can't give them, so they're waffling," Joseph said. "We could, with all this, arrest both on suspicion, but then have to release them if the prosecutors won't proceed. The only thing that will make the prosecutors move is a confession, so how to get one? When you had your headless duo, how did you manage that?"

"I had chapter and verse on the movements of my two suspects," Marieke replied. "Then I took them through everything they had done from when they first landed in Zambia, to crossing the Zambezi and entering Botswana, it was interesting to see how the story changed as they realised I had all the evidence. In the end, they both blamed each other for the actual killing and beheading."

"So, do we have chapter and verse on our suspect's movements in Zambia?" Joseph asked.

"We do," Hippo replied. "We know when they landed in Lusaka, then in Mfuwe, we have statements from the staff at Lundwe, then Mushika, we have statements about who collected what seeds where, even photographs of the trees and vines themselves, we have the means they used to grind the seeds into powder and the capsules that were removed to allow for the adulterated ones to be added."

"So, you think that presented with all this, one of them would crack?" Joseph asked.

"I think that between you and Superintendent Zimba, you can work them with details and minutia so that they're uncertain about what you actually know," Marieke suggested.

"You wouldn't want to be part of that?" Joseph asked.

"I think this has to be a wholly Zambian team, otherwise I could see some clever defence counsel coming up with arguments that the interrogation wasn't properly conducted," Marieke replied.

"You are right," Joseph said. "We have to take it from here, inspector, you were present at all the interviews?"

"I was," Hippo replied. "Some I also conducted in Nyanja, which commissaire Englebrecht has told me she does not speak."

"We have statements from the guides and the ZAWA scout?" Joseph asked.

"We do," Hippo confirmed.

"I think the next step is to detain Macmillan and Davis before they leave the country," Joseph said. "Paula, can you get me Chief Super Sejani for me?"

"He's on the line, Sir," she said.

"Harry, Joseph here, we'd like you to pick up two tourists, should be staying at the Royal Livingstone, Mr David Davis and Dr Tom Macmillan, both Americans, both wanted for questioning in the death of one Dr Alberto Juarez," Joseph said. "If you can't get them today at all, they're booked to leave on the SAA flight tomorrow morning for Jo'burg, stop them. The rest of their party is free to go if they want. Should alert immigration too, in case you miss them at the airport or they try and walk across the bridge to Zim. Let me know as you as you can that they're in custody, and we'll work out how to ship them here."

The telephone rang a few minutes later, and Joseph answered it.

"Harry, let me put you on the speaker," he said. "You have them, good, hold them, and I'll have Inspector Chikonde come and get them. What did the rest decide to do?"

"Mrs Davis told Mr Davis that she was getting a divorce lawyer and said that she was leaving as planned on the SAA flight," Harry replied. "The doctors Davis, also said they were leaving as scheduled, and Dr Sofia Macmillan just shook her head and told her husband that he was on his own."

"Happy families," Joseph said.

"Happy indeed," Harry said. "We picked them up all headed for the Vic Falls bridge and Zim, the immigration chaps held them until we came. Did they really kill this Dr Juarez?"

"We believe so," Joseph said. "The challenge now is to prove it."

"They both asked for consular access," Harry said.

"I'll talk to the American Embassy and they can send a chap over to talk to them when they get here," Joseph said. "Tell me, did you search the bags of Davis and Macmillan?"

"Customs did that for us at the border; they have wider powers than we do, at least at the border, in Macmillan's bags, they found 31 bags of various seeds," Harry replied. "The customs chaps said that there was no problem as far as they were concerned with them taking the seeds, none are on any protected species lists."

"Thirty-one, not thirty-two?" Joseph asked.

"No, definitely 31," Harry confirmed.

"Did you see them?" Joseph asked.

"I did," Harry confirmed.

"Do you remember seeing any lucky beans?" Joseph asked.

"I don't remember seeing any, but I wouldn't swear to it," Harry said.

"Anyway, thanks, David and thank the immigration chaps for me," Joseph said.

"So, it would seem that we no longer trouble you further, Matshwane, Madame Garnier, besides which, once you leave for France, you will not want to come back here for what could be a lengthy trial," Joseph said. "Thank you for your help in this matter."

"We are pleased to be able to help," Marieke said. "We hope you are able to conclude this successfully."

"So do I," Joseph said. "So do I. Inspector, I need more of your time. Perhaps you could arrange for someone to help with transport to the airport and return here."

Marieke and Melisende were dropped at the airport, and they made their way to the Air Safari office to find Will.

"Hey, all done here?" he asked.

"We've done all we can," Marieke replied. "It's up to the Zambia Police now, they've got a pile of circumstantial evidence and I think know how to use it to get someone to talk."

"I can get you on this afternoon's flight," Will said.

"That would be super," Marieke said.

"Shall we get some lunch while you wait?" Will suggested.

"That would be appreciated," Marieke said.

"Let me call Bridget, and she can meet us for lunch," Will suggested. "There's a new hotel just opened, Latitude 15, they do a really good lunch."

"Latitude 15 because we're pretty much on that latitude?" Marieke asked.

"That's what I understand," Will confirmed. "There's another one, Latitude 13, that's in Lilongwe."

"Clever," Melisende said.

Will drove them from the airport to the hotel, a fairly straightforward route, except for the detour around the Lusaka City airport. The hotel itself was in a leafy neighbourhood, and Bridget was already there waiting for them.

"All done?" she asked. "Can you talk about it?"

"I'm sure the bush telegraph has a lot already," Marieke said. "You know that the guest Alberto Juarez died, well, it seems highly likely that he died of abrin poisoning, something he was exposed to in Lower Zambezi, so nothing to do with Mupundu."

"That's a relief," Bridget said. "If it had been something like food poisoning, we'd have had an issue."

"Definitely not food-related," Marieke confirmed. "It seems to be related to the eternal triangle."

"Who between?" Bridget asked.

"Alberto Juarez and Monica Davis," Marieke replied. "Just before we left the police headquarters, they got word that they had detained two of the other guests at the Vic Falls Bridge, apparently on their way to walk over to Zim. David Davis and Tom Macmillan were the ones detained; the others elected to leave them and go home."

"So the spouses left?" Bridget asked.

"The report we heard was that lawyers could be involved in the future in the States, so happy marriages all around," Melisende added.

"Are you flying back out to Lufupa this afternoon?" Bridget asked.

"Will got us seats," Marieke confirmed. "We should take some more printer paper and ink cartridges, we used up a lot printing photos and interviews."

"I've got some at the airport, I'll give it to you when you leave," Will said. "So, we should eat."

"What's good?" Marieke asked.

"They do a Kariba bream that is really good," Bridget said.

"Sounds good," Marieke said.

"I'll have that as well," Melisende added.

They ate, they talked, dancing around what Marieke and Melisende had actually found on their trip to the two parks. Bridget assured them that details of the case would leak out over time and that the public would probably divide into the two inevitable camps, those pro the detainees and those against.

"Even if they walk away from here," Marieke said. "They'll have problems at home, divorce lawyers being among them."

"So, what did we learn from the point of view of the camp?" Bridget asked.

"They had to move the body fairly quickly," Marieke replied. "As Grace said, if they hadn't, they would have attracted predators and scavengers. As it was, the vultures had gathered and were perched in trees all around. If they had waited for the police to arrive, they probably would have had to guard the body all day and all night so as not to lose anything."

"Perhaps we need to develop a suitable protocol for what to do if we have a death," Bridget thought. "Maybe something similar to our medevac policy of calling in a helicopter to take a sick person out, only in this case, the sickness is fatal. When you found those two dead profs in Botswana, I remember we had a guard on them all night until the police surgeon and his forensic chap arrived."

"I didn't want to just dig them up without trying to learn something about how they were buried and how long it had been," Marieke said. "The other thing that you might look at is what you do if guests gather seeds, make sure they know what they're collecting and if there are any risks associated with them."

"You think the chaps that collected the lucky beans knew what they were doing?" Bridget asked.

"Certainly," Marieke said. "One is a poison plant expert, so my guess is that he researched things before coming here and knew just what to get."

"I think we should look at our knowledge of trees, bushes and vines and make sure we at least know which ones to avoid, or be very careful of," Bridget said. "Our guides know them, I'm sure, but it wouldn't hurt to have a review and make sure."

"Ah, here's lunch, dig in," Will said.

The afternoon flight to Lufupa was full, and Marieke and Melisende just took the empty seats that were left after all the paying passengers had boarded. Marieke had a seat next to a woman who introduced herself as Vivian Harris from Reading. She was on her own and going to Mupundu, which would be her first stop before moving on to Luangwa. Marieke introduced herself, and then Vivian wanted to know if she had been to Mupundu.

"I have," Marieke confirmed. "I'm related to the owners and have visited their camps before, this time being the first to Mupundu, which only opened this year."

"Will I see many animals?" Vivian asked.

"You should," Marieke replied. "There's plenty around. Are you with the others on the plane?"

"No, I just met them all at the airport," Vivian replied. "I like to go places on my own. Is Mupundu safe?"

"It is," Marieke said.

"But I heard that someone died there," Vivian said.

"A man did die," Marieke confirmed. "But it was a condition he had contracted elsewhere in Zambia, and it just happened to show up when he was at Mupundu."

"So, nothing to do with the food, the water or animals?" Vivian asked.

"Nothing at all," Marieke assured her. "I have just been in Lusaka giving my statement to the police, and they are looking at other places."

"That's good to know," Vivian said. "Did he die in his tent? I wouldn't want to sleep in a bed where a bloke had died."

"He died outside on a path," Marieke said. "He was found by the housekeeping staff. The Zambia Police came out and investigated, and as far as I know, are still investigating."

"What do you do when you're not visiting relatives?" Vivian asked.

"I'm retired," Marieke said. "And you?"

"I have a software company," Vivian replied. "We write software for hotels and the hospitality industry."

"Is it a large company?" Marieke asked.

"Large enough, we have 1280 programmers, analysts and others at the moment," Vivian said.

"We could have used you a few days ago," Marieke laughed. "The booking software that they use at Mupundu had a glitch, we worked out what it was and sent a note off to the supplier."

"What package is it?" Vivian asked.

"BookWithUs," Marieke replied.

"One of ours," Vivian said. "Let me know what the glitch was, and I'll make sure it's fixed when I get home."

"How long will you be staying at Mupundu?" Marieke asked.

"Two weeks," Vivian replied. "I've been putting off any kind of holiday for years, and I saw this place advertised at a trade show, so just decided to take the time off and come."

"I hope you won't be disappointed," Marieke said.

"I've no expectations, so what it is, is what it is," Vivian said. "Do you know where we are?"

"Flying over the area known as the Kafue Flats," Marieke replied. "We have to make a detour around an air force base, so we follow the river for quite a way. We should be there in about half an hour."

"OK, folks, we're coming into the Ntemwa strip," Chad, the pilot, said. "If you're going to Lufupa or Ngoma, stay in your seats, we'll only be on the ground for about ten minutes."

They landed, and four people got out and two got in, and true to Chad's word, they were off the ground in ten minutes.

"Next stop, Lufupa," Chad said. "Be there in about ten minutes."

They were on the ground at Lufupa in eleven minutes, not ten, not that anyone noticed.

"Chad," Alessandra said as she greeted the plane.

"Alex, got nine for you," he replied. "Two returning and seven new."

"Good afternoon," Alessandra said to the guests as they deplaned. "I'm Alex Martin with the Mupundu camp, we'll just get your bags, then we've a short ride to the boat dock, then a ride up the river to the camp."

"Vivian, this is my partner, Melisende Garnier," Marieke said, making the introduction. "Melisende, this is Vivian Harris, we could have used her when we first arrived with the booking software glitch, it's her company's"

"Nice to meet you, Melisende," Vivian said.

"Vivian had heard that Mupundu had had a death and was concerned that it might be food or water," Marieke said.

"Neither food nor water," Melisende said. "Respiratory failure caused by breathing in the wrong things at another camp, the symptoms took a little while to show, and by the time they did, it was too late for the poor chap."

"OK, folks, I've got all the bags loaded. If we could all climb aboard, we'll run over to the boat," Alessandra said.

Once at the camp, Alessandra was busy for the next hour or so, settling in the new guests and attending to some minor issues, then she sat down with Marieke and Melisende to hear all about their adventures.

"So, tell me all," she said.

"Not a lot to tell," Marieke said. "We met with the commissioner in Lusaka, told him our tale, then he asked us to go with his inspector to Luangwa and Lower Zambezi to see what we could find."

"And you must have found something because I heard from Tiffany that a couple of blokes were detained as they tried to walk across the Vic Falls bridge," Alessandra said.

"I suppose we did," Marieke confirmed. "At Lundwe in Luangwa, Robin sends her regards by the way, we learned that Alberto was in good health and Tom and David went for two walks and collected 32 small bags of seeds of one type or another."

"Including lucky beans?" Alessandra asked.

"Including luck beans," Marieke confirmed. "They picked them up on their second walk. In Lower Zam, it looks like Tom smashed up some beans to fill capsules."

"How did he do that?" Alessandra asked. "I wouldn't want to do that."

"We found some plastic bags, bags within bags within bags, and a couple of flat stones that had evidence on them of plastic," Marieke explained.

"Where was this?" Alessandra asked.

"The chalets there are up on platforms, and this stuff was buried in the sand under the chalet," Marieke explained.

"I was worried about her poking around and digging up things," Melisende said. "If this stuff is as toxic as she says, then I was worried that she might breathe some in and get sick."

"I did wear a mask and gloves," Marieke said. "And I think Tom bagged things up carefully so that he didn't kill himself, so I felt quite safe. Inspector Hippo Chikonde took charge of all the evidence and took statements from the staff at both lodges, and at Mushika had two of their guides witness all that we found under the chalet, so if it comes to trial, they can give evidence."

"What happens now?" Alessandra asked.

"There's still no readily available, reliable test for abrin, so they can't prove that's what it was," Marieke said. "They can only say that the respiratory failure is consistent with the signs of abrin poisoning. Unless they can somehow magically get prints from the insides of the gloves used to handle the lucky beans and the capsules, they have only got circumstantial evidence, so it's going to need a confession to get any kind of conviction. That's up to the Zambia Police."

"Can they do it?" Alessandra asked.

"Possibly," Marieke said. "If I were them I'd have all the evidence handy and trot it out when I needed to shake their story."

"Like *Columbo*," Alessandra said.

"*Columbo?*" Marieke asked.

"Old American TV show, detective played by Peter Falk, usually knows very early on who did it, then works to prove how, famous

241

for the line, just one more thing," Alessandra explained. "Very Un-American, no guns involved, just brain work."

"That's very cynical," Melisende said.

"That's how I see it," Alessandra replied. "Anyway, you've done your bit, dug up incriminating evidence and handed it over to the cops, now it's time to have a holiday."

"One of your new guests, the single, Vivian Harris, owns the company that does your booking software," Melisende said. "We told her that we had worked on a glitch, so perhaps when she leaves, you might tell her what it was."

"Good idea," Alessandra said. "You're right, do it when she leaves, she's here on holiday, not to solve our problems, but if I tell her when she goes, she'll know what to tell her people to look at."

"So, what shall we do tomorrow?" Marieke asked.

"I'll talk to these people tonight," Alessandra said. "If some of them fancy a drive and a longer day out, I thought it might be nice to go back to the Chibemba Salt Pan and see what's there."

"I like that idea," Marieke said. "If there's room, we'll come with you."

"I'd better get ready for the new guests," Alessandra said. "We may have had a death, but we can't shut up the camp; have to be ready for the next batch."

The new guests drifted into the *boma* and were helped with drinks before dinner. It was also a time for introductions as, unlike the last group of guests, the current group were not together.

"Let's see," Alessandra said. "We all met briefly at the airstrip and on the boat, time, I think, for more formal introductions. This is Grace, she's the manager here, this is her husband, Abel, who is one of our guides, and this is Adam, our other guide. All of us as guides are walking qualified, so during the week we'll trade off duties to give you varying perspectives of what we may see. I also have two guests with me who are staying in one of the staff tents, my aunt, Marieke Englebrecht and her partner in crime, Melisende Garnier. I say that somewhat literally as they are both police officers."

"Were you here when the dead man was found?" a guest asked. "Sorry, George Adams, my wife, Elizabeth."

"I see the bush telegraph is as busy as ever," Marieke said. "We were here and have been helping the Zambia Police with their inquiries."

"Not in the sense that we normally think of when that's said, I trust?" George asked.

"No, we actually did go to help," Marieke laughed. "I have worked with the Zambia Police before."

"Vivian Harris," Vivian added. "I had already asked Marieke if the death was related to food or water and have been assured that it was not, but merely pure chance that the chap died here and not elsewhere."

"Vincent and Millicent Bishop," were announced next.

"I suppose that leaves us, Charles and Ann Dewhurst," Charles said.

"I want to assure you all, that no matter what stories may be out there on the bush telegraph, that the unfortunate death of a previous guest was due entirely to something acquired at another place, and as Vivian has said, it was pure chance that he died here and not elsewhere," Alessandra said. "I hope that you'll enjoy your stay with us and not worry about things that happened before."

"Just curious," Vincent said. "Being a doctor myself. What did he die of?"

"Respiratory failure," Marieke replied. "In hindsight, he would have been better staying in Lusaka and seeking medical attention."

"In fact, his wife had made arrangements for them to leave here early and go to Lusaka for just that," Alessandra added. "Sadly, she left it a day late."

"Always the way," Vincent said, nodding his head sagely.

"Good, that's out of the way," Alessandra said. "Now before we go for dinner, tomorrow, who would like to do what? We can offer you a game drive, a boat ride with the possibility of game viewing from the river, or a walk."

"A boat ride sounds fun," George said. "What do you think, Betty?"

"I'm game for that," Elizabeth replied.

"Count us in for that, " Ann said.

"We've been talking and we rather like the idea of a walk," Vincent said.

"That leaves me, I don't suppose a game drive is possible with just one?" Vivian asked.

"It's perfectly fine," Alessandra assured her. "Adam will take the boat, Abel will take the walk along with our ZAWA scout, and I'll take the drive. Would you object to a picnic lunch, Vivian?"

"No, that would be lovely," Vivian replied.

"A couple of housekeeping items," Alessandra said. "In the morning you'll get a wake-up call at five-thirty, if you don't get one, stay where you are, because it means that there's something between here and your tent, when you're ready use the walkie-talkies that we showed you in your tents to call and someone will come and get you. Breakfast at six, then the morning activity, back by lunch, then quiet time until three, meet here for tea, coffee, biscuits, then an afternoon activity. During the day, feel free to come and go as you please between here and your tents, but if you do see something, just wait here or in your tent or call us."

"What might we see?" Ann asked.

"Possibly elephants, perhaps lions," Alessandra replied.

"How exciting," Millicent said.

"After dinner, when you're ready to go back to your tents, we'll escort you back," Alessandra said.

"I suppose you don't need another death," Charles said.

"Indeed not," Alessandra agreed. "Now, I think dinner calls."

"Ready for this again?" Alessandra asked Marieke and Melisende as they left in the morning for the drive to the salt pan.

"You've been to this place before?" Vivian asked Marieke.

"That's where we were when we got the radio call to go back and attend to an issue," Marieke replied.

"What might we see there?" Vivian asked.

"Elephants, lions, buffalo, dogs, zebra, antelope of all kinds, we won't know until we get there and just sit and watch and wait," Alessandra replied.

"Who's the best guide you have?" Vivian asked Alessandra.

"Adam and Abel are both excellent," Alessandra replied. "Adam has a lot of the folklore and seems to have this uncanny ability to find leopards, Abel is a little more academic and scientific. I try and deal with both, but Adam will always have more of the folklore."

"Where did you learn your guiding?" Vivian asked.

"My folks ran a bush camp in northern Botswana," Marieke replied. "I started guiding essentially when I was tall enough to not be considered prey. I'd usually go out with one of the Botswana guides, and they were amazing teachers, coaches and examiners," Alessandra replied. "I'd have to say, though, that Auntie Marieke is a better tracker than me, maybe even better than Adam or Abel."

"Where did you learn to track?" Vivian asked Marieke.

"I grew up on a farm in Namibia," Marieke replied. "The San who lived on our farm taught me from when I was very young."

"The San?" Vivian asked.

"The people they used to call the bushmen," Marieke explained.

"Oh, *The Gods must be Crazy* people?" Vivian asked.

"That's right," Marieke confirmed.

"When you said you were helping the police with their inquiries, did that include tracking?" Vivian asked.

"I suppose it did," Marieke said.

"It did," Melisende added. "It was amazing what she saw and how she saw it."

"So, there's villainy afoot?" Vivian asked.

"Let's just say that some people have some explaining to do," Marieke said.

"Excuse me, what's that over there?" Vivian asked.

"Those are roan antelope," Alessandra replied. "They're one of our larger antelope, third largest in fact for here, fourth if you go north and include the bongo."

"And the largest?" Vivian asked.

"The eland," Alessandra replied.

When they reached the salt pan it was busy with all types of antelope, but they disappeared when some lions arrived. They did not stay long and the antelope all drifted back when they felt it was safe to do so.

"This place is amazing," Vivian said. "It's so quiet here, but there's so much going on."

"Worth the drive?" Alessandra asked.

"Absolutely," Vivian replied.

"We'll park over there in the shade and just watch, then we'll have lunch when everyone goes to ground in the heat of the day," Alessandra suggested.

"Look, everything has just disappeared," Vivian said. "Almost as though someone sent out a signal."

"Heat of the day," Alessandra said. "We'll get some lunch, then just relax until activity picks up again."

"Sorry to bring this up again, but how did you deal with a death?" Vivian asked.

"It wasn't the best thing that's happened," Alessandra admitted. "We've had a heart attack at another of our camps; we medevaced him out, but it was too late."

"No animal-related deaths?" Vivian asked.

"We haven't had any," Alessandra replied. "It's possible and it has happened, but not to us."

"I suppose in some ways you're like a hotel, can't shut the whole place down for one death," Vivian said.

"It may be necessary for a day or two while police investigate," Alessandra said. "But that's only for suspicious deaths, and we're like anyone else there, always wanting to know when we can reopen. If we were shut down for a week or so, we'd probably have to rebook people elsewhere, they won't want to cancel trips."

"Well, I for one am very glad you didn't have to do that," Vivian said. "This is just delightful."

"We think this is a magical place," Alessandra said.

There was no radio call summoning them back to the camp, so they were able to enjoy the rest of the day.

"We must have seen hundreds of animals," Vivian said when they got back to the camp and compared notes with the others.

"I've also been there when there's been almost none," Alessandra cautioned in case the others thought that sightings at the salt pan were a surety. She was gratified to hear that the others had also had good days, and the conversation over coffee seemed to be about when they might come back, music to Alessandra's ears as return bookings took less marketing. The next few days until the departure of the guests were without incident, which was far more normal than the death, which in reality was quite a rarity. The time came for Marieke and Melisende to leave.

"You will come back?" Alessandra asked them.

"We will," Marieke promised. "Hopefully, the next time you won't have any deaths."

"God no," Alessandra said. "Deaths in the camp are bad for business, even if they have nothing to do with the camp, word gets out on the bush telegraph, then the booking agents hear about it and you have to spend ages explaining and pointing out that it was mere chance that he died here."

Epilogue

Three months after the holiday in Zambia, Marieke received an email from her cousin, Katrina, in Hawaii. Attached to it was a newspaper cutting from a Utah paper.

"Listen to this," she told Melisende.

"Renowned scientist at the USDA poison plant lab in Logan convicted of conspiracy to commit murder. Dr Tom Macmillan of Logan and Mr David Davis of Los Angeles were both recently tried and convicted for the murder of Dr Alberto Juarez of Atlanta. The trio were part of a group of friends on a safari in Africa, and Dr Juarez died of what at first was classified as a snake bite. That was proven to be incorrect, and the death was actually respiratory failure caused by the inhalation of a toxin derived from a local seed. The motive for the killing was infidelity on the part of Dr Juarez and Mrs Davis. A spokesman from the Zambia Police said that they had been able to track the movements of both Macmillan and Davis and show how, when and where they collected the seeds, and how and where they had been ground into an inhalable powder which was then introduced into capsules used by Dr Juarez to counter the effects of asthma. Davis, who reportedly actually gave the adulterated capsule to Dr Juarez, was sentenced to death, as is the law in Zambia, but it has been the practice to commute many death sentences to life in prison. Dr Macmillan was sentenced to life in prison. The United States Embassy in Lusaka, Zambia, has expressed concern over the death penalty and will be pressing for clemency and asking for the sentence to be commuted to life. It is of note that the last death penalty actually carried out was in 1997."

"I'd forgotten that Zambia still has the death penalty," Melisende said.

"I don't think I'd want to be in a Zambian prison," Marieke said. "Botswana prisons weren't that great, and I can't imagine that the Zambian ones are much different."

"Well, this was certainly one holiday I won't forget in a hurry," Melisende said. "I'm still amazed that you can see all these things in the bush, track individual people and even have a fairly good idea of when they were where."

"It's just a matter of observation," Marieke said. "In the same way that you can watch people and tell when they're lying."

"I'm still amazed, though, you were as good as the guides they have at the lodges," Melisende said.

"You're easily amazed," Marieke laughed.

"I'm just glad that when we go off to wild places that you're with me, I know you'll get us home safely," Melisende said.

"There's another email," Marieke said. "This one's from Bridget and it's got a Times of Zambia cutting attached."

"What does that one say?" Melisende asked.

"Two visitors convicted for the murder of a third: Last week the High Court handed down its verdict of guilty in the trial of Mr David Davis and Dr Tom Macmillan, both of the United States. They had been accused of the murder of Dr Alberto Juarez, also of the United States. The prosecutor painted a picture of planning and execution that led to the death, planning that started in the States and continued here in Zambia. The three were part of a group of eight who came to visit the Luangwa, Lower Zambezi and Kafue National Parks, and the circumstances of the case took investigators to all three parks to gather evidence and obtain statements. A police spokesman praised the staff and guides of the various camps for their assistance and also thanked ZAWA for their assistance. The prosecutor laid out the events that occurred, from gathering lucky beans in Luangwa, to the crushing of those beans in Lower Zambezi and then the filling of asthma capsules, which were then substituted for others used by Juarez. The death from inhalation of abrin, the toxin associated with lucky beans, occurred in Kafue, and the body was transported to the Teaching Hospital in Lusaka for a postmortem examination. The police recovered items used to crush the beans and load the capsules from Lower Zambezi, and when presented to the accused, it is reported that one of them became a witness for the prosecution in return for a lesser sentence. Found guilty of murder, Mr David Davis now joins the several hundred that are on death row awaiting either clemency or a death order by the President. The United States Embassy has petitioned for clemency, asking for the sentence to be commuted from death to life in prison. We in Zambia are having a continued debate about the ethics of the death penalty, which at the moment is a mandatory sentence for murder, but which has not actually been used since 1997. Dr Tom Macmillan was sentenced to life in prison. Both men have filed appeals with the Zambia Supreme Court."

"Interesting," Melisende said. "They must have shown Macmillan all that you found under his chalet and then pointed out that murder carries the mandatory death sentence, and he decided not to risk a jury trial that might find him guilty, so made a deal with the prosecutors."

"Bridget also says that the paper had an editorial piece about abrin and the dangers associated with it and a caution for people who would use the lucky beans to make rosaries and other jewellery," Marieke added.

"So death in the bush camp does get resolved," Melisende said. "Largely thanks to you and your knowledge of the bush and, dare I say it, the criminal mind. Have you heard from the Zambia Police?"

"There is another email here from Commissioner Bwalya thanking us for our help," Marieke said.

"As it should be," Melisende said.

Selected Bibliography

1. Ashley, Nikki, *The Kafue National Park, Zambia*, CBC Publishing 2012.
2. Bancroft, J. Austen, *Mining in Northern Rhodesia*, The British South Africa Company, 1961.
3. Benson, C.W., *Check List of the Birds of Northern Rhodesia*, Department of Game and Tsetse Control, 1957.
4. Broadley, Donald G., Doria, Craig T., Wigge, Jürgen, *Snakes of Zambia: An Atlas and Field Guide*, Edition Chimaira, 2003.
5. Bull, Schuyler, *Along the Luangwa: A Story of an African Habitat*, Soundprints, 1999.
6. Carr, Norman, *A Guide to the Wildlife of the Luangwa Valley*, Save the Rhino Trust, 1987.
7. Carr, Norman, *Kakuli*, CBC Publishing, 1996.
8. Carr, Norman, *Return to the Wild*, Collins, 1962.
9. Carr, Norman, *Valley of the elephants: the story of the Luangwa Valley and its wildlife*, Collins, 1979.
10. Chen, Hsiao, et al. *Abrin and Ricin: Understanding the Toxicity, Diagnosis and Treatment*, Biological Toxins and Bioterrorism: pp 79 - 102, 2021.
11. Chinyama, Martin, *The Application of Death Penalty Law in Zambia: What is the Justification.* University of Zambia, School of Law, 2012.
12. Clark, John., Loe, Ian., A *Guide to the National Parks of Zambia*, Anglo American, 1974.
13. Dickers, Kirsten J., et al, *Abrin poisoning*, National Library of Medicine, 2003.
14. Ellison, Gabriel, *Common Birds of Zambia*, Zambian Ornithological Society, 1990.
15. Estes, Richard D., *The Behavior Guide to African Mammals*, University of California Press, 1991.
16. Estes, Richard D., *The Safari Companion*, Chelsea Green Publishing Company, 1993.
17. Felder, Eva, et al, *Simultaneous Detection of Ricin and Abrin DNA by Real Time PCR (qPCR)*, Toxins (Basel) 2012.

18. Gabel, Creighton, *Stone Age Hunters of the Kafue: The Gwisho A Site*, Boston University Press, 1965.

19. Gilges, W., *Some African Poison Plants and Medicines of Northern Rhodesia*, The Rhodes-Livingstone Museum, 1955.

20. Govender, I., Tumbo, J., *The management of snakebite in South Africa*, South African Family Practice, 2019: 61(3):51-58.

21. Guy, P. R., *Riverbank erosion in the mid-Zambezi valley below Lake Kariba*, Biological Conservation, vol: 19, issue 3: February 1981, pp 199 - 212.

22. He, Xiaohua, et al, *Detection of Abrin Holotoxin Using Novel Monoclonal Antibodies*, National Library of Science, 2017.

23. Hupe, Ilona, *Luangwa - Unique Wilderness in Africa: HUPE Nature-Guide Luangwa Valley*, Hupe Ilona Verlag, 2016.

24. Kalsi, Rhythm, Modak, Aryaman, Choudhary, Bhumika, *Abrus Precatorius (Rosary pea) - Medicinal Uses and Toxicological Overview*, Agri-India TODAY, 01/VII/01/0721.

25. Lawrence, Barbara, Editor, *African Wildlife Safaris*, Spectrum Guides, 1989.

26. Leigh, Kellie, *Evaluation Report: Kangaluwi Open Pit Copper Mine in the Lower Zambezi National Park*, Zambia, University of Sydney, 2013.

27. Leonard, Peter, *Important Bird Areas in Zambia*, Zambian Ornithological Society, 2005.

28. Letcher, Owen, *Big Game Hunting in North-Eastern Rhodesia*, John Long, 1911.

29. Liebenberg, Louis, *The Art of Tracking: The Origin of Science*, David Philip, 2003.

30. Liebenberg, Louis, *A Field Guide to the Animal Tracks of Southern Africa*, David Philip, 1990.

31. McIntyre, Chris, *Zambia*, Bradt Travel Guides, 2013.

32. Mitchell, B. L., Ansell, W. F. H., *Wild Life of Kafue and Luangwa*, Zambia National Tourist Board, 1965.

33. Musambachime, Mwelma C., *Before the Rise of the Modern Copperbelt*, Xlibris Publishing, 2017.

34. Mwima, Henry, *A Brief History of the Kafue National Park*, Koedoe - African Protected Area Conservation and Science, 2001.

35. Nolting, Mark W., *African Safari Journal*, Global Travel Publishers, 2000.

36. Owens, Delia, Owens, Mark, *The Eye of the Elephant*, Houghton Mifflin, 1992.
37. Palgrave, Keith Coates, *Trees of Southern Africa*, Struik Publishers, 1997.
38. Robertson, Michael James, *Kitumba - a new kind of copper deposit in a Zambian context*, The Southern African Institute of Mining and Metallurgy Base Metals Conference, 2013.
39. Roodt, Veronica, *Trees and Shrubs of the Okavango Delta*, Shell Oil Botswana, 1998.
40. Saganuman, Alhaji, *Toxicosis of Snake, Scorpion, Honeybee, Spider and Wasp Venoms: Part 1*, Medical Toxicology, 2021.
41. Storrs, A. E. G., Pierce, G. D., *"Don't Eat These": A Guide to some local Poisonous Plants/Poisonous Mushrooms*, Forest Department, Zambia, 1982.
42. Tapson, Winifred, *Old Timer*, Howard Timmins, 1957.
43. Wainwright, Geoff., *Hunting for Trouble*, Safari Press, 2007.
44. Walker, Clive, *Signs of the Wild*, Struik Publishers, 1996.
45. White, F., *Forest Flora of Northern Rhodesia*, Oxford University Press, 1962.